A BID FOR LOVE

A BID FOR LOVE

CAROL FINCH

KENSINGTON BOOKS

KENSINGTON BOOKS are published by

Kensington Publishing Corp.
850 Third Avenue
New York, NY 10022

ISBN 0-8217-5300-2

First Zebra Paperback Printing: May, 1994
First Kensington Hardcover Printing: September, 1995

Printed in the United States of America

This book is dedicated to my husband Ed and our children, Christie, Jill and Kurt, with much love.

A very special thanks to Willena Shales. I wish you love, laughter and happiness!

Chapter One

Elizabeth Smith Sutton stared at the shiny silver Cadillac that whizzed down the gravel road toward her ranch. A Caddy? Good God, she knew she shouldn't have let her long-time friend and business consultant persuade her to meet with the auctioneer from Oklahoma City, even if the man came highly recommended. One look at that car and Elizabeth knew Wyatt McKenney wasn't the man for her. What could a city slicker possibly know about the value of livestock, farm machinery and ranch property in Osage County?

It was bad enough that she was being forced to sell Heartstrings Ranch—the homestead that had been in her family for generations. But agreeing to let a citified shark handle the arrangements for the auction? Damn, she must have been out of her mind!

Elizabeth's dark eyes narrowed in critical scrutiny when the Caddy wheeled through the arched gateway, kicking up a cloud of dust. This meeting might have been less awkward if Jerry Patterson could have accompanied his "ole buddy" from college days, Elizabeth mused as she watched the car roll to a stop. But Jerry had called a half-hour earlier to inform her that he had been detained at one of the ranches near Hominy and that he would be a couple of hours late.

The minute Wyatt McKenney unfolded himself from the plush leather seat and stood up, Elizabeth groaned. The supposedly successful auctioneer, highly praised by Jerry for his expertise, looked completely out of place on this ranch. McKenney could have been an executive who belonged in a penthouse in a high-rise building. Elizabeth wanted a down-home auctioneer she could relate to, one who could understand her situation, not some lah-de-dah yuppie with an ego the size of a hot-air balloon.

While Elizabeth drove a broken-down pickup that had seen its better days years ago, Wyatt McKenney cruised around in a fully loaded, late-model Caddy. Elizabeth was wearing a chambray shirt, Lee jeans and Justin Roper boots. McKenney was decked out in a three-piece suit that had cost as much as a sizable payment on the outstanding loans Elizabeth's husband had bequeathed to her. Wyatt McKenney was so far out of his element, it was laughable. And worse, he sported a mustache. He probably doesn't have an upper lip, Elizabeth decided. Most sharks don't.

Although she was doing her damnedest to list everything she didn't like about McKenney, she had to admit the man had a certain sensual appeal that might arouse the interest of urban women. She, however, was countrified and damned proud of it. She was too sensible to be bowled over by a lean, masculine physique wrapped in expensive clothes, or by dark hair—sparsely sprinkled with gray around the temples—capping a handsome, distinguished face.

Physical appeal befuddled young girls into thinking they were in love; Elizabeth was a practical, mature woman. And anyway, Wyatt McKenney, nationally known auctioneer, wouldn't be staying long enough to pique her interest. She wasn't about to hire this high-class city slicker to sell her ranch. He could climb back in his Caddy and hightail it to the nearby town of Pawhuska. He had wasted his time, and she had a dozen chores to tend to before dark.

"Mrs. Sutton?"

Nice voice, Elizabeth begrudgingly admitted. Of course, an auctioneer needed a rich baritone to command attention. It went with the territory.

"Mr. McKenney." Elizabeth extended her hand in polite greeting when Wyatt stepped onto the porch.

"I presume Jerry called to tell you he was tied up with another client."

"Yes, he did." Elizabeth darted a glance toward the shiny town car, enviously speculating on how much money McKenney blew on expensive transportation while she scrimped and struggled to make ends meet. "Nice car."

"It gets me where I need to go," Wyatt said.

"And in style," Elizabeth muttered, half under her breath.

"Excuse me?"

"Nothing." Elizabeth heaved a sigh and decided to be blunt rather than pussyfooting around the issue. "I'm afraid you have made a long drive from town for nothing, Mr. McKenney."

"Why? Because I drive a nice car?" he asked, his green eyes twinkling with the kind of amusement that nothing in the conversation could account for.

"No, not because of the car." Well, okay, maybe she did hold that against him—among other things.

"You've decided not to sell your ranch?"

"I didn't want to sell my ranch in the first place," she clarified, staring across the rolling hills that had been her home since the day she was born. "This is a matter of necessity, plain and simple. I don't have to like it. I just have to do it."

"Then why have I wasted my time in coming?" Wyatt questioned, following her gaze across the pasture to where a herd of cattle grazed.

"Look, Mr. McKenney—"

"Wyatt," he corrected.

"Look *Mr. McKenney,*" she continued formally, "I don't think you are quite right for this particular auction. To be perfectly frank, I don't imagine this run-down ranch will offer the kind of commission you're accustomed to receiving. And being from Oklahoma City, I doubt you are familiar with procedures and practices in this part of the state."

Wyatt bit back a wry smile and surveyed the five-foot-five-inch lady rancher who was all but looking down her nose at him because he was an "outsider" driving a souped-up Caddy. "In other words, you don't think I know beans about the value of ranch property, livestock and machinery."

"As a matter of fact, no," she said honestly. "Most auctioneers I know drive pickups and dress in boots and jeans. They can accurately estimate the value of a tractor or pastures of grassland in thirty seconds flat."

"I see."

"I'm glad you do. You and this ranch simply aren't right for each other. It's nothing personal, you understand."

Wyatt chuckled at Elizabeth whose windblown auburn hair was swirling around her attractive face, tangling in her long curly lashes. He liked the lady's looks and style. She was honest and plain spoken, nothing like the pretentious females who usually gravitated toward him the minute they learned he was making a killing in his line of business. Elizabeth had an earthy, wholesome quality about her, and her dark eyes shone with an inner spirit it was impossible to ignore. Wyatt didn't bother trying to overlook the appealing way Elizabeth filled out her Western wear, either.

Wyatt was enjoying the company he was keeping, even if Elizabeth was trying to shoo him away as if he were a pesky mosquito. "Even if you don't think I'm the man for this job, would you object to letting me take a look around the ranch until Jerry shows up?" Wyatt questioned.

"It won't change anything," she insisted. "And I have work to do."

"I've got time to kill. If you have chores to do, I don't mind helping you."

Elizabeth couldn't control her gurgle of laughter. "Do chores in that suit?" God, the man didn't have a clue as to what sort of things he could step in around here.

"It'll wash," Wyatt assured her.

"Don't bet on it."

"I'm offering to help. Where do we start, Mrs. Sutton?"

Elizabeth looked the tall, citified auctioneer over and decided he needed a lesson in humility, even if he was Jerry Patterson's friend from college days at Oklahoma State. By the time Elizabeth finished with this dude, he wouldn't *want* to make arrangements to auction Heartstrings Ranch to the highest bidder.

Elizabeth swallowed an ornery smile. "You're sure?"

"I'm sure," Wyatt confirmed. "Where do we start?"

Elizabeth, you should be ashamed of yourself. You are a mature forty-five-year-old woman with two grown daughters. You shouldn't be playing pranks at your age, and especially on this city slicker who probably hasn't been closer to a horse than watching one trot by in a parade.

Well, he asked for it, Elizabeth silently reminded her nagging conscience.

"Follow me, Mr. McKenney."

When Elizabeth strode through the breezeway of her uniquely arranged home-in-the-middle-of-nowhere, Wyatt caught himself watching the hypnotic sway of her jeans-clad hips. He felt guilty for all of two seconds before telling his conscience to take a hike so he could admire the stimulating scenery. He might be forty-eight years old, but he certainly wasn't dead. And there was nothing wrong with his eyesight that a pair of reading glasses couldn't correct. Good-looking women had drawn masculine appreciation since time immemorial, so who was he to resist basic instinct? Besides, it had been a long time since Wyatt had experienced instantaneous sexual attraction. Why shouldn't he enjoy it? It would help soothe the sting of rejection he had noticed in Elizabeth's onyx eyes.

According to his physician, he had been pushing himself too hard. The doctor had advised him to slow his pace before he drove himself into an early grave. This, Wyatt decided, was a good time to start changing his hectic life-style. The scenery was pleasantly distracting . . . and the rolling prairies of Osage Hills weren't bad, either . . .

"Did you change your mind about doing chores?"

Wyatt glanced up from his preoccupation with Elizabeth's well-shaped derriere and smiled. "No, I'll be there as soon as I put my jacket in the car."

"I'll meet you in the barn."

Elizabeth smothered another mischievous grin. This high-class auctioneer would think twice before he volunteered to help with ranch chores again. Serves him right, Elizabeth decided. She hoped he'd split the seams of his Armani slacks and scuff his black Cole Haan shoes.

Shame on you, Elizabeth. You are being spitefully childish.

"Oh, shut up," she muttered at her annoying conscience. She was entitled to a little amusement occasionally, wasn't she? She had been working her butt off for nine years to put her daughters through high school and college and keep this ranch operating as best she could. So what if she put this city slicker in his place? He might as well learn what ranch living was all about—the hard way.

The minute Elizabeth stepped into the barn, her eyes narrowed thoughtfully on the spirited horse her older daughter had used to barrel-race in rodeos. The sturdy sorrel gelding could turn on a dime and run like streak lightning. Definitely not a mount for a man who probably wouldn't know how to guide his mode of transportation without a steering wheel and an emergency brake.

Putting Wyatt McKenney on the sorrel was going a bit too far, Elizabeth decided. He would probably wind up flat on his back the first time the horse switched directions. Then this city slicker would sue the pants off her, and that was the last thing Elizabeth needed on top of her outstanding debts and expenses.

Be sensible and put the man on the strawberry roan, Elizabeth told herself. The mare had an unflappable disposition and was better suited for a tenderfoot. Elizabeth set a saddle on the roan. She had just fastened the girth strap when Wyatt strode inside in white dress shirt, slacks and shoes already coated with a layer of the dust that had floated up from the straw-covered floor.

Wyatt walked over to stroke the mare's velvet muzzle. "What's first on the agenda?"

Elizabeth watched the sorrel gelding perk up its ears when she slid the blanket on its back. "After the hired man and I fed the cattle this morning, we noticed one of the yearlings was limping. Foot rot, I expect," she diagnosed. "The calf needs to be doctored and isolated—"

"Here. Let me do that," Wyatt insisted, lifting the second saddle from Elizabeth's arms.

After he set it on the sorrel, Elizabeth shifted it forward and reached under the gelding's belly to grab the dangling cinch. Before she could step into the stirrup, Wyatt tapped her on the shoulder.

"Why don't you let me ride the sorrel. The mare is a little too short for my taste."

Dark eyes twinkled up at the six-foot-two auctioneer. "If you ride Chicago, you ride at your own risk," she warned him.

"Chicago?"

Elizabeth indicated the stockings that marked the gelding's back legs. "White socks."

Wyatt chuckled and gestured his dark head toward the docile mare. "Philadelphia filly, I presume?"

"No, that's George." When Wyatt arched a questioning brow, Elizabeth elaborated. "There was a typo on the Quarter Horse registration form, and I didn't catch it until it was too late. The mare was supposed to be called Georgie . . . Come here, Damn It!"

Wyatt blinked at Elizabeth's unexpected shout. He half-turned when he heard a panting dog trotting down the aisle in the barn. "Damn It?" he repeated curiously.

Elizabeth pulled herself onto George's back. "Best cow dog in the county. He does the work of three hired hands."

Wyatt swung onto Chicago while Elizabeth studied him in silence. He knew what she was thinking. She had pegged him as a greenhorn because of the cut of his clothes. Rather than deny her misconceptions, Wyatt decided to play along. It would serve *her* right for prejudging him, just because he wore a suit and drove a Caddy.

When Elizabeth trotted off, looking more comfortable on a horse than most women did in luxury cars, Wyatt trailed after her. It didn't take him long to realize the gelding he'd volunteered to ride was born to run. The horse fairly danced beneath him, tossing its proud head at regular intervals and sidestepping impatiently.

Elizabeth's discreet glances implied that she expected him to be unhorsed before he reached the pasture gate. Wyatt merely smiled and kept the prancing gelding under control. He was enjoying this test of his abilities by a woman who obviously had ranching in her blood. Elizabeth Smith Sutton belonged in the great outdoors. She moved in perfect rhythm with the mare she straddled. She was an integral part of these obscure hills and wooded valleys, and she relished life's simplicities.

A sense of contentment overshadowed the hypertension that had become Wyatt's constant companion. He inhaled a cleansing breath as he trotted across the sloping prairie, the wind in his face and a powerfully built animal beneath him. He *had* been living in the fast lane too damned long, driven by a need that had become an obsession these past few years. He had awakened too many mornings with his teeth clenched and his hands knotted in fists, unable to relax, even after several hours of sleep. Jerry was right. This was the therapy he desperately needed, even if Elizabeth considered his presence an inconvenience.

Because necessity had demanded it, Wyatt had transformed himself into a moneymaking machine, and he had become accustomed to keeping a relentless pace. But here, on this sprawling prairie of bluestem and Indian grass in the Osage Hills, he felt himself unwinding despite a decade of being coiled tighter than a spring.

Touring Heartstrings Ranch put him back in touch with the simple pleasures he had almost forgotten existed. He would be sure to thank Jerry Patterson for insisting that he drive up for the weekend.

I could get used to this, he thought with a contented sigh. He was enjoying himself immensely, even if Elizabeth Smith Sutton resented his intrusion on her private space.

When Elizabeth reached the pasture where the lame yearling grazed, she concentrated on the business at hand. Surprisingly, Wyatt appeared to be competent in the saddle. Of course, he wouldn't be a damned bit of help if the calf spooked and tore off across the prairie.

She had been riding and roping since she was old enough to walk. With Damn It's help, she could corral the steer and doctor its infected hoof. The city slicker could sit and watch. That was what "his kind" did best.

"Have you seen many cases of foot rot in your livestock?" Wyatt questioned while Elizabeth carefully appraised her cattle.

"We've had more problems than usual this year," she replied absently. "It was a wet winter. The cattle slopped around in too much mud, and bad weather conditions lend themselves to bacterial and viral complications. We've treated some of the livestock for pneumonia and we've already lost three steers.

"The ranch operation has already been cut back till it's as lean as it can get; we can't afford profit reductions. Jerry Patterson suggested I increase the mineral and cattle-cube supplements—which I did—but extended periods of cold weather and excessive rain have been hard on disease control . . . Damn It!"

Upon command, the speckled dog nipped at the heel of the calf Elizabeth had singled out. The steer limped toward the small corral located in the southwest corner of the pasture. Things were going smoothly until the calf balked at being separated from the herd. It veered off to the west, following the fence row and avoiding the open corral gate.

Wyatt would have joined in the chase, but he found himself

marveling at Elizabeth's abilities. She was an accomplished rider and Damn It's herding skills were nothing to sneeze at, either.

The look on Elizabeth's face indicated that she was doing more than a required task. This was her chosen way of life—a life she thoroughly enjoyed. Wyatt wondered what this lady rancher was going to do with herself when she sold her property. Somehow, he couldn't visualize this vital, energetic woman crocheting doilies while sitting in front of a television in a modestly priced house in town. He predicted that she would be climbing the walls in less than a month, just as he had done those first few years when he'd been forced to adapt to *his* new life-style.

While Wyatt sat there admiring the picture Elizabeth and her cow dog presented, the twosome turned the ailing calf in the opposite direction and herded it along the fence. At Elizabeth's command, Damn It nipped the calf's tail to ensure the animal didn't cut and run when it reached the corral gate.

In a flash, Elizabeth bounded to the ground to secure the gate.

"I'm duly impressed."

She glanced around to see Wyatt smiling down at her. He had an engaging smile, though she had been so immersed in her task she had almost forgotten about him. "Thanks, but it's all in a day's work."

Disappointment tweaked Wyatt's male ego; he had been momentarily forgotten in her thrill at the chase. He wasn't accustomed to being ignored by those of the female gender. Women were attracted to him—or at least to his money. He had fended off divorcees galore who considered him "low maintenance" and "prime prospect." Elizabeth, however, appeared to be immune to his charms, and he couldn't help but wonder why. Hell, he showered regularly and dabbed on expensive cologne. So what was the problem . . . ?

"I thought you volunteered to help," she prompted as she dug into the saddlebag to retrieve the medication. "Or is this strictly a sightseeing tour?"

Wyatt gave himself a mental slap for dawdling and swung to the ground. "Sorry, capable as you seem to be, I doubted you needed my help."

"I don't," she assured him. "If you'd rather not break a sweat, now's the time to say so."

"Maybe you'll find sweat more appealing," Wyatt murmured as he grabbed the rope that hung over the pommel of Elizabeth's saddle.

Her hand stalled in midair. "What did you say?"

" I said . . . maybe you'll—"

"I heard you."

"Then why'd you ask me what I said?"

Luminous obsidian eyes narrowed on him. "What was that wisecrack supposed to imply?"

Wyatt leaned an arm against the mare's rump and met Elizabeth's unblinking stare. "Without being purposely rude, you have made it clear that you don't have much use for me. I was just wondering why."

"Are you always this straightforward with strangers?" she asked.

"Usually. Do you always try to avoid direct questions?"

"Only when I'm trying not to be rude."

Wyatt chuckled and shook his head. "Okay, out with it. What did I do to annoy you besides drive up in a Caddy, wearing a suit?"

"Nothing."

"So that's the *whole* problem? You don't approve of me because of my clothes and my car?"

Elizabeth scowled at his persistence and at the pleasing scent of cologne that fogged her senses. She did *not* want to like this man. He wasn't her type. They had nothing in common except a mutual friend. She had grown accustomed to working from dawn until dusk with no spare time and no spare money. And what the hell did this citified shark expect from her anyway? Flirtation and fawning? Well, he'd come to the wrong place for that kind of reception. Elizabeth had been out of circulation far too long for the sort of games he was probably accustomed to playing with women.

"The problem is exactly what I specified at the onset," she told him bluntly. "This business arrangement won't work. This ranch won't sell for the kind of money you expect to make." Her arm swept up in an expansive gesture. "Take a good look around you. The fences don't need to be *repaired;* they need to be *replaced.* In order to make this ranch more appealing to buyers the outbuildings need a fresh coat of paint and the bar ditches should be mowed. Prospective ranch buyers make note of such things when they're estimating property value. Every project that will require time, effort and money will automatically be deducted from the amount they are willing to pay."

"So you don't want to have anything to do with me because you don't think your ranch is going to bring as much as it's worth?" Wyatt asked straight-faced.

"No, damn it!"

The dog barked and came trotting to Elizabeth when its name was called. "Not you, Damn It," Elizabeth muttered. "Go corner that calf."

Wyatt sighed audibly. "Look, Elizabeth, all I want is to have a good look around. If you don't want me to handle the auction, at least let me evaluate your property while I'm here. A second opinion won't hurt anything, now will it? I came here as a favor to Jerry. For some reason, he seems to be fond of you. And I would appreciate it if you would shrug that chip off your shoulder for the next couple of hours."

Her head snapped up. "I don't have a chip on my shoulder."

Wyatt's green eyes sparkled in a teasing challenge. "No? It sure as hell doesn't look like dandruff."

Elizabeth glowered at him. "What is it you want from me?"

"Nothing more than to be treated with common courtesy and respect."

She accommodated him. "Fine. *Please* bring the rope and try to stay out of my way while I tend to business." With that, she wheeled around and stalked off.

Wyatt smothered a chuckle. They came easily around this

spirited female. Damned if he didn't like Elizabeth's spunk. She was such a refreshing change from the women who led sedate lives and vowed to age gracefully.

Forever young, eternally vital, that was Elizabeth Smith Sutton. And aggressively independent, stubbornly proud.

Still chuckling, Wyatt let himself through the gate, only to find the coiled rope snatched from his grasp. It was evident that Elizabeth was no stranger to doctoring cattle. While Damn It snarled and nipped at the calf, forcing it down the narrow wooden chute, Elizabeth positioned herself by the head gate. When the calf tried to leap through the opening, she jerked down on the lever, securing her four-legged patient. The calf, eyes bulging, bawled its head off when Elizabeth bound its hind legs with rope to prevent being kicked.

Pretty damned impressive, Wyatt thought as he strolled forward with the medication Elizabeth had slapped in his hand a few moments earlier.

She plucked up the syringe and swiftly injected the calf, then secured the medicated wrap to the infected leg while the calf bellowed at being restrained. Wyatt was still standing there admiring Elizabeth's efficiency when she released the calf from the head gate and rounded on *him*.

"It's the mustache," Elizabeth said out of the blue.

Wyatt blinked, bemused. "What?"

She recoiled the rope and dusted off her hands. "I never did like a man in a mustache and a business suit. Not my type. Any more questions?"

"Yes. Anything else?"

"Don't get chummy with me because you're a man and I'm a woman," Elizabeth ordered, annoyed that Wyatt was grinning at her as if she were providing him with amusement—at *her* expense. "I only brought you along because I have things to do that won't wait. And if you spend more than eight bucks on a haircut and styling I don't like *that,* either."

"Are you about finished?" he asked, swallowing the smile she obviously resented.

"No. In fact, I'm just getting wound up. I can be more in-sulting if you prefer."

"It gets worse?" Wyatt's throttled laughter only irritated her further.

"You better believe it, mister."

"You do a lousy John Wayne impression," Wyatt didn't hesi-tate to say.

"So do you. A man who can't hold his own with cattle is as worthless to me as—"

"Lady, I don't have to hold my *own*," Wyatt assured her. "There are those who are glad to do it for me."

"Well, don't expect *me* to be interested in your basic appli-ances. I would get more thrills turning on my washing ma-chine," she flung back, appalled that she had reduced herself to exchanging off-color remarks with a man who delighted in annoying her. Damn him, he was silently laughing at her! She'd like to kick him. Or better yet, let Chicago do it. The nine-hundred-pound horse would leave a bigger impression on this tenderfoot.

Wyatt couldn't help himself. He burst out laughing.

Elizabeth stalked back to her mount. The first chance she got, she intended to inform Jerry Patterson that he had the absolute worst taste in friends.

Chapter Two

For the most part, Elizabeth ignored her companion during the second leg of their ride, across pasture stocked with registered Limousin cows. She did, however, break the silence occasionally to point out various defects, purposely downgrading the ranch to discourage Wyatt's interest in handling the sale. He was *not* going to convince her to let him make arrangements for the auction, especially since he derived pleasure from irritating her.

Elizabeth was far more aware of this city slicker than she preferred to be. It made her decidedly uncomfortable that she *couldn't* shrug him off as easily as she would have liked . . .

Her thoughts trailed off when she spotted a cow that was staggering to its feet at the sight of intruders. It was obvious the cow was having difficulty birthing. And worse, by the position of the new calf's protruding hooves, the delivery was coming breech. Elizabeth muttered under her breath. Now was a time when she needed a competent hired man with her, not this pesky tenderfoot.

When the cow trotted off, halfway through her difficult delivery, Elizabeth reached for the lariat coiled on the pommel of her saddle. To her surprise, Wyatt snatched the rope from her hand.

"I'd better do this," he said somberly. "I'm riding the faster horse."

"Now is not the time for you to practice your rodeo skills," Elizabeth grumbled. "I can't afford to lose that cow or the calf . . ."

Her voice dried up when Wyatt gouged his heels into Chicago's flanks. The gelding gathered itself in and then uncoiled its powerful body in a lunge. To Elizabeth's stunned amazement, Wyatt shot off as if he were an old hand in the saddle. While Chicago thundered toward the retreating cow and Damn It gave chase, Wyatt circled the lariat over his head.

Elizabeth shook herself loose from her trance and raced off to haze for a man who was probably going to turn out to be an incompetent roper. She tried to keep the trotting cow near the fence so the animal could be dallied and restrained, *if* and *when* Wyatt managed to lasso it.

Good grief, what was the man trying to do? Impress her? More than likely he would wind up making a fool of himself and the laboring cow would die before giving birth to a calf that was attempting to make its entrance into the world—backward.

Despite Elizabeth's and Damn It's attempt to herd the cow along the fence, the animal panicked and decided to go *over* the fence into the neighbor's pasture. Elizabeth cringed, expecting to see the cow slashed by barbed wire before charging across the adjoining pasture.

To her utter amazement, Wyatt swung the loop just as the wide-eyed cow reared up to make her leap to freedom. The lasso settled over the cow's neck, bringing her down onto all fours and leaving her bawling in outrage.

Elizabeth had the sneaking suspicion—judging by the way Wyatt had flung the lasso and wheeled Chicago around to keep the rope taut—that he wasn't the greenhorn she had presumed him to be. Now, *she* felt foolish. No wonder Wyatt was silently laughing at her. And worse, when time allowed, she was going to have to apologize for behaving like a reverse snob. But now time did not allow. The next few minutes were critical to the survival of the unborn calf.

Reflexively, Elizabeth positioned her horse in the cow's path, forcing it toward the fence. Chicago did his duty by backing up, keeping tension in the dallied rope while Wyatt strode forward to restrain the terrified cow.

"Damn It, back off," Elizabeth ordered abruptly, bringing the snapping dog to heel.

Wyatt cast Elizabeth a quick glance before he realized she was talking to the dog. He met a pair of anxious obsidian eyes that were not nearly as condescending as they had been a few minutes earlier. Wyatt felt ten times better, even if he did have his hands full with a thousand-pound cow that made a second attempt to jump the fence, rope and all.

Hurriedly, Wyatt lunged toward the nearest steel fence post to dally the rope. With an abrupt yank he brought the cow's head down, making it impossible for her to take a flying leap. When the cow's left side slammed into the fence, Wyatt tossed the trailing end of the rope toward the post that stood eight feet away, trapping the cow.

"Tie down the lariat," Wyatt ordered Elizabeth.

She grabbed the rope and lashed it around the post. The minute the bellowing cow slid to the ground, Elizabeth looped the lariat around her back legs for complete restraint.

"Where did you learn to ride and rope like that?" she questioned accusingly.

"Watching John Wayne movies?" he ventured with a wry grin.

"Not likely," Elizabeth mumbled. "You should have told me instead of letting me make an ass of myself."

Wyatt chuckled as he strode over to where Elizabeth stood, assessing the situation. "Why? You seemed to be enjoying yourself at *my* expense."

Elizabeth clamped her mouth shut and sheepishly looked away.

Wyatt let the matter drop and glanced back at the two horses. "Did you bring a birthing chain to pull this calf?"

"No."

"Then we'll have to improvise."

"With what?"

Wyatt unbuttoned his shirt, and Elizabeth squawked in objection. "You can't use your shirt to pull the calf. It's too expensive."

A rakish grin tugged at his full lips. "It's either *your* shirt or *mine*. Are you volunteering?"

Elizabeth noted the twinkle in those vivid green eyes flecked with gold; and she blushed for the first time since she couldn't remember when. She had to admit Wyatt McKenney had irresistible charm when he smiled. His mischievous nature appealed to her, too, reluctant though she was to admit it.

"Take off your shirt," she ordered, battling her blush.

He waggled his eyebrows suggestively. "I thought you'd never ask."

Elizabeth tried to look the other way, but feminine curiosity kept her eyes glued to the dark matting of hair, peppered with a touch of gray, that covered his well-muscled chest. There was no question that Wyatt McKenney had kept himself in good physical condition. Muscles rippled down his arms and across his lean belly when he doffed his shirt. Elizabeth was embarrassed by her need to stare at the lithe contours of his physique.

A gurgle of laughter bubbled from his lips. "Thank you."

She dragged her eyes up to his lopsided grin. "For what?"

"You figure it out, Elizabeth," was all he said before he twisted his expensive dress shirt like a braided rope and turned his attention to the serious matter at hand.

Elizabeth mulled over his comment as she positioned herself behind the downed cow—and more specifically, behind the man whose broad back and narrow hips kept distracting her. She wondered if Wyatt had thanked her for noticing he was all man rather than the nuisance she thought him to be. Probably. She had come on a little strong, allowing her assumptions and first impressions to dictate to her. Whatever else Wyatt McKenney was, he was a fun-loving individual who didn't take himself quite as seriously as Elizabeth had been taking herself since he'd shown up. She was the one who needed to lighten up. Maybe she would after the calf had been delivered, but for now two lives were in jeopardy and the difficult delivery demanded attention.

Wyatt tied the sleeves of his shirt to the calf's protruding hooves and braced his feet. "We could use a Come-Along right about now. If this oversize calf is coming backward, we might not be able to save it."

Elizabeth crouched beside Wyatt, placing both hands on the makeshift chain, prepared to put every ounce of strength into pulling the calf. "Make sure you pull downward, not up."

He smiled over his shoulder. "Whatever you say, boss. Any other tidbits of instruction before delivery?"

"Yes." Elizabeth flung him a quick glance as her arm brushed his bulging biceps. "The calf may already have smothered, but if it shows signs of life, pick it up and sling it around the second it hits the ground. If the calf doesn't start breathing pretty quick, your shirt will have been ruined for nothing."

"On three," Wyatt commanded, coiling himself into position to tug on the breech calf.

Side by side, Elizabeth and Wyatt strained and cursed. The cow bawled her head off. Progress was so slow that Elizabeth was certain the calf wouldn't survive long enough to inhale its first breath.

"Take the halter and reins off George and attach it to Chicago's saddle," Wyatt ordered between pants of breath. "Even between the two of us, we don't have enough strength for this task. The calf is too damned big."

Elizabeth bounded up and rushed off to do as Wyatt suggested. After she had anchored the halter to the saddle, she tied the trailing reins to the middle of Wyatt's twisted shirt. Tapping Chicago on the chest, she urged the gelding backward, one step at a time. To Elizabeth's relief, the unborn calf's head appeared.

"Keep backing Chicago up," Wyatt said through gritted teeth. "Slow and easy . . ."

The instant the lifeless calf plopped onto the ground, Wyatt bolted up to sling the newborn to and fro. Elizabeth rushed forward to clear the membrane from its nostrils, but in her haste to help she accidently slammed Wyatt broadside, knocking him off balance. They tumbled to the ground in a tangle of arms and legs, sending the calf rolling like a barrel.

Elizabeth's breath came out in a grunt when Wyatt made a pancake landing on top of her. The feel of his body grinding into hers suggested he was all muscle and masculine strength. It had been a long time since Elizabeth had found herself flat on her back, staring up at a man at close range.

Instant and total awareness streamed through her as she peered up into a handsome face and green eyes that were studying her intently. For a moment, the cow and calf were forgotten. Dormant sensations burst to life and tantalizing speculations tapped at Elizabeth's mind, leaving her wondering . . .

The feeble bawl of the newborn calf was sweet music to Elizabeth's ears. "We did it," she wheezed, consciously aware of the intimate position she shared with this man who was full of unexpected surprises.

One thick brow lifted in teasing amusement, assuring Elizabeth that he had given a drastically different interpretation to her statement. "Yes, we did, didn't we? Was it as good for you as it was for me?"

Elizabeth squirmed and then went as still as stone, realizing she had only made matters worse in her effort to escape the tingling sensations that had no business assaulting her.

Wyatt's dark brow elevated even higher as he stared down at her flushed face. "What exactly is it that you want, Elizabeth?" he asked in a soft caressing voice that caused her female hormones to act up.

"I want you to get off me—now!" she insisted, cursing her body's betraying reaction. "We hardly know each other!"

Wyatt propped his forearms beside her shoulders and

grinned outrageously. "How can you say that when we have just delivered our firstborn together?"

Elizabeth grinned in spite of herself. "You are impossible."

"Nothing is impossible, Elizabeth . . ." His head dipped downward until his sensuous lips were only a hairbreadth away.

Elizabeth swallowed audibly, afraid he might kiss her and wondering if she would like the feel of his mustache brushing against her lips, wondering if the hot flashes she was suddenly experiencing were chronologically or sexually induced, for heat seared through specific regions of her anatomy, causing her heartbeat to stampede in her chest, which was mashed against a bare—and exceptionally male—torso.

Good God! This wasn't supposed to be happening. She wasn't some inexperienced schoolgirl on the threshold of womanhood. She should *not* be having an anxiety attack simply because Wyatt had landed on top of her when she'd accidentally tripped him up in her haste to deliver a calf. But so much for her cool head and dignified reserve. Elizabeth didn't honestly know what she was going to do if Wyatt decided to kiss her . . .

And she wasn't sure how she would react if he *didn't* . . .

When his gaze lingered on her parted lips, Elizabeth inwardly groaned. He smelled good; he looked good; he felt even better. She shouldn't be thinking what she was thinking, not at a time like this. She should be spouting indignant protests . . .

But she wasn't.

For more years than she could remember, she had placed her own personal needs on hold to ensure that her daughters were formally educated. She had poured time and effort into the ranch, had refused to let herself think in terms of her own happiness. Because her obligations had piled up, she had worked her fingers to the bone, cutting corners and making good use of all her time. She had sacrificed her own identity to make ends meet.

Now, all those years of neglecting her own needs were placed in perspective by Wyatt's proximity, reminding her that she was

still very much a woman. Too bad it was *this* man who reminded her of her deprivation. Why did it have to feel so right
when she knew it was all wrong?

Wyatt gazed into those dark, haunted eyes and felt the rapid
heartbeat that matched his own racing pulse. He wanted to
kiss Elizabeth, he really did. But the way she was staring up
at him prevented him from doing what he was sure would have
been a pleasurable conclusion to an unusual afternoon—the
most unusual one he had ever spent with a woman. But considering Elizabeth's preconceptions about him, Wyatt doubted
she would approve of being kissed after the delivery. Yes, it
would be ill advised. Too bad he was having trouble convincing
his male body that his timing was all wrong.

When the cow struggled to gain her feet to tend her floundering calf, Damn It barked, shattering the sensuous spell.
Wyatt drew his knees under him, straddling Elizabeth's prone
body, and then reluctantly stood up.

Awkward silence descended as he walked over to untie his
shirt from the calf's hooves. That done, he released the restrained cow and backed away. Lowing quietly, the cow licked
her calf, casting the intruders cautious glances at regular intervals.

Wyatt pivoted toward Elizabeth who was replacing the bridle
on George's head. His assessing gaze ran the length of her
denim-clad body as he remembered the feel of her generous
curves beneath him. She was soft but firm . . . and exceptionally feminine.

The thought caused Wyatt's unruly body to clench in frustrated awareness. Damn, wasn't he getting too old for this sort
of thing? Apparently not. He didn't know whether to be
pleased or dismayed that he could be so easily aroused. God,
maybe he was turning into a dirty old man before his time.
Or, if men did reach their sexual peak at seventeen, he was
entering his second adolescence. Whatever the case, he was
fiercely attracted to Elizabeth Smith Sutton. He wondered if
she felt the same degree of sensual awakening.

"Thank you," Elizabeth said as she ambled over to retrieve the discarded lariat.

"For what?" he asked, his voice one octave below normal.

She grinned impishly. "You figure it out, McKenney."

When she tossed his words back in his face, Wyatt chuckled. The awkward tension evaporated. He appreciated that about her—the ability to make him smile, to let what might have been an uncomfortable silence die a graceful death.

"I'll buy you a new shirt," Elizabeth insisted as she swung into the saddle.

"That isn't necessary."

She was glad he hadn't taken her up on the offer. Money was tight. All the same, Elizabeth felt indebted.

She flicked a glance in Wyatt's direction when he stepped, bare-chested and noticeably virile, into the stirrup. Clearing her throat, she sought distraction.

"Now, would you mind telling me where a man who wears three-piece suits and drives a Caddy learned to ride and rope with such ease?"

His face closed up suddenly, and he shrugged a broad shoulder. "I used to work on a ranch in central Oklahoma before I became a full-time auctioneer." This was the extent of his explanation, reluctantly offered.

Something akin to pain flashed in those green eyes, and Elizabeth decided it best not to pursue the topic. It really was none of her business, after all.

"Wanna race to the pasture gate?" Wyatt challenged abruptly.

She didn't bother accepting; she kicked George into a canter and took off. Since she was riding the slower mount she needed a head start to compete. Chicago was long and leggy, making the gelding a natural for long distances. The compact mare was better for quick starts and short runs.

Halfway to the gate Wyatt overtook her and waved teasingly as Chicago stretched out in a run that ended in a skidding halt beside the gate. The cloudy haze that previously overshadowed the sparkle in his green eyes had faded by the time Elizabeth reined up beside him. Whatever gloomy thought had dampened his spirits was forgotten.

Even though she had lost the race, Elizabeth was exhilarated. She had needed this brief distraction. It had been a long time since she'd had time to enjoy the ranch, because she had become a slave to this heritage she had fought so hard to keep—and would eventually lose . . .

"Hey, don't pout," Wyatt said, teasing her back into good humor. "You still came in second."

"Now there's a consoling thought."

When Elizabeth reached from atop her horse to unlatch the gate, Wyatt reined in closer. His hand brushed over her fingertips in a light caress. "Thank you, Elizabeth, for letting me share the excitement and challenge with you. I had almost forgotten how much I missed it."

Although she wished he would explain what he meant, she smiled playfully. "Now I know why your name sounds familiar. *Wyatt* . . . Aren't you the tough hombre who tamed Dodge City in your younger days?"

Wyatt's crack of laughter wafted across the pasture. "Yep, and that must have been about the time you were ruling England, *Elizabeth.*"

"In a previous life," she assured him. "That must be why I'm so bossy—all those peasants to lord over from my lofty throne. This life of making ends meet must be my comeuppance for languishing in luxury all those years."

"You have it made, Elizabeth," Wyatt said in all seriousness, staring across the rolling hills. "It gets no better than this."

Like an arrow, the comment struck that secluded corner of Elizabeth's heart—that place she protected from the rest of the world. She was about to lose her roots, her heritage. In a few months there would be no galloping romps across land that had been known to generations of proud ancestors. Heartstrings would be a tormenting memory, the reminder of Elizabeth's failure to hold onto what her forefathers had provided for her. God, how was she going to live with herself, knowing that the property that had been in her family for a hundred years would be auctioned off to the highest bidder?

No, Elizabeth didn't have it made at all. She silently corrected Wyatt. She had failed miserably. All she could do was cherish what time she had left on this open range and pray that her ancestors who were buried in the remote plot beside Bird Creek wouldn't roll over in their graves and curse her. But then, her family had been disappointed countless times before, hadn't they? Elizabeth cringed, knowing she was going to be labeled as the final disappointment for all eternity . . .

When the horses had been unsaddled, Eliza- beth invited Wyatt into the house. Still bare-chested, he paused at the doorway of a living room lined with pecan paneling. He admired the Early American furniture and antiques, with the experienced eye of a man who auctioned some of the finest collectables in the country.

Wide, spacious windows permitted a view of undulating hills, making the quaintly furnished room seem larger than it actually was. The living room, dining room, kitchen and master bedroom adjoined each other, while several bedrooms were connected on either side of the main house by the breezeways that opened onto the U-shaped portico on the south, shaded by two gigantic pecan trees.

Wyatt's curious frown prompted Elizabeth to smile at his reaction. "A half-century ago, this was the bunkhouse, home to ten cowboys." She motioned for Wyatt to follow her through the living area to the breezeway door and beyond to the succession of bedrooms, all of which opened onto the shaded portico. "I always loved this bunkhouse. When profit on Heartstrings was plentiful, my husband decided to modernize this structure and use the original house for hired hands. Modern farming practices cut the number of employees needed to keep this five-thousand-acre ranch in operation."

Elizabeth leaned back against the door of what had been her youngest daughter's bedroom. "I thought my husband was a little too extravagant when he decided to refurbish. I liked the rustic wood look just as well as the new limestone rock exterior. But the memories of days gone by are still here, echoing within these walls and across the covered patio. When I was a child, I used to come down from our house at night to listen to the cowboys sing ballads and tell tall tales of things they had done and places they had been."

Wyatt could tell by the expression on Elizabeth's face and the mist in her eyes that these memories were dear to her. His first impression of her had been accurate. She was as much a part of this bunkhouse as she was of the land itself. Proud and strong-willed though Elizabeth was, her attachment to the place was deeply ingrained. He could well imagine that she had done everything humanly possible to retain ownership of the ranch, that she had fought to survive until overwhelming odds had finally defeated her.

Elizabeth smiled tremulously and wiped away the betraying tears that pooled at the corners of her eyes. "Of course, my daughters would have preferred to move to town during their high school years. They thought their social life was suffering because they were miles from their friends." She sighed and shook her head. "To hear them talk, you would have thought nine miles made Pawhuska light years away from civilization. I guess they aren't old enough to appreciate their heritage, or perhaps I didn't instill the need for family traditions in them. Whatever the case, they were anxious to move closer to the fast lane."

Wyatt inwardly winced. He'd had his fill of the fast lane, toward which the youth of the world gravitated. *This* was heaven, in his estimation.

"I take it that your daughters are eager for you to sell out and move away."

Elizabeth nodded her dark head. "In their opinion, the sooner I leave the better. Now that I'm by myself, my daughters are convinced that I need the security of close neighbors. And of course, Julia and Lana drop in every so often to reassure me that I will love town life and all its conveniences."

"Will you, do you think?"

Elizabeth glanced up into liquid green eyes that glistened with sincere curiosity. "I think I'm going to have one helluva time adjusting after being so involved and active on this ranch," she answered honestly. "But I suppose I'll survive."

He noticed she didn't say she would be happy or satisfied. Wyatt doubted a woman with Elizabeth's background could truly be content with neighbors crowding her space. And she was too independent and assertive for early retirement. She would hate city living. He would bet on it.

Elizabeth shook herself out of her pensive trance and pushed away from the wall. "If you would like to wash up, you can use the large bathroom off the master bedroom. I'll fix us some refreshments."

After she had shown him to the spacious bedroom with its inviting king-size bed covered with a colorful, old-fashioned, quilted comforter, Wyatt made his way to the vanity to freshen up. He stared into the mirror, distracted by the homey room that indicated Elizabeth's taste in antique furniture. True, the drapes and bedspread looked to be long used and in need of replacement, but the place appealed to Wyatt's senses—as did the woman who spent her nights sleeping alone in that bed . . .

Wyatt gave himself a mental slap for allowing his wandering thoughts to detour down arousing avenues. Women like Elizabeth didn't do much bed-hopping. Wyatt guessed she preferred to remain off the beaten path, content in her isolated world, and undoubtedly too busy to have spare time or the energy for bedroom gymnastics. He knew that feeling well. His days of coordinating auctions and jet-hopping to conventions took their toll. He reluctantly admitted he was too damned tired to do much else except sleep by the time his head finally hit a pillow. That is, until just recently.

His dead battery had received several volts of stimulation during the afternoon's activities with Elizabeth. Finding himself sprawled on top of her was like being hooked up to jumper cables. His male motor was suddenly humming, and he had to admit he enjoyed feeling vital and alive again.

Inhaling a refreshing breath, Wyatt stuck his head under the faucet and slapped cold water in his face. His hectic lifestyle now seemed a million miles away. He was beginning to relax, to enjoy life instead of being ruled by the driving obsession that had kept him going at a grueling pace—one his conscientious physician assured him would earn him a date with the mortician if he didn't watch out.

Chapter Three

Elizabeth didn't hear the two cars pull into the driveway while she was making lemonade and thawing out the half-batch of cookies in the microwave. The creak of the front door brought her around to see her two daughters standing in the living room. Julia and Lana took one look at their mother's mussed hair and frowned.

"Whose car is in the driveway?" Lana questioned. "And what have you been doing?"

It was then that Wyatt, his hair damp and his chest still bare, came strolling out of Elizabeth's bedroom. As the young women's suspicious gazes zeroed in on him, he silently groaned. Once again, he was making a bad first impression. He could tell by the expressions on those two lovely young faces that he had just been consigned to perdition. A half-naked man sauntering nonchalantly out of Elizabeth's bedroom lent itself to lurid speculation—which Lana and Julia were pursuing at the moment. Good thing lynch mobs were outdated. Otherwise Wyatt was sure he'd have been a prime candidate for an old-fashioned necktie party.

Elizabeth's gaze darted across the wide space that separated her from him, and she blushed to the roots of her hair. She didn't know whether to deny what her daughters were thinking or to simply ignore their erroneous assumptions. She decided to make the necessary introductions and act as if nothing had happened—it hadn't.

"Julia, Lana, this is Wyatt McKenney from Oklahoma City. He is the auctioneer Jerry Patterson suggested I consult about selling the ranch."

Wyatt surveyed the tall, curly-haired blonde whose pale blue eyes and fair skin indicated she had inherited her father's coloring. Julia looked to be twenty-two or -three and she was built like a model who could have graced the pages of *Vogue*—if not for her sporty T-shirt and trim-fitting Levi's.

Lana looked to be about the same age as her sister, but she had her mother's dark eyes and auburn hair and she stood two inches shorter than her statuesque sister. Attractive though both young women were, there was nothing pretty about the condemning expressions on their faces. Wyatt was as welcome here as a plague of rattlesnakes, having been judged guilty of a whirlwind seduction and labeled a Casanova. Elizabeth undoubtedly was viewed as the helpless victim since she was Julia's and Lana's mother. Gawd, Wyatt had never felt so awkward in his life.

"Nice to meet you," he said, extending a hand in greeting.

Julia and Lana stared at the proffered hand— attached to the bare arm and chest—as if his fingers dripped poison. Self-consciously, Wyatt dropped his arm and stuffed his hands in his pockets.

Elizabeth spoke up. "We were about to have lemonade and cookies. Would you girls like to join us?"

Well, Julia and Lana certainly weren't about to leave! Their intrusion was all that was preventing this bare-chested Romeo from seducing their mother—again.

"Sure," Lana replied as she strategically placed herself between Wyatt and Elizabeth. "Sounds good."

"So . . . have you decided on a date for the auction?" Julia questioned her mother, ignoring their unwanted guest.

"We haven't got around to making the arrangements yet . . ." Elizabeth inwardly groaned. She had unwittingly implied that she and Wyatt had been engaged in more rigorous activities than discussion. Damn, it was going to require surgery to have her foot removed from her mouth.

"Oh, really?" Lana spared Wyatt a pensive glance. "Then how much progress have you made this afternoon?"

Elizabeth stuffed a glass of lemonade and some cookies in each daughter's hand. "We were just having a look around the ranch so Wyatt could get an idea of Heartstrings' value."

The knock at the front door was a godsend. Elizabeth fairly sagged in relief. The tension in the living room was so thick she could have chopped it in two with a meat cleaver.

"I'll answer it," Wyatt volunteered. "That should be Jerry." He hoped.

The minute Wyatt was out of earshot, Lana and Julia rounded on their mother.

"Are you out of your mind?" Julia asked. "This is the twentieth century, you know, Mother. Women don't have to tolerate the suave come-ons of middle-aged Don Juans. You can actually discuss business arrangements without having to succumb to illicit activities."

"If you would stop waving your women's lib flag in my face and listen—" Elizabeth tried to object, only to be interrupted by reinforcements from the left flank.

"Now, Mother, I can understand that you might have gotten lonely with Julia and me out of the house. That is exactly why we have insisted on your moving to town to associate with other widows your age."

This from a first-year teacher of psychology and sociology in the Skiatook school system, Elizabeth mused. She noted that Lana had failed to mention that widows of her "own age" might like to share the company of a M . . . A . . . N.

Good grief, suddenly her two daughters had appointed themselves to the position of *Mother,* lecturing *her* on proper social and moral protocol. For years Elizabeth had heard Lana and Julia complain that they were too grown up for lectures. Now, all of a sudden, *they* were delivering advice to *her.*

Ironic, wasn't it, that Lana and Julia believed the worst about their own mother? Where was that bond of trust mothers and daughters were supposed to share? You raised your kids as best you could, making all sorts of personal and financial sacrifices and *wham!* They attacked their parent like starving wolves.

"There are many cases of lonely women turning to men for companionship," Lana continued diplomatically, as was her custom. "But you must remember that meaningful affection should not be mistaken for desperation. And who knows how many partners Wyatt McKenney has had? With communicable diseases running rampant, caution is extremely important."

"Oh, for God's sake," Elizabeth groaned.

"She's right, Mother," Julia chimed in. "You should listen to Lana. After all, she is certified in psychology, and she understands the stimuli and responses of behavioral patterns. We realize that you miss Dad, but you have let yourself be taken in by a virtual stranger. Granted, I can see why you might consider this man attractive—for his age."

Elizabeth choked back a laugh. For his age? To hear Julia talk, Wyatt had escaped from a senior citizens' retirement home. The poor girl had no concept of masculine beauty if she couldn't see that he was physically appealing, even at the ripe, decrepit old age of forty-eight.

"Wyatt McKenney is *extremely* attractive—at his age," Elizabeth felt compelled to say in his behalf. "But the fact is—"

"All right." Lana, the amateur psychologist, was patronizing her. "For the sake of argument, we agree that the man is good looking in a mature, distinguished sort of way."

Elizabeth flung Lana a withering glance.

"But there's more to a positive, supportive relationship than physical appeal," Lana continued, regurgitating all the information she'd acquired in her college classes. "There must be respect, common interests and similar socioeconomic backgrounds to form a stable foundation. Loneliness often manifests itself in—"

Elizabeth's hand shot toward the sofa. "Both of you sit down, now!" she commanded, resorting to her *mad mother* tone of voice.

When Julia opened her mouth, Elizabeth glowered her into submission. "I said *sit.*"

Reluctantly, both daughters sat.

"Now then . . ." Elizabeth inhaled deeply and formulated her thoughts. "In the first place, what you think happened did not happen. And in the second place, if it *had* happened it would be my business, not yours. I have spent nine years struggling to keep this family afloat and to ensure you were educated, well fed and respectably dressed. I have neglected my own social life and have taken a part-time job to make certain you had every op- portunity to make successes of yourselves. That is not to say that you haven't helped to support yourselves," she added. "But—"

"With all due respect, Mother—"

"Clam up, Lana. I'm not finished yet. When I'm doing the talking, you're going to do the listening. You should be able to relate to that now that you have a classroom full of students to discipline and instruct."

"We're only trying to keep you from getting hurt," Julia insisted. "You're out of touch with the singles scene. There aren't many men like Dad left in the world."

Thank God for that, Elizabeth thought, but she kept the comment to herself. Julia and Lana knew Bob Sutton as a father, not as a husband. There was a big difference, and Elizabeth preferred not to shatter her daughters' perceptions of the "beloved father" who didn't take the time to be with his children when he could have done so.

"I don't think you should let Wyatt McKenney organize the auction," Julia advised.

"Why? Because you think I slept with him, despite my denial?" Elizabeth challenged.

"Why don't you tell us why he was wandering around with his hair damp from a recent shower and without a shirt," Lana calmly suggested. "If you explain, perhaps we won't be jumping to any more conclusions."

"Fine," Elizabeth snapped, annoyed with her daughter's condescending tone. "We used his shirt as an improvised rope to pull a calf that was having a difficult delivery. It was his shirt or mine. Would you have preferred I volunteered to go topless?"

Lana and Julia sat there contemplating the explanation for a half-minute before the psychology expert replied diplomatically, "That sounds reasonable, I suppose."

"Would you like to check the bed, just to make sure?"

"No of course not," Julia grumbled. "If you say nothing happened, then I guess nothing happened."

"Your unfaltering trust overwhelms me." Elizabeth smirked. "But in the future, I expect you to let me handle my own affairs. Let me rephrase that. I expect you to accept my mature judgment." She inhaled deeply, mustered a smile and bounded off to another topic like a kangaroo. "So . . . how are the jobs going?"

Wyatt stood on the portico, confronting Jerry Patterson's curious stare. "No, I have not been to bed with Elizabeth," he insisted. "I used the shirt off my back to deliver a calf. And I was just on my way to retrieve a clean shirt from the suitcase in my car."

Jerry Patterson chuckled at his friend's defensive tone. "Don't tell me Julia and Lana caught you half-naked."

"They did," Wyatt muttered as he ambled across the lawn. "I seem to be having trouble with first impressions."

"Do you want me to go to bat for you? I'll be glad to serve as a character witness. Should I tell them about some of your college antics?"

Wyatt flung his teasing friend a disgruntled glare. "No thanks. I'm sure you would delight in making matters worse." Wyatt opened the trunk and rifled through his suitcase for a shirt. "Why don't you just tell me the real reason you invited me up here for the weekend."

Jerry clasped his hands behind him, rocked back and forth on his heels and smiled slyly. "You said your doctor suggested that you take a vacation. I thought this would be the perfect place for you to relax. Besides, I haven't seen you in six months."

"And?" Wyatt prodded as he fastened himself into his shirt.

"And I wanted you to have a look around Heartstrings," Jerry insisted. "Helluva place, isn't it? I sure would hate to see some cattle corporation move in and take over. You've got good connections in the National Cattlemen's and Stock Feeder associations. I'd like to see you become involved in this auction rather than someone who views the ranch strictly in terms of dollars and cents."

Wyatt eyed Jerry for a long moment before his gaze strayed to the shadowed silhouettes in the window. He could probably save himself a lot of trouble and grief if he walked away from Heartstrings and its complications.

"Come sit down on the portico and drink your lemonade," Jerry requested. "It will be another hour before Nancy has dinner ready."

Wyatt followed along behind the stocky nutrition consultant who had been assigned to the northern districts of the Stocker Feed Company. Wyatt and Jerry had become acquainted during their college years and had kept in touch since graduation. Because of their professions, the two men often crossed paths. Wyatt knew Jerry well enough to realize his friend had something up his sleeve. It didn't take a genius to determine Jerry's ultimate motive, either.

When Wyatt sank down on the wooden bench on the U-shaped portico and felt the wind whispering through the breezeways that connected the bedrooms to the main house, an odd sensation swept over him. He stared past the towering pecan trees, across the valley toward the creek. The spectacular view eased the tension that had become so much a part of his fast-paced life, leaving him amazingly content. Wyatt could have sat there for hours, watching grass grow, feeling the wind brushing over him like a relaxing massage. He glanced back through the window of time, remembering his childhood and the peacefulness that had become overshadowed by heartbreak and tragedy.

He could sympathize with Elizabeth's anguish over losing something that was a part of what she was. He understood better than she knew, more than he had allowed himself to remember for years . . .

"Are you okay, Wyatt?" Jerry questioned, scrutinizing him closely. "You *are* okay, aren't you? I mean, this business with your physician—?"

"I'm fine," Wyatt assured his concerned friend. "I just need to get away from the killing pace for a while, away from the telephone."

"Tell me about it." Jerry snorted. "Alexander Graham Bell has become the curse of my life."

As if on cue, the phone in the living room blared and Jerry muttered. "I'm really beginning to hate that sound."

Wyatt leaned back to sip his lemonade. "I need background information on this ranch," he requested. "Everything, even insignificant details. How did it become financially unstable? From what I've seen so far, Elizabeth is anything but extravagant and wasteful."

Jerry chuckled. "She is as practical and conscientious as they come, and she's a damned good manager. She inherited debts from her husband that place the property in jeopardy."

"He was the extravagant one?" Wyatt queried.

"From what I know personally and have heard, Bob married this ranch. Elizabeth became an only child after her brother died in a farming accident when he was a teenager. She was the heir to the ranch and to an Osage headright by which money was paid to tribal roll members for oil leases on reservation land.

"During the oil boom, Bob Sutton decided to purchase more property, even at increased prices. When he was at the height of his glory, he was wheeling and dealing in the cattle market and buying machinery, pickups and livestock as if they were going out of style. He tried to expand too fast and borrowed hundreds of thousands of dollars."

"Elizabeth didn't object?" Wyatt questioned.

"Sure she objected, for all the good it did." Jerry leaned back and laced his fingers behind his head, staring at the peaceful scene before him. "You would have had to know Bob to understand. He could be a real charmer when he wanted to be. When Elizabeth grew concerned about their finances he shrugged her off, insisting that he could handle the growing business. But it was always Elizabeth who kept this ranch running. Bob spent more and more time at the coffee shop, boasting of his success, and in the office he rented in town."

"And then the oil boom went bust." Wyatt sadly shook his head. "Land was devalued and bankers called in debts to cover their losses."

"That's about the size of it. The oil royalty for Osage headrights hit rock-bottom, and Bob lost the five thousand acres he had bought, plus the cattle he had purchased to graze it. He was scrabbling around like a madman, taking out double mortgages without the banks in the county knowing what he was doing. When Elizabeth found out that he had tried to sell off part of the original Osage homestead, the shit hit the fan. She is a quarter Osage, and her family heritage means a great deal to her. Bob committed the ultimate sin when he tried to pull *that* fast one."

Wyatt glanced toward the house. "Did she toss him out on his high-rolling ass?"

"She might have." Jerry took a sip of Wyatt's lemonade and then handed the glass back to him. "Unfortunately, Bob was killed the following week during a thunderstorm. His . . . um . . . secretary who worked at the office he rented in town was driving her car over winding, rain-slick roads and lost control. They both went over the guard rail and ended up in the wooded canyon below. Sutton Cattle Company closed down operation and Elizabeth has been struggling to hold things together at Heartstrings ever since."

"Secretary?" Wyatt's gaze narrowed on Jerry, who was rolling his eyes and shaking his sandy red head.

"That's the story Julia and Lana were told, the one Bob had always used to keep up the pretense."

"That son of a bitch," Wyatt muttered sourly.

"You must have known Bob Sutton better than I thought," Jerry chuckled. "He was a status seeker and a ladies' man from the word go. Elizabeth did all the work, while he tried to see how many female challenges he could conquer."

"I've met my share of Bob Suttons, thank you very much. Too many of them around to suit me," Wyatt said.

"He was definitely a skirt-chaser, and Elizabeth was his meal ticket. Now she's paying for all his mistakes while raising her daughters all by herself."

Wyatt was well acquainted with paying for the mistakes of others. He had paid—and paid.

"What about present operations and investments?" Wyatt wanted to know. "Is there any way for Elizabeth to acquire a loan?"

Jerry shook his head. "Not with Bob's credit rating hanging over her like a guillotine. She was paying interest on the loans as best she could until her girls enrolled in college. The extra expenses devoured any profit and what little money she was getting from the Osage headright. Two hard years of extreme weather conditions took their toll. She still works her night job at Tall Grass Prairie Cafe for spending money."

"Good Lord," Wyatt groaned.

Jerry laughed aloud. "What are you moaning about? You're a fine one to talk about burning candles at both ends. Elizabeth isn't any different. She's doing what she has to do to survive, no matter how many hours a day it takes."

Wyatt muttered under his breath. He and Elizabeth were two worker bees buzzing around their hives, rarely taking time to rest their wings. It was a wonder *her* doctor hadn't prescribed an extended vacation for her.

"At present, Elizabeth is running one hundred and fifty cows on fifteen hundred acres and fifteen hundred yearlings to sell to feed lots on twelve hundred acres of pasture. I cut her the best deal I could on cattle cubes from the feed company, and she bales her own hay to ensure her livestock are making good weight gains. But three hundred tons of feed at one hundred and fifty dollars a ton doesn't come cheap. Elizabeth works nights to make ends meet and she drives a beat-up pickup that buzzards circle. Her hired man does most of the repairs on the farm machinery, to save on expenses. She has cut every ounce of fat from this operation, works her tail off every damned day and she still breaks less than even because of the outstanding debts.''

"Didn't dear Bob ever hear of life insurance?''

"Yeah, he heard of it, and he mortgaged his own life to buy part of the expanded property. One of the banks in Tulsa now holds the deed to that land. Elizabeth didn't get one red cent.''

"Well, shit.''

Jerry patted Wyatt on the shoulder. "That's why I called you. You're the man to handle this particular auction. You take the time to get details instead of putting a property on the block and looking the other way when a rancher goes under.''

Wyatt raised a thick brow and surveyed his smiling friend. "Anybody ever tell you that you are one shrewd bastard, Patterson?''

"You did.'' Jerry chuckled, undaunted. "Besides, you never could take a vacation. Always did have to be doing something. This is the perfect project for you.''

"Set me on a sinking ship and watch it go down, is that it?'' Wyatt queried. "That should do wonders for the stress my doctor insists I avoid.''

Jerry rose to his feet and worked the kinks out of his back. He grinned enigmatically as he appraised the grand view from the shaded portico. "Like I said, Wyatt, this is one helluva place Elizabeth has here. Sure would hate to see it fall into the wrong hands.'' He strode toward the breezeway. "Come on, Nancy should have dinner ready pretty soon. She's anxious to see you. It's been two years since you stopped in for a visit.''

Wyatt frowned pensively as Jerry sauntered off. Without a word to the Suttons, he got up and left. He figured Lana and Julia preferred it that way.

Chapter Four

After the afternoon's fiasco that had left Julia and Lana casting speculative glances at their mother, Elizabeth was relieved to have an excuse to leave the house. Julia was in a bitchy mood—something about the jerk of a veterinarian she worked for at the animal clinic in Bartlesville. But then, Julia was full of spit and fire, so who would know exactly what the problem was with her boss. And Lana was still dropping subtle psychological comments when Elizabeth strode off in her waitress uniform.

Keeping her fingers crossed that her jalopy pickup could make another run to Pawhuska, Elizabeth roared off. When she was alone, her thoughts immediately turned to the man whose appearance had caused such commotion.

She had come to the conclusion that there was a lot more to Wyatt McKenney than just a distinguished face and muscular body. The incident in the pasture testified to the fact that he was no stranger to cattle and horses. He obviously had more experience in ranching than she'd given him credit for. Yet, all of Julia's and Lana's warnings had raised doubts in Elizabeth's mind again.

Wyatt appeared to be a man who kept his own counsel. Elizabeth knew very little about him, other than the fact that she was physically attracted for the first time since Bob Sutton had swept her off her feet. That romance had lasted a sum total of four years, the marriage sixteen.

Oh sure, Elizabeth had been hit on countless times while she worked the evening shift at the Tall Grass Prairie Cafe which was situated beside Pawhuska's finest motel. But she'd had sense enough not to take those pick-up artists seriously. And she'd had no time for dating, not with a ranch to run by day and a part-time job by night.

Her encounter with Wyatt McKenney was different, she admitted. It was a sensual reawakening, a reminder that she was still very much a woman who had put her feminine needs in cold storage after being hurt by Bob's infidelity. Wyatt had reminded her that there was more to life than work. And yet, there was no future with a man like Wyatt McKenney. He would be here today and who knew where tomorrow. And for heaven's sake, the man could even be married for all she knew. Jerry had never discussed Wyatt's personal life, only his professional credentials.

Well, what difference did it make now? Elizabeth asked herself sensibly. Wyatt hadn't even taken time to say good-bye and he probably wouldn't be back, since she had insisted that he wasn't the man for the auction. They had gotten off to a bad start and had ended on a sour note, thanks to Julia's and Lana's unannounced arrival. But in the middle . . .

A smile tugged at Elizabeth's lips as she drove to town. She and Wyatt had certainly met in the middle. Even now, she could feel sensual heat channeling through her body. Remembered sensations and images of a tanned face hovering over hers were spotlighted in her mind. Now she wished Wyatt *had* kissed her, even with that mustache . . .

"Good grief, Liz, how old did you say you were? Twenty?" Elizabeth glanced in the rearview mirror. Definitely not twenty. "Forget him," she lectured herself. "McKenney is gone and best forgotten."

Elizabeth clung to that practical thought as she applied the brake and parked outside the restaurant. She could use a distraction right about now. Good thing Irene Truman was working the night shift with her. The forty-seven-year-old, twice-divorced waitress was amusing company. Irene was sure to provide her own unique brand of entertainment to take Elizabeth's mind off Wyatt.

"You're on duty tonight? Good, sugar," Irene said, latching onto Elizabeth's arm the minute she sailed through the door. "Boy, have I got some juicy gossip to share."

Irene stuck a pencil in the dyed blond hair that was piled up on her head like cotton candy and then she leaned close. "You know Aaron Black, the city councilman? Well, you're never going to guess who Anna Mae Hillman saw him with last night after the council meeting."

Elizabeth reached for her order pad and grinned. "Ole Aaron has changed girlfriends again? Does he have his wife's permission?"

"Are you kidding? I don't know what color the sky is in Jessica Black's world, but she doesn't have a clue that Aaron has been running around on her for years. Aaron's latest lady friend is your neighbor's ex-wife," Irene confided. "Can you believe that woman? What could Patty Hollis possibly see in chubby ole Aaron? Gawd, the man has a belly to match a bloated horse. Every time he comes swaggering in here and gives me the eye I want to slap him. He reminds me so much of my first husband it gives me the creeps. To this day I don't know why I married that loser." Irene scooped up the coffee pot and headed toward the empty cups that awaited her attention. "I'll fill you in on all the sordid details when we have a spare minute."

Elizabeth didn't have any spare time for the next two hours. The cafe was jumping with customers. The rodeo at the fair grounds had been good for business, but it was hard on Elizabeth's aching feet. She needed track shoes to keep up the pace. She had filled enough coffee cups and tea glasses to float a yacht and she had served enough hot beef sandwiches to feed the national guard unit. There was no doubt that she would sleep like a rock tonight. And if her pickup failed her on the return trip, she would camp out on the seat. God, *tired* didn't begin to describe her condition!

Finally, the crowd thinned out and Elizabeth plopped into the corner booth beside Irene, who was fussing over a broken fingernail.

"Will you look at this?" Irene grumbled. "I just had these claws polished and buffed."

Elizabeth self-consciously curled her fingers into a fist. Farm chores didn't tend to produce gorgeous nails. Work gloves were all that prevented her from having calluses one inch thick.

That thought reminded Elizabeth of Wyatt McKenney. How it could have the slightest connection she didn't know. But then, the man had been so much on her mind the past few hours, everything reminded her of him. *He* was probably accustomed to cavorting with women who never missed weekly appointments at hairdressing salons, women who dressed elegantly and who got manicures.

When Elizabeth considered this ridiculous fascination she was harboring she realized she was deluding herself if she thought Wyatt might have a real interest in someone like her. He had been toying with her that afternoon, more than likely silently laughing at her because she had misjudged him. He was only amusing himself with a country bumpkin because there were no cosmopolitan females around. Gad, now she really did feel like a fool!

Irene sipped coffee to lubricate her vocal chords and took up where she had left off earlier in the evening. "You'll never believe where Aaron and Patty Hollis were getting it on last night." She snickered devilishly. "The backseat of a car. Can you believe it? I swear Aaron will never grow up. He still thinks his sexual prowess determines how much of a man he is. If you ask me, a man who does it so poorly a *hundred* times with dozens of different women is having trouble doing it right, just *once.*"

Elizabeth burst out laughing. "How long have you been working on this theory, Irene?"

"Don't scoff," Irene said in feigned offense. "I don't think Aaron's wife is the least bit cold in bed. There is no such thing as a cold woman, only awkward, insensitive men. If Aaron could do it right at home, he wouldn't have to keep changing bed partners when the novelty wears off . . . Damn, who is *that?*"

Elizabeth glanced over her shoulder to see who had drawn Irene's rapt attention. To her surprise, Wyatt McKenney ambled into the cafe and took a seat. He was dressed in jeans, boots and a Western shirt. Irene was drooling all over herself.

"Keep your seat, sugar," she insisted. "I'll wait on the future love of my life." She stood up and brushed a preening hand over her hair. "Maybe the third time around will be the charm. You think Aaron would mind if I borrowed the backseat of his Lincoln?" she asked with a wink and a naughty grin.

Elizabeth sipped her drink and assured herself it was the caffeine that was giving her sluggish body a jolt. Her gaze darted to Wyatt, who offered Irene a smile in greeting. Damn, he *would* have to be wearing trim-fitting jeans and a pearl-snapped shirt. It should be a criminal offense for a man to look that good in whatever he chose to wear. And what quirk of fate, Elizabeth would like to know, had landed Wyatt in Tall Grass Prairie Cafe? Wasn't he supposed to be visiting with Nancy and Jerry Patterson?

As Wyatt's deep, resonant voice carried across the cafe, Elizabeth swallowed another gulp of coffee, pretending the mere presence of the man didn't affect her. Should she stroll over to say hello, or rather good-bye? She really should apologize for Julia's and Lana's behavior. But Wyatt probably didn't care to see her again, and she *was* on duty.

Excuses, excuses.

Go talk to the man. You know you want to.

"Don't you ever shut up?" Elizabeth scowled at that honest

little voice that was nagging her to death. Besides, what was the point? Irene was falling all over herself to rush back to Wyatt's table with a pot of coffee and containers of cream.

"God, what a hunk," she whispered on her way down the aisle. "Did you get a close look at this guy? Bedroom eyes, if ever I saw any."

On legs that felt like spaghetti, Elizabeth picked up her cup and aimed herself toward the kitchen. She might as well fill a few salt shakers while Irene talked Wyatt's ear off. No sense in wasting time; that was Elizabeth's motto.

Obviously it was Irene's motto, too. She'd always been a sucker for a handsome face, and she'd had the worst luck with men. Her ex-husbands had used her and her men friends had only wanted temporary sexual satisfaction.

Maybe Elizabeth should be thankful she didn't have time to become involved with men. One husband had been plenty. Bob had been charming and attentive until after he'd married her. In the following years, he seemed to have forgotten everything he knew about courtesy and consideration. Marrying money had gone to his head, and Elizabeth had watched the man she thought she loved be transformed.

Julia and Lana might believe their father to be perfect, but Elizabeth had dealt with the reality of living with a man who took more than he ever intended to give. He talked a success story. As Elizabeth remembered it, she had worked the dawn to dusk shift while Bob was supposedly supervising the ranching operation from the driver's seat of his pickup. He'd turned out to be a far better *operator* than Elizabeth had even imagined!

Irene poked her head inside the kitchen door to flash Elizabeth an accusing glance. "Why didn't you tell me you knew that hunk?"

The cook perked up immediately. "What hunk?"

"The one who wants to talk to Elizabeth. Put in a good word for me, will you sugar?"

Elizabeth set the salt and pepper shakers aside and reversed direction, suddenly feeling as nervous and self-conscious as a schoolgirl on her first date. Her hands were clammy and she wasn't even running a fever. Lord, what was the matter with her?

Wyatt watched Elizabeth approach and smiled to himself. There was no other way to put it: she looked adorable in her prim white blouse, red bow tie and black skirt that extended to three inches above the knee. Nice legs, he noticed, and the extra touch of makeup accentuated those big brown eyes that reminded him of melting chocolate.

An odd thrill riveted him as his gaze descended to the full swells of her breasts and then dipped to the trim curve of her hips. Wyatt distinctly remembered the feel of her supple body meshed intimately to his. Judging by the way his male juices percolated at that thought, he could have sworn it had been minutes instead of hours since he and Elizabeth had been sprawled in the pasture. Damn, he was getting aroused by a memory!

"Did you want me to warm your coffee?" she questioned, extending the freshly brewed pot.

Wyatt chuckled. "You just did, from inside out."

Elizabeth frowned, unable to decipher his quietly uttered words. "Come again?"

"I don't think this would be the suitable place for it, but thanks for asking."

Elizabeth eyed his smile with wary consternation. "I'm not sure you and I are having the same conversation."

Green eyes twinkled, and the left corner of his mouth kicked up. "No, I don't think we are." He gestured toward the opposite side of the booth. "Sit down, Elizabeth. I need to talk to you."

Elizabeth slid onto the seat. "You didn't even bother saying good-bye." She slammed her mouth shut and inwardly groaned.

Real subtle, Liz. Next thing you know foreign ambassadors will be calling to enroll in the Smith Sutton School of Tact and Diplomacy.

Wyatt felt inordinately pleased that she had wanted him to say good-bye rather than walking off, never to reappear. "Under the circumstances, I thought it best to make a dis- creet exit," he explained. "Julia and Lana didn't seem thrilled to have me underfoot. Since Nancy Patterson had dinner waiting, I decided it best to leave *bad enough* alone."

"I'm sure what Nancy served was more appetizing than the ham sandwiches we had for supper." Elizabeth sank back in the booth and forced herself to relax. There was absolutely no reason for her to be nervous around Wyatt. Other men didn't make her jittery.

But other men aren't as appealing to you as Wyatt McKenney.

"Gimme a break, will you," Elizabeth muttered, half under her breath.

"Pardon?"

"Nothing. We're having one of those double conversations again," Elizabeth informed him.

Wyatt chuckled, wondering if she was having the same trouble controlling erotic thoughts as he was. He could only hope. If she was, it was an encouraging sign. It indicated the attraction wasn't one-sided. That revelation gave Wyatt the confidence to present his proposition. He hoped Elizabeth wouldn't reject it as quickly as she had earlier in the day.

Bracing his elbows on the table, he leaned forward. "After my brief tour of Heartstrings this afternoon, I really would like to take a closer look at your operation and inventory."

The tension flooded out of Elizabeth. He would be back. That pleased her—more than it should have.

"I know you don't think I'm the right man, but I've auctioned registered cattle and horses— sold farms, ranches and machinery many times in the past. In fact, most of my clientele are involved in agriculture, though I have done Western art auctions and charity benefits on occasion." He paused and smiled that crooked smile that could melt Elizabeth's knees. "The only reason I was wearing a three-piece suit today was because I just got off a plane from California after doing a highbrow Arabian horse sale for a celebrity."

Elizabeth returned his smile. "And the Caddy?"

"Is comfortable for long drives. Compact cars leave me feeling as if I'm sandwiched between two pieces of bread. And by the way, you're a snob for judging me because of my choice of automobiles."

Funny, Wyatt thought, most women had the exact opposite reaction to seeing a man in an expensive car. Usually, dollar signs registered in their eyes, and they showed increased interest when they noted there wasn't a wedding ring on his finger. But not Elizabeth. She was put off by expensive vehicles and designer suits. Nothing seemed to appeal to her as much as scuffed boots and well-worn jeans. That suggested she was more impressed by a man who was willing to work as hard as she did.

"I really did intend to apologize for misjudging you," Elizabeth said. "But Julia and Lana showed up, and they were far more interested in what you were doing in my bedroom without your shirt. I got sidetracked, and then you left."

Wyatt couldn't conceal the grin that quirked his lips. "Did you finally convince them we weren't fooling around?"

"Would you have been convinced, given the incriminating circumstances?" she questioned.

His gaze locked with those luminous obsidian eyes that were surrounded with thick sooty lashes that looked to be three inches long with the emphasis of mascara. "No, probably not. But I'm wishing I could have enjoyed what I have been accused of doing," he said in a husky voice.

A jolt of awareness shot through Elizabeth, swift as a round of ammunition pumped from an automatic weapon. There had been times during the past hours that she had found herself wishing the same thing . . .

"You're blushing," Wyatt noted with an ornery smile.

"Change of life—hot flashes and all that."

He eyed her dubiously. "Don't you think forty-five is a little young?"

"Apparently not . . . Are you married?" she blurted out.

Wyatt blinked at the question that came straight from left

field. "I used to be, but I'm not now. What does that have to do with hot flashes?"

"A lot, considering you just indicated you wouldn't have minded being guilty as accused by the hanging judges." Elizabeth nodded toward the waitress who was aiming herself in their direction, employing the drumroll walk she reserved for special male customers. "Irene was just telling me about one of our mutual high-school acquaintances who left his wife at home while he was fooling around with a divorcee. I wondered if you practiced that policy."

"Can I get you a slice of pie?" Irene questioned with her brightest smile. "Lemon, butterscotch or chocolate?"

"No thanks," Wyatt declined. "I was just leaving."

"Well, you come back any ole time, sugar. This is the best restaurant in town. Good food and *fast service,*" she added with a suggestive wink.

Elizabeth burst out laughing at Irene's outrageous remark. She was a hopeless tease who never met a stranger.

"God, Irene, give the man a break. The regular customers are used to your flirtatious routines. Wyatt McKenney will think you're serious."

"Who says I'm not?" Irene said, batting her fake eyelashes at Wyatt. "Coffee is on the house for first-timers. Next time it'll cost you."

When Irene sauntered off, giving Wyatt the rear view of her May West walk, Elizabeth shook her head. "Irene isn't really like that. She simply delights in setting men back on their heels, just for shock value. With two broken marriages behind her, she is actually very particular about the company she keeps these days."

"And you're not?" Wyatt inquired. "I'd imagine with your striking looks you've had your share of invitations from male customers."

"None of which I take more seriously than your comment about being caught doing what didn't happen."

Wyatt took a sip of coffee before staring at Elizabeth over the rim of his cup. "Maybe I was serious."

Elizabeth felt as if she were the one who had just downed steaming coffee. "I thought you were just leaving," she prompted in a croaking voice that would have done a frog proud.

His unblinking gaze probed into her. "I am, as soon as I have your answer. I'm taking a couple of weeks of vacation and I would like to spend it here. I like the looks of Heartstrings." *I like the looks of you.* "Let me organize your auction, Elizabeth."

The expression on his handsome face and the raspy sound of his voice suggested more than a business arrangement. Elizabeth froze up. This could be a very risky business, considering her vivid awareness of Wyatt McKenney. He was tempting her. Their unplanned tumble in the grass had escalated her attraction to him, so she had to proceed with caution. She already knew the feel of his muscular body molded all too familiarly to hers. He had indicated he wouldn't be averse to enjoying the erotic activities Julia and Lana thought they had already participated in.

Elizabeth was wading into quicksand here. If she wasn't careful she was going to lose more than the ranch to which she was sentimentally attached. When the auction was over Wyatt could very well be gone, having had a fling and collected his commission. And how did she know for sure that he didn't make a habit of this sort of thing? It was common practice for Aaron Black, after all.

"Elizabeth?" Wyatt exhorted, scrutinizing her intently. "I'm waiting for an answer."

"I'm thinking it over."

"Do you want a résumé of my professional credentials?"

"No, a character reference if you have one on you."

He smiled. "You don't trust me?"

"I don't know you. The last man I entrusted Heartstrings to has cost me my family's ranch," Elizabeth said more bitterly than she intended. "I don't like losing Heartstrings, but selling it for less than it's worth would be a killing blow."

"I'll make certain your ranch gets a fair price on today's market," Wyatt promised.

No guarantees, Elizabeth noted. *On today's market.* Twelve years ago, the ranch would have brought double the price. Of course, she wouldn't have considered selling it for any price unless she'd been forced into it.

Now she was.

"I'm staying at the motel next door," Wyatt said finally. "You can think it over and come by to give me your answer. I'm in room twenty-two."

Catch twenty-two, Elizabeth thought to herself.

Leaving Irene a generous tip, Wyatt unfolded himself from the seat and walked off. Elizabeth watched him disappear out the door. She was still staring after him when Irene plunked down, all eyes and catlike curiosity.

"Well?" Irene probed.

"Well what?"

"What's the scoop on Wyatt McKenney?"

"He's forty-eight years old."

*"Per*fect," Irene purred.

"Drives a plush Caddy."

"Really? My favorite kind of man."

"He's an auctioneer who headquarters in Oklahoma City, and he organizes sales for the rich and famous."

Irene slapped her hand down like a gavel. "Sold."

Elizabeth rolled her eyes and flung Irene a withering glance. "He only offered to conduct the auction of my ranch," she tried to explain.

"Forget the damned ranch and take *his* bid," Irene insisted. "Are you blind, sugar? The man is interested in you."

"Since when did you become an expert on sexual nuances?" Elizabeth teased her. "I thought you said you were a terrible judge of men."

"For myself, yes. But I can spot possibility for you at twenty paces. Go for it, Liz. You've been tied to Heartstrings for too many years. A woman can't fool around with horses and cattle all her life, you know. Another kind of ride wouldn't hurt on occasion—"

"Irene!" Elizabeth gasped.

"How long has it been?"

"None of your business," Elizabeth muttered, flustered by the outrageous question, though she shouldn't have been considering who'd posed it. She had known Irene since grade school. Irene wasn't afraid to say anything to anyone.

"Well, if you ask me, you should give the man a chance," Irene decreed. "You were widowed too young, and you isolated yourself on the ranch. Life is passing you by. You need to live a little, sugar."

"I will accept your free advice for what it's worth."

"You're going to up the bid?" Irene asked, grinning devilishly.

"No, I'm going to up *and leave,*" Elizabeth said, rising. "It's closing time."

"Fine, be an old fuddy-duddy," Irene taunted as Elizabeth collected the cups and coffee pot. "But keep in mind that a man with Wyatt's credentials could draw outside bidders to raise the price on your ranch. He probably has connections galore. I always did say if you wanted to do it right, start with the best and go from there. And let yourself enjoy his company while you're at it. What have you got to lose?"

Elizabeth paused and smiled ruefully. "Heartstrings. That's bad enough. Having my heart broken in the process would be even worse."

Chapter Five

Elizabeth grabbed her keys and propelled herself toward her pickup on weary legs. Her gaze was magnetically drawn to the motel where the silver Caddy shone beneath the neon sign. Irene's comments were getting to her. She was tempted to take the risk, to pursue moments of pleasure and enjoyment.

And why not? she asked herself. She was losing everything else. The ranch, her daughters' trust. Why not risk her heart, too?

Maybe she should simply place a phone call to Wyatt after she returned to the house. That would be sensible.

Elizabeth piled into the battered truck and switched on the ignition. The starter whined and groaned until the motor finally growled to life.

Should she or shouldn't she?

Oh, what the hell, Elizabeth decided. Her suddenly protective daughters already thought she had tripped the light fantastic at home. Why not at the local motel, too? Might as well do it up right.

Elizabeth steered across the parking lot and pulled up beside the Caddy. If ever two vehicles were mismatched, it was these two. *And so are we.* Elizabeth silently commented. What could a man like Wyatt McKenney possibly see in a woman like her, except a careless fling?

She must be out of her mind!

Cursing herself up one side and down the other, Elizabeth reached for the gearshift to put the truck in reverse. When the door to room twenty-two opened and Wyatt's muscular physique filled the doorway, Elizabeth's hand betrayed her. Instead of reversing direction, she turned off the ignition.

Give the man a sporting chance. You prejudged him once. Doesn't he deserve a second opportunity? Don't you?

"Whose side are you on anyway?" Elizabeth asked that infuriating little voice that had been hounding her to death since Wyatt McKenney walked into her life.

"Talking to yourself again, Elizabeth?" Wyatt teased when he heard the inarticulate sounds floating from the open window of the truck.

"The hell with it." Elizabeth inhaled a fortifying breath and climbed down from her perch. The door creaked as she shut it behind her—or was that her aching joints? Both could do with some WD-40 lubricating oil.

"I've thought it over, and I've made my decision," she announced, drawing herself up in front of him.

Wyatt stepped aside, inviting her inside with a sweep of his arm. Elizabeth closed the motel door behind her, glanced at the bed that dominated the impersonally furnished room and clung to the doorknob as if it were her lifeline.

"I would like you to handle the auction," she blurted out on a shaky breath. Good gawd, she was so uptight about being alone with Wyatt in the motel room that her knees were quivering. Must have been the long hours on already tired legs.

Doubt it, came that inner voice that was really starting to aggravate Elizabeth.

"Would you like to sit down?" Wyatt invited.

Elizabeth released her stranglehold on the doorknob and half collapsed in the chair beside the small round table. Wyatt positioned himself on the seat across from her, watching her with quiet intensity. He was too close for her comfort. Elizabeth squirmed nervously.

"Relax," he said in a soothing voice. "Nothing is going to happen. This is a business conference. I'm not the Big Bad Wolf your daughters probably made me out to be."

Elizabeth slumped noticeably in her chair.

Nothing could have been more indicative of her lack of participation in sordid affairs than her antsy behavior. Wyatt had the reassuring feeling that her afterhours at Tall Grass Prairie Cafe never included tête-à-têtes at the local motel. He was reasonably certain there had been few men in her life—if any—since the loss of her husband.

"As I said earlier, I would like to take a thorough look around Heartstrings the next few days," he began in a businesslike voice. "I will need to evaluate your line of farm equipment, check the registration certificates of your cattle and assess the structural stability of the barns, sheds and house.

"There is a strong possibility that feed-yard owners from western Oklahoma, Texas and New Mexico might be interested in bidding on the property. If I contact them, they will each send a representative to bid on Heartstrings. There are also ranchers in other parts of the country who need a place to resettle after being forced out by restrictive environmental groups. Investors in property near metropolitan areas are constantly being bought out and are forced to relocate their agricultural operations. Osage Hills has been a prime area for corporate ranching, with ties to western feed lots and northern stocker associations. I'll have the auction notices printed up and put on the mailing list to prospective buyers as soon as I check my schedule and set the date for the sale."

Elizabeth approved of the way Wyatt got down to business. When it came to the ins and outs of organizing details for sales, he was definitely efficient. Of course, she would never drop everything into his hands as Bob had insisted she do before he'd wheeled and dealed Heartstrings into near bankruptcy. But Wyatt was not Bob, Elizabeth reminded herself. He appeared to be experienced and knowledgeable.

"I do, however, propose upgrading the appearance of the ranch," Wyatt went on to say. "A fresh coat of paint and mowed ditches will increase sale value by thousands of dollars. Polish and shine catches eyes."

"I don't have extra cash right now," Elizabeth confessed. "I have an interest payment due at the bank at the end of the month. My spending money includes and extends only as far as my tips and salary at the cafe. I'm sorry to report that my greenbacks aren't made of Spandex."

"Would you object to letting me record the price of paint, fuel for tractors and fence post replacements on my expense account and then settle up after the auction?"

"Is that standard procedure?" Elizabeth questioned warily.

"No, it's a favor to you and our friend Jerry, who is as disappointed about having to sell Heartstrings as you are—almost."

Elizabeth regarded him for a meditative moment. "Why are you offering to do this?"

"I already told you, I'm on vacation and I would like to spend it here, away from congestive crowds, doing a little work from the neck down rather than from the chin up. Physical labor is the best therapy I know for mental stress."

Elizabeth gaped at him, owl-eyed. "Painting the outbuildings and mowing ditches is your idea of a vacation?"

He chuckled at her astounded expression. "Yes, and I *do* know how to handle the butt end of a paint brush and the gears of a tractor. I will also have time to make the rounds in the district with Jerry, contacting *his* connections as well as my own. The more interest we can generate the better the bids for Heartstrings. If I'm going to organize this sale, I intend to do it right, to get as much for you as I possibly can."

Flashbacks of Irene's proclamation rang in Elizabeth's ears. Always go in style, Irene maintained. Elizabeth, however, had been forced to apply the make-do policy for a decade. Her conservative philosophy was being tested. She hated spending money she didn't have.

"I really want to do this, Elizabeth," Wyatt insisted. "And I

want to know the background of your ranch, how it was origi-
nally acquired. Often, a well-placed comment with a sentimental touch spurs the lull in bidding. Buyers like to have a
personal overview, even large corporations who use historic
information as promotion in their campaigns to attract investors. Anything you can tell me about traditions and ancestry
will improve the sale. I need to know your ranch inside and
out in order to do the best job I possibly can for you. If I
know your procedures in the farming operations as well, I can
relay that information to prospective buyers."

Elizabeth peered into those mesmerizing green eyes that
sparkled with specks of gold and asked herself when was the
last time she'd looked so deeply into a man, wanting to believe
in him, wanting to trust him to keep her best interest at heart.
Either Wyatt McKenney was sincere or he was one whale of
an accomplished salesman. Elizabeth was certainly sold. But if
she put her complete faith in him and found herself betrayed,
it would be worse than simply losing extra dollars per acre on
the ranch. She was attracted to this man. He could make her
more vulnerable than she had been in years.

"If I agree, how much time will I have left?" she asked
grimly.

She reminded Wyatt of a condemned prisoner on the way
to the death chamber. She looked so apprehensive and miserable that he wanted to hug her to him and reassure her that
everything would be all right, but he forced himself to stay
where he was.

"I'm sorry I can't tell you exactly when the auction can be
held," he replied. "I have other obligations, so I'm not sure
when I can fit Heartstrings in. Without looking at the schedule, I would say it might be sometime in May or the first of
June."

Elizabeth nodded pensively. That would give her time to adjust to the idea of leaving Heartstrings permanently. By that
time, she would have the pastures burned to remove the dead
forage of weeds and new spring grass would be abundant, giving the ranch a productive appearance. The end of May, she

mused. The end of life as she knew it. Damn, this was going to take some getting used to.

Wyatt came to his feet and walked around the table to tower over her. "Do we have a deal?" he asked, extending his hand.

Elizabeth stared at his hand, hesitated for a few agonizing moments and then accepted his offer. She found herself drawn to her feet, her hand still clasped in his.

The air conditioning in the room must have shut down completely. She couldn't breathe without inhaling anything except the tantalizing scent of expensive cologne. Wyatt was temptingly close, so incredibly appealing to her awakened senses. The need to be held and comforted very nearly overwhelmed her. It had been so long since she had had anyone to lean on, anyone who really gave a damn about what she was feeling.

Elizabeth shivered when Wyatt removed his hand from hers and settled both of his palms on her hips. His head descended toward hers until she could see the dilated pupils of eyes that were fanned by long lashes Irene would have killed for. Elizabeth could feel that dynamic male aura drawing her within its perimeters, pulling on her like a current.

She wasn't an expert on nuclear reactors, but she was convinced that splitting atoms couldn't generate more heat than the internal combustion that exploded in her when she was close to Wyatt. Her heart was trying to beat her to death, and her hands were sweating. For the life of her she couldn't find her tongue. It felt glued to the roof of her mouth. And if she didn't breathe soon, she was going to faint!

It must be time for a physical, Elizabeth decided. All her involuntary bodily functions were breaking down. She needed hormone injections—or something. How could she be so instantaneously aware—so physically aroused—by this man she had only met? This didn't seem normal! Damn, even her skin didn't seem to fit correctly when she peered into those hypnotic eyes and felt his hands resting familiarly against her.

When his fingertips gently drifted up her ribs, a coil of heat burned in Elizabeth's lower regions. Her flimsy white blouse might as well have been on the floor, for all the good it did in concealing the pebbled peaks of her breasts. When Wyatt's gaze fastened on the buttons of her blouse, and he smiled in pure male satisfaction, Elizabeth wanted to whack him. He knew perfectly well how she reacted to him, and he was gloating.

"What are you doing?" she muttered.

"Watching me affect you the same way you affect me," he replied in a voice that was husky with disturbed awareness. His knuckles brushed one taut nipple, making her shiver in helpless response. "Body language, Elizabeth. I speak, you answer and then I start aching all over."

Her wide-eyed gaze drifted down the expanse of his chest to his belt buckle. He was aroused, either that or he was carrying a concealed weapon in the fly of his jeans.

The thought caused Elizabeth to giggle. If nothing else, her laughter eased the sexual tension that was frying her alive.

"What's so funny?" he asked hoarsely.

"Nothing." Eyes dancing, she tried to conceal another snicker—and failed.

His arms slid around her waist, bringing her body into direct contact with the hard evidence of his arousal, molding her sensitive nipples to the solid wall of his chest. Elizabeth stopped laughing, stopped breathing. Her lashes swept up to survey his suddenly somber expression.

"Make no mistake, Elizabeth Smith Sutton. If you agree to this arrangement, business is not all I would like to conduct with you. You make me feel young again, very much alive—and feeling deprived. I want you to be aware of the possibility that I might ask for more than you want to give, going in." His forefinger traced the lush curve of her bottom lip, and he feasted on her mouth with hungry eyes. "I'm too old for games, Bet. I'm willing to offer you however much you want— on your terms. And if you take a step toward me in the future, I won't be shrugging off the gesture the same way I did Irene's playful innuendos. Do you understand what I'm saying?"

Elizabeth swallowed visibly and tried to take in a normal breath. She couldn't. Her lungs felt as if they were filled with prairie sod. "You're saying that you're willing to handle the auction as long as I provide fringe benefits."

Wyatt scowled, dropped his arms and stepped back a pace. "Damn, that didn't come out quite right."

She was amused by his disgusted expression. Wyatt didn't know that he had earned several Brownie points for being put out with himself for sounding as if he were propositioning her.

Although Elizabeth had always tried to be sensible, this man was making it difficult. She liked his straightforward honesty. It was better than fumbling around, never knowing what to do or expect next. Bob had never been honest with her. He had played a charade for her benefit, and Elizabeth had been too naive and trusting not to see him for what he really was until it was too late. Now she was older and wiser—she hoped.

"I'll make *you* a deal," she offered. "If you're willing to play the hired hand to spiffy up the ranch, I'll provide room and board. A hard day's work for a hot, home-cooked meal."

Julia and Lana will have a cow!

Let them.

Wyatt raised his dark head and appraised the curvy silhouette outlined in dim light. He inwardly groaned, wondering how he could resist temptation while being under the same roof as Elizabeth.

"I don't think I can do that," he admitted on a ragged sigh.

"Why not? I'm not *that* bad a cook."

He smiled rakishly at her. "It's not *your* cooking that worries me; it's *my* appetite. You might find yourself on my dessert menu."

Elizabeth grabbed her purse and wheeled toward the door. She paused to glance back over her shoulder and mimicked Irene's Southern drawl. "The work day at Heartstrings begins at six-thirty Monday morning. If you've still got energy to burn after dark, then we'll see what we can do about it, sugar."

Wyatt chuckled at her playful quip, but he still said, "I'm not kidding around, Elizabeth. I'm not sure I can keep my hands off you. I already proved that to you and myself tonight.

It'll only get worse. I keep remembering how good you felt beneath me this afternoon, and my hormones revolt." ..

Elizabeth remembered the afternoon and the warm pleasure of his touch this evening. It *had* felt good—too good, too natural. Every minute she spent with Wyatt was taking her another step closer to what her betraying body craved and the practical side of her brain cautioned her to avoid. And yet, he stirred her as no other man had in a very long time. Could what felt so good be bad?

For a long moment Elizabeth scrutinized his masculine profile, the evidence of his need, his striking features. "How fond are you of that mustache?" she questioned out of the blue.

Wyatt did a double take. Elizabeth always startled him when she jumped from one subject to another, like a grasshopper. "I've had it for ten years."

"Pretty partial to it, I'd guess."

"I guess," he said with a shrug.

A cryptic smile pursed her lips as she pulled open the door. "Then I suppose that's when I'll know."

On the wings of that baffling comment she walked out and quietly shut the door behind her. Wyatt half-turned to stare at his reflection in the mirror that hung over the dresser.

"That's when she'll know *what?*"

His reflection couldn't come up with an answer, either.

Sighing heavily, Wyatt plopped on the bed and plucked up the remote control to the television. He needed to hear the drone of voices. The room felt extremely empty, lonely.

God, he had really made a poor showing tonight, hadn't he? He'd sounded like a damned Don Juan, offering to swap favors for favors. Geez, what finesse!

Well, what had he expected? Elizabeth would throw herself at his feet? He would have been surprised if she had. He was dealing with an extraordinary female whose morals differed from those of the women who pursued him. But he still had to be extremely careful, even if he was trying to be straightforward with Elizabeth. He never wanted to be used again.

And he didn't want to become anybody's credit card, either. He simply wanted to be wanted and accepted—for himself.

Wyatt needed to escape the grind of everyday life, and he wanted to enjoy Elizabeth's company. At Heartstrings he could relax and give the ranch the facelift it needed and deserved. As Jerry had said, Heartstrings was one helluva place—a special, isolated world all its own, a throwback to a simpler lifestyle in which a man could live in harmony with nature.

There was an intriguing lure about that obscure ranch in the Osage Hills, a compelling whisper in the wind that smoothed the wrinkles from Wyatt's soul. He imagined Heartstrings would be spectacular beneath a vault of night sky sprinkled with starlight. At Heartstrings there was peace and quiet and . . . Elizabeth . . .

Unconsciously, his hand lifted to stroke his mustache. When it finally dawned on him what Elizabeth had meant by her mysterious remark, he grinned in amusement.

"Helluva woman, Elizabeth Smith Sutton," he murmured as he kicked off his boots and sprawled on the bed. She didn't seem interested in his money and she didn't appreciate his citified clothes or shiny Caddy. To her, those things were obstacles between them that made her feel as if they were worlds apart.

From what Jerry had said that afternoon, Wyatt had the feeling Elizabeth had learned not to expect much from a man. She had seen what greed and a lust for power and prestige could do to one. To her, flashy cars and fancy clothes symbolized what had become of her husband—a pretty package for heartache. She had also become accustomed to doing without everything except necessities.

Wyatt frowned, wondering how long he could endure doing *without* to prove to Elizabeth that she wasn't just time he was killing, a new challenge to be conquered. He couldn't really blame her for being cautious about becoming involved in what she perceived to be a dead-end relationship. Wyatt had avoided meaningless affairs himself, so who was he to criticize? But it was different with Elizabeth, and only time would convince her that he didn't want cheap, temporary thrills any more than she did. If it couldn't mean something to both of them then it simply wasn't worth taking chances with their hearts . . .

"Go to sleep, Wyatt," he grumbled at his reflection in the mirror.

He went to bed, but he found himself mentally listing the supplies he would need to begin the refurbishing project on Heartstrings . . . and tingling with the kind of energizing desire he hadn't experienced in years.

"She has freaked out completely," Julia declared as she slumped against the passenger door of Lana's car. "I was afraid something like this might happen after we left home and Mother had to sell the ranch."

"She's facing a crisis, and she's very susceptible right now," Lana quoted from her psychology textbook. "Her nest is empty, and her nurturing instincts have no external release. She feels frustrated and unneeded by her independent offspring. Furthermore, she's about to lose Heartstrings, and you know how attached she is to it. Mother is floundering, trying to find herself—"

"By shacking up in the local motel with a man who is practically a stranger?" Julia sniffed, disgusted. "All your clinical explanations aren't going to solve the problem that Mother is sleeping with a man she just met. I think I would have been happier if we hadn't driven by the cafe to check on her tonight, only to find her pickup parked at the motel beside the Caddy. Lord! The woman is forty-five years old. How can she do it twice in one day?"

"According to the latest findings, a woman reaches her sexual peak at sixty," Lana reminded her sister. "Maybe Mother is trying to satisfy her need to be needed by rediscovering her sexuality."

"Well damnation, couldn't she have simply turned into a chocoholic or something? What are we going to do? Convince her to come live with one of us?"

"I suppose we aren't going to have a choice if this behavior pattern continues," Lana said logically. "Maybe after six months she'll begin to adjust to her new life-style and she'll want to relocate in Pawhuska. Or maybe she'd prefer a home in Bartlesville or Skiatook where we can keep an eye on her." Lana frowned consideringly as she turned onto the gravel road and headed for Heartstrings. "Perhaps I should suggest counseling."

"I've got a better idea. Why don't we run Wyatt McKenney out of town. He's only using Mother for his own pleasure. Maybe we should confront *him* and deliver a few ultimatums about preying on a vulnerable widow who's overwrought about losing her family ranch. We could threaten to create a scandal if Mother does decide to hire Wyatt for the auction—to ruin his reputation if he doesn't cease and desist."

"I think a psychological campaign directed toward strengthening Mother's resolve against reckless desperation would be the most beneficial approach," Lana advised. "Mother is still influenced by our opinions. If we voice our disapproval without issuing ultimatums to her, perhaps she'll come to her senses and realize that she's grasping for straws and destroying her own self-respect. She needs to be aware that there are con men in this world who practice this sort of scam."

"I still say tar and feathers isn't a bad idea," Julia grumbled. "I'd like to try it out on my boss at the animal clinic first, to see how it works."

"Just what is your problem with this John W. Casey III character?" Lana questioned her disgruntled sister. "Maybe I could help pinpoint the difficulties in your working relationship."

"He's an ass, plain and simple," Julia said hostilely. "Psychology doesn't work on mules, does it?"

"Have you tried a two-by-four?" Lana teased.

"Starting next week I might." Julia frowned sourly. "If he doesn't drop that domineering, superior male routine by Wednesday, I may crack him over the head and take control of the bookkeeping files and handle our four-legged patients *my* way."

"He's still the owner and the boss," Lana calmly pointed out.

"I don't need *your* reminder when *he* calls it to my attention a dozen times a day. I have a mind of my own and a degree to prove my capabilities, but he treats me like an idiotic go-for. To hear him talk, you'd think I can't give an injection of an antibiotic without screwing up."

Lana pressed down the accelerator and sailed down the last two miles of graveled road to ensure that they beat Elizabeth home. "I'm afraid you're going to have to put your problems with Casey on the back burner for the weekend. We need to deal with Mother first thing in the morning. Maybe after she sleeps on this fling with Wyatt McKenney she'll be more receptive."

Julia grimaced. She wished Lana could have employed another cliché besides *sleeping on*. The thought made her uncomfortable. "Do you think we should tell Mother that we know where she went after she got off work?"

"No, that would only make her defensive. The social and psychological dynamics of this situation could send Mother running to Wyatt to escape our criticism. We're going to have to be subtle."

Julia sniffed in contradiction. "I still say a two-by-four might work well for Wyatt and John W. Casey III. Once we have their attention we can adjust their attitudes."

"How long have you been plagued with these violent tendencies?" Lana wanted to know.

"Since I went to work for the high and mighty Casey III," Julia grouched. "I swear the man delights in infuriating me."

"I see, and how does it make you feel, knowing he is making sport of you?"

"Don't give me that psychotherapy crap. Just drive, Lana. Make sure the dust has settled before Mother gets home or she'll suspect we've been spying on her."

Lana floorboarded the accelerator and zoomed over the hill, mentally organizing a campaign to save her mother from making a ghastly mistake.

Chapter Six

Elizabeth hauled Julia and Lana out of bed at the crack of dawn to help with the chores. She intended to make them pay for annoying her the previous afternoon by depriving them of sleep. She gave Vic Henderson, her hired man, the day off to spend with his wife and two young children.

Bleary-eyed, Lana piled into the one-ton truck and drove up beside the overhead feeder bin while Julia climbed the ladder to dispense the ration for hungry cattle. When several truck loads and two thousand pounds of feed had been delivered to the eight sections of pasture, Elizabeth asked Julia to check the health condition of the cattle.

Since Julia had a degree in veterinary medicine, she was also sent to examine the cow that had delivered its calf backward.

"The cow isn't getting around very well," Julia reported when she returned to the truck. "She's still suffering partial paralysis in her hind quarters. I don't think it would hurt to give her an antibiotic as a precautionary measure, although King Casey III would probably apply his wait-and-see policy."

Elizabeth documented the cow's ear-tag number and health

condition in the log book and made note of Julia's resentful tone. After motioning for Lana to drive over to drop a private supply of feed for the ailing cow, Elizabeth stared pensively at Julia.

"Are you having a professional conflict with your boss?"

"Personal and professional," Julia corrected before flinging her mother a discreet glance. "But you know how men are. You can never be certain of their ulterior motives. In my case, I'm not sure if Maharajah Casey III wants to fire me because I disagree with some of his practices or if he intends to prod me into resigning. And then again, he could be testing me."

"What's he like?" Elizabeth questioned curiously.

"Like a pain in the —"

"Do his clients like him?" Elizabeth cut in quickly.

Julia expelled a sigh. "Oddly enough, yes. But men can be deceiving in certain relationships. With his clients, Casey is all charm and cooperation. With me, he's an antagonist."

Elizabeth surveyed the herd of registered Limousin cattle that crunched noisily on the rations that had been strung across the pasture. Pensively, she glanced in Julia's direction. "If you have a personality conflict, why did he offer you this job, and why on earth did you take it? As I recall, you had several options when you finished school."

Julia peered directly at her mother. "I honestly don't know. I guess I just wanted to get settled into my new life and this job was the closest to home. Maybe I was overanxious and misjudged the man." She paused strategically and added, "I suppose we all do things we later regret."

Elizabeth bit back a smile. She had the inescapable feeling this conversation carried a double meaning. She had anticipated a lecture from her daughters on the topic of Wyatt McKenney. It seemed that instead she was to be treated to subterfuge and innuendos strategically directed toward her "tryst" with a stranger.

"I *wanted* to take the job because I thought I should stay fairly close to home," Julia reiterated. "I wasn't as particular as I probably should have been. What we often *think* we want, what seems right for us at the time, isn't always exactly what we *need,* nor is it always in our best interest, either."

This was *definitely* a discreet lecture, Elizabeth decided. Julia was taking her turn before Lana applied her psychology skills. Good grief, these two armchair therapists thought they had the world figured out, and before they'd reached the age of twenty-five. Did they have a lot to learn! It would be decades before they realized how *little* they knew.

A familiar voice blared over the CB as Lana eased the truck alongside the cattle. "Elizabeth? I was wondering if I could talk to you. Are you about finished with your chores?"

Elizabeth stepped up on the running board to respond to Griffin Hollis' request. Her neighbor sounded aggravated. She wondered if he'd heard that his ex-wife was screwing around with Aaron Black. Probably. News travels fast in one-horse towns.

"I wonder what Griff wants?" Lana questioned as they bounced across the pasture toward the house.

"No telling. I'll talk to him while you're loading the next round of feed," Elizabeth said.

"Are these chores going to take all day?" Lana questioned, glancing at her watch.

"Haven't they always?"

"Well, yes, but Brad was planning on flying up this afternoon. We haven't been able to see much of each other since he took the job as a pilot for the oil company in Tulsa and I accepted the teaching position."

Elizabeth was fond of the young man Lana had dated for the past year. In fact, he seemed more partial to Heartstrings than Lana and Julia did. Brad Phelps was country born and bred, a regular farm boy at heart. Too bad Lana and Julia didn't have a need to cling to their heritage, Elizabeth thought regretfully.

"Brad is concerned about how you're handling the upcoming auction," Lana continued conversationally.

Oh, goodie, thought Elizabeth. Here comes the second

round of psychological sabotage from the self-proclaimed expert.

"How sweet of him to worry about me," she replied with a straight face.

"Yes, he is sweet—and considerate," Lana contended. "He is also respectful and sensitive to my feelings and needs. Some men aren't and they never will be. The Pleasure-Seeker Syndrome is prominent in today's society. Too many women fall prey to con- quering males. Loneliness and desperation often play preeminent roles in creating unproductive relationships."

"Is that so?" Elizabeth glanced out the window and tried not to laugh at her well-meaning daughter. She supposed she should be flattered that Lana and Julia were concerned about her ability to handle those of the male persuasion—Wyatt McKenney in particular.

"Sadly, yes, it is so," Lana continued. "Too late, women realize they have been taken for the ride of their lives and then left by the wayside, their self-respect in shambles. They perceive themselves as deserving exactly what they have gotten and they begin the self-destructive process again."

"And you think Brad is trustworthy, unlike these pleasure-seeking males?"

"Certainly." Lana seemed surprised that Eliza- beth would question *her* judgment. "I have gotten to know Brad exceptionally well over a long period of time. I have studied his moods and analyzed his personality to determine his depth of character. He is fundamentally sound and receptive to constructive suggestions."

"What a wonderfully mature approach to dating," Elizabeth managed to say without snickering.

"Well, a woman can hardly evaluate the strengths and weaknesses of a man in a relationship overnight, now can she? The process takes time and has to be viewed through a variety of situations, not to mention studying behavioral responses to certain stimuli."

"Naturally. And after listening to you, I'm sure your high-school students find you to be as much of an intellectual inspiration as I do."

Lana smiled in self-satisfaction. "Do you really think so?"

"Of course," Elizabeth confirmed. "I'm considering buying myself some laboratory mice and testing their behavioral patterns by matching them up with various mates to see how they respond to the good, bad and the ugly of rodent society."

"Mother! Lana is serious," Julia scolded. "Would you prefer that she jumped into this relationship with Brad on a purely physical level?"

"From the sound of things, your analytical sister is too busy documenting a case study of Brad's social and psychological behavior to get physical." She turned to Lana. "Good grief, don't the two of you ever kiss? Or do you simply sit around with your checklists, taking surveys of each other's responses to stimuli?"

Elizabeth swung her firepower on Julia when Lana sat there with her jaw gaping and her eyes popping. One couldn't show favoritism toward one's offspring, now could one? "And it seems to me, Julia, that you and John Cassity—"

"John W. Casey III," Julia scowled in correction.

"Whatever," Elizabeth said with a careless flick of her wrist. "You and John need to sit down and air your griefs before what sounds like professional jealousy and competition evolves into petty spite. I'm not sure either of you could agree on the treatment to cure a ham, much less sick livestock."

"You don't know what a toad John can be," Julia sputtered.

"Just how old is this guy?" Elizabeth questioned.

"Thirty, when he's acting his age. Thirteen when he isn't."

"Well, maybe you should kiss this jerk and see if you can turn him into a prince."

When the one-ton truck rolled to a stop beside the overhead storage bin, Elizabeth hopped out. "It was nice to have this chat with you girls. I'll have lunch waiting when you finish feeding. And Julia, give the pregnant heifers a careful check, will you? A half-dozen of them are beginning to bag up. If we're going to have to deal with difficult first deliveries, I want to keep on top of the situation and go to the pastures prepared. Using a shirt to pull a calf in an open field was not my idea of good management. I don't want that to happen again."

When Elizabeth walked off, Julia glanced at Lana. "She really thinks we fell for that hogwash about the shirt?"

"Sounds like it to me," Lana replied. "A likely excuse, that's what it is. We both know Mother never went unprepared to a pasture in her life."

"I don't think that subtle approach fazed her," Julia said. "I vote for the two-by-four treatment on Wyatt's head." She hitched her thumb toward the door of the truck. "It's your turn to climb onto the storage bin. Maybe while you're up there, Brad will fly over and you can blow him a kiss."

Lana glanced calmly at her mischievous sister. "Very amusing, Julia. And maybe Mother had the right idea. You should try kissing the breath out of John W. Casey III. Maybe you can suck his male chauvinist tendencies right out of him."

"Oh, he'd love that," Julia grumbled. "It would indicate that I admitted defeat and agreed to play the subservient role in his veterinary kingdom."

"No," Lana contradicted as she climbed down from the truck. "It would get you close enough to him to whack him with the two-by-four while he's distracted. Then the vet empire you secretly covet would be in your hands."

Julia wagged a finger in her sister's face. "Let me tell you something, Miss Would-Be Analyst, you have yet to realize that Mother has us squabbling rather than focusing our energy on *her* problem."

Lana blinked her dark eyes. "Good Lord, you're right! I should have seen that immediately. We'll start a new campaign over lunch. You can suggest having her move in with you in Bartlesville after the auction."

"Me? I've got enough trouble dealing with my obnoxious boss. How am I supposed to cope with Mother's traumatic adjustment period when I have my own crisis to resolve?"

"She could serve as a distraction from your problem," Lana insisted.

"But you're the one qualified to counsel her," Julia argued. "She can be your live-in patient. You seem to get your kicks out of analyzing everybody. Why not give Mother a whirl?"

"Fine, I'll make the suggestion." Lana climbed up the ladder to drop a load of cattle cubes—some of which landed on the truck cab, setting off a racket above Julia's head. "Sorry about that."

Julia glanced up at her sister and smirked. "I'll just bet you are."

Sure enough, Lana wasn't. Calm and controlled though she always tried to be, there were times when Julia managed to ruffle her feathers.

Elizabeth noted the frown plastered on Griff Hollis' face as she ambled through the breezeway to find him perched on the wooden bench. Griff was chewing on a blade of grass and staring down the hill toward the pond where cattle had gathered to drink. For the past few years she and her nearest neighbor had volunteered services to each other when it came time for cattle roundups and pasture burnings that required more hands than either of them kept on payroll. By sharing chores, Heartstrings and Lazy H ranches had remained in operation. The only difference was that Griff's line of credit obviously didn't have the black marks against it that Elizabeth's did, thanks to her husband's reckless spending sprees.

After Griff's divorce three years earlier, he had invited Elizabeth out, but she had never accepted an official date. She had, however, offered to fix supper for Griff on occasion. He had made a pass once or twice, but she had laid down the ground rules. It wasn't that her forty-six-year-old neighbor wasn't reasonably attractive and compatible. It was just that she felt no spark of attraction. She considered Griff a neighbor, and she made certain their relationship never altered.

When Griff heard the click of boot heels on the concrete portico he glanced sideways. His hazel eyes drifted over Elizabeth's appealing physique before lifting to meet her greeting smile.

"Hi, Griff, what's up?"

When Elizabeth sank down beside him, Griff draped his arms over the back of the bench and crossed his feet at the ankles, stretching out his six foot-one-inch length in a leisurely sprawl. "I came by to see if you were ready to burn the dead weeds off the pastures next week. The meteorologists are forecasting rain in the middle of the week. It should be dry enough by then to get a fast burn, unless we have a cloudburst."

Elizabeth nodded agreeably, wondering at the reason for Griff's clipped undertone. Something was bothering him. She had noticed the irritation in his voice on the CB. "The end of next week should be fine. That will give us time to round up and corral our cattle."

"Good. My hired man is laid up with a sprained wrist, so I'll need more help than usual."

"What happened to Chuck?" Elizabeth questioned curiously.

"He was competing in the rodeo last night and took a fall. He got launched off a bucking bronc and tried to brace himself instead of rolling out. The damnfool kid thinks he's a world-class rodeo champion."

"I could use a Coke, Griff." Her long-winded debate with Julia and Lana had parched her throat. "Would you like to join me?" Elizabeth asked, rising.

"Sure, might as well lubricate my vocal chords." Griff gathered his legs beneath him and stood up. "I have something else I want to discuss with you, Liz."

Ah-ha, thought Elizabeth. Now they were getting to the real reason Griff was in a huff.

"I heard you called in some highfalutin auctioneer to sell Heartstrings."

Elizabeth strode into the kitchen to fix the drinks. "Where did you hear that?"

"Jerry Patterson stopped by my place this morning to look over my cattle. In between telling me that I was scrimping on rations he mentioned the possibility of your auction."

Elizabeth dropped ice cubes in the glasses. "I'm considering it."

"I was hoping to get first chance at buying the property since we're neighbors."

Elizabeth glanced up, surprised. "You can get a loan that size to expand?"

Griff looked the other way. "I think I can make the arrangements, yes."

Elizabeth didn't want to sell to Griff. She was of the opinion that he overgrazed his pastures and kept his cows undernourished while they nursed their young calves. Taking from the land without giving back and half-starving livestock didn't appeal to Elizabeth. Never had, even when times were lean, as they were now. Elizabeth didn't think she could stand knowing Griff was draining Heartstrings' natural resources.

"I've got a deal for you, Liz," Griff announced before sipping the Coke she handed to him. "You know I'm fond of you, always have been. We could form a partnership that would prevent you from having to sell out at all. I know how much you love this ranch and I hate like hell to see you lose it."

"A partnership?" she questioned dubiously. "What kind of partnership?"

Griff slid his arm around her waist and pulled her closer. "I'm talking marriage, Liz. You and I have always gotten along well. And you already know how I feel about you. We could make it work."

Elizabeth blinked, too stunned by the unexpected offer to voice a reply. *Her* married to *Griff*? She wondered how he would feel about separate bedrooms. No, make that separate homes, she amended. She just couldn't see them sharing the same space—more specifically, the same bed.

"I could get a loan to pay off the interest and part of the principle on the outstanding debts Bob left you. Between the two of us, and your competent hired man, we could put this operation back on its feet. I could save money by letting Chuck Ryburn go. His salary alone could pay the interest on a new loan. You wouldn't have to give this ranch up when I know it means more to you than anything else."

Griff made the offer sound tempting. Elizabeth had to consider the possibility, even though she had never been romantically inclined toward him.

Her thoughts trailed off when the back door creaked open and Julia and Lana appeared. Well damn, here we go again, Elizabeth muttered to herself. Griff had his arm wrapped around her as if they were intimately acquainted, and Julia and Lana were frowning at the presumption that their mother had turned into a full-fledged sleaze. Elizabeth wasn't in the mood to explain Griff's proposal at the moment. Let her darling daughters think what they would.

"We just came in to grab a soda before hauling the next load of cattle cubes," Lana announced as she surged toward the refrigerator.

Griff dropped his arm from Elizabeth's waist and stepped back into his own space. "How are you girls doing with your new jobs?"

"Fine," Julia lied, telling herself she would be fine after she assassinated her domineering boss.

"Glad to hear it. And it's nice to see you girls show up to help your mother on weekends. She keeps a busy schedule."

"Doesn't she though?" Julia smiled around her gritted teeth. "I don't know where she finds the energy to maintain her hectic pace. Must be a healthy dose of Vitamin E."

Elizabeth slanted her elder daughter a disparaging glance, wondering if the child was too old to have her fanny paddled.

Lana scooped up the drinks and headed for the back door. "Gotta run. We have two more loads to deliver," she said as she buzzed off.

"You've got nice kids, Liz," Griff complimented when Lana and Julia were out of hearing range. "I always did like them."

"Wanna adopt them?" It popped out, and Elizabeth wished it hadn't. That wasn't the kind of sarcastic remark to make to a man who had just proposed to her. Griff took her seriously.

"Yes, as a matter of fact, I would." His arm snaked around

Elizabeth's hip, and he gave her an affectionate squeeze. "I think the whole lot of us can make this arrangement work. I know I would be more than satisfied. We share the same interest.

"My ex-wife never liked ranch life. She only stayed until our sons were grown before flitting off to pursue her own career. I've been lonely, Liz. I know you must be, too. What do you say we put Heartstrings back on its feet and keep doing what we both love best?"

Elizabeth sidestepped and swallowed a mouthful of Coke. "I'll have to think about it."

Griff nodded acceptance of her request. "You do that, hon. We could rent out my house and a couple of acres around it, live here since you have more space. I know you're really partial to this house of yours."

While Elizabeth was mulling over the offer, thoroughly distracted, Griff dropped a kiss on her lips. "Just tell that auctioneer friend of Jerry's to buzz off, and let's keep this ranch going—together. You might wind up selling out to some foreign investor if we don't work out arrangements. I know it would kill you to see your ranch in some uncaring stranger's hands. And I'd never have the neighborly cooperation I have with you."

He paused in the doorway and smiled charmingly at her. "We can make it work well, Liz. You'll never have to leave Heartstrings because our combined efforts will get the bank off your back."

When Griff walked out, Elizabeth slumped against the counter and frowned pensively. Although she had no romantic interest in Griff, *he* had managed to keep *his* ranch afloat. Elizabeth thought he cut too many corners in the wrong places, but the lure of not having to sell Heartstrings was undeniably appealing.

But you don't love Griff.

"Well, so what?" she scowled at her noble conscience. "Lots of women my age marry for reasons other than love, don't they? Why shouldn't I?"

Look at all the sacrifices she had made to hang onto Heart-strings? She had taken a part-time job to provide extra cash. She had driven a rattletrap pickup and repaired run-down machinery instead of purchasing newer models, just to hold onto this ranch and ensure her daughters received the best education she could provide. Marrying a man she didn't love would be just another sacrifice on an extensive list. It is practical, Elizabeth told herself.

It would also prevent her from feeling like a failure. To sell Heartstrings was to become a traitor to generations of proud ancestors who had managed to survive difficult times. Weren't long-held traditions and deep attachment worth a few sacrifices?

Griff Hollis would never become as extravagant or power hungry as Bob Sutton, Elizabeth assured herself. He was more of a tightwad than a spendthrift. That had been the major problem in Griff's first marriage, as Elizabeth heard it told. He reverted profit back into the ranch operation rather than splurging on his wife, who resented playing second fiddle to cattle herds, pickups and farm machinery. Now Griff's ex-wife was going in style, wasn't she? Elizabeth thought with a dry smile. Patty Hollis was fooling around in the backseat of a Lincoln. Patty had always wanted a fancy luxury car rather than a pickup. Now she had the use of one.

Elizabeth took another sip of her Coke and pondered the tempting proposal. True, Heartstrings probably wouldn't get the facelift Wyatt McKenney thought it deserved, but at least Elizabeth would still have control of her ranch. That was her top priority.

And besides, she reminded herself. Griff would be there to appease this rioting need Wyatt had awakened. She could learn to develop a physical interest in Griff, couldn't she? It was a matter of positive thinking. How bad could fifteen minutes once a week be? If Griff was no more sexually demanding than Bob had been, Elizabeth could endure.

She had endured sixteen years of a bad marriage. What could be *worse* than that?

She could save Heartstrings. What could be *better* than that?

Griff had made his bid for the ranch, one that could work to Elizabeth's advantage. She would be a fool not to accept and regain her shattered pride before being forced to admit defeat.

But you don't love Griffin Hollis.

"I like him well enough." Elizabeth scowled.

Do you really?

"Okay, so he suffers from the He-Man Complex, but I can tolerate that if I have to."

Tolerate, Elizabeth? This is marriage we're discussing, not a one-night stand.

Elizabeth muttered at her conscience, chugged her Coke and stamped over to grab a skillet and sauce pan. She had dinner to prepare and a house to clean before Lana's boyfriend flew in for a visit.

The thought of Lana's analytical deductions about her year-long relationship with Brad made Elizabeth chuckle. Maybe she should apply Miss Psychology's clinical process of checklists and metaphysical equations to this marriage proposal. Lana would appreciate that sensible approach. She and Julia would both approve of the match, Elizabeth predicted.

Elizabeth had known Griff for years, worked with him on a regular basis, socialized with him on occasion. Practical, sensible, that's what the marriage would be. She and Griff could cohabit in a symbiotic relationship, arranged for the benefit of both parties concerned . . .

Good grief, Elizabeth was beginning to sound like a therapist herself! God forbid, Lana and Julia's psychological warfare was actually working!

"Well, what do you suppose *that* little scene was all about?" Julia asked as she drove through the pasture to unload the cattle cubes for the herd that bawled and trotted behind the truck.

"I'm beginning to think Mother is more starved for affection and companionship than we previously suspected," Lana diagnosed. She reached over to push the button on the hydraulic lift, sending a string of cattle rations tumbling from the up- lifted bed of the truck. "At least the fling Mother appears to be having with Griff will be more productive than one with a total stranger. Maybe she's trying to make Griff jealous enough to offer marriage. She's subconsciously searching for a way to prevent severing ties with her past life and avoiding an uncer- tain future."

"By damn, I think you might be onto something here," Julia declared as she circled the pasture to check the condition of the cattle. She glanced at the steers that gathered around the truck. "Number eighty-two is limping. Record it in the log book, Lana. Number seventy-four looks a little droopy. I need to give it a dose of antibiotic for shipping fever."

Lana jotted down the notes in her mother's black book. "If we encourage Mother's liaison with Griff she may be swayed by our approval." She glanced somberly at Julia. "Problem is, how are *we* going to cope with Mother's second marriage, if it should come to that? We can't encourage a relationship with- out being aware of the ramifications in our personal lives."

"God, you sound like a walking textbook again," Julia groaned.

Lana eyed her sister. "Your avoidance reaction suggests that you have misgivings about the prospect of a stepfather. We may have to deal with the situation sooner than we think, Julia. Mother is susceptible and desperate. She has decisions to make, and they must be made swiftly."

"Not necessarily," Julia argued. "Mother could visit Griff's ranch for a few years when she becomes homesick for her old life-style."

"So you balk at the idea of a second marriage?" Lana as- sumed.

"Don't you?"

"I'm trying to be objective. We both have to think in terms of what is best for Mother, not ourselves. If Mother *is* trying to wrangle a marriage proposal from Griff by testing his affection for her, he might act quickly in response to this stimulus."

"Mother has been widowed for nine years. Surely this is no more than a natural reaction to losing the ranch."

"In other words," Lana paraphrased, "you are going to resent being saddled with a stepfather."

Julia released a rush of breath. "Yes."

"Well, you'd better start warming to the idea," Lana advised. "Considering the behavioral pattern we have witnessed this weekend, I think Mother is grasping for stability and security. We've tried to reassure her that it's time to move to town, that losing the ranch is not the end of the world. Outwardly, she has tried to accept the inevitable, but inwardly she is terrified. She is making a silent cry for support, for a more acceptable alternative."

"By sleeping with an auctioneer while she's fooling around with Griff? How long do you suppose *this* affair has been going on? Since we left for college?"

"I doubt it," Lana said reasonably. "It probably developed when Mother initially realized she couldn't afford to keep Heartstrings. Subconsciously, she began reviewing possible options."

"Then where do you think this citified auctioneer fits in?"

"Maybe it's his money," Lana replied thoughtfully. "He seems to have a great deal of it, and Mother doesn't. I'm simply not certain why she became involved with him, except to gain Griff's notice or to attach herself to the wealth she lost. I just haven't figured Wyatt McKenney out yet, or determined Mother's true motive. But I'd say directing her toward Griff is our safest bet."

"Fine, I'll outwardly approve," Julia said. "But I still don't think marriage is advisable."

Lana was silent for a moment while they drove back to load the last portion of feed. "Dad is gone, Julia. We can't think in terms of Mother replacing our father, but in terms of her seeking a mate. She's the one left alone during the second half of her life. If she needs companionship we'll have to provide it or she'll find someone who will."

Julia forced herself to consider the possibility of her mother intimately involved with Griff. She supposed it wouldn't be so bad to have Griff as a stepfather. She had known Griff forever.

Maybe Lana was right. Maybe Julia was being selfish by objecting. Besides, things could be worse. Mother could continue throwing herself at strangers, looking for satisfaction in all the wrong places.

Griff was the logical choice, Julia assured herself. If her mother could adjust to losing a ranch for which she had such a strong attachment, Julia could certainly adapt to the idea of Griff as a prospective stepfather. Better than the "outsider" Mother had latched onto the minute he showed his face in Osage Hills!

Chapter Seven

Elizabeth was in a terrible dilemma, torn between a man who provided entertaining companionship, and who had awakened dormant desire, and another who could save Heartstrings. She wished Griff had presented his offer a few days earlier. Things wouldn't have been so complicated . . .

"Don't you agree, Mother?"

Elizabeth, jolted from her musings, saw Lana and Brad Phelps staring at her from across the living room. "I'm sorry. My mind was wandering. What did you say?"

"I said its's very neighborly of Griff to co-op roundups and spring burnings since Julia and I aren't around as much these days to help you out."

Elizabeth's dark eyes narrowed as she wondered what new campaign Miss Psychology and her sidekick were on now. "Yes," she agreed. "It saves manpower. Griff and I work reasonably well together."

"If you need an extra hand, I could fly up next weekend," Brad offered.

"Thanks, but Griff and I can handle the burnings."

"I'm really sorry about your having to sell this—ugh! What

was that for?" Brad questioned when Lana gouged him in the ribs with her elbow.

Elizabeth bit back a grin. Her well-meaning daughters were trying to protect her from reminders of her upcoming loss.

Pulling her feet beneath her, Elizabeth rose from the sofa and pivoted toward her bedroom. "I have to get ready for work. I'll see you tonight."

"You're leaving for work already?" Julia queried suspiciously. "I didn't think you went on duty until five o'clock."

"I don't, but I have an errand to run first."

"One that's going to take a full hour?"

Elizabeth frowned at Julia. "It may only take fifteen minutes, but I don't want to have to rush."

Julia and Lana exchanged wary glances before peering at their mother.

"I can run the errand for you," Julia volunteered. "What do you want me to do?"

"This is something I have to do myself."

The comment confirmed Julia's and Lana's belief that Elizabeth was trotting off to a rendezvous with her lover.

"Why don't we invite Griff over for Sunday dinner," Lana suggested. "Brad and I can feed the cattle while you and Julia cook."

Elizabeth studied her daughters for a ponderous moment. "What's the sudden interest in Griff?"

"We have always liked him," Julia explained as nonchalantly as she knew how. "Now that he's alone, he would probably enjoy a home-cooked meal."

"Fine, invite him," Elizabeth said before she strode off to shower and change clothes.

"What the heck is going on?" Brad questioned Lana.

"Mother isn't adjusting very well to selling Heartstrings. She doesn't need any reminders of impending doom."

"Sorry, I didn't mean to upset her."

"Just guard your tongue," Julia advised. "We're the official support group and we're trying to help Mom cope."

Brad nodded in compliance before settling back on the

couch beside Lana. Julia took the cue and found something to do outside so Lana and Brad could have their privacy.

Why, Julia wondered, couldn't she and John W. Casey III be as comfortably compatible as her sister and Brad? The atmosphere at the clinic was riddled with tension, some of which Julia reluctantly admitted she instigated. But damn it, the man riled her. Maybe she should resort to her mother's drastic strategy of sleeping around in the hope of easing *her* frustration.

No, Julia told herself realistically. That would prove nothing. One hussy in the family was plenty!

Elizabeth straightened her red bow tie and ran a quick hand through her hair before knocking on Wyatt's motel door. Things had changed dramatically since the previous evening when she had talked to him. She was not anticipating this conversation.

Apprehensively, she waited for Wyatt to answer the door. After several seconds he appeared—bare chested and bare-footed. From all indications he'd just stepped out of the shower, looking altogether too appealing.

The welcoming smile on Wyatt's lips nearly melted Elizabeth in her Keds. Why did *this* have to be the man who attracted her and not Griff?

"On your way to work, I see," Wyatt observed as he motioned her into the room.

Elizabeth inhaled a fortifying breath and sallied forth. "We have to talk, Wyatt."

The sound of her voice provoked Wyatt's wary frown. "What's wrong?"

She plunked into the nearest chair and formulated her words carefully. "I have had an offer to save Heartstrings, and I am seriously considering it," she said for starters. "My neighbor, Griff Hollis, has proposed an arrangement that will keep Heartstrings off the auction block."

"What kind of an arrangement? A top dollar offer?"

Elizabeth fidgeted beneath Wyatt's probing gaze. "Not exactly."

"Then what exactly?" he persisted.

"Would you mind putting your shirt on, please?" Elizabeth asked out of the blue.

Wyatt was growing accustomed to her leapfrogging from one topic to another. Instead of blanching in surprise, he simply grinned at her. "Yes, I would mind, as a matter of fact. If it bothers you, take *your* shirt off so you won't feel overdressed."

Elizabeth slanted him a narrowed glance, refusing to be amused and trying very hard to ignore the sleek expanse of hair-roughened chest, the narrow hips. It wasn't easy. Too bad Wyatt wasn't built like Aaron Black, then she could glance at him without admiring his well-proportioned physique. This conversation was difficult enough without tantalizing distractions—which Wyatt definitely was.

"Now, what is this offer you mentioned?" Wyatt insisted on knowing.

Oh hell, she might as well be honest and straightforward and get this over with. Elizabeth took a deep breath and said, "Griff proposed that we marry. He offered to cover my outstanding debts with a new loan. I can keep Heartstrings."

There, she had said what she had come to say. She didn't feel a blessed bit better, but she was glad the truth was out.

Wyatt stood very still, studying Elizabeth through slitted green eyes. "I've already bought paint, barbed wire, fence posts and fuel. We had a deal, Elizabeth."

Elizabeth winced and swallowed the lump that had collected in her throat. "We don't have a contract," she reminded him.

"No, we have something more binding and honorable than that," Wyatt qualified. "Where I come from, a handshake between two trustworthy individuals is all that's needed. Last night you accused me of making my offer to renovate Heartstrings just for the fringe benefits I wanted you to provide. Today, you're telling me you're willing to give yourself to your neighbor to save your ranch. Would you like to explain how you have rationalized your integrity with this new turn of events?"

Elizabeth avoided his disparaging stare, feeling as tall as the chair she was sitting in. Damn it, didn't he understand what Heartstrings meant to her? Apparently not. How could he know how it felt to lose something that was a part of what she was, of what she perceived herself to be? Besides, he wasn't accustomed to making sacrifices to keep what he had. *He* had the world in the palm of his hand. She was holding on by her . . . her heartstrings!

"Are you in love with Griff Hollis?" Wyatt questioned while Elizabeth squirmed uncomfortably in her chair.

"It's the—"

"Answer me," he demanded in a gruff voice.

Elizabeth exhaled slowly. "No, I'm not."

"But you would do anything you had to do to save your precious ranch? Would you even sleep with me every time I happened through town if I agreed to float you a loan at lower interest rates so you could keep your ranch in operation?"

Her head snapped up, and she glowered at him.

Wyatt braced his arms on the table and leaned down to stare her squarely in the eye. "Well, would you? If you're selling sex to your neighbor, why not to me?" he asked cuttingly. "With him, you'll have to consider his decisions in ranch management. If you choose me, you'll maintain your independence, just for dancing the horizontal two-step a few times a month."

"You're a genuine bastard," Elizabeth hissed at him. "It must come with having so much money to burn."

"If I'm a bastard, just what does that make you, Elizabeth?" he asked in a biting tone that cut all the way to the bone.

She vaulted to her feet, itching to slap the insulting smirk off his face and rearrange his mustache. Wyatt caught her hand before it connected with his cheek. Too bad. Elizabeth was really anxious to leave her mark on him after he had slashed a wide gash in her pride.

"Temper, temper, *sugar,*" he drawled. "Don't strike out at

me because your conscience is giving you hell. Did you already tell Hollis you'd marry him?"

"I said I'd think about it," she snapped, wresting her hand from his steely grasp.

"Would you also think about it if I arranged for a corporation to assume your debts and let you become the caretaker for Heartstrings? Cattle corporations are paying a dollar a head for feeding and caring for livestock. They also pay the veterinary bills. You wouldn't have to move away from home at all. You wouldn't have to sell yourself to me or Hollis."

"And I would no longer own Heartstrings," Elizabeth contended. "I know several ranchers who opted to become caretakers. They can't even call their property their own these days."

"Because *they* were in debt up to their eyebrows," Wyatt clarified. "You aren't in extreme straits. Financial difficulty, yes. But because of your conservative management procedures the past nine years, you'll have something left when all is said and done."

Elizabeth backed up a step, defying the gravitational attraction that had obviously been skin deep to begin with. "I can't see what difference it makes to you what I decide to do. If you don't auction my ranch you'll auction something else. That's your business, after all. And Jerry made a point to mention—repeatedly—that you're very much in demand. I'm nothing to you but a prospective client."

"Are you? Think again, Elizabeth." He took a step forward, pinning her to the wall without actually touching her. "This deal matters to me because *you* matter to me. I told you that last night. Nothing has changed."

"Everything has changed. I—"

He pressed his index finger against her trembling lips, shushing her. "Has it? Or have you decided to ignore what you *can't* change? I think *I* matter to *you*, too. But we'll never know if you accept Hollis' offer without giving us the time we need to really get to know each other."

Elizabeth sniffed caustically and removed his hand from her

mouth. "The time to know each other? What for? To see if we are compatible in bed? Why wait? Why don't we find out right now? I've got thirty minutes to kill."

"Thirty minutes won't be enough," he assured her with a rakish grin.

"Oh, really? My husband never needed more time than that," she smirked.

"Then your husband obviously wasn't doing something right."

Elizabeth choked on a laugh. "And you're an expert, are you? So you *do* do this sort of thing on a regular basis."

He scowled at her. "No, I do not."

"Then you're simply a slow operator," she taunted him. "What's the matter, McKenney? Age catching up with you?"

"I'm very thorough," he guaranteed, his eyes dancing with sensual challenge as he moved ever closer. "Would you like a demonstration?"

Elizabeth didn't appreciate the throbbing heat that pulsed through her betraying body or the devilish gleam in his eyes. And furthermore, she did not want to respond when Wyatt's thumb brushed over her breast, circling the suddenly rigid peak that burned with heightened sensitivity. When he freed the buttons of her white blouse and made disturbing contact with bare skin, Elizabeth's breath caught; her heart flipflopped in her chest. Splinters of fire prickled her flesh and swirled into a coil of flames deep inside her.

When his knee insinuated itself between her thighs, pressing suggestively against her, her legs turned to jelly. It was demoralizing to realize that *his* touch could devastate her and that *his* supporting arm was all that prevented her from crumbling at his feet.

Wyatt held her gaze as his fingertips migrated across the fabric of her bra to tease her nipples. He drew her ever closer, his hips pressing firmly to hers, his mouth hovering inches from her lips. When Elizabeth struggled to draw breath, he caressed her again—and again. Her pulse hammered against his wandering hand, assuring him that he was disturbing her in the most sensuous ways imaginable.

When his caress drifted down to the hem of her hiked skirt and his hand scaled the silky flesh of her inner thigh, Elizabeth felt her traitorous body aching with forbidden anticipation. His fingertip traced the leg band of her panties, gliding against the moist heat of desire he had so easily called from her. Elizabeth half-collapsed against the wall, hating him for making her want him with a maddening obsession, hating herself for being so susceptible to his seductive charm. He was bending his will into her own . . . Or had she simply tried to deny the truth of her own ardent needs?

"Two weeks, Bet," he whispered as he caressed her, leaving her to burn with each skillful stroke of his hand. "Give us two weeks before you decide what to do about Hollis. I will keep my end of our bargain."

His warm breath hovered over the throbbing column of her throat, causing gooseflesh to pebble her skin. "If you decide it's him you want instead of me, then I'll back off and you can repay me for the expenses of upgrading Heartstrings whenever you can afford to."

His fingertips brushed over the fabric of her panties again, feeling the heat of her response against the back of his hand. His body clenched in answering response and his voice dropped to a husky pitch. "But whatever you decide to do, Bet, don't make Hollis your crutch, and don't try to convince yourself you'll be happy if you don't love him. I've seen it happen before. It never works, not for either party. No matter how strongly you feel about your ranch, you have to be true to yourself. Living a lie won't make you happy or keep you satisfied."

His left hand drifted down from the swell of her breast and folded around her fingertips. He brought her hand down between their bodies until her palm rested against the denim jeans that concealed the rigid evidence of his need. "What we do to each other isn't something that happens unless two people are totally aware and wildly attracted to each other. Not only do I thoroughly enjoy your company, but you arouse me. We're both old enough and mature enough to recognize what's happening between us. Ignoring it isn't the solution.''

Wyatt removed his hand from hers, vividly aware that *she* had not removed *her* hand from his hard male contours. "Don't *settle*, Bet,'' he urged her huskily. "There can be much more if you're willing to take the time and the risks to find out for certain. I'm willing to try. But the question is: Have you locked your personal needs away for so long you've forgotten how good it can be? Or have you ever really known what lovemaking is like when a man takes the time to pleasure you instead of thinking only of himself?''

"I don't know what you're talking about,'' she said shakily, ashamed of herself for touching him and yet unable to find the will to withdraw her hand when he had given her every chance to do so.

"I'm talking about complete satisfaction with someone you care about,'' he murmured against her shoulder. "I'm talking about slow, unhurried lovemaking, not recreational or obligatory sex. *Lovemaking*, Bet, the kind that makes you ache to return the pleasure you've received because it demands to be fully shared . . .''

His raspy voice and erotic words were painting visual pictures that left Elizabeth quivering uncontrollably. His hand was whispering over the exposed flesh of her stomach and tracing the underswell of her breasts, sketching designs that burned like branding irons. Her body instinctively arched up in answer to his masterful touch, but Elizabeth valiantly reminded herself of what she stood to lose if she surrendered to a passion that might only become temporary appeasement for long- denied needs.

Wyatt made no promises; Griff did. Wyatt was forcing her to make choices that demanded costly sacrifices. If she pleased herself, she could lose Heartstrings—or at least real control of her ranch operation. If she appeased her deep-seated need to hold onto Heartstrings, she would inevitably find herself married to a man she might never come to love, whose farming practices didn't coincide with hers and with whom she would inevitably argue.

How many sacrifices was she supposed to make? Which choice was the right one to suit the uncertain future that lay ahead? How could she live with herself if she yielded to Wyatt's request and found herself holding shattered dreams when he walked away . . . ?

Elizabeth's eyes fluttered shut when his hand skimmed her hip, gently sliding her panties out of his way, letting them drop to the floor at her feet. She breathed a shuddering sigh when he eased the discarded garment out of his way and nudged her legs farther apart. When his fingertips tested the damp heat he had summoned from her, brushing tenderly against her sensitive flesh, Elizabeth moaned in helpless abandon. This sensual wild man was sending the world spinning off in a dizzying blur, leaving her to focus on nothing except the white-hot sensations that seared her to the very core.

Her hand contracted around the hard length of him, wishing there wasn't a layer of denim between her questing fingertips and his potent flesh. She wanted to touch him as intimately as he was touching her, to feel him hard and pulsing in her hand, to know that the fire that splintered through her was raging with the same intensity inside him . . .

She was absolutely shameless! She was placing herself in the same degrading category as Patty Hollis. And yet, as Elizabeth's maddening needs multiplied with each bold caress, she couldn't help but wonder if she *had* missed something rare and fulfilling all these years, something her marriage had never provided. There was an undeniable hunger in her that demanded to be appeased, and Wyatt's masterful seduction was making her vividly aware of that overpowering need.

But this was purely physical, Elizabeth tried to remind herself, even while her hand glided down the fly of his jeans, caressing him while he caressed her. There was more to life than sexual pleasure, more than feeding hungry desire . . . If only she could remember what it was . . .

"God, Bet," Wyatt breathed hoarsely. "I feel like I'm burning." He nuzzled his chin against her shoulder, inhaling the feminine scent of her, fighting to restrain what was quickly becoming overwhelming.

Something more demanding and intense than common sense tugged at Elizabeth. "I . . . want . . . you . . . too," she reluctantly admitted to him, to herself.

"Then delay this decision that will affect the rest of your life," he requested as he traced her tenderest flesh, feeling the soft rain of her desire spilling onto his fingertips, filling him with the need to bury himself in the silken fire that he knew awaited him. "Two weeks, Bet. Give us two weeks."

Very slowly, maddeningly, he penetrated the secret warmth of her body and then gently withdrew his fingertip. Her intimate response shimmered through him like sensual lightning, and he suppressed a groan of unappeased need. It was all he could do to retreat when his male body was throbbing with aching desire. He wanted nothing more than to slide into that liquid fire and burn alive.

He should be ashamed of himself for making such a brazen play for a woman who had enough difficulty without his complicating her life. But he couldn't back away, not from something he sensed could become very special to both of them.

Elizabeth tried to button her gaping blouse—with ten thumbs. When she fumbled, Wyatt took up the chore, his knuckles brushing against her beaded nipples, fanning the fires Elizabeth couldn't extinguish, though she tried.

"Stay a while, Bet . . ." he murmured, his eyes smoldering with the promise of unbridled passion.

"I-I have to g-go to work," she stuttered between ragged breaths.

"Tomorrow then?"

Elizabeth swallowed down her heart when it catapulted into her throat. Each time his hands glided over the throbbing crowns of her breasts and went down her body in a gentle sweep the sensations intensified. She squeezed her eyes shut and fought the deliciously tantalizing feelings he called from her. "I can't."

"Hollis?" he questioned quietly, exploring the curves and swells of her pliant body.

Elizabeth nodded mutely. "Julia and Lana invited him to dinner."

"So they approve of him," Wyatt assumed, his hands stalling.

"Yes," she managed to get out on a shaky sigh.

"But not of me."

"I'm sorry to report that you're being jeered by the peanut gallery." Elizabeth tried to retreat, but his scintillating caresses were making it difficult to do more than attempt to speak. "They think you come on too fast, too strong." She licked her bone-dry lips and peeked up at him through thick lashes. "They're right, you know."

His hands lifted to frame her face, holding her level gaze when she would have self-consciously looked the other way, afraid she would feel the compulsive need to answer the hunger in his eyes—again.

"For once in your life, Bet, think of yourself first—what you want and need to be content. Don't think of your daughters' opinions or of your heritage, only of yourself." His thumb brushed over her parted lips like a feathery kiss, but he refrained from pressing his mouth to hers, even when she looked as if she wanted his kiss as badly as he wanted to offer it. "I've got a feeling this craving to save Heartstrings goes deeper than you're willing to admit. I think you know you made a mistake in your marriage, one that almost cost you the ranch that was entrusted to your care.

"It's guilt, isn't it?" he whispered. "It's a feeling of failure that you're trying to overcome. You keep wondering how you could have corrected the problems early on, how you could have prevented these last nine years of scratching and clawing that never would have come to pass if the ranch had been under your control."

He was hitting exposed nerves, bleeding her emotions. A mist of tears clouded Elizabeth's eyes. How could he read her private thoughts, sense her deepest secrets? How had he seen past her strong, stubborn facade?

Wyatt gathered her close, lifting her to his bare chest, nuzzling his cheek against the fabric that covered her breasts. Her breath stirred softly against his forehead, and he felt her tears moisten his shoulder. He relished the quiet intimacy of the moment, cherished the feel of this strong but tender woman in his arms.

"You haven't failed, Bet," he assured her. "When you have done all you can, then you have a right to be proud of your accomplishments, your tireless efforts. Just be careful that winning for the sake of winning doesn't become your obsession. Ask yourself if you'll truly be at peace, if you'll truly be happy if you save Heartstrings and sacrifice your own happiness. Where's the sense of accomplishment if you lose more than you've won?"

"How can you possibly know what I'm feeling?" Elizabeth choked out as her arms reflexively wrapped around him, absorbing his strength, savoring the incredible security she discovered in his embrace.

He pressed a kiss to her temple and smiled. "Because my driving obsession to make money these past years has become nothing but a way of keeping track of how far I've come from what I considered rock-bottom. But there's no peace, no satisfaction in it anymore. I accomplished my purpose. I proved to myself that I could succeed. Now I find myself asking if this is all there is. Is this the best my life can be? Where is the fire that has been missing? What's the purpose of having plenty of money when all accruing it has become is a compulsion that brings me no pleasure? Now, you're the pleasure I want, the one thing that seems to give me a purpose."

Wyatt leaned back to trace her soft lips, staring deeply into her cloudy eyes. "You and I can burn down both ends of the night, Bet. Even after only two days you know it as well as I do. There is something between us. I can feel the answering fire in you, and I know you can feel it in me." He pressed her against him, reminding her of how quickly he reacted to her. "Give us two weeks," he implored softly, urgently. "For two weeks, let's pull out all the stops and hold nothing back.

Let's forget the past and the future and just live every day as it comes. Let's see how hot this fire can burn between us and where the flames will lead."

"And then?" she questioned, matching his intense gaze.

"And then we evaluate priorities, both yours and mine."

"You don't know what you're asking me to do—the risks, the chances I'll have to take. I could lose everything—"

"Or have it all," he added with a tender smile. "How will either of us know for certain what we have to gain or lose if you walk away now? I'll always wonder how good it could have been, Bet. Will you?"

"But what if—"

His thumb skimmed her lips again; he was refusing to let her flounder in doubt. "In the business I'm in, I've learned that you don't make a bid for something unless you want it very badly and you're willing to pay the price. Money isn't the only medium of exchange. We're dealing with something far more valuable, something that could be worth every risk. Think about it."

Wyatt reached over to open the door for her. "You must be at work, and I'm due at Nancy's and Jerry's for supper again tonight. If you don't leave now, I may not find the willpower to let you go."

Elizabeth drew in a steadying breath and struggled to gather her composure. It was virtually impossible. Her mind was still reeling, warring with the unruly desire that had overwhelmed her. Her body was still humming like a tuning fork, long after Wyatt had released her from his hypnotic spell.

After she drove off in her beat-up truck Wyatt closed the door to face the empty silence that became more noticeable each time Elizabeth came and went. Dispirited, he pivoted around . . . and stopped dead in his tracks when he noticed the article of clothing still lying on the floor.

A deep skirl of laughter reverberated in his chest as he scooped up the bikini panties, wondering how long it would take Elizabeth to realize she would be working the night shift without her underwear. The thought left a smile pursing his lips long after Elizabeth had left.

"Good Lord!" Elizabeth groaned a half-hour later while she was on her way down the aisle to deliver fried chicken and mashed potatoes to the corner booth.

"What's the matter, sugar?" Irene questioned, turning away from the table where she had just taken an order. "Are you feeling all right? You look flushed."

No kidding! thought Elizabeth. "No, I'm fine. I just remembered something I forgot to do." Or rather, something she should *not* have done. Sweet mercy! Wyatt had her so rattled she was scuttling around, wondering why there was such a cool draft in the cafe.

Irene swiped the two plates from Elizabeth's shaking hands and gestured with her dyed blond head toward an empty table. "I think you better sit down awhile."

"No!" If she sat down, someone might see right up her short skirt!

Irene frowned at the near hysterical protest. "I think you should have called in sick tonight, sugar."

Elizabeth thought she should have called in insane.

While Irene bustled the food off to the waiting customers, Elizabeth self-consciously made her way to the kitchen and propped herself against the wall. She couldn't believe she had been so reckless, so oblivious! How could a woman not remember that she forgot her undies?

Irene marched into the kitchen, hands on hips. "Okay, sugar, now tell me what's wrong with you."

"I'm having a nervous breakdown," Elizabeth declared.

"Why? Because of the auction? Do you need some help around the ranch? Even though I don't know much about cattle, except how they look when they're cooked medium rare and lying on a plate, I'll be glad to lend you a hand. All you have to do is ask."

"Thanks, Irene. I appreciate the offer."

"So out with it." Irene demanded. "What is the trouble?"

Elizabeth's face flamed like grilled shish kebab. "I can't discuss it."

"Order up!" The cook called out.

Irene flung up a hand in a deterring gesture when Elizabeth reflexively pivoted toward the counter. "I'll get it. You stay here and practice deep breathing for a few minutes until your face returns to its natural color. You look like a beet wearing a bow tie."

Elizabeth took Irene's advice and breathed in several gallons of air before resuming her duties. She did, however, walk a bit more carefully than she had the previous hour.

Julia dropped her car keys in her purse and strode through the front door to see Brad and Lana propped side by side on the sofa, watching a flick on television.

"Could you spare me a minute, sis?" Julia requested as she propelled herself toward the kitchen.

Lana appeared in the doorway. "Well?"

"She was with *him* again at the motel," Julia bleakly confirmed.

Lana frowned pensively. "Then we're going to have to make sure Mother knows she has our blessing tomorrow when Griff comes to dinner."

Julia nodded grimly. "I think we had better come back next weekend, too. Hopefully, Romeo McKenney will be long gone by then."

"Of course, he will," Lana predicted. "Men like that are always on the prowl. Mother will be depressed and guilt-ridden when she finds herself discarded like a used toy. She'll definitely need our support and compassion."

"God, I never dreamed we were going to have to start taking care of Mother so soon," Julia said with an incredulous shake of her blond head. "She was always so strong, reliable and independent."

"Midlife crisis," Lana diagnosed. "But we will get Mother pointed in the right direction."

"Or have her committed," Julia said pessimistically. "She may have to have shock therapy after being humiliated by this sordid affair."

"You're overreacting, as usual," Lana noted as she pirouetted around. "Mother will be back on track with a little coaxing from us. Griff is the answer."

"I just hope Mother doesn't crack up so badly she can't even remember the question!" Julia muttered to the room at large.

Elizabeth glanced up at five minutes before closing time to see Wyatt McKenney strolling into the cafe. She nearly groaned aloud at this visual reminder of a reckless moment when she had lost her head and given in to a desperate need.

Wyatt was standing at the cash register with his back to Elizabeth, talking to Irene who was entertaining him with another of her Mae West routines. He was wearing a colorful Mo'Betta shirt and trim-fitting jeans that emphasized his masculine physique. Elizabeth tried to ignore him. It was like trying to ignore the sun when it rose.

With a trembling hand, Elizabeth picked up the tip on the table she was cleaning and deposited the dollar bill in the pocket of her skirt. Heart palpitations made it difficult for her to breathe normally. She didn't dare look in Wyatt's direction for fear their eyes would meet across the cafe and her legs would turn to liquid, leaving her a puddle on the floor, just like the Wicked Witch of the West when Dorothy doused her with water.

Even when Irene's sudden outburst of laughter carried across the room, Elizabeth kept her eyes trained on the second table she was wiping clean. No doubt, Irene was flirting outrag-eously and Wyatt had offered her a clever rejoinder. Against her will, Elizabeth's gaze drifted toward the cash register.

Wyatt turned around, holding a coffee-to-go in one hand

and sporting a smile that affected every feature on his face. Elizabeth's fumbling fingers bumped the glass of water, sending it tumbling to the carpet. She stared at Wyatt in stupefied disbelief.

Wyatt McKenney had shaved off his mustache! She thought he looked almost ten years younger with nothing to conceal the rakish grin on those full, sensuous lips.

Elizabeth had duly noted that each time they had been together, he had never once dared to kiss her after she'd announced that she didn't like mustaches. Good grief, maybe things wouldn't have gotten so far out of hand—or so far *in* hand, as the case happened to be—if she had settled for a mustached kiss to start with.

Doubt it. It was her annoying conscience again.

Elizabeth reluctantly agreed as she scooped up ice cubes and blotted up the spill on the carpet. For some unexplainable reason she and Wyatt couldn't seem to be alone together without touching. It was the darnedest thing she'd ever experienced.

Self-consciously, she tugged at her skirt as she climbed to her feet. She had just gathered up the coffee cup and saucer from the table when tanned fingers slipped a note into her empty hand. Startled, Elizabeth glanced up to see Wyatt towering over her, his green eyes dancing with mischief, his mouth curved in a smile as wide as the Osage Hills. He said not one word before he ambled toward the door.

Elizabeth stared at the note he had tucked in her quavering hand.

I'll be waiting outside for your answer. And by the way, if you're wondering why I'm smiling, it's because I'm wearing your bikini underwear.

The cup and saucer clanked on the floor, and Elizabeth's face turned fuchsia. As the clatter of fallen dishes echoed around the empty cafe, Irene's voice rang out like a pealing bell.

"I don't know what's wrong with that woman tonight," she

told Wyatt as he pushed open the door. "She's been flushed and shaky since she got here."

"Oh, really?" Wyatt glanced back at Elizabeth. In raffish glee, he watched her self-consciously tug at her skirt as she knelt to clean up her mess. "Maybe she's coming down with the flu."

"This late in the season?" Irene said skeptically.

"Never can tell after you've been caught in one of those cool spring drafts," Wyatt replied.

Elizabeth promptly dropped the cup she had just picked up from the floor. She swore she heard Wyatt snickering as he swaggered out the door.

Chapter Eight

Wyatt was leisurely propped against the battered farm truck in the parking lot when the lights flicked off inside the cafe. Four silhouettes appeared beneath the neon sign. Wyatt sipped his coffee, still grinning in devilish amusement. He wondered what kind of reception awaited him after he had unmercifully razzed Elizabeth about her forgotten undies. This was going to be a test of her temperament, he predicted. He probably shouldn't have teased her when their future was on the line, but he couldn't resist the playful temptation.

When Elizabeth strode toward him, Wyatt felt himself tense in apprehension. The time of reckoning had come. Tonight was either going to be an exciting beginning or a disappointing end. He had left the decision entirely up to Elizabeth. She already knew what he wanted.

"Get in, you rascal," Elizabeth muttered at him, grabbing her keys.

Wyatt opened the cab door for her and walked around to the passenger side of the truck. "The devil made me do it," he told her as he slid onto the seat.

Elizabeth perched beneath the steering wheel and stabbed

the key into the ignition. A grinding sound preceded the erratic growl of a motor obviously in need of tuning.

"Elizabeth?" Wyatt ventured softly, studying her alluring profile in the dim light.

She said nothing as she stomped on the accelerator, almost causing Wyatt to suffer whiplash and slopping hot coffee in the crotch of his jeans. He braced an arm against the dashboard when Elizabeth wheeled up beside the Caddy and stamped on the brake. More coffee dribbled over Wyatt's hand and splattered in his lap.

"Okay, I guess I deserved that," he said good-naturedly.

"Damned right you did," Elizabeth agreed as she cut the engine. She stared directly at his crotch. "Would you like me to blot up that spill, too?"

"After what happened between us earlier tonight, there isn't room on the seat of this truck to do what would come next if you put your hands on me." He told her frankly.

"Why did you shave your mustache?" she asked, displaying her customary habit of switch- ing topics in midconversation.

"Because I knew you didn't like it, and because you implied last night that you would know how serious I was about what has been simmering between us if I gave up something I was partial to."

"And that's also why you've done practically everything *except* kiss me, because you knew I didn't like the 'stache?"

"Yes," he said simply. "It sure as hell wasn't because I didn't want to kiss the breath out of you since we were sprawled in the pasture."

"Where's my underwear?"

"I told you. I'm wearing it." He tried out her technique of bounding from one subject to another like a jackrabbit. The suspense was killing him. "Where do we go from here, Bet?"

Elizabeth slumped against the door, staring at the muscular silhouette outlined by the motel lights. "I think you could cost me Heartstrings." *You could also break my heart, Wyatt McKenney. Don't you know that?*

"That's what you *think*." Wyatt scooted toward her, close

enough to jolt her pulse and remind her of how perfectly his body molded to hers. "But what do you *feel?*" he murmured in question.

Wyatt sketched her lips with his forefinger, holding her wide-eyed gaze, leaving her craving the breathless pleasure she knew awaited her if she was willing to take the risk.

"You're tearing me apart," Elizabeth whispered brokenly. "You know that, don't you?"

"And you're leaving me aching in places I thought I was too old even to feel anymore. Do you know what it's like to sit through a dinner with friends, unable to keep your mind on conversation, hungering for something a plate full of gourmet food can't begin to satisfy?" His hand splayed over her thigh, tracing the hem of her skirt. "Do you know what I feel when I touch you? I want to go on touching you, holding you until we've fed this gnawing hunger, but I know you think I'm already moving too fast for your comfort."

Elizabeth shivered in response to the caressing huskiness of his voice, the alluring scent that tortured her senses, the light touch of his fingertips. Her hand clamped on the steering wheel to prevent her from reaching toward him. She was feeling all the things he had described, those sensations were her constant, tormenting companions. Wyatt was clouding her mind and tearing at her heart, not to mention what his words and touch were doing to her body.

"If we let go, Bet, there will be certain risks for both of us. You're not the only one taking chances. But neither of us will know until all the walls come tumbling down.

"I can be myself with you. I like how I feel when I'm with you. I've begun to relax and enjoy living instead of merely existing. It's been too long. I'd almost forgotten what it's like to feel so vital, so hungry"—his voice hit a gravelly pitch—"and so aroused . . ."

Elizabeth looked into that handsome, distinguished face—devoid of mustache. She remembered those wild, breathless moments when they were alone in his motel room, the playful note he handed to her in the cafe. She forgot everything but this raging need that was as basic as life itself—the need to touch and be touched, the need to enjoy being a woman again, not an inanimate machine.

She remembered what Wyatt had said about making the first move toward him. That was what he was waiting for now, for her to decide whether keeping her ranch was her only heart's desire.

Elizabeth stared at his full lips, and she knew what she wanted. She hungered for his kiss and the fulfillment of sensual promise in those glistening green eyes. She didn't want to settle for Griff Hollis. He couldn't make her feel wild and reckless. He had kissed her that morning and Elizabeth had known that if she accepted his offer she would be *settling* in order to save her ranch.

Her gaze fastened on Wyatt's mouth again, and she began by letting go, by taking the risk she no longer cared if she came to regret. For the first time in more years than she could remember, Elizabeth ignored duty and obligation, considered only what she wanted and needed.

She leaned into Wyatt, her lips settling tentatively against his, feeling him breathe new life into her at first kiss, her body sparkling with radiant pleasure. His hand swirled over her leg, gliding up and down her bare hip, pausing to pay particular attention to that sensitive spot on the inside of her knee. His teeth playfully nipped at her bottom lip, tugging at it in the same way erotic sensations were tugging at her body.

When she moaned, he answered with a low growl. The tip of his tongue sketched her lips as his thumb retraced a path across her thigh. When his palm settled between her legs, Elizabeth's breath faltered and her ribs threatened to shatter beneath the fierce thud of her heartbeat. His hand brushed against the heated response he had called forth from her, and Elizabeth felt uncontainable desire coursing through her.

He caressed her feminine flesh with thumb and fingertip while he guided her legs farther apart with the gentle pressure of his elbow. He explored her, aroused her by tormentingly tender degrees. His tongue glided between her lips as his fingertip penetrated deeper, holding her suspended in the grip of a fiery passion that promised to burn out of control—here, now.

When his hand eased between her legs again, probing and then withdrawing with the same maddeningly tender motion that his tongue delved into the moist recesses of her mouth, all her senses keyed on his incredibly skillful seduction. The deliberate, unhurried strokes of his hand and lips set a synchronized rhythm, luring her deeper into the sensual web, until time could only be measured by the beat of his heart against her breasts. Space became no more than hands and lips offering unbelievably gentle pleasure as they traveled on a journey of intimate discovery, igniting a maelstrom of heated responses.

This was not the way Elizabeth remembered her romantic encounters. Sex had been another wifely duty she'd been expected to perform. *This* was smoldering need and exquisite torture that turned bone to glowing coals and flesh to scattered ashes.

Wyatt traced the hidden secrets of her body with teasing tenderness while he nipped at her quivering lips with his teeth. He could feel the sweet pressure of her contracting around his fingertips, caressing him as gently as he caressed her. When she melted around him, bathing him in a warm spring of shivering desire, his body tightened with the kind of throbbing pleasure that left nerve and muscle strung as taut as fence wire. He was burning with her, aching to become the flame flickering within the hottest and sweetest of fires.

"Oh, God . . ." Elizabeth gasped when the indescribable sensations uncoiled inside her. Her fists knotted in the sleeves of his shirt, anchoring her to him when the world threatened to slide out from under her. Pleasure expanded in her; consumed her until she was shuddering helplessly in his arms.

This can't be happening! Elizabeth thought wildly.

When Wyatt felt her answering his intimate caress, felt her body convulsing in warm, sultry response, he clenched his teeth against the ravenous need that hammered at him. He wanted nothing more than to lead her to his room, to his bed. He wanted to appease this wild ache that was eating him alive. But it was too soon. He had already gone too far, and he dared not do more than leave her with the shattering knowledge that this *was* the beginning of something unique and special and unbelievably satisfying.

Elizabeth's mind was still clouded with hesitation and doubts, Wyatt knew that. If he made love to her completely he might lose her forever, especially with her daughters waiting at home to assure her that he was a man who cared only for meaningless flings. When he did make love to her, he wanted to be there the morning after to reassure her that he was no fly-by-night Romeo who performed disappearing acts at the break of day.

And so, Wyatt did no more than hold Elizabeth close until the rippling sensations that had burst inside her ebbed, echoing softly from her pulsing body and whispering through his.

Having gained full command of her attention, he slowly withdrew his fingertip and lifted that same hand to trace her parted lips with the nectar of her own response. Her eyes widened at the intimate gesture, and he smiled at her before he tasted her need—on her lips and then on his own.

Elizabeth tried to speak . . . and couldn't. What could a woman say to a man after she had come unraveled in his arms, proving to him that he could fully arouse her with his gentle caresses? He now knew that he made her lose control. Did he also know that she wanted him so badly she could barely breathe, that leaving now would bring on a tormenting ache that might never go away?

"If I survive the weekend, I'll see you Monday morning," he whispered as he eased back to his side of the truck.

Wyatt smiled when Elizabeth continued to stare at him with onyx eyes that glowed with the passion he had aroused in her. "Irene was right. You do look a little flushed tonight." His grin broadened knowingly. "She said you didn't feel well, but when you're in my arms you *feel* absolutely marvelous."

The teasing remark snapped Elizabeth back to her senses. "I need my underwear," she blushed.

He chuckled huskily. "I told you, I'm wearing it. Since this is the closest I'll come to having you around me, I think I'll keep it."

Provoked by the visualization of his hushed words, Elizabeth made a ragged sound that testified to the sensual torment he was putting her through.

He opened the creaking door and glanced back at her as the light flicked on in the cab. His expression mirrored the unappeased need that churned inside him. His intense green eyes riveted on her. "I'd rather be wearing nothing but you, Bet," he said before he closed the door and let himself into his room.

Elizabeth did not remember driving home that night. She did not recollect what she said to Julia, Lana and Brad before she walked into her room to undress for bed. All she could recall was the feel of Wyatt's hands bringing her body to life, his lips playing gently upon hers, his muscular flesh pressed so close . . . and yet so intolerably far away that her forbidden dreams followed her into sleep.

"Mother?"

Elizabeth froze, her hand wrapped around her fork, poised inches from her mouth. She glanced across the dining-room table to see Lana peering questioningly at her.

"I said . . . don't you think Griff looks nice today?"

Elizabeth manufactured a smile and nodded in agreement. "Yes, you do, Griff. I meant to compliment your shirt earlier. Teal green becomes you."

"Thanks, Liz." Griff beamed in satisfaction and took another bite of steak. "The food is delicious. I haven't eaten so well in weeks, not since the last time you invited me to dinner."

"Mother is a wonderful cook," Julia put in. "Busy as she is, she always manages to put a great meal together."

"She has always had the ability to do more than one thing at a time, too," Lana remembered. "I don't ever recall seeing Mom talking on the telephone that she wasn't dusting furniture or picking up discarded objects within reach of the long cord. She could fix a meal and prepare vegetables and fruits for canning in the pressure cooker at the same time, making both tasks look as if they required no effort."

Elizabeth absently listened to further testimonials that sang her praises. Her mind wasn't on the man who had come to dinner, but on the one she had invited into her life the previous night. She was going to have to tell Griff that she couldn't accept his offer. If she did accept the proposal, she could no longer live with herself, not when she had learned the difference between settling and satisfying.

There simply was no comparison. Elizabeth had settled in her first marriage, thinking that was all there was and expecting no more. But Wyatt had taught her how wrong she'd been, how much she had missed. As much as she loved this ranch and felt obliged to hold onto the heritage and traditions, Elizabeth wanted—just once in her life—to let go of all inhibitions, to embrace heartwarming enjoyment and fulfilling pleasure for as long as it would last.

Wyatt was right. She had *not* failed. She had succeeded. She had two well-educated, successful daughters to her credit, a ranch that Bob would have lost years earlier if not for her conservative management and tireless efforts. She had raised her children, guided them through the critical stages of life with very little assistance from Bob, who had had no interest in being a good husband and father.

Elizabeth had simply been afraid to let go of the past because the future was so uncertain. But she had already proved she was a survivor. She could cope with whatever this new phase of her life dealt her. And before Wyatt had to go away, she was going to live again—really live—and amuse herself.

After Sunday dinner Lana and Julia volunteered to clear the

table. Griff took Elizabeth by the hand and led her onto the portico to lounge on the bench that overlooked the sloping meadow.

"I always did love this view," he said appreciatively. "Your grandfather selected the best location on this ranch to build this bunkhouse. But I never could figure out why he didn't build his own home here instead of setting it back where the view was blocked by that monstrosity of a barn."

Elizabeth absorbed the spectacular scenery and she smiled, remembering. "My grandfather always said it was the men who worked this ranch who deserved the best view. They were the ones who made it a success. He wanted them to have the same sense of pride and belonging that he harbored for Heartstrings. And the hired hands did feel that. They considered the ranch their home all the years they worked here, breaking green colts and herding cattle."

Griff laid his arm over the back of the bench, toying with the fabric of Elizabeth's pastel pink blouse. "We'll do well together here," he assured her. "This ranch will be back on its feet after I add more livestock to the pastures."

"It is already filled to capacity without dam- aging the grass," Elizabeth contended. "Overgrazing is hard on the land."

"My cows do all right grazing one animal to two acres."

Elizabeth begged to differ. Hollis cattle were malnourished. She could count their ribs from the far side of the shared fences. Hollis calves were scrawny, and they didn't gain weight as quickly as they could have if the mother cows were in better physical condition. That was one of the reasons Hollis cattle broke through Heartstrings fences so often. The herds were hungry.

"I still think livestock are more productive if the land is conserved and protected. Grubbing pastures lends itself to bacterial disease in cattle," she said tactfully.

"Well, you can let me worry about all that after we're married, hon," he replied with a dismissive shrug. "You can sit back and relax after working so hard the past few years."

"Griff, I—"

"I think we should hold the ceremony right here at Heart-strings," he cut in. "There's no sense waiting more than a week since we've known each other so long."

Elizabeth drew a deep breath and blurted out, "Griff, I don't think I should marry you."

He sat upright, stunned. "But I thought this invitation to dinner was—"

"Just that: an invitation to dinner," Elizabeth told him firmly. "As much as I love this ranch, as much as I appreciate your promise to keep it afloat, I'm not sure it would be fair to either of us."

"I certainly have no complaints, Liz," Griff grumbled. "We're more than compatible."

The wind swept through the breezeway, tossing Elizabeth's dark hair around her face as she stared into the distance and smiled sadly. "I want more than compatibility, Griff. If I do decide to sell Heartstrings to the highest bidder, I'll pay my debts and start all over again."

"Damnation, Liz, you'll wither away in town," he prophesied. "And I don't want to lose a good neighbor. Some cattle corporation will probably bulldoze its way in here and you'll cringe when you discover what overgrazing really can do. The grass will be grubbed down to the roots, and the manager won't keep your hired man on payroll. Vic Henderson and his family will be left out in the cold."

Elizabeth grimaced at the reminder. She felt bad enough about dismissing Vic without Griff rubbing it in.

"Just you wait, Liz. You'll go stir crazy when you're cooped up in town. You'll come driving out to take a look around, but you won't recognize the ranch that once belonged to your family.

"What the hell do you think you're going to do with yourself in town anyway? Bale up the grass on your lawn? Confine Damn It to a fenced backyard? Neither one of you will be happy when you're no longer doing what you were born to do, what you really know how to do well."

Elizabeth turned to Griff with a mist in her eyes. "It's time

to stop looking back. I intend to make the necessary adjust-
ments. I'll find something to do," she insisted determinedly.
"I know how to work hard. There're always jobs for those
who are willing to put in the time and effort. That won't
change."

"Fine, work full time at Tall Grass Prairie Cafe," he muttered bitterly. "At night you can go back to your cracker-box
house where you can't turn around without rubbing elbows
with your next-door neighbors, where the only scenic view
is the house across the street or the one across the alley."
He stood up, his chest swollen with offended dignity. "You
could have me—and you still can if you come to your senses
before it's too late. I'll give you another week to think it
over, Liz. Consider what you have to gain and what you
could lose."

Elizabeth sighed heavily. "All right, Griff, I'll give it more
thought if that's what you want, but—"

"That's what I want—the time to change your mind." Griff
stared straight ahead, fighting to control his temper. "We'll start
burning pastures after we round up the cattle. I'm sure you'll
want to get that done so the fresh spring grass can be waving
in the wind if you go ahead with the auction." He glanced
back at her, his expression cold and hard. "Just when *is* the
auction supposed to take place."

"I haven't set a date."

"Well, if you decide to set a *wedding* date instead, you know
where you can find me. I'll be where I've always been and
always want to be—at home, working my butt off to keep what
I've got."

On that parting shot, Griff stalked through the breezeway
and piled into his late-model Ford truck. Elizabeth envied him
that. Her clunker pickup hadn't purred like that in years, and
it knocked and rattled from too many trips over washboard
roads and rough pastures.

That hadn't gone very well, Elizabeth thought to herself. She
hoped by the time she and Griff joined forces to move cattle
and burn dead forage, he would have recovered from her re-

jection. The man had survived divorce, after all. This was only a proposal that hadn't lived up to his expectations. Although he had given her more time to consider his proposal, Elizabeth doubted she would have a change of heart, not when she looked at Griff and compared him to Wyatt. There was simply no comparison.

"Where is Griff going in such a rush?" Julia quested as she wandered onto the portico.

"Back to work."

"I like Griff," Julia enthused.

"I'll be sure to tell him you said so, next time I see him."

"Is something wrong, Mom?"

"Not a thing," Elizabeth said more cheerfully than she felt.

"Well, Lana and I want you to know we approve of Griff. You two are good for each other."

"So you indicated at lunch. Thinking of adopting him, are you?"

Julia raked her fingers through her long blond hair when the wind whipped it in her face. "To tell the truth, Lana and I were wondering if maybe Griff was considering adopting *us.* Is he?"

"He suggested it, but I have my doubts about it," Elizabeth said as she rose from the bench and pivoted toward the door.

"Why? Because of that auctioneer you've been seeing on the sly?" Julia blurted out. Lana would strangle her for refusing to employ subtlety. To hell with Miss Psychology. Julia had always been the up-front, confrontational type of individual who didn't mince words. "We know you've been meeting him. Does Griff know, too?"

Elizabeth wheeled around, her dark eyes popping with disbelief. "You have been following me?"

It was obvious Lana was also becoming an expert at stakeouts, for she appeared in the doorway.

"We've been concerned about you. You know that, Mother," Lana hastened to explain. "Selling this ranch has caused emotional upheaval. We understand that you're trying to find yourself."

"I know exactly where *I* am, thank you very much," Elizabeth snapped. "I just didn't realize *you* were two steps behind me. And for your information—"

Lana flung up a hand to forestall Elizabeth. "Denial is a defensive reaction provoked by guilt and shame, neither of which you want to face. Just because you have made three mistakes—"

"Three?" Elizabeth howled.

"Friday afternoon, Friday night and Saturday evening," Julia contributed. "Lord, Mother, doesn't that kind of schedule tell you something about the man? Fast and furious is usually a good indication of short and sweet—as in it was fun while it lasted."

"Julia!" Lana chastised her outspoken sister. "You're making matters worse."

"I'm bringing matters out in the open where they belong," Julia contested before she focused on her mother. "If you aren't considering a respectable relationship with Griff, then you should consider coming to live with one of us after the auction."

Elizabeth almost burst out laughing at the motherly expression on her daughters' faces. "You want me to come live with a potential murderess who is plotting to dispose of her asinine boss, or with the pseudo-intellectual ostrich who constantly has her head poked in a psychology book?"

"I'm not planning on killing him," Julia protested. "I'm only going to knock some sense into the male chauvinist pig."

"Oh, fine, you'll expect me to raise bail after you're charged with assault and battery. Sounds like fun. We'll call in Miss Psychology to counsel Miss Psycho."

"I resent being referred to as a pseudo-intellectual ostrich, Mother," Lana inserted in her characteristically controlled manner. "And I wish you would take us seriously. We're trying to help you cope with the upcoming changes in your life. Together we can make a smooth transition." She clasped her hands in front of her and smiled that patronizing smile Elizabeth itched to wipe off her face. "We can defeat every crisis together, Mother. You can depend on us for moral support."

Lana had always been an imperturbable and precocious child, Elizabeth recalled. Always seeking analytical solutions, always stuffing her nose in a book when the chores were done. Very tame in temperament, too, Elizabeth reminded herself. Lana was like the air bubble in the liquid tube on a level—always equalizing every situation to maintain stability. She was the counterbalance to neutralize her feisty sister.

Poor Brad, thought Elizabeth. If he married Lana he could expect to have every facet of their relationship perfectly equalized, stabilized and analyzed to death. Yes sir-ee, life in the bubble of a level. How thrilling.

"Julia and I are coming home next weekend to do what we can to get the ranch ready for auction."

"That won't be necessary. I can handle it." Elizabeth insisted.

"But we *will* be here," Julia declared in no uncertain terms. "And please give some thought to coming to Bartlesville or Skiatook for a few months."

"Fine, I'll give it some thought. Thank you for the offers."

"We have to get back to our jobs," Lana calmly informed her mother. "I'm taking Brad to the airport before I drive home to prepare my lesson plans for the week."

Julia grinned spitefully. "And I have to sharpen my scalpel so I can make a few more incisions in John W. Casey III's overinflated male ego."

"God, now she is planning to carve the man up for dinner," Elizabeth said melodramatically.

"Good-bye, Mother." Lana gave Elizabeth a peck on the cheek. "We'll be back Friday night."

"Thanks for the warning."

"Lose the auctioneer. He's bad news." This from Julia.

"Just try to hold on until we get back, Mom," Lana urged before Brad appeared with their luggage.

"I'll try to get a firm grip," Elizabeth promised in mock seriousness.

When offspring and the boyfriend drove away, Elizabeth asked herself if it was abnormal for a parent to be glad to see her children gone.

Chapter Nine

At promptly 6:30 A.M. the silver Caddy rolled beneath the gateway of Heartstrings Ranch, refurbishing supplies bulging from the trunk.

Vic Henderson frowned curiously from atop the overhead feed bin. "What's going on, Liz?"

Elizabeth poked her head outside the truck window. "Wyatt McKenney volunteered to polish up the ranch before the auction."

Vic looked skeptical. "I didn't know painting and fencing were part of the deal. Buster Simmons doesn't paint before he holds an auction."

"Buster Simmons isn't Wyatt McKenney," Elizabeth assured him. "Wyatt is also an exceptionally good sport . . . or he will be if he tries to paint the peak of the barn while clinging to the roof by his fingernails."

Vic glanced toward the gargantuan barn. "Long fall. Hope his insurance is paid up."

"Health insurance?" Elizabeth questioned.

Vic shook his shaggy brown head. "Nope. Life insurance. All the king's men couldn't put him back together if he lost his footing up there. Hope he's got a disassembled scaffold in his trunk."

"Good morning, Elizabeth," Wyatt greeted as he ambled up beside the one-ton truck that looked as run-down as her di-' lapidated blue pickup.

"Good morning." Elizabeth made no attempt to conceal her pleasure at the sight of him. She was through with guilt-ridden inhibition. She was going for the gusto in life. "Wyatt, this is Vic Henderson. He's been working for me the past seven years. Best help in the country, by the way. He and his wife Donna, who is a cashier at the bank, have two adorable grade-school-age children."

"I heard you do windows, or something to that effect," Vic called down to Wyatt. He hitched his thumb toward the barn. "Watch that first step out of the loft. The ground can come up and hit you pretty fast."

Wyatt peered up at the looming peak of the barn and nodded consideringly. "Did the last man who painted that monstrosity live to brag about it?"

"Nope, buried him down by the pond," Vic teased. "At least what was left of him."

"Be careful. You look better all in one piece," Elizabeth insisted. "Lunch will be served at high noon, if you haven't given up and gone home by then."

"I'll be there, even if I have to crawl," Wyatt promised.

Heat, like summer sunshine, poured through Elizabeth's body in response to that probing gaze. One look triggered an awareness of foretold pleasures. It had never been like this with Bob. He had never been attentive before or after a night of lovemaking—or whatever one called the hurried meeting of bodies after dark and before sleep. She wondered if her husband had been more romantic and considerate with women who weren't his wife. She also wondered what she might have done to prevent him from turning to other women for affection. Would Wyatt tire of her as quickly as Bob had?

Wyatt frowned pensively when he noticed Elizabeth's smile dissolve and the sparkle in her eyes dwindle. Was she suddenly having second thoughts? Was she asking herself what he intended to give in exchange for the chance he'd asked her to take?

"See you at noon," Wyatt murmured before he pivoted toward his car.

"So that's the high-rolling auctioneer Julia mentioned," Vic said as he climbed into the cab of the truck. "She didn't care for the man, but he seems a likable sort to me."

"Julia doesn't like much of anyone at the moment," Elizabeth explained as she shifted gears and drove toward the pasture gate. "She's having trouble with her boss."

"The vet? What's his problem? Having difficulty dealing with the fact that his assistant is an extremely competent woman?"

"I guess." Elizabeth shifted into second and took the slope of the pasture at an angle to prevent breaking an axle. "Lana, of course, is trying to counsel Julia through the difficulty."

Vic chuckled at that. "Julia always was a firecracker, and Lana's all wound up in the psychotherapy business, isn't she?"

"It always amazes me how two children, raised in the same environment, can turn out different," Elizabeth mused aloud. "I wonder if Lana has a theory on that, too. Probably does."

"Well, it's a mystery to me," Vic replied. "My two kids are nothing alike. Whatever one of them doesn't think to do, the other gets into. They're handfuls in their own rights at just eight and ten."

"It will get worse," Elizabeth guaranteed.

"Thanks for the encouragement," Vic grumbled.

"Just wait until they get old enough to think *they* can tell *you* what to do, and how to live. Enjoy lording it over them now. They can become real tyrants when they develop minds of their own and decide *you* have completely lost yours."

She waited until Vic returned from opening and shutting the second set of gates before striking up a more serious conversation. "Vic, I don't want to have to let you down," she murmured apologetically. "If I do decide to auction Heartstrings, it won't be easy for me. I'll feel as if I'm abandoning you."

Vic propped an arm on the open window and stared straight ahead. "I'd miss the ranch," he admitted. "It feels like home. But there's a job opening up at the feed store in Pawhuska in November. Sonny Swartz is retiring. Jerry Patterson said he would put in a good word for me since he deals with the owner on a regular basis. Don't worry about me, Liz. Donna has a good job and we'll be fine. I just hope you'll be satisfied if you go through with the auction."

Elizabeth grimaced and tried not to look too far into the future. She was taking one day at a time, reaping every benefit along the way. She had considered the risks going in, and she would accept the consequences.

One day at a time, she told herself. Don't look forward and don't look back . . .

The fifth day after Wyatt's arrival at Heartstrings, Elizabeth breezed through the kitchen door to fix lunch. She screeched to a halt when she noticed the monstrous bouquet of flowers— every variety and color under the sun.

Elizabeth pivoted toward the door to admire the triangular peak above the loft opening that glowed in the sunlight. Barn red—a wild splash of color to complement the red-tile roof of the house. Her gaze settled on Wyatt who was standing on the pyramid of hay bales and the ladder he had placed by the barn to reach the towering peak. The man did work fast, she'd give him that. He hadn't dillydallied since the day he'd arrived.

At this rate, he'd have finished the barn by early afternoon and have a second coat of paint on the adjoining shed by dark. Elizabeth was impressed. Hard work didn't appear to be a stranger to Wyatt McKenney. He attacked a chore with amazing enthusiasm.

He was also incredibly thoughtful, she mused as her gaze circled back to the bouquet. She didn't recall ever having flow-ers await her during her marriage—not even on a birthday or

Valentine's Day. Bob hadn't been into gifts, at least not for Elizabeth. She couldn't speak for the women in the wings.

Elizabeth popped leftover roast beef in the microwave and set a sauce pan on the stove to make gravy. While the meal was cooking she started a load of laundry and cleaned up the kitchen, following her standard policy of wasting no time. In a few minutes hot beef sandwiches were ready and waiting.

"Hungry, Picasso?" she questioned when Wyatt ambled into the room, his shirt and face splattered with paint.

"I'm starved," Wyatt told her.

"What's with the flowers?"

Wyatt fielded the abrupt question with a smile and a shrug. "I just felt like getting you something since you have been on my mind the past few days. It must be this skin-tight bikini I'm wearing that keeps reminding me of you."

Elizabeth groaned as she set the plates on the table. "Am I ever going to live that down?"

"A classic like that? Are you kidding?" He grinned outrageously and said, "I never intend to take these undies off, except to wash, of course." He winked and sank down behind the wall of flowers that partially blocked him from view. "I'm thinking of giving up clinging cotton briefs forever."

"Pervert," Elizabeth mocked playfully.

Wyatt peeked around the sprawling bouquet and waggled his thick brows at her. "You're the one who left without them so you could give the customers at the cafe a thrill. Just how long *did* it take for you to remember what you forgot?"

"Shut up and eat, or you'll find your ladder pulled out from under you."

"God, this tastes good," Wyatt complimented. "My stomach has been growling at me for two hours."

"It's the arsenic in the seasoning that enhances the taste. I wanted you to enjoy your last meal."

Wyatt was silent for a moment, his ruffled head bent over his heaping plate. "I'm glad I'm here, Bet," he murmured.

Elizabeth suddenly felt limp as the gravy dripping over her hot beef sandwich. Wyatt had the knack, she decided. He walked in and suddenly mundane activities became the high-lights of her day. She had looked forward to seeing him at lunch and supper since he had come to Heartstrings. She would remember how he looked when he stepped inside, pep-pered with paint, that disarming smile of his even more ap-pealing without the mustache.

His appreciation of the home-cooked meals she managed to provide despite her chores made her efforts worthwhile. The thoughtful gift of flowers that suggested he'd been thinking of her was touching. Perhaps her well-meaning daughters wouldn't approve of Wyatt being here, but Elizabeth was thor-oughly enjoying herself.

He had kept his distance from her, and she had refrained from venturing close enough to test her resistance. They had been taking the time to know each other, while sharing the same space. It felt . . . good, comfortable, natural, but not completely fulfilling as it would have been if they crossed the final threshold . . .

"I was wondering if you would have the time in the next day or two to show me around the various pastures," Wyatt said between bites. "I'd like to gather information about the divisions and sizes of the pastures and the farm ground."

"I should have a couple of free hours this afternoon before I go to work. Vic and I have to doctor the quarantined calves for foot rot and then spray the herd for flies and lice first, though."

"What time?"

"Around two-thirty."

"Good, I should have the north peak of the shed painted by then."

Elizabeth glanced over the bouquet, surprised. "Good grief, how many hands do you have?"

"Two, last time I checked."

"Do you always work like a house afire?"

He met her gaze between the carnations and roses. Green eyes, flecked with gold nuggets and surrounded by lashes fringed with red paint, gleamed at her. "Since last Saturday night, I *have* been a house afire, Bet. Working allows me to let off steam while I'm trying so hard to keep my hands off you."

"Sounds like gastrointestinal problems," she replied with an impish grin. "It must be the tight underwear that's causing the trouble."

His dark brows flattened over his smoldering eyes. "Or maybe it's the woman who owns the underwear who sets me afire. I hope you appreciate the restraint I've shown since I got here. It's been five days of hell, in case you're wondering."

Elizabeth took a sip of iced tea to cool the flame that burned inside her, knowing it probably wouldn't help. It didn't. His comments only served to remind her of how uncomfortable it had become *not* to have him touch her.

Thus far, Wyatt had been courteous and considerate, and he had maintained a respectable distance. She appreciated that, or she supposed she should. Funny, wasn't it? she mused as she strolled out the door to tackle the waiting chores. Wyatt had been very much the gentleman, and here she was wishing he would be less so.

Go figure . . .

"Come on, Damn It, hop in Old Red. We're going to tour Heartstrings," Elizabeth called to the dog.

Wyatt frowned when the speckled dog jumped into the bed of the faded blue truck Elizabeth always drove to work. "Damn It must be color blind."

"Nope." Elizabeth slid onto the seat and gestured for Wyatt to join her. "This is Old Red."

"Then *I* must be color blind. It damned sure looks blue to me."

Elizabeth held her mouth just so and turned the key in the faulty ignition. The starter groaned and finally sputtered to life. "I call this truck Old Red because that's the name of the mechanic in Pawhuska who works on it. From the sound of things, the truck is due for another tuneup at Red Gibson's shop."

Wyatt knew for a fact that the farm vehicles and machinery Elizabeth used for her operation were in sad condition, because he had evaluated them over the past few days. The tractor and fork lift he'd used to stack hay bales so he could reach the peak of the barn were undependable. He had poured enough oil in the tractor to choke a horse. It definitely needed to be overhauled—to the tune of a thousand dollars.

Setting his wandering thoughts aside, Wyatt concentrated on evaluating the cattle that grazed along the path Elizabeth followed down the rolling hillside. "Good-looking Limousins," he complimented.

"Registered reds," Elizabeth said proudly. "Jerry Patterson keeps insisting I could make more profit if I dry wintered four-hundred-fifty-pound yearlings entirely, rather than keeping cows and calves. I realize part of the pasture receives no rest, and I did compromise by selling some of my cows to buy yearlings, but I never had the heart to give up completely on the cow-calf operation. These young calves have been inoculated and branded, and their feed is supplemented with range cubes to save wear and tear on the pastures."

"Three pounds of cubes per animal per day? Twenty percent protein rations?" he quizzed her.

Elizabeth nodded, pleased that Wyatt was up to date on farming practices. "By August, the steers should have gained a half-pound per day, and I can sell them to Kansas feed yards as top-choice livestock. The problem I've had with yearlings is treating shipping fever. I don't have that trouble when I fatten my own weaning calves. There's little shrinkage because my yearlings haven't been transported by truck from God knows where. Although the yearling operation turns a profit, my veterinary expenses increase and I run a higher risk of losing sick calves."

"I agree with you," Wyatt replied as he studied the slick coats of the Limousin cows and their healthy calves. "A combination of cows/calf units and short-term yearlings seems a wise choice in this part of the country. You can defray costs of importing yearlings and doctoring them by raising your own feed-lot-destined steers."

Elizabeth was delighted to hear Wyatt approved of her methods. But, she reminded herself, by summer she would be living elsewhere . . .

She glanced sideways when she felt lean fingers curl around her forearm in a gesture of compassion.

"You've done well, Bet, exceptionally well," he said when he noticed the sparkle evaporate from her expressive eyes. "From what I've learned thus far, you inherited financial difficulty, you didn't invite it. If you don't mind my asking, what was the source of the debt that forced you to increase your larger loan?"

Elizabeth stared across the pasture that was just beginning to show signs of tender, green spring growth. "The estate taxes for Heartstrings and the funeral expenses were almost fifty thousand dollars," she confided. "That, added to the loan Bob signed to buy all new equipment and a fleet of trucks two years before he died, broke my back."

Wyatt recalled what Jerry had told him about Bob mortgaging his life insurance to secure loans. He hadn't done his wife any favors, had he?

"I'll be able to pay off the smaller loan at the end of this month. But because of this year's uncooperative weather conditions, the cattle didn't grow out as well as usual. Minimal profits made it impossible to pay on the loan I've had to let slide the past few years to cover my daughters' college expenses. Now that cursed loan has become an impassable mountain."

Before Elizabeth sank into depressing reflections on what she was about to lose, Wyatt gestured toward the adjoining pasture. "I see you also raise Salers cattle. I've heard good things about the breed. Pure bred and crosses have been bringing top dollar when I run them through auctions. They're in big demand as beef cattle."

Elizabeth veered toward the gate to enter the next pasture.

"I'm well pleased with the Salers. I've been running two of the bulls with Limousin and Angus cows. Salers bulls are known for producing small calves that present less problems in delivery, especially for first-time heifers. Although the calves start small, they compensate with quick weight gains and match the Limousins and Angus by market time."

"Do your spring and summer pastures hold up well with one animal to four acres without extra supplemental feed?"

"Yes, unless we have a dry spring," Elizabeth responded. "Griff runs one yearling to two acres and each year his pastures are slower in recovering. At that rate, the nutritional value of the grass and land will be depleted in a decade. I cringe to think how hard he is on his cattle and property. Always taking and never giving back."

"He's not much of a land conservationist," Wyatt snorted. "I've seen ranches ruined by trying to cut back in the wrong places. Your neighbor should take advice from you."

"Right." Elizabeth laughed humorously. "Griff drives a new four-by-four pickup, starves his cows and grubs his pastures. I have healthy cows, drive a rattletrap truck and can't pay my debts. I've got it made, don't I?"

"You can replace a pickup eventually, and a helluva lot cheaper than you can restore needed minerals and nutrients to soil," Wyatt reminded her. "The land has to last forever; trucks are dispensable."

Elizabeth smiled appreciatively at him. "Thanks, you're doing wonders for my sagging spirits. It's nice to know you don't think I've made bad decisions."

Those hypnotic green eyes keyed on her, bringing her entire body to a higher level of awareness. His hand lifted, gently stroking her arm from shoulder to wrist before his hand folded around hers. "You impress me, Bet. I admire what you've done. Never doubt that. I only hope you don't regret your most recent decision, because I can't think of anywhere I'd rather be or anyone I'd rather be with . . ."

Her skin tingled beneath his lazy caress, and her body burned with a sensual flame. One look, one touch and she stopped counting her losses and enjoyed her blessings. Wyatt McKenney made her feel young, vital and alive. When he smiled that sinfully sexy smile the sun shone twice as bright. There were times, like now, that what she stood to lose didn't compare to the happiness and contentment she had discovered when she was with him.

Wyatt leaned over, erasing the distance between them, pressing a feathery kiss to her lips. "You're really something, Bet. Other women might have bailed out when the going got tough. You dug in your boot heels, made your sacrifices and raised your daughters. I'm not sure even Heartstrings deserves a remarkable woman like you."

Elizabeth looked away, fighting the flood of sensations evoked by his kiss, his words. Her gaze landed on the barely visible cottage that stood in a grove of red cedar, persimmon, pecan and post oak trees on the rise above the spring-fed creek.

"You don't think Heartstrings deserves my efforts?" she questioned as she headed for the log cabin that had been her favorite childhood haunt. "Heartstrings deserves the sacrifices. You'll see why in a minute."

Wyatt frowned curiously when Elizabeth zoomed off. He also wondered how Old Red passed safety inspection when it sounded as if it was spitting out its muffler and was hitting on only four of its eight cylinders. Wyatt glanced overhead, swearing vultures were circling the clunker of a truck.

"You want background information on Heartstrings, do you?" she challenged with a proud smile. "Come with me, McKenney. You'll see why this ranch has come to mean so much to me, why I held onto it as long as I could."

Wyatt climbed from the truck, following along behind Damn It who veered off to hunt rabbits. He came to an abrupt halt as he rounded the obscure cabin. Shade trees formed an arched pathway from the front porch of the cottage to the pond that rippled over a ledge of limestone rock. The clear pool, surrounded by trees, reminded Wyatt of an oasis.

He had greatly admired the view from what had once been Heartstrings' bunkhouse. But this . . . God, if this wasn't heaven it was as close as he needed to come to it without actually dying. He defied any state in the nation to match this view of rolling hills and wooded valleys, offering the kind of serenity that ironed the wrinkles from troubled souls.

"This is No'n-Dse-Waspi, the very soul of Heartstrings," she told Wyatt in a voice thick with sentiment. "When the Osage tribe was restricted to Indian Territory at the turn of the century, the clans established four settlements. The Upland Forest and Big Heart clans built villages to the north and south. The Thorny Thickets and Heart-Stays clans settled on Bird Creek, close to the Indian Agency at Pawhuska. This creek was the home of my ancestors from the Heart-Stays clan."

Elizabeth felt that familiar sensation of peacefulness pour over her the minute she sank down on the porch step and peered through the trees, watching the gurgling spring dance over the rocks and sparkle in sunlight.

"When the government forced the Osage to sign the tribal roll and take land allotments of six hundred and fifty-seven acres, they objected, for all the good it did them. In the first place, Indians disliked being counted and numbered. They thought cows and horses could be counted, but never men who possessed souls and spirits. Of course, Indians were considered ignorant savages by the whites during the nineteenth century, so their objections were overruled and conveniently ignored."

Elizabeth smiled ruefully, remembering the stories she had heard from her grandparents when she was a child. "To the Heavy Eyebrows—as the Osage called the white men—owning land was the secret to prosperity and success. The whites thought Indians were too stupid to understand the importance of laying claim to land. They were oblivious to the Indian point of view that land could not be owned because it belonged to Wah Kon-Tah, great spirit of the Osage. The tribe believed *ho e ka* was the snare that trapped all living creatures and separated man from the Spirit Path. *E patsa ta* was the four winds that gave the breath of life.

"They were a band of people who actually *felt* the land beneath their feet and the wind in their faces. They lived in harmony with creation. Tearing the Sacred Earth with plows, reckless disregard for animal life and seizing land for greedy purposes were terrible violations of the natural order of the environment. To the Osage, the land was like the air they breathed—something that couldn't be owned or divided, something to be respected and revered. Nonetheless, government officials allocated property to the tribe's members, and they sold the surplus land supposed to have been a resource for the Osage as long as grass grew and rivers flowed."

"And so," Wyatt murmured, "although it took whites three thousand years to become westernized, we forced the Indians to change in less than two hundred years."

Elizabeth nodded and smiled tremulously. "So much for discarded beliefs, broken promises and shattered dreams. My family took what the government insisted they take and settled on this tributary of Bird Creek. They came to love this land because it was their last stronghold. This is where the Heart-Stays . . ."

When her voice trailed off like a fleeting spirit drifting in the wind, Wyatt saw the mist that clouded Elizabeth's eyes. His heart went out to her as she surged to her feet to stroll toward the spring-fed creek. No matter how willful she tried to be, he knew that severing her ties to this land on which the Heart-Stays clan had resided was difficult for her.

It humbled Wyatt to realize just how great a sacrifice Elizabeth had made by allowing him into her life and delaying her decision about Griff's proposal. He felt selfish for keeping her in a dilemma, but he relished the chance to really know her, to test this fierce attraction that still hounded him each time he drew breath, each time he crawled into the empty bed in the room Elizabeth had designated as his.

"How did your family come to have the name of Smith if the Heart-Stays clan of the Osage settled this region?" he questioned as he paused behind Elizabeth, reflexively circling his arms around her waist, holding her as he had refrained from doing—until now.

She instinctively leaned back against him, admiring the

beauty and tranquillity of the antiquated homestead and its freshwater spring. "Government employees were uninterested in preserving the honor and significance of Indian names when listing them on tribal rolls," she explained. "Unpronounceable names were quickly discarded. The Indians were expected to sacrifice their identify for the white man's convenience. That's why there are so many Smiths, Joneses and Browns among Indian tribes today.

"Some Indians were given names of famous people for the agents' amusement—George Washington, John Adams and Thomas Jefferson, for instance. My family's names were long, difficult to spell and to pronounce. They became Smith, which is a far cry from the hard-earned heritage my ancestors acquired because of their bravery and courage. Mo'n-Ko'n-Nika-Shinkah and Ni-Zhiu-Mo'n-I'n became Mr. and Mrs. Smith—short and simple. And now those who traveled so far, making sacrifices that I never will begin to make . . ."

Wyatt brushed his index finger over her quivering lips to silence her. "If your purpose is to make me feel exceedingly guilty for asking for this time together, despite Griff's tempting offer, you have succeeded. Where the Heart-Stays isn't just a name, is it, Bet? To you, it's a life force, an innate feeling tied to Heartstrings." He sighed audibly. "I'm sorry, Bet. I wasn't trying to tear your heart out by the taproot by asking for these two weeks together. I only wanted to be with you."

"I didn't mean to make you feel—" She tried to object, only to have his fingertip settle on her lips again.

"I know you're afraid you'll lose something that was handed down for you to cherish and preserve for generations to come, but I was afraid I'd lose something that could become as precious as life itself," he whispered before his lips replaced his fingertip.

All thought drained from Elizabeth, but hungry need burgeoned in her when he kissed her. She felt as if there were no tomorrow as he held her to his muscular torso. God, could what felt so right be wrong? Could she trade these wild, pulsating sensations, this feeling of belonging and being cherished, for Griff's proposal of a financial merger? How could she consider marriage to save Heartstrings when her heart longed to feed the fire Wyatt McKenney so quickly ignited in her?

This quaint cabin was the *house* from which generations of customs and traditions had sprung. But Elizabeth had become a trembling shell that housed a dozen different needs that shouted for release. She was holding a double-edged sword that was going to draw blood, no matter which way she turned. No matter what she did she was bound to lose, but for now she was going to live and enjoy . . .

When his palm glided inside her shirt to caress her breasts, flames of passion leaped through Elizabeth's nerve endings. Her tongue fenced with his as their breaths merged, as their bodies inched closer to share the same thundering pulse beat.

The need to touch him was overwhelming, and she responded without hesitation. Her hand tunneled under the hem of his shirt, feeling corded tendons and muscles flex and relax beneath her exploring caress. Enthralled, she counted his ribs with investigating fingertips, encircled his male nipples, brushed her hands over the crisp matting of hair that covered his chest, provoking a hoarse groan.

"The heart that is supposed to *stay* in my chest is going to *pop out* if you keep that up," Wyatt rasped when her palm swept over his belly and trailed along the band of his jeans.

Elizabeth smiled wickedly as her palm swirled over the bulge in his jeans—pulsating testimony that she affected him as dramatically as he affected her. "Would you be offended if I confessed it is not your heart that demands my attention at the moment?"

His thumb and fingertip teased the peak of her breast, causing her breath to trip out in a shaky sigh. "Not if you don't mind hearing that getting my hands on your body is demanding *all* my attention at the moment."

"I'm not sure Mr. and Mrs. Smith would appreciate us fooling around on their homestead," Elizabeth said, even as her hand dipped beneath his waist band to make bold contact with his aroused male contours.

The clever comeback Wyatt might have voiced became entangled in a husky moan when her thumb grazed his sensitive flesh. "God, Bet, I vowed to take it slow and easy with you, but I don't know how much longer I can pretend I don't want to touch and taste every inch of you. I feel like a damned kid battling rioting hormones. I thought I was too old to feel like this."

Elizabeth peeked up at him through dark lashes as her hand folded around that place where he was very much a man. "You mean you *felt* different when you were younger? Don't see how you could have had a *harder* time then than you do now."

He wanted to laugh; he wanted to scream in tormented pleasure. He also wanted the time they didn't have. If he and Elizabeth didn't get a grip on themselves—instead of each other—she was going to show up for work stark naked, because she would have no time to dress after he got finished making a feast of her.

Damn, he'd like to ask her to quit her night job so they could spend every evening alone together . . .

Hadn't he asked enough of her already? he asked himself critically. Today he had come to realize just how great a sacrifice she had made when he had offered no guarantee. And why? Because he'd become cautious. He could make no promises, no commitments. If he did, he could never be certain of her feelings for him.

Wyatt had been burned once—and badly. He wasn't going through that torment again. Especially now. He had to be absolutely certain this attraction could survive without his money and connections and without Heartstrings—with nothing except who he and Elizabeth really were and what they felt for each other. If only there were time enough for them both to know for sure . . .

When Elizabeth withdrew her fingertip from his aroused flesh and limned his lips with the moist response she had drawn from him, Wyatt was jolted. When she tasted him in the same erotic way he had tasted her essence that night an eternity ago, Wyatt cursed clocks and work schedules and noble intentions. He wanted her so badly that he ached all over!

He certainly wasn't too old for this sort of thing, he realized. His pulse rate was shooting through the roof, and his capillaries were threatening to spring leaks. This vital lady rancher had him dangerously close to blowing a gasket. He'd feel ten times better if they could finish what they started, but since they couldn't, he was doomed to suffer the devastating symptoms of deprivation.

Elizabeth glanced at the watch strapped around her wrist, wondering if withdrawal from a drug could be worse than what she now experienced. She doubted it.

"I'll be late for work if we don't leave now," she got out.

"And I'll be dead by the time you get back," Wyatt said with a groan. "I think I'm having a stroke."

"You *have been* stroked," she teasingly corrected.

Wyatt tipped her head back to meet her playful smile, and his pulse made another mad dash to catch up with his ragged breath. Hour by hour, day by day, Elizabeth was shrugging off all restraint, coming to life before his eyes. She was warm and generous and spirited, and he delighted in her impish sense of humor, her sensuality, her inexhaustible energy.

The bouquet of flowers he'd given her hardly seemed enough to express his admiration and respect. When he stared into those twinkling black diamond eyes his blood ran hot, and there were no words to communicate the sensations she aroused in him. Every day with her was a tormenting test of self-restraint.

Wyatt inhaled a steadying breath and told himself to get his mind on something else—and damned quick.

"When you get back from work, supper will be on me tonight," he promised in a hoarse voice that testified to his simmering desire.

One dark brow elevated. "Sounds good. Is that all you'll be wearing?"

The picture that leaped to mind put Wyatt on another scalding burn. He really did adore her wit.

"Come on, Damn It!" she bugled abruptly. "As John Wayne would say, 'We're burning daylight.' "

Wyatt followed Elizabeth to the blue truck she called Old Red, watching the hypnotic sway of denim-clad hips. Forget burning daylight, he thought in tormented anguish. All he wanted was to take Elizabeth in his arms and burn down the night . . .

Chapter Ten

Wyatt paced the floor and glanced at his watch for the umpteenth time since the antique clock on the mantel chimed 11:30. Elizabeth should have been home by now. Wyatt hated this waiting game. It reminded him of too many nights from the unpleasant past.

"Well, damn it!" he scowled.

The speckled dog that lay outside the screen door whined and barked.

"Not *you*, mutt, *her!*" Wyatt barked back.

He would wait ten more minutes and that was it . . .

Thunder rumbled in the distance, and he swore under his breath. According to the six o'clock weather report, a line of thunderstorms had built along the cold front sweeping across Kansas. He had kept a watchful eye on the mountain of vaporous clouds that had been piling up like overstocked cauliflower in the produce department, hoping his fresh paint job would have time to dry, wishing Elizabeth would get the hell home—now!

The wind switched to the north as Wyatt stepped onto the portico. Lightning flickered and another grumble of thunder drowned his curse. Elizabeth was going to have to drive that jalopy of a truck home in a downpour. He doubted Old Red had windshield wipers, at least not the kind that functioned properly.

Wyatt had insisted she take his car to work, but she had adamantly declared that she wouldn't be caught dead in a Caddy, that her pickup truck was *her* limousine. And off she'd gone in her bow tie and short black skirt. At least she was wearing underwear . . .

Thunder boomed and raindrops pattered on the tile roof. A cold wind whistled through the breezeways that connected the bedrooms to the main section of the house. Wyatt glanced at his watch—again.

God, how he despised this waiting and not knowing. If he remembered anything about his marriage, he remembered that.

Five more minutes, Wyatt decided. If Elizabeth's headlights weren't beaming on the road in that space of time, he was going looking for her. He should've been more insistent when Old Red's starter groaned and the engine sputtered like a drowning victim. He should've driven her to town and gone back to pick her up. But he'd planned to have a candlelight dinner waiting for her. He'd made the only dish he could prepare well—spaghetti.

When the sky opened and lightning illuminated the roiling clouds, Wyatt fished into his pocket to retrieve his keys. Time was up. He was out of here!

Elizabeth pleaded, prayed and then resorted to swearing when Old Red's engine choked and lost power. The damned thing had been cutting out since she reached the gravel road. Fuel pump, she diagnosed as she steered the pickup toward the ditch. Time to call her faithful mechanic.

Raindrops dribbled down the windshield, and Elizabeth glanced heavenward. "Anything else that can go wrong?" she asked as she opened the door and stepped out. "Never mind, just surprise me."

Lightning streaked across the sky, like fireworks on the Fourth of July. Elizabeth glanced northwest at the threatening clouds. She hadn't heard the weather report, but she knew the last place she wanted to be when a tornado struck was in a truck sitting on the incline of a ditch.

Her gaze darted northward. She was only three-quarters of a mile from the Heart-Stays cabin. Better to wait out the storm there, she decided. She had always felt safe and secure within the confines of that cottage.

She hiked off down the road and turned onto the dirt path that led to the cabin. She hadn't gotten far when torrential rain and howling winds descended, soaking her to the bone.

Bad idea, Elizabeth thought as she jogged toward the cabin. Maybe Old Red would have been a safe port in the storm after all.

The minute Elizabeth burst through the cottage door, she groped along the wall to locate the antique pie cupboard where she kept matches and a kerosene lantern. The shadows retreated to the far corners of the room when the lantern blazed to life. Although rain drummed, like impatient fingers, on the window panes, that old familiar serenity settled over Elizabeth.

Where the Heart-Stays, she mused as she unclipped her bow tie. This was home to the gone-but-not-forgotten clan of people who had been forcefully removed from their hunting grounds that had spanned what now was Kansas, Missouri, Arkansas and part of Oklahoma. Now that Elizabeth thought about it, she realized that she was about to be uprooted, just like her Osage ancestors. They had been relocated three times, so who was she to complain about having to relocate only once?

Perhaps, if she couldn't keep the refurbished bunkhouse that had been her home, she could arrange to keep this plot of land and the access path that led to the cottage. At least then she could hold onto the very roots of her heritage.

The thought was comforting to Elizabeth. She would insist

on keeping Heart-Stays. She wouldn't have to lose everything that was near and dear to her.

She propelled herself across the room to toss kindling and logs in the limestone hearth. Within a few minutes a blaze crackled and firelight danced around the room. Elizabeth draped her blouse over the wooden rocking chair that had belonged to her grandmother. Her skirt joined the blouse to dry.

Perfectly content to wait out the storm in the cabin, Elizabeth ambled into the small bedroom to retrieve the sleeping bag stored in the closet. The bed with its feather ticking had long ago been discarded, having seen better years. But Bob's sleeping bag, once used for hunting trips, was still in passable condition. He had camped out here when he and his friends had hunted quail, pheasant or deer.

Elizabeth wondered if the bedroll had seen other uses on occasion. She wouldn't have been surprised. This out-of-the-way cabin would have been perfect for a rendezvous.

She shook out the sleeping bag and checked for varmints hiding within, reflecting on her marriage to a man who had been an expert at taking what he wanted from others without giving of himself. Bob had never bothered to make time for her. He had been too busy feeding his oversize ego and trying to prove to the world that he had made a success of himself, though it was at Elizabeth's expense.

Give the man a break, Elizabeth told herself. She certainly hadn't been without fault in those early years. She had never been sure of herself around men as a teenager, and Bob hadn't encouraged or invited the kind of loveplay she had enjoyed with Wyatt that afternoon. Wyatt had been receptive and encouraging when she'd become playfully daring. It had felt good to let go, to explore and expand the boundaries of her own sexuality and her relationship with a man—Wyatt McKenney in particular.

Elizabeth shivered, not from the chill but because of remembered sensations, smoldering glances that Wyatt cast in her direction. His attentiveness kept amazing her.

Would he be concerned that she was late? she wondered. Bob had never been home long enough to fret about her and the kids. Elizabeth remembered countless times when difficulty arose and she was left to handle it—with two young children trailing behind her. That must have been where she learned her independence, she decided. She had become accustomed to fending for herself long before she lost Bob.

While the storm raged outside, she nestled beside the cozy fire, wishing for the company of the man who occupied her thoughts, the one who had brought her to life like a match set off the flames leaping across the logs. Because of her undependable pickup she would not be sharing a late-night dinner with Wyatt McKenney. But at least she had a roof over her head and the comfort of a sleeping bag. It wasn't as if this was the first time Old Red had left her by the side of the road. Indeed, that was the one thing Elizabeth *could* depend on—being stranded somewhere or other.

Wyatt let loose several foul oaths when he happened onto Old Red, sitting with two wheels on the edge of the gravel and two wheels in the ditch. In two shakes, he was out of the car, stalking forward, frustrated enough to read Elizabeth the riot act when he got within shouting distance.

Another curse flew off his lips when he yanked open the door to find her gone. Wyatt wheeled around, only to be slapped in the face by wind-driven raindrops. Desperation closed in on him. Had she tried to walk home and been struck down by lightning? Had she been lying in the ditch, unnoticed, as he whizzed by? Or could she have been picked up by a passing motorist?

A passing motorist on this lonely stretch of gravel road at midnight? Wyatt doubted that. The only traffic in this secluded part of Osage Hills was local ranchers, most of whom were bedded down for the night. The only one out running around in a rattletrap truck that had angels floating around it was

Elizabeth, determined to hold her part-time job to pay off at least one of her loans.

She is perfectly fine, Wyatt told himself. Or at least she would be until he got hold of her. Then he would strangle her for objecting to driving his Caddy and for worrying him sick.

He jogged back to his car, wondering why he hurried since he was already soaking wet. Hell, he knew that wasn't the reason. He plunked himself onto the leather seat. He was apprehensive. He hadn't been in a position to worry about anyone for a long time. When last he had been, it had been a bad experience, and he hoped this didn't turn out to be like that.

A dim glow of distant light caught Wyatt's attention after a brief flare of lightning plunged the night into darkness. He wasn't familiar enough with the area to know exactly where he was, but there seemed to be a sign of human life in the distance. Either that or a UFO had touched down nearby.

Reversing direction, Wyatt cruised down the road, studying the fence row. When he spotted the cattle guard that opened into pasture, he followed the muddy path down the hill toward the beacon of light. He was upon the secluded cabin before he recognized it for what it was—the cottage Elizabeth had shown to him that afternoon. They had followed the route through an adjoining pasture to reach the old homestead. But Elizabeth must have walked to the cabin from the road after her truck broke down.

Wyatt switched off the headlights and sagged in relief. Then he asked himself how he was going to react when he confronted her. He could pretend he hadn't been pulling out his hair for the past hour, that he wasn't concerned about her. Yes, he could, but that wouldn't be honest. He was annoyed as hell because she'd refused to take his car. He'd had a bad feeling about Old Red when it had sputtered that afternoon.

There were times when Elizabeth was too stubborn and independent for her own good. This was one of them, and Wyatt intended to tell her so, if only to relieve the anxiety he hadn't had to deal with in years. He didn't like being reminded of the old days, those fretful nights when he'd walked the floor.

With his mouth set in a grim line, he stalked onto the porch and barged through the door. The scene before him launched all resentful thoughts into orbit. There, lounging contentedly before the hearth, was Elizabeth, wearing a demi-bra, bikini panties and a look of shocked disbelief. A jolt equal to that of lightning sizzled through Wyatt. He feasted on the alluring sight before him as Elizabeth self-consciously wrapped herself in the bedroll.

Lord! That view of cleavage and firm bare legs nearly put Wyatt into cardiac arrest. *Playboy* centerfolds had nothing on Elizabeth Smith Sutton. Not to Wyatt. He would choose this sexy lady rancher over bouncing Bunnies anytime. He had never been a man who clung to his lost youth by chasing younger women. He wanted a companion who understood him, who shared his interests and matched him stride for stride.

Wyatt savored the tantalizing sight of Elizabeth—the woman he wanted and very badly.

Elizabeth tucked the sleeping bag around her and stared goggle-eyed at the drenched man who loomed by the door. His clothes clung to him like a second skin, outlining his powerful shoulders, broad chest, trim waist and muscled thighs. His hair was plastered against his head. Raindrops sparkled like diamonds on those incredibly long lashes which rimmed intense green eyes—the ones bearing down on her like laser beams.

"What are you doing here?" she asked in a bewildered tone.

Wyatt stopped fantasizing long enough to realize she was actually surprised to see him. "What am I doing here?" he repeated stupidly.

"That was the question," she acknowledged with a wry smile.

His frustration spewed over like a hissing tea kettle. "What the hell do you think I'm doing here? I came looking for you, of course," he grumbled.

Elizabeth stared up at him as if she were unable to conceive such a notion. "Why?"

"Why?" Wyatt parroted.

Damn it, didn't she think he cared that she was late? Didn't she realize he'd imagined all sorts of disasters striking her? Or wasn't she accustomed to having someone awaiting her return, at least anyone who gave a damn if she met with ill luck.

Elizabeth chuckled and sat up, modestly pulling the sleeping bag around her. "You seem to be having trouble with simple questions. Does your brain shut down after midnight or what?"

Wyatt appraised her in the golden light, realizing that she hadn't expected his concern or consideration. Had her husband been so oblivious to her that he'd completely taken her for granted? How could any man take a woman like Elizabeth for granted?

Bob Sutton was an utter fool, Wyatt concluded.

"I was worried about you," Wyatt replied as he ambled over to sink down into the rocking chair that had become Elizabeth's clothesline.

"You were?"

"Yes, I *were,*" he assured her with a grin. "And thanks loads for being concerned that *I* might worry. Damn, you let a woman get her hands on you and then you're discarded and ignored like a worn-out boot."

The suggestive reminder of their afternoon interlude caused heat to rise in Elizabeth's face, all the way to the roots of her damp hair. "I didn't mean to worry you."

"Well, you did," Wyatt scolded. "And my spaghetti sauce turned as thick as tar. If you didn't bother to consider how well I might hold up, waiting for you to return, you should at least have considered my ruined sauce."

It had been ages since anyone had fretted over her. Elizabeth had forgotten what it was like. It felt . . . good.

When Wyatt stood up to peel off his shirt, Elizabeth's gaze focused on an expanse of muscle covered with a thick matting of hair. "What are you doing?"

"Drying out," he said as he hung the shirt beside her blouse. "Got a problem with that?"

When he unfastened his jeans, the rasp of the zipper matched Elizabeth's sudden intake of breath. "I've only got one sleeping bag," she wheezed, all eyes and pounding pulse.

He paused, thumbs tucked in the band of his jeans, his gaze locked with wide onyx eyes. "So I see. Got a problem with my sharing it with you?"

Elizabeth looked up at him, knowing what he was asking, pleased that he *had* asked. He was giving her the chance to call a halt if she wasn't ready to know him in the most intimate sense. The fact that he allowed her the choice, that her feelings mattered to him, caused a lump to gather in her throat.

She supposed she had subconsciously been testing him, waiting for him to make a critical mistake, which would verify Julia's and Lana's concern that he was only interested in a careless fling before he returned to his own world. But Elizabeth hadn't asked for guarantees. She'd learned not to expect too much from a man, wasn't sure she even wanted promises that might be broken. Life, thus far, had offered no guarantees, and she'd stopped thinking in terms of past and future. She'd adopted the philosophy of relishing every moment.

Her mind had been on Wyatt while she was at work, despite Irene's constant yammering. She had debated making that first step toward Wyatt when she returned home that night, wondering if it was too soon, wondering if he would interpret the gesture as her customary policy with men. She didn't want him to think she made a habit of jumping into bed with just anybody.

Did he wonder if she had been intimate with Griff or other men in the community, since she'd been widowed at a young age? Did he really care if there had been other men? And where, she couldn't help but wonder, did *she* fit into *his* line of female companions?

When Elizabeth tarried so long in thought, Wyatt heaved a sigh and drew his jeans back in place. He shouldn't have pushed the issue, he chastised himself. He was still moving too fast for her. She obviously wasn't ready yet, even if he was eager to become her lover. As badly as he wanted her, he refused to rush her into something she might regret.

"Don't put them back on," Elizabeth requested in a throaty voice.

Wyatt glanced down at her, his expression somber. "Are you sure, Bet? I don't want you to have the slightest misgiving about what's going to happen. I have something more in mind than just drying clothes. You realize that, don't you?"

She chortled. "I may have been isolated in my little corner of the world for a decade, but I'm smart enough to figure that out all by myself." She paused to fling him a provocative glance. "But how can *you* be certain I didn't expect you to come looking for me so I could seduce you?"

"If I thought that, I would have been here a helluva lot sooner," he assured her as he kicked off his boots and slid his jeans down his hips.

His breath clogged in his throat when her dark eyes drifted down his torso in a wandering caress. Damn, he could almost feel her hands swirling over his cold skin, warming him from inside out. Her appreciative gaze made him feel desirable, wanted.

Dressed in briefs that concealed little about his aroused condition, Wyatt walked over to douse the lantern. When he pivoted around, Elizabeth was grinning at him, her eyes twinkling in the firelight.

"Now what's wrong? Do I have a sign stamped on the back of my briefs that says Kick Me?"

"No. You said you were wearing my underwear."

He smiled scampishly. "I lied, so shoot me."

Elizabeth watched him saunter toward her in slow, deliberate strides. She studied his well-honed physique in the glowing light, while sizzling sensations filtered through her, eager to touch him as freely and thoroughly as her gaze had devoured him.

When he knelt in front of her, pushing away the sleeping bag she held to her chest, inhibition abandoned her. There was no doubt that he approved of what he saw. It was in his eyes, in the expression that settled on his features when his gaze dropped from her parted lips to the exposed swell of her breasts, to the curve of her hips.

"You're beautiful, Bet," he whispered as his knuckles brushed her cheek and then glided down to the pulsating column of her throat.

"I'm forty-five years old—"

He interrupted her. "Age has nothing to do with anything." His hand dipped down to trace the lacy edge of her bra, evoking a quick intake of breath that assured him his light touch was enough to stir her. "You are exquisite, everything I could ever want in a woman."

Any apprehension that he might not find her appealing because she had lost her girlish figure dissolved when he looked at her as if she were a priceless work of art to be cherished and admired.

"Wyatt, I—" She swallowed nervously. "Despite what you might think, it's been a long time since I—"

His thumb grazed her lips as he drew her to her knees and bent his head, his mouth hovering above hers. "And it's going to be a *long time* before I'm through savoring you."

Elizabeth wasn't accustomed to unhurried lovemaking that allowed her to fully enjoy each shimmering sensation. She wanted to touch him as gently as he touched her, to assure him that she appreciated a slow, gentle hand rather than a heated rush that spoke of only physical need.

When his hands swept down her hips, she instinctively arched toward him. He kissed her with penetrating thoroughness before withdrawing just enough to playfully nip at her lips. Then his hand ascended across her abdomen to swirl over the rising swell of a breast, and Elizabeth gasped for breath, startled by the vivid sensations that assaulted her.

He smiled against her lips as he teased her nipple to a taut bead. He could feel her trembling beneath his caress, wanting it as much as he cherished touching her, pleasuring her.

His left hand trailed over the elastic leg band of her bikinis and wandered off to stroke the sensitive flesh of her inner thigh. Her fervent reaction caused hungry need to clench inside him. But Wyatt vowed to take his time with her. If the world came to an end tomorrow, this was going to be one special night, nothing like the thunderstorm raging outside the cabin. This was going to be like a slow, gentle rain that soaked into their senses. Like each raindrop that fell, every sensation and caress would be an entity unto itself, provoking its unique brand of pleasure.

His lips skied down the slope of her shoulder, finding that sensitive point at the base of her neck that made her quiver helplessly in his arms. As his kisses trailed deliberately over her breast, his tongue flicked at the rigid crest he gently caressed with his fingertips. He felt her arms gliding around him, holding his head against her soft flesh as he suckled and carefully tugged at her with his teeth. He was rewarded with a raspy moan and the flexing of her fingers in his hair.

When Wyatt offered the same dedicated attention to the other taut nipple, Elizabeth's ardent response rippled through her, and he heard her whisper his name. He retraced the band of her bikinis before his fingertip slid beneath the silky fabric to stroke the secret petals of her femininity. He felt the dewy softness on his fingertip and savored the scent of the woman he longed to arouse until she came completely undone in his arms.

He traced the smooth flesh of her inner thigh as he took one dusky crest in his mouth and cherished the taste of her. His tongue teased her nipple while his fingertip teased the delicate nub of passion. Sizzling pleasure coursed through him when he probed deeper, feeling her body contracting around him, answering each tender stroke with a secret caress.

And when he eased her onto her back, still holding the trembling essence of her in his hand, her lashes fluttered down to shield her from the intensity of the eyes and hands upon her.

"No, Bet," he whispered before his lips returned to hers. "Don't ever be ashamed of what you're feeling. I want to watch you burn in my arms. I want to know that every touch is pleasurable. I want to discover all the ways you like to be loved."

Elizabeth wasn't accustomed to such openness in lovemaking. It took a great deal of courage for her to meet his gaze while his hand cupped her, teased her to the limits of sanity.

He smiled at her tentative expression and kissed her again, his tongue imitating the gliding stroke of his fingertip. He felt the moist heat of need burning around him, felt her tremble, heard her gasp as pleasure uncoiled, radiating from her body and burning through him.

"Oh . . . God . . ." Elizabeth gasped when wild, undefinable pleasure engulfed her. Was this supposed to be happening? She remembered nothing so tormentingly devastating as this. She was about to plummet into a mindless abyss and would never be able to find her way back. "No—!"

His mouth came down on hers, silencing her cry of disbelief, intimately caressing her until the sensations that had assailed her converged again, and again, destroying what little composure she had left.

Just when she was certain nothing could ease the haunting ache that turned her wrong side out, she felt the hard, satin length of him filling her with pulsating heat, flinging her into oblivion.

It's too soon! Elizabeth thought as the blind rush of hungry passion consumed her. She had wanted to arouse Wyatt to the same intense degree, but the muscular columns of his legs had glided between her thighs and the penetrating thrust of his passion had demanded that she surrender to the phenomenal rapture that exploded inside her—again.

Still gasping for breath, she watched him uncoil above her, lifting her to him, teasing her with his thumb as he moved gently within her and then slowly withdrew. And when he felt her body contracting around him, and she clutched at him in helpless abandon, he clutched her to him. With a groan of unrestrained release he gave in to the ecstasy that rippled through every fiber of his being.

Elizabeth held him to her as the aftershocks of passion

surged from her body to his and back again. Her palms drifted over his shoulders, down the corded tendons of his back, to the curve of his hips. She kissed the ridge of his cheekbone, his chin, his collarbone and felt contentment fill her to over-flowing.

She smiled to herself as she absently stroked Wyatt's shoulders. This man might very well be a terrific auctioneer, but he was also an incredibly sensitive and attentive lover. He had given of himself to arouse and satisfy her—so much so that Elizabeth felt guilty that she hadn't returned the exquisite sensations, caress for caress. He deserved far more than she'd given.

"I'm sorry . . ." Elizabeth heard her thoughts translated into words and felt Wyatt stir above her.

He braced on his elbow and stared inquisitively at her. "That bad, Bet?"

She chortled at his expression. "No, that *good*. *Too* good. I wanted you like hell blazing."

He grinned as he eased down to cradle her in his arms. "Beggin' your pardon, ma'am," he drawled playfully. "But I believe you just *had* me like hell blazing. Or did I dream it all—again?"

"I meant I wanted to touch you, to give you back the pleasure you gave me, to share . . ."

He smiled as he trailed his forefinger over her kiss-swollen lips. "I have no complaints about lovemaking as satisfying as this, Bet. You gave me more pleasure than you can imagine."

The reply soothed her guilty conscience, but it wouldn't appease her for very long, Elizabeth was sure of that. She wanted to explore every virile inch of him to learn how to make him burn as she had burned beneath his slow, erotic touch. He would know all the sublime sensations she had experienced— one by one—until maddening need sent him plunging into the dimensions of passion she had discovered when in his arms.

"It's stopped raining," Elizabeth noted several minutes later.

"Mmmm . . ." he responded drowsily.

"You won't be able to complete your masterpiece, Picasso, if you spend the night sleeping on this hard floor."

He opened one eye as a smile spread across his sensuous lips. "Hang the barn. The only masterpiece I care to complete is you."

Elizabeth returned his grin. "My bed is more comfortable."

"But my bed is empty, and has been for five tormenting days."

Her eyes met those glistening pools of emerald flecked with slivers of gold. "That was an invitation, in case you didn't notice."

"I was just checking. I'm not living on presumptions, Bet. I told you that we were going to move at your pace, however you want it. If tonight wasn't—"

She touched his lips to silence him. "It was incredible," she assured him. "And if I didn't have to drag myself out of bed at six-thirty in the morning, I'd demand equal time with you."

His thick brow quirked teasingly. "You're into time-sharing, are you?"

"I'm into equality, mister. What I get, I give, and you better believe it."

Wyatt chuckled. "John Wayne, you're not."

"That's okay." Elizabeth leaned close, her lips a hairbreadth away from his mouth, her body brushing provocatively against his masculine contours. "I only want to be *me* . . . with *you.*"

On that quiet assurance, she reached for the discarded undergarments Wyatt had seductively stripped off her. Or had her clothes simply melted beneath his masterful touch? Elizabeth honestly couldn't remember. All she could recall was warm lips and gentle hands whispering over her, arousing sensations that defied description.

They dressed in silence, each allowing the other the privacy of thought, the time to contemplate the threshold they had crossed.

Elizabeth glanced back at the cozy cabin, watching the dwindling coals glow in the hearth. They would burn themselves out eventually, she mused. But she wondered if the fire Wyatt McKenney had ignited in her ever would . . . even after he was long gone.

Chapter Eleven

Although Elizabeth had spent a physically and emotionally satisfying night, nestled in Wyatt's arms, the weekend got off on the wrong foot. Right off the bat, Vic Henderson made a wisecrack about Wyatt making tracks before Lana and Julia showed up. The truth of the matter was, Elizabeth had requested that Wyatt rent a motel room to avoid being verbally harassed by Julia and analyzed to death by Lana. Even though Wyatt was reluctant to leave, she knew he enjoyed the time he spent with Jerry and Nancy Patterson. It had to be better than doing combat duty, dodging oncoming verbal missiles all weekend.

Having the dissenting troops march home to invade and sabotage had disturbed Elizabeth's sense of well-being. She had delighted in the companionship of a man who treated her with the consideration and respect she hadn't received in her marriage, yet her well-meaning daughters had tried to dictate her conduct. Elizabeth didn't appreciate it one damned bit.

When Lana and Julia finally drove away Sunday afternoon, she was more than ready to see them leave, and to have a couple of hours of peace before she went to work.

* * *

The phone call Elizabeth received Monday while she was preparing lunch disturbed her more than she was willing to admit. The woman who called for Wyatt had an extremely sultry voice; Elizabeth wished she hadn't noticed. She took the message and relayed it to him. He nodded mutely and strode off to place the return call in the privacy of Elizabeth's bedroom.

Wyatt, Elizabeth knew, was not a man who volunteered to discuss his past. He seemed determined to keep his professional life separate from this private world at Heartstrings—a world that fit into the designated time slot of two weeks. The first week had flown by at supersonic speed, in Elizabeth's estimation. She was afraid the second was going to blast past at the same swift rate.

Since all Wyatt had ever said was that he had been married and now he wasn't—case closed—Elizabeth didn't know if the woman who called was his daughter, a close acquaintance, intimate friend or secretary. "Tell Wyatt to call Deidre" didn't give Elizabeth much to go on.

Should she pry or keep her trap shut?

Elizabeth cast a discreet glance in Wyatt's direction when he ambled through the back door to take a Coke break, in between mowing the ditches. He had been distracted since he had received the phone call that morning, and curiosity was eating Elizabeth alive.

Something was wrong, she sensed it; yet she was hesitant to interfere in Wyatt's "other" life as her daughters were trying to interfere in hers.

"I'll be leaving for work in a few minutes," she announced as she handed him a Coke.

"Take the car."

"Thanks, but—"

"Take . . . the . . . car," he said slowly and emphatically.

"Like I told you before, *over my dead body.*"

"I'm trying to prevent you from ending up with a *dead body*," he insisted more harshly than he'd intended.

Wyatt heaved a frustrated sigh. The phone call hadn't done a damned thing for his disposition. Only Deidre had the nerve to badger his secretary into giving her the phone number at Heartstrings. Talking to her always stirred up memories he preferred to keep tucked in the farthest corner of his mind.

Elizabeth's refusal to be reasonable wasn't helping matters, either, Wyatt mused irritably. He knew she was independent and unaccustomed to being told what to do, but he would feel ten times better if she would drive his car to work.

"I would rest easier if you were in a dependable vehicle," he said as diplomatically as he could.

"You don't have to feel responsible for me," she assured him. "I've been looking out for myself for years."

Wyatt hooked his arm around her waist, drawing her familiarly against him. His hand curled beneath her chin to lift her face to his. "What I *shouldn't* have to feel and what I *actually* feel are two entirely different matters. Unless you want me to wear holes in your carpet, wondering if you'll make it to town and back without trouble, you'll take the car."

Elizabeth blinked. "You're serious," she realized it and said so. "You'd actually pace the floor, worrying about me? The pick-up truck broke down, but the one-ton truck is in better working condition. It won't fail me."

"That's what you said about Old Red before it dumped you beside the road during a thunderstorm," he argued. "Take the car."

Up went the chin. "No. It's yours, not mine."

"Elizabeth . . ." he said warningly. "You're being unnecessarily stubborn."

"And you're squeezing the stuffing out of me. You wanna ease up there, Atlas?"

"Sorry." Wyatt hadn't realized he was holding onto her so tightly. The gesture was an expression of the inescapable feeling that he was going to lose her if he let go. The phone call had put him on edge, and the tension he'd thought he had shed had returned in full force.

Inhaling deeply, Wyatt blurted out, "I have to go back to the City next weekend, and I want you to come with me."

Discovering that she was going to be deprived of Wyatt's company for another weekend was disappointing. "You know I can't. I have daily chores to tend."

"I'll ask Jerry Patterson to fill in for you."

"You can't do that. This ranch isn't Jerry's responsibility."

"He's a friend. He won't mind helping you out."

"I appreciate the offer, but I can't go."

Elizabeth was relieved to know Wyatt wasn't ashamed to invite her into his world, despite Lana's and Julia's remarks to the contrary. But her wardrobe was limited, and she would not make a good showing if she strolled into Wyatt's world in faded jeans and the outdated dresses she wore to church.

Some women had a weakness for outfits with shoes to match. Elizabeth's weakness was supporting a ranch that spent more time clad in *red* than in *black*—with *no* shoes to match.

"You're making excuses, Bet. Why won't you go?" he insisted on knowing.

She tiptoed around the question by asking, "What do you have to do in the City?"

"I have to handle the auction for the Quarter Horse show at Heritage Hall. I declined the first time they offered the job to me. But the auctioneer who took the job—a close friend of mine—landed in the hospital for an emergency appendectomy," Wyatt explained. "I didn't want to leave you this past weekend and I sure as hell don't want to lose our last weekend together. The only way for us to be together is for you to come with me. I'm not giving up our last two days."

He did not mention that he didn't want Elizabeth's daughters sabotaging her thinking about him during his absence. He knew Lana and Julia didn't approve of him and that they spent all their time assuring Elizabeth she was better off without him.

Wyatt had become fiercely protective of the special bond

developing between him and Elizabeth. He wanted to spend every spare minute with her, and he had the unshakable feeling that nothing would be the same after he returned from the two-week circuit of auctions on his calendar. Call it intuition, call it instinct . . . call it a frustrating fear of losing something that he hadn't enjoyed in years.

Elizabeth toyed with the buttons of his shirt, her eyes monitoring her restless hands. "I really don't belong in your world, Wyatt. I think we both know that."

"Bullshit."

Her gaze darted upward, and she grinned impishly. "That's what I have in *my* world."

He adored that about her—the way she could smile and tease him back into good humor, the way she could relieve his tension in nothing flat. "Come with me," he requested before dropping a kiss to her lush mouth. "I'll let you have your way with me anytime you please."

"Even at the auction?" she asked in mock shock.

"With the exception of that," he amended with a chuckle. "I draw the line at performing before an audience. Will you come with me?"

"I'm going to be late for work," she said, withdrawing from his arms.

She was starkly aware of the emptiness that enveloped her when Wyatt wasn't within reach. The past weekend without him had been lonely, even with a house full of family to distract her. Wyatt was beginning to matter too much, to consume all her thoughts.

Enjoy him, but don't get too attached to him, Elizabeth cautioned herself. Nothing lasts forever, you know that.

"Come with me, Bet," he softly implored.

"I'll think about it."

"While you're driving my car to work?" he asked hopefully.

"No, while I'm tooling off in the one-ton truck," she corrected.

"Then I'll drive you to town."

Elizabeth declined. "No, Irene would hound me to death if I drove up in a Caddy or climbed out of a chauffeured car."

He eyed her ponderously. "You don't want anyone to know about us, is that it?"

"I'm trying to avoid outside interference. I've faced enough already with Lana, Julia and Griff. And when you tell Irene anything, you're broadcasting the news to the whole town," Elizabeth assured him. "I like Irene immensely, but she loves to gossip."

Wyatt sighed in defeat. When Elizabeth had changed and prepared to leave, he followed her outside, wishing he had brought his mobile phone so he could insist that she take it with her. But he had been determined to avoid as many calls as possible.

"Be careful," he requested.

"*That* from a man who has been practicing trapeze routines while painting barns and sheds?"

He grinned as he propped his hands on the door. "I was only trying to impress you with my daring feats."

"You don't have to dazzle me with your bravado, Picasso. I'd rather you and your paint-brush stayed in one piece."

"Good. I'll save a few *strokes* for tonight," he said with a wink and a smile.

Elizabeth's bubble of laughter sent Wyatt's lingering tension gushing out of him. With a wave and a grin she drove off, and he stared pensively after her. He hoped that damned truck made it round trip without a hitch. With Old Red in the shop for repairs, Elizabeth was bound and determined to drive the one-ton truck. If it collapsed in a pile of nuts and bolts, she would probably fuel up the tractor!

By the time Elizabeth arrived at work she had made her decision about going to the City with Wyatt. Gusto-grabbing demanded that she accept the offer, even if she were modestly attired in the latest fashion of five years before. Wyatt wanted to be with her. She would have the opportunity to see him in his natural environment. If Julia and Lana did come home for the weekend, as they had promised to do, they could do the daily chores. Of course, they would have a conniption fit when they discovered their mother had driven off with Wyatt.

Elizabeth grimaced. Lord, she could almost hear Julia howling in protest and Lana calmly listing all the symptoms of middle-age craziness. Was it worth it?

That familiar voice deep inside her answered, *Yes.*

Having made her decision, Elizabeth requested to switch work schedules. Even if she'd have to work seven days straight, she vowed to do it in order to spend her first weekend away from Heartstrings in years. It would be a good test of her ability to function without the ranch, she reminded herself.

After several hours of running her legs off, Elizabeth finally collapsed in the corner booth to ingest enough caffeine to get her to closing time. Tall Grass Prairie Cafe had been a hubbub of activity until the past fifteen minutes. Elizabeth had just begun to rejuvenate her energy when Griffin Hollis stalked inside, a frown stamped on his leathery face. She couldn't decide whether he looked mad enough to shoot somebody or he already had.

Griff plunked down in the booth and glared at Elizabeth from beneath his Stetson. "I can't believe you put me on hold so you could shack up with that citified auctioneer," he said without preamble.

Elizabeth nearly strangled on her coffee.

"I tried to catch you before you left for work, and I found that McKenney character vacuuming your living room. Good Lord, Liz, what kind of twink vacuums carpets?"

Elizabeth didn't appreciate the implication that sweeping carpets was woman's work. Nor did she appreciate Griff calling Wyatt a twink. That was utterly preposterous.

"Wyatt offered to refurbish the ranch before the auction, and I offered him room and board for the free labor," she explained, nobly refraining from dumping her coffee on his head.

It was touch and go for a few seconds before she decided

not to christen Griff with scalding liquid, even if he did deserve it.

Griff snorted disdainfully. "You can have your ranch, Liz, if you get rid of that live-in twerp."

If he called Wyatt another derogatory name, she was sure enough going to baptize him with coffee.

"We're neighbors and friends, Griff," she managed to say without snarling at him. "I don't tell you what to do with your life and you have no right to interfere in mine."

"We can have it all, Liz. Tell McKenney to pack up and get out. I'll go to the bank and get the loan. You'll be making the worst mistake of your life if you don't accept my offer."

She would be making another mistake if she settled for more of the same life she'd had with Bob. She shook her head and then listened to Griff expel several muttered curses.

"What not me, Liz?" he grumbled. "What's he got that I don't?"

Keeping a straight face, Elizabeth looked him squarely in the eye and said, *"He* vacuums carpets, and *you* don't."

"Oh hell." Griff slumped in his seat. "I didn't mean to make you mad. I was just trying to talk sense into you. I'm afraid the possibility of losing Heartstrings has sent you off the deep end. You aren't yourself these days, flitting around as if you don't have a care in the world. Letting that silver-tongued auctioneer move in with you testifies to that fact."

A lot he knew! She was herself for the first time in years, and glad of it. And furthermore, she enjoyed having excitement, amusement and companionship in her life again.

"I'm not changing my mind, Griff."

"I'm not giving up on you, Liz," he vowed as he got to his feet. "You need a man who can take care of you for the years to come, not some yuppie who'll sell you out, take his commission and walk away without looking back. *I'll* still be around by summer's end. *He* won't."

Elizabeth gnashed her teeth as Griff stamped off. She didn't need to be reminded that eternity only lasted two weeks. But if she wound up with nothing else, she would have one brief blaze of glory, one shining moment to cherish. Being with Wyatt felt good, and he was not a twerp, a twink or a yuppie!

Elizabeth parked the truck beside the Caddy and stepped down. A curious frown puckered her brows when she heard the Caddy crackle and pop like Rice Crispies, same as her truck. When she walked over to lay her hand on the hood, she could feel the heat from the engine that had been running recently.

Her gaze darted to the lights in the house. If she hadn't missed her guess, and she doubted she had, Wyatt had been on the prowl. And if he had come to check on her after putting up a fuss about her driving an undependable vehicle, she was going to let him have it.

For what? For caring enough to be concerned about your welfare and safety? You always wanted Bob to worry about you, but he never did. So which is it?

"I'm really getting sick of you," Elizabeth muttered at her conscience. "You're spoiling all my fun."

She strode up the sidewalk to the breezeway and paused to stare across the moonlit pasture where silhouettes of grazing cattle dotted the countryside. Inhaling a breath of air, she entered the house to see Wyatt perusing the newspaper.

"Did you enjoy your drive into town?" she asked casually.

The newspaper that shielded his face slowly lowered. He said nothing; she smiled mischievously. He waited for her to launch into a feminist, flag-waving tirade; she didn't.

"How did you know?" he asked finally. "I thought I was exceptionally clever."

"Your car is hot and metal pops when it contracts and cools down," she said very technically.

"Let me guess. You majored in science in college. Right?"

"Correct," she affirmed, tossing her purse aside.

"And you aren't angry with me?"

"Correct again. Would you like me to be?"

"I'd rather you wouldn't be. I just didn't want a repeat of Friday night's performance."

One dark brow elevated in amusement. "Once was enough for you?" she teased him.

"That performance is *not* the one I'm referring to," he amended with a rakish grin.

Elizabeth glanced down at the freshly swept carpet and nodded approvingly. "Thanks for cleaning up. I appreciate it."

"Your friend Griff doesn't." Wyatt laced his hands behind his head and lounged on the sofa. "He thinks I'm a sissy."

And a twink, a twerp and a yuppie, Elizabeth silently added. "Griff has Neanderthal tendencies. He wouldn't touch a vacuum cleaner if his life depended on it. He thinks it would destroy his machismo. He hires a lady to clean once a week so he doesn't have to step down from his throne to dabble in menial tasks." Elizabeth chuckled in afterthought. "I should remind Griff how *men*ial is spelled."

Elizabeth strode off to the bedroom to change clothes and glanced up to see Wyatt propped leisurely against the doorjamb. "Your phone rang off the hook tonight. I didn't answer it."

"It may have been Julia and Lana calling to check on me. I usually don't work this night shift, but I traded with one of the other waitresses so she could take a personal business leave." She flashed him a sententious glance. "You aren't the only one checking up on me. My daughters think I've lost my grip on reality."

"Because of me," he presumed.

"Because, according to the psychology instructor at Skiatook High School, I'm trying to *find myself.* Julia's prognosis is that I lost my mind and will never recover. She always was more of an alarmist than Lana."

Wyatt appraised the weary look on Elizabeth's features. As much as he wanted to take her to bed and make love to her, she was exhausted. He would have preferred to be the one who exhausted and satiated her, but it was probably best if he bunked out in his own room, because if he lay down beside her, he wasn't going to be able to resist temptation.

"Good night, Bet," he murmured, pushing away from the door.

She blinked when he strode off to switch off the living-room light. "Where are you going?"

"To my own room. I think you need extra sleep, and you aren't likely to get it if I join you in bed. If you hear a howl during the night, it won't be Damn It. It will be me."

Elizabeth chuckled at the remark and sighed at the realization that Wyatt was aware of her needs. He was a nice man, even if Griff and everyone else around her didn't think so. And after she'd had a few hours' rest, she would slip into Wyatt's room to repeat their wondrous performance at Heart-Stays. All she needed was a catnap, she assured herself as she collapsed in bed.

At 6:15 A.M. Elizabeth bolted awake to realize she had wasted another night of her limited time with Wyatt.

Disappointment settled over her when she found the note he had left on the kitchen table. He had made arrangements to ride with Jerry Patterson on his rounds in the district, consulting other ranchers, taking orders for feed to be delivered for livestock.

When Elizabeth walked outside, she paused to admire the fresh coat of paint. Heartstrings was more impressive than it had been in years. She simply had been too busy saving for interest payments and college expenses to do the ranch justice. True, the girls had offered to apply for educational loans to help out, but at the time, Elizabeth considered *loan* a four-letter word. She wouldn't wish debt on her worst enemy, much less her daughters.

Griff happened by around noon—to check up on her, Elizabeth speculated. Her neighbor perked up when he noticed the Caddy was gone, but his mouth turned down at the corners when Elizabeth informed him that Wyatt would be back. After several snide comments about Elizabeth's taste in men, Griff reminded her of the dates he had selected to move the livestock before burning the dry forage off the pastures.

After listening to him ridicule her house guest, Elizabeth decided she'd had just about enough interference in her personal life. Everybody seemed to know what was best for her and passed out free advice like it was going out of style.

When she returned to the house to shower and change for work, the phone was ringing. Lana had called to give her triweekly lecture on avoiding association with deceitful, untrustworthy men. Elizabeth's good mood had taken a beating. She was ready to pack up and drive to Oklahoma City—now.

The crunch of gravel heralded Wyatt's arrival. Grateful for a pleasurable moment, Elizabeth greeted him with open arms on the portico and hugged him to her as if he had returned from the dead.

Wyatt cuddled her close and chuckled at the zealous reception. "What did I do to deserve that?"

Elizabeth tipped her head back, her obsidian eyes dancing. "You make me happy."

The careful reserve Wyatt had tried to project the past few days, flew away through the breezeway. Elizabeth's simple but eloquent declaration streamed through him. His hand glided down her hips, guiding her into the cradle of his legs, reminding both of them of the intimacy they had shared, the pleasure they had given each other.

When he bent his dark head, his hungry gaze focused on her parted lips. Elizabeth surrendered to the warm tide of emotion that crested in her. Her body arched into his masculine contours, absorbing his strength, his scent, his taste. She wanted nothing more than to lead him to the bedroom, to peel away the garments that prevented her from exploring him, teasing him with provocative kisses and caresses, taking him to her, holding him until the sweet fires that burned in her body and soul had been fed.

"God, Bet," Wyatt said hoarsely. His hands contracted on

her derriere, molding her to him, assuring her of his instantaneous response. "I want you . . ."

He kissed her hard and demandingly, feeling her answering promise in the way she arched toward him, the fervid way she returned his devouring kiss.

The rattle of gravel flying around the speeding vehicle that skidded through the gateway forced Elizabeth and Wyatt apart, still panting for breath. A muffled groan tumbled from Elizabeth's lips when she recognized the compact car. She knew her eldest daughter had witnessed the amorous embrace and winced, knowing how Julia would react.

Julia bounded out of her car and glared in their direction.

Disgusting, illicit, that's what it was, Julia thought as she stalked toward the house. Her mother had become a pleasure-seeking lush. And at her age! Wyatt McKenney, the suave, fast-talking auctioneer, was taking her for the ride of her life. He wasn't here to organize an auction, Julia assured herself. He was here to seduce and conquer another lonely widow! Men! she fumed. Young and old alike, the male of the species was the curse of a woman's life.

"Julia? What are you doing here in the middle of the week?" Elizabeth asked her scowling daughter.

Julia was in the worst of all possible moods. Her temper had been simmering during her forty-five minute drive from Bartlesville. "The question is: What is *he* doing here?" she demanded, looking down her nose at her mother. "Have you no shame?"

Wyatt took quick offense at the crack directed at Elizabeth. "I think your mother deserves more respect from you than—"

"Respect?" Julia cut in waspishly. "And how much respect is she getting from you? Is it professional policy to fool around with every prospective client? My God, couldn't you at least have the decency to go into the house instead of pawing each other on the porch!"

"Julia!" Elizabeth snapped in outrage. "Apologize this instant."

Blue eyes sparked as Julia gave her blond head a defiant

toss. "I wasn't the one groping on the patio. Why should I apologize?"

"That's enough," Wyatt growled at the belligerent young woman.

"My sentiments exactly," Julia flashed back.

Elizabeth thrust herself between Wyatt and her daughter, shocked by Julia's disrespectful outburst. True, Julia had always been outspoken, but never had she disgraced herself so thoroughly as she had now, and in front of a guest. Julia's conduct was inexcusable!

"If you aren't going to apologize then I think you better leave, Julia," Elizabeth demanded.

"And *he* stays?" she retaliated snidely. "God, Mother, where are your priorities? I will always be here for you. He won't . . ."

The roar of another approaching vehicle caused Julia to glance down the hill. "Damn him!" she railed. "Where's the shotgun?"

Elizabeth watched Julia storm into the house, slamming the door so hard the house rattled. Bemused, she pivoted to see a brilliant blue short-bed pickup wheel into the driveway and skid to a stop. A tall, sandy-haired young man of thirty, or thereabouts, strode hurriedly toward the portico. He flicked a glance toward the front door before focusing his attention on Wyatt and Elizabeth.

"Mrs. Sutton?" the young man ventured.

"Elizabeth Sutton." She introduced herself. "And this is Wyatt McKenney."

The young man extended his hand in greeting. "I'm John Casey."

Elizabeth appraised the attractive veterinarian and then glanced at the closed door. Things were beginning to fall into place. From all indications, Julia and her boss had come to blows—or near enough to unleash Julia's flighty temper.

While Lana logically responded to what she *thought,* Julia reacted to what she *felt.* And whatever Julia felt for John W. Casey III was obviously fierce and intense. That was Julia. Love or hate, the emotion was always potent.

Now all Elizabeth had to do was figure out if this was a case of love or hate. If John W. Casey III had closed down his animal clinic to chase Julia all the way to Heartstrings that suggested he *felt* something for his high-strung assistant. If John was a *feeler* rather than a *thinker,* it was little wonder he and Julia got along like a cobra and mongoose.

Elizabeth smiled wryly. "Julia didn't by chance quit, did she?"

John's mouth tightened in a grimace. "As a matter of fact, she did."

"Was that *before* or *after* you fired her?" she questioned perceptively.

John blinked in surprise and then glanced around as if he had just realized where he was. Elizabeth wondered if blind instinct had provoked John to follow wherever Julia led. The poor guy had it bad and didn't know it yet.

John shifted awkwardly from one booted foot to the other. "She quit immediately after I fired her," he mumbled.

"And now you want to rehire her?" Wyatt asked with an amused grin. "You do like to live dangerously, don't you?"

"I guess," John murmured lamely. "I don't even know how it happened. We were having one of our usual arguments over little or nothing, and she made one of her snide remarks. All of a sudden I fired her and she told me I couldn't fire her because she quit." His anxious gaze darted toward the closed door for the tenth time. "Where is Julia?"

Elizabeth curled her hand around the young man's elbow and steered him forward. "She went to get the shotgun. Why don't you come in and have a glass of lemonade while she's loading for bear—or veterinarians, as this case happens to be. Better to have a drink now. Later, you might be filled with so much buckshot you'll spring leaks."

"This isn't funny, " John grumbled.

Wyatt gave him a consoling pat on the shoulder. "It will be after you and Julia cool off enough to realize how ridiculous this spat is."

"This isn't a spat," John insisted as he strode toward the

kitchen. He glanced around, noting the pecan paneling and quaint antiques. "Nice place, Mrs. Sutton," he added.

"Thank you, John. Julia likes it, too. She must. This seems to be the first place she comes when trouble gets the best of her."

"Heart-Stays?" Wyatt questioned.

Elizabeth nodded affirmatively.

"Heart-Stays?" John repeated, bemused.

Elizabeth smiled remorsefully. The roots of Indian heritage obviously ran deeper than Julia and Lana realized. They had insisted that the Sutton family didn't need to hold onto a ranch, and Elizabeth had convinced herself that she could walk away and begin the new phase of her life without Heartstrings. But this would always be home, the place her family came when the outside world crowded in on them.

And if Elizabeth couldn't keep this house, she would definitely keep and refurbish the cabin by Bird Creek. It was the heart of this family, the soul of heritage and tradition.

Perhaps it would be years before Julia and Lana fully realized their sentimental attachment. They were still young and out to show the world they could succeed at their chosen endeavors. But deep down inside—where the Heart-Stays—their heritage from a clan of people who had been called a vanishing race by white expansionists had endured, had survived. Julia and Lana belonged here; they would always belong here, no matter how far they roamed.

This land and the inborn need to preserve a heritage, would eventually whisper to them, compelling them to preserve the customs of a proud people who defied the intrusion of outsiders. The log cabin on Bird Creek was the life force of Heart-Stays, the very pulse of Heartstrings. There would always be that, Elizabeth vowed fiercely. She would keep the cottage, no matter what!

Inhaling deeply, she tucked that thought deep inside her and focused on the problem at hand—preventing John W. Casey III from being turned into a human sieve, compliments of Julia and her loaded shotgun.

Chapter Twelve

While Wyatt was keeping John company in the kitchen, Elizabeth strode off to find Julia who was washing away her tears in the bathroom that adjoined the master bedroom.

Julia met her mother's gaze in the mirror. "Has he left yet?"

"Who? Wyatt or John, the jackass of a boss?"

"The jackass," Julia muttered.

Elizabeth ambled over to retrieve the shotgun from the top shelf of the closet. "You're right, Julia. The man is an absolute jerk, following you all the way home after he fired you. The nerve of him! I think we should shoot him and be done with it. We'll bury the evidence in one of the remote pastures and no one will be the wiser. Then you can take control of the animal clinic and run it your way. I'll pay Vic off, just in case he noticed the flashy blue truck in the driveway."

Julia wheeled around, a horrified expression on her face. "Mother!"

"What?" Elizabeth asked calmly as she cradled the weapon in her arms. "The man is causing you undue stress. He's making you a victim in his transactional games—as your sister would say. If the annoying stimulus—which provoked you to lash out at everyone within shouting distance—is removed from your life, you can function normally."

Elizabeth made a spectacular display of slapping the shotgun against her shoulder in precise military fashion. "As your mother, it's my obligation to resolve this situation. When an investigation is opened, I want you to truthfully be able to say that you had nothing whatever to do with what happened to your boss."

Julia stared at Elizabeth as if she had sprouted devil's horns. "Good God, Mother!"

"I thought you despised the man," Elizabeth reminded her goggle-eyed daughter. "I thought he was ruining your life. I thought you agreed with the theory of slaughtering male chauvinist pigs rather than wasting time rehabilitating them."

Julia swore her mother had flipped her wig. She was standing there, holding a weapon, planning the demise of the source of Julia's exasperation.

"Give me the shotgun, Mother," Julia requested as calmly as Lana would have done if she had been there.

Elizabeth cuddled the weapon protectively against her. "No, you'd get your fingerprints all over it. Can't have that." She pivoted toward the door. "You stay here, Julia. You won't want to watch. This could be very messy."

"Mother, for God's sake! I don't want John dead!"

Very slowly Elizabeth turned around to face her apprehensive daughter. A smile quirked her lips. "Then how, exactly, do you want John?"

The frustration that had sustained Julia during the drive home came pouring out like a flood bursting through a dam. "I don't know what's the matter with me." She inhaled a shuddering breath and slowly exhaled. "Everything that man does rubs me the wrong way. It's the look on his face, that glint in his eyes, his very stance when we're debating clinical procedure or prognosis. I swear, he argues with me for the sport of it. He pushes me, just to see how much I'll take."

"And you reciprocate in like manner," Elizabeth speculated.

Julia raked her fingers through her windblown hair and nodded reluctantly. "Nit-picking, he calls it."

"There is often a fine line between love and hate that can be very exasperating, Julia." Elizabeth patted the barrel of the shotgun and grinned impishly. "Maybe I should shoot both of you and put you out of each other's misery."

Julia managed a feeble smile. "I thought mothers were supposed to support their daughters, no matter what."

"I have for years, financially and emotionally," Elizabeth contended.

"And to repay me for being a bothersome burden you're taking sides with the jackass vet," Julia muttered.

"I've tried to be objective in my affection," Elizabeth said with pretended seriousness. "I'm sad to report that neither you nor your sister are perfect. We all have weaknesses which neutralize our strengths."

"So does John W. Casey III," Julia grumbled, staring at the bedroom door . . . and beyond.

"So vaccinate him," Elizabeth playfully suggested. "You're a vet. Find a cure for what ails the man."

"Yeah," Julia replied wickedly. "I can put him down."

"Julia, please. This is your mother you're talking to."

Julia blushed profusely. "That is not what I meant."

Elizabeth replaced the shotgun on the shelf and steered Julia toward the door. "Doesn't the fact that your bullheaded vet shut the clinic and followed you all the way to Heartstrings tell you anything?"

"Yes, he'll sacrifice love and money to badger me," Julia mumbled, digging in her feet when they reached the door.

Elizabeth laughed softly and gave her dark head a shake. "No, Julia. Beneath all that bluff and bluster the man cares about you. And you care about him, so don't bother denying it. You want his respect, attention and his recognition of your ability. And he apparently wants the same thing from you. The two of you are too much alike—dominant personalities with feisty temperaments."

Julia inhaled a fortifying breath. "I suppose you're going to make me confront him all by myself."

"Sure am," Elizabeth confirmed, glancing at her watch. "I have to go to work. If you need a referee, ask Wyatt, though why he would help you out after the shameful way you treated him I don't know, except that he is a far better man than you have given him credit for being."

"I still don't think he's trustworthy," Julia insisted. "He could be a shyster for all I know."

"And a jackass for all *I* know."

Julia noticed the mocking grin that bracketed Elizabeth's mouth. "So maybe I was a little hard on the man."

"And Wyatt, too," Elizabeth added with a wink.

"Maybe," Julia conceded. "But I'm reserving judgment on both men." Drawing herself up to her full height, she marched off to the kitchen—without the shotgun.

When Elizabeth scurried off to work, Wyatt followed her outside, determined to see her behind the wheel of a dependable vehicle. He propelled her toward the Caddy instead of the run-down one-ton truck. When she opened her mouth to voice a protest, he kissed her into silence and tucked the keys in her hand.

"I'm not taking *no* for an answer this time," he told her in a no-nonsense tone. "You either take the car or I'm driving you to work, kicking and screaming, if need be."

"You may need your car to make a fast getaway, in case Julia and John open fire on each other."

"I'll keep a low profile and stay out of rifle range," Wyatt promised with an amused grin. "You hightail it out of here in the car before hell breaks loose."

"Oh, all right," Elizabeth muttered as she sank down on the leather seat. "But I'm not going to like it."

"Fine, don't. Just be safe so I don't have to worry about your making it home without another breakdown."

When Elizabeth drove off, Wyatt breathed a relieved sigh.

He didn't fault her for being so independent and determined to make do with what she had, and he could understand that she wanted to avoid gossip at the cafe where she worked, but this was one time when her pride was going to have to take the back-seat—*in his Caddy*—to ensure her safety.

Wyatt sincerely wished he could whisk Elizabeth away from her hectic schedule and outside influences, away from faulty vehicles, meddling children and habitual gossips. Nothing would please him more than to sweep her off to some uncharted island until they were certain enough of each other to take on the world.

He cast a glance around the ranch with its freshly painted barn and outbuildings. This was going to have to be their enchanted island for the time they had left. His gaze darted back to the house, and he wondered how many of the natives he was going to have to kill to ensure privacy. But the way things were going, the hot-tempered couple might just finish each other off and save him the trouble.

Elizabeth found herself the object of Irene Truman's speculative glances from the moment she arrived at Tall Grass Prairie Cafe. It didn't take long for Irene to broach the subject that was on her mind, either.

Irene brushed past Elizabeth while they were carrying dinner orders to tables. She leaned close and whispered, "Griff tells me you've been seeing that good-looking Wyatt McKenney."

Elizabeth turned an artificial smile on her customers and set the plates on the table. After a cheerful "I hope you enjoy your meal," she pivoted to find Irene standing shoulder to shoulder with her.

"Well?" Irene demanded.

"Well what?"

"Are you dating my latest heartthrob or aren't you?" Irene wanted to know.

"If I say yes, are we going to become the latest news on the grapevine?"

Irene flung her a withering glance. "Of course not. I think it's wonderful. The man is a hunk. If I can't land him, there's no one I'd rather see have him. You were widowed too young, and you haven't taken any time for yourself. It's time you did."

Elizabeth ambled down the aisle toward the kitchen with Irene on her heels. "I'm not trying to *land* McKenney. I'm simply enjoying his companionship for as long as he's in town."

Irene nodded consideringly. "Ah yes, I do remember hearing you proclaim a few years back that one marriage was plenty for you. I assume you simply intend to shame Wyatt and send him on his way when he no longer amuses you . . . hmmm?"

"Good grief, you make me sound like a femme fatale."

Truth was, Elizabeth hadn't dared mention the M-word or refer to "them" in the future when talking to Wyatt. She had adjusted to living for the moment, ignoring the future, and he had been as cautious as she in that regard. For him, there was only the eternal present—quality time spent together. The happiness and contentment she experienced with Wyatt was worth it, Elizabeth assured herself. She was no more interested in destroying the fragile bond between them than he was.

Okay, call it nearsighted, tunnel visioned or whatever you wanted, Elizabeth thought to herself. But no matter what it was called, she wanted it left alone. *If it isn't broken, don't fix it* had been her motto for the past few years. The theory applied to her relationship with Wyatt McKenney. Things were good between them—period, end of sentence.

"I think you should go for it," Irene advised. "The man is obviously a first-class meal ticket. He could provide for you after you sell the ranch. He's attractive, he's wealthy—hence the silver Caddy—and he has all his own teeth. Not that *I* would look a gift horse in the mouth, mind you."

"Maybe you should have," Elizabeth playfully popped off. "You might not have so many marriages to your credit."

Irene pulled a face and then chuckled good-naturedly. "All right, so everybody knows I'm a pathetic judge of men when it comes to my own life. But I know a sure-fire winner for *you* when I see one. McKenney is a prime prospect and he looks good, whether he's walking toward you or away."

Elizabeth burst out laughing at that. "You are simply awful, Irene. No shame whatsoever."

Irene struck a sophisticated pose and ran a preening hand over her stiff blond hair. "You think it doesn't cost a lot to look *this good* and *this cheap?* It's the shameless image I'm after here. Haven't you heard that country and western song by Confederate Railroad, insisting that they like their women on the trashy side—with clothes too tight and hair that's dyed?"

Elizabeth, who had just taken a sip of Coke to wet her whistle, choked and sprayed a stream of soda through the air. Irene reached over to whack her between the shoulder blades.

"The point here is that even *I,* poor judge of men that I am, can see that McKenney is a gold mine." She winked wickedly and added as she sauntered off, "If all you're getting is the *shaft,* you're cheating yourself out of the gold nuggets that could go with it."

Elizabeth sucked in her breath and strangled on her Coke—again. If you didn't like blunt, then you'd better steer clear of Irene. She was the female version of Howard Cosell.

After Elizabeth recovered from near-strangulation on her soft drink, she strode off toward Irene, who was flirting outrageously with one of the regular customers.

"If I hear rumors circulating about Wyatt and me, it will be your head, Irene, even if it does cost you an arm and leg to keep your roots dyed blond," she warned in mock seriousness.

"Mum's the word," Irene assured her. "Since I approve, and since you're my best friend, I don't want anything to spoil your happiness." Her expression sobered. "But Griff Hollis is carrying a grudge. Every time he comes in here, he shoots off his mouth to anyone who will listen. I *accidentally* dumped water in his crotch this afternoon when I heard him telling some of his buddies that you were giving McKenney fringe benefits while he's staying at Heartstrings. The cold water shut him up—temporarily."

"Thanks, Irene, I appreciate your loyalty."

"What's with Griff anyway?" Irene asked curiously.

"He offered to marry me and assume the loan on Heart-strings. I keep telling him it won't work, and he keeps insisting I need more time to think it over."

"You and Griff?" Irene turned up her pug nose. "Male chauvinist of Osage County? God, don't make me gag! Even I wouldn't marry him, and I've married practically every-body else around here!"

"He's a good neighbor," Elizabeth felt inclined to say in Griff's behalf. Why she didn't know. Griff certainly hadn't been very neighborly lately.

"A good neighbor? With a six-strand barbed wire fence between you, *maybe,*" Irene amended. "But I'd demand a fence stretched down the middle of the bed if I accepted that proposal."

Elizabeth was glad to know that Irene felt marrying Griff would be a mistake for her, even if Heartstrings would be sacrificed. Irene, who considered future security and low-maintenance men with thick wallets important, had flatly rejected Griff as potential marriage material.

If Elizabeth harbored any lingering doubts about rejecting Griff's proposal, that dissolved them. And furthermore, Griff had begun to show his true colors when he didn't get his way. He had a tendency to turn spiteful. No wonder Patty Hollis had left the man and was fooling around with Aaron Black. Aaron was no prize—the two-timing Casanova—but then, Patty wasn't accustomed to having the best, was she?

The last thing Irene said to Elizabeth as they walked out into the parking lot after work was, "Go for it, Liz. I think you owe it to yourself after working so hard for so many years. And if I were you, I'd make that handsome auctioneer a bid. Why not? You never know. He just might take it."

Elizabeth discarded another earful of free advice from her well-meaning friend and wandered off to where she had inconspicuously parked the Caddy. She wasn't going to issue ultimatums or expect promises and commitments. She didn't want to become so materialistic that she weighed Wyatt's worth in terms of financial statements and viewed his steady income as an endearing trait. That seemed cold-blooded to her.

And come to think of it, Griff had been cold-blooded himself, with that proposal. Oh, he had sugar-coated the arrangement, making it sound as if Elizabeth would receive all the benefits of the merger. But look what he had to gain. He was angling for control of Heartstrings—five thousand acres of rent-free pasture, herds of registered cattle and increased work production. He would expect to use Vic Henderson, would want Elizabeth to put three hot meals on the table every day and labor on the ranch—right up to the minute when he confined her to the kitchen.

Well, phooey on Griff Hollis! She wasn't going to be *his* meal ticket. He wanted to do all the taking and none of the giving. Elizabeth had been there before—with Bob. She wasn't going through that again, not even for Heartstrings . . . !

Her attention shifted to the rearview mirror. Headlights followed the cloud of dust she was kicking up on the gravel road. Elizabeth was unfamiliar with the Caddy and all its push buttons. She'd already bumped the electric window button with her elbow and had fumbled around, while trying to turn on the dash lights. Having another vehicle closing the distance behind her made her nervous. If flying gravel put a nick in the Caddy or a crack in the windshield she would never forgive herself.

Suddenly bright headlights flared in the side mirror, practically blinding her. It took her a moment to react to the vehicle that roared toward her in a fog of dust. She clamped onto the steering wheel when the driver of the other vehicle whizzed past her like a maniac, causing gravel to pepper the side of the Caddy.

Elizabeth swerved toward the ditch to avoid a collision and glared at the unidentified vehicle. A fog light flared to life beside her, and she stamped on the brake, fishtailing on the edge of the road.

The passing vehicle shut down all its lights, making it impossible for her to read the license tag or get a make or model. Like a prehistoric monster sinking into a black sea, it disappeared over the hill, leaving Elizabeth to inhale panting breaths to bring her heart rate down below the danger zone.

She sat there shaking for several minutes until she had regained her composure. When she had recovered her wits, she shifted into drive and cruised down the road. Beer cans were strung out in front of her like Hansel's and Gretel's bread crumbs, reflecting off her headlights.

"Damn pranksters," Elizabeth muttered. From all indications, a carload of teenagers were boozing it up, getting their kicks by scaring the living daylights out of a poor defenseless driver. Where was her shotgun when she really needed it?

The thought reminded Elizabeth of Julia's surprise visit. Thankful for the distraction, she turned her mind to her daughter and John W. Casey III. She wondered if those two had resolved their differences. They obviously needed Lana's counseling skills to overcome their difficulties.

Elizabeth smiled to herself. Perhaps she would give John W. Casey III a call, asking him to do her chores while she was out of town for the weekend—which she had definitely decided to be. She would let Lana, Brad, Julia and John take charge during her absence.

The *feelers* and the *thinkers* could cohabit for a couple of days. The time could become a retreat for bonding, consciousness-raising and all that. And who knew? Maybe the four of them would sift themselves out. A *thinker* might gravitate toward a *feeler.* Or maybe the two firecrackers would ignite a few sparks in the intellectual analyzers. It might even turn out that the analyzers neutralized the combustible temperaments of the firecrackers. Of course, Lana would apply all the proper technological psychobabble to the encounter. Elizabeth wasn't up to date on the jargon because it had been years since her college sociology and psychology classes. Still whatever happened when opposing magnetic fields collided, repelling and/or setting off static charges, Elizabeth was sure Heartstrings would be standing when she got back.

Chapter Thirteen

The incident on the road was immediately forgotten when Elizabeth walked through the front door to find a neatly wrapped package on the sofa, candles flickering on the dining table . . . and Wyatt wearing nothing but her apron!

The man definitely knew how to gain a woman's attention. If he turned around, he would receive even more of her attention!

Elizabeth propped herself against the wall and tossed her purse toward a nearby chair, missing it by a mile. Her gaze was glued to the roguish grin on Wyatt's face, the ladle in his hand and the long columns of muscled legs that extended from the hem of her red checkered apron.

Forget the awaiting meal, Elizabeth thought. Wyatt McKenney looked good enough to eat.

"Dinner is served, madam," Wyatt announced with an exaggerated bow. "Would you care for iced tea or coffee?"

"Is it included in the price of the meal, or do you charge extra for beverages? I'm on a tight budget." She eyed him thoroughly and deliberately. "And what, I'd like to know, are you serving for dessert?"

He flashed her a naughty grin that said it all.

"I see," she said.

"Do you?" Wyatt tugged at his revealing apron. "I was trying to be careful about turning my back."

"If you're running around in nothing but an apron, you have already been exposed to risks," she pointed out.

"I've been considering that," he murmured cryptically, then motioned her toward the chair he pulled out for her.

Elizabeth sashayed forward, plucking off her red bow tie and clipping it to the top of his apron.

"Thank you, madam. I needed that touch of sophistication."

She reached around to pat his bare tush and grinned. "I suppose you got the idea for this indecent ensemble from me," she said as she took her seat.

"I did," he confirmed as he backed toward the kitchen. "If you can serve customers without underwear, I thought I'd try it without clothes. All of this, of course, is strictly experimental. I'm considering opening a unique restaurant."

"I'm sure you'll have a female clientele beating down the door," Elizabeth assured him. "Will *Bare*varian Cream Pie and *Backside*-Down Cake be listed on the menu?"

His burst of laughter wafted from the kitchen.

Wyatt returned with garlic bread and two heaping plates of spaghetti, doused with sauce. After he had placed the meal in front of Elizabeth, leaning close enough to brush his bare arm against the swell of her breast, he sank into his own chair.

"You are absolutely no fun at all," Elizabeth grumbled when he managed to sit down without exposing his backside.

Two dark brows jackknifed. "You aren't amused? That was the whole point."

"Why do I need to be amused?" She sank back in her chair and stared at him in feigned dismay. "You aren't trying to soften the blow of bad news? Julia didn't take after John W. Casey III with the shotgun, did she?" Elizabeth jerked back from the table. "God, don't tell me we are disposing of the evidence with dinner!"

Wyatt chuckled and shook his head. "No, this is not à la

John. Julia didn't put the vet out of *her* misery by blowing him to smithereens. They discussed their differences like two hot-headed young adults, cast a few aspersions and then drove off in two clouds of dust."

"What did they say to each other?"

"I don't know. I was mowing the bar ditches."

Elizabeth frowned, disappointed. "How am I to know what's going on in my elder daughter's rocky personal and professional life if you aren't sneaking around spying on her for me?"

"Do I look like Mata Hari?"

"No," Elizabeth admitted. "Mata didn't have a hairy chest and legs. She did, however, dance on tables." Her brows waggled suggestively. "I'd like to see you try it in your apron."

Wyatt took fork in hand to sample his efforts. Elizabeth had been a few minutes late, and the sauce was a little too thick for his taste. Between bites, he let his gaze dart to her. "I envy you, Bet," he said seriously.

Elizabeth blinked, amazed. She, who had little or nothing that the bank wasn't trying to take from her, was envied by a man who appeared to have everything going for him? "You have got to be kidding!"

He smiled ruefully. "You have children. I have none of my own."

Elizabeth was surprised that Wyatt had revealed even that much about his past. He wasn't exactly secretive, but he'd volunteered very little information.

"If you want children, I'll give you mine," she generously offered. "You can prevent Julia from murdering the vet, and you can listen to Lana analyze everything that moves and some things that don't. I'll have the adoption papers brought around tomorrow after I pick up Old Red from the mechanic's."

"I mean it, Bet, your daughters may give you headaches, but they've kept you involved and vital. I was feeling very old and very used up before I came to Heartstrings. Being here has brought me back to life."

Elizabeth would have leaned across the table to hug him,

but she didn't want to smear spaghetti on her white blouse. The sauce might have been mistaken for blood when the news came out that the vet had met with a bad end.

Elizabeth and Wyatt ate in companionable silence, casting glances and smiles that were bathed in flickering candlelight. She tried to remember a time when Bob had been so playfully romantic. She couldn't come up with one endearing memory.

Wyatt McKenney had already taken control of her body and had set up residence in her heart. If she wasn't careful, her soul would be his. She could be destined to lose more than her heritage in this ranch, she realized. She might lose these newfound pleasures, this precious time when she embraced life with open arms.

Before long, these sweet dreams would filter through her hands like stardust. When the ranch was auctioned off to the highest bidder and she whispered her last good-bye to Wyatt, she was going to be tormented. Her new beginning would be agonizingly empty, she just knew it!

After the meal, Wyatt backed out of the dining room to retrieve the neatly wrapped package. "For you, madam. A door prize for the restaurant's first patron."

"A matching apron?" Elizabeth guessed.

"Yes," Wyatt declared with a scampish smile. "We'll be a perfect match. I'll be wearing a backless apron and you'll be attired in a frontless apron. However, I don't know where *you're* going to pin *your* bow tie."

Elizabeth giggled at his playful antics and opened the package. A gasp burst from her when sparkling sequins winked back at her. Good grief, the black evening gown must have cost a fortune!

"Where in the world—?"

"I checked the clothes in your closet to determine your size and picked up the dress in Bartlesville while I was accompanying Jerry on his appointed rounds. Do you like it?"

Elizabeth was thunderstruck. "Wh-why . . . ?"

"Is that a yes or a no?" Wyatt questioned, grinning at her reaction to the gift.

"Of course, I like it. I never owned anything so elegant," Elizabeth blathered once she recovered her powers of speech. "But why?"

Wyatt strolled up to close her gaping jaw. His green eyes twinkled down at her. "Because you make me happy, Bet."

Elizabeth sighed heavily and stared at the expensive gown. "I can't accept this."

"I wanted you to have something new to wear to the cocktail party we have to attend the night before the auction in the City."

Elizabeth blinked. "I thought you were just going to sell off a few horses."

"I am."

"These horses are so ritzy they have a cocktail party first?"

"This is a multimillion dollar business," Wyatt explained. "Not your run-of-the-mill horse sale."

"I can't wear this dress."

"Fine, but you aren't going naked. I want you for my eyes only." He tried to look properly threatening—if a man could do that while wearing nothing but an apron. "It's this dress or a saddled blanket. Take your pick."

"I haven't even said I'd go yet," she reminded him.

He clasped her hand in his, drawing her fingertips to his lips. "Please come with me. I don't want to lose even an hour of a day I could spend with you. I like the way you make me feel when I'm with you."

Elizabeth peered into those entrancing green eyes, fanned by lashes as long as paint brushes, and felt her heart melt. She reached down to scoop up the sequined dress, noting the shoes beneath it. "Not matching shoes, too!"

Wyatt quirked a wondering brow. "Did you want one black one and one white one?"

Elizabeth let out a long sigh. "And I suppose I'm going to have to ride in that damned Caddy again."

" 'Fraid so. It's a long trip to the City by horseback."

She slumped defeatedly. She had loudly proclaimed that she didn't do Caddys or flaunt expensive clothes, much less sport matching shoes. Truth was, luxury cars and extravagant spending had been a sore spot with her since the early days when oil headrights had made the Osage the wealthiest tribe in the country. Some of the tribe's members had spent their money foolishly. If their fancy Lincolns or Caddys broke down on the road, they simply left them there and purchased new ones. Elizabeth had never forgotten her family's remorse at seeing some members of their clan waste the money from the mineral rights.

Now Elizabeth was forced to eat her words, and they tasted like sour grapes. "Oh, all right, but I hope you realize you're turning me into a hypocrite."

"I wasn't trying to turn you into a hypocrite. I was only trying to turn you *on.*" Wyatt clasped her hand in his and led her toward the bedroom, his backless apron revealing his naked form to her consuming gaze.

He had accomplished that easily enough, Elizabeth mused as she surveyed the tantalizing scenery. Irene was right. Wyatt McKenney looked good coming and going, and she intended to appreciate everything about him until he was gone . . .

The thought reminded her of the pact she had made with herself after the night Wyatt had made wild sweet love to her, fulfilling every possible need he had aroused in her. Tonight she was going to return that pleasure as gently and tenderly as it had been bestowed on her. She was going to savor Wyatt until he filled up her senses, until she absorbed him completely.

Elizabeth grabbed the apron string as Wyatt sauntered through the door, leaving the garment dangling around him. When he pivoted toward her, she drew the apron over his head and tossed it aside. Her gaze flooded over him as her hand swept across the padded muscles of his chest and circled his male nipples. She was rewarded with a muffled groan that encouraged her to continue her explorations. As her lips feathered over the curve of his chin, she inhaled the tantalizing scent of his cologne and her fingertips trailed over his belly and swirled upward, drawing a shuddering sigh from him.

When Wyatt reached for her, she stilled his hands and murmured against his chest, "Tonight I want to seduce you, but when you touch me I forget how to think." She settled his hands on her hips and grinned playfully at him. "Now, be a good boy and don't distract me."

"You don't have to—"

Her lips brushed over his sensuous mouth, shushing him. "But I do, you see," she softly assured him. "Because touching you makes me immensely happy . . ."

Wyatt's body contracted with ungovernable need when her fingertips skimmed his chest. Lips as soft as rose petals feathered over his skin, sending sensual lightning pulsing through him, and when her hands glided over his hips and skied over his inner thigh, he was reasonably certain his knees had turned to rubber.

Then things got progressively worse. Wyatt's legs melted down to the consistency of jelly when Elizabeth gently cupped him. The sweet pressure of the hands stroking the throbbing length of him had him staggering to maintain his balance. He was shaking with a hunger so profound it was recoiling on itself, burgeoning until it consumed his body, mind and soul.

A tormented groan rumbled in his chest when her whispered kisses trailed up the wedge of hair on his chest and drifted back down again. She knelt before him, her hands sweeping from thigh to ankle, sensitizing every inch of his skin. Butterfly kisses wafted over his rigid flesh, and he felt her moist breath hovering . . . so close and yet so maddeningly far away. He shivered uncontrollably when she measured him with the tip of her tongue, and torrid pleasure multiplied with each intimate kiss, each tormentingly tender caress.

When she took him into her mouth, flicking at the velvet tip of his manhood with her tongue, Wyatt heard his sharp intake of breath. Desire clawed at him like sharp talons, dragging him ever closer to the crumbling edge of restraint. She nuzzled her cheek against his thigh while her hand folded around him, her fingertips drawing lazy circles on his aroused flesh. A silvery drop of need betrayed his attempt to hold himself in check when she plied him with another round of exquisite torture. This, Wyatt decided, was the kind of erotic torment a man could die for without regret.

He moaned shakily when her lips brushed over him again, tasting him, suckling him. Her hands swept to and fro like the surf caressing the shore. Wave after wave of pleasure rippled through him. His blood was running so hot and heavy that he swore he could feel his pulse beat flowing through him, hear his lungs shudder in their desperate attempts to draw in air.

When she drew his hands along with hers while she caressed him, Wyatt nearly went out of his mind. But then, he asked himself, how could a man go out of his mind when he didn't have one left after being seduced with such exquisite tenderness? Her gentle assault had emptied him of all thought and had filled him with such phenomenal sensations, *feeling* was the only reality he understood. There was only the sweep of her hand, the gentle pressure of dewy lips. He was living through her touch, aware of nothing but the indescribable sensations that knotted in the very core of his being, burning on a white-hot flame; and each bead of need she kissed away drew another . . . and yet another.

Hands and lips skimmed his thighs and belly, making him shudder. She rose to her feet ever so slowly, splaying kisses across his chest until she was standing before him. Her hand folded around him once again, teasing him until his body answered her caressing summons. She traced him with her thumb as she lifted up on tiptoe to circle his lips with her tongue, provocatively imitating the motion of her fingertip on his rigid flesh.

Wyatt could taste his own need on her lips, feel it on her fingertips. Every barrier of restraint came toppling down around him. "God, Bet . . . If you don't stop what you're doing to me, I won't survive the night."

Wyatt didn't mean to clutch her so fiercely to him, but he felt like Mt. St. Helens on the verge of eruption. She was melting him down until every bone and muscle was liquid fire begging for release.

Sweet merciful heavens! If he didn't reach the bed—and quickly—he was liable to collapse. And if he didn't draw breath soon, he wouldn't have to bother with breathing at all because he would be going, going, gone . . . lost forever.

A sense of satisfaction coursed through Elizabeth as Wyatt took her down onto the bed with him. She could hear him panting for breath, feel his heart hammering in his chest like a wild hawk fighting for freedom. Perhaps now he knew how she had felt when he'd sent her soaring far away without leaving the circle of his arms. If she had ignited all the hot, fervent sensations in him that he'd aroused in her, she would be content. She wanted him to understand how completely he had devastated her with his loving touch.

Every shred of willpower deserted Wyatt when Elizabeth took him in hand, brushing his throbbing flesh against her inner thigh, teasing him with the silky warmth that awaited him. He was losing control, bulletlike sensations riveting him until self-restraint became impossible.

"No, Bet," he groaned as she urged him ever closer to the honeyed fire of her answering passion. "Not like this . . ."

If he thought she wasn't eager and willing to take him and hold him covetously to her, he was mistaken. She wanted him, just as he was—as hungry and desperate as she had been that first time, so oblivious that need had become a tangible force that lived, breathed and consumed.

"Yes, Wyatt," she assured him as she arched toward him, feeling his velvet strength filling the aching emptiness inside her. "Exactly like this . . . completely out of control . . ."

Wyatt clutched her to him when ungovernable passion seized his body and smothered all rational thought. He thrust against her, burying himself deeper and deeper with each frantic thrust. He was moving too fast, and he must surely be depriving her of the pleasure he had wanted to give her before they both tumbled over rapture's waterfall and plunged into blissful infinity.

Too late. Wyatt could no more control the pulsating hunger

than he could sprout wings and fly to Mars. And even as desire offered him wild, fulfilling release, he cursed himself sourly.

"Damn it to hell . . ." he muttered in the aftermath of mindless passion.

Elizabeth laughed softly and pressed a kiss against his shoulder. "You're calling the dog at a time like this?"

"No, but I may have to call an ambulance," he grumbled as he braced up on an elbow and glared down at her. "What are you trying to do, woman? Kill me before my time?"

She smiled sadly as her fingertips smoothed away his disgruntled frown. "No, I'm trying to love you while there is *still* time."

"Bet, I—"

"Don't say anything," she cut in. "Just let me enjoy you, enjoy us . . ."

He went very still, watching her, studying her with vivid intensity. "You want no promises? You expect nothing from me after—?"

She shook her head slowly. "Nothing," she quietly assured him. "What you've given me is more than I could ever have hoped to find."

"You want nothing from me," he repeated. When she shook her head again, he smiled mysteriously and bent to press a tender kiss to her lips. "I didn't think you would."

Elizabeth was left to ponder the enigmatic expression that settled on his shadowed features, the cryptic comment he'd uttered before he eased away. There was some hidden meaning in his words and his smile. Elizabeth didn't have a clue to what he was thinking, but she refused to dig too deep for fear she would become like her younger daughter who often tied herself in analytical knots. She just wanted to relish the spontaneity, the reckless abandon in her life before reality returned.

Then again, what if Lana and Julia were right? Elizabeth found herself thinking as she snuggled against Wyatt's shoulder. What if she really had walked off the deep end, letting herself be taken in by a man who *seemed* sincere in his attraction to her, but who refused to speak of his past? What if this was some sort of midlife crisis in which she was trying to assure herself that she was still desirable, still vital and capable of drawing a man's interest? Perhaps it was a desperate attempt to boost her self-esteem after facing failure.

Elizabeth lay awake a long time, mulling over the disturbing smile that settled on Wyatt's face. She had defied her family's and a neighbor's warning. The only person who seemed to approve of this whirlwind affair was Irene. Elizabeth reminded herself that the poor dear had had no luck at all in her relationships with men.

Well, she wasn't going to start second-guessing herself now. She had made a vow and she was sticking to it. For better or worse, she was going to follow her heart. She'd known the risks going in, known she might come to care so deeply that Wyatt's leaving would be as traumatic as losing Heartstrings.

She had begun to fall in love with him, she admitted. But she wasn't expecting commitment or promises. That was the truth. He was not the paycheck she sought, not her future security. When he returned to his world and she was left behind in what was left of hers, and when time and distance dissolved what had been a kaleidoscope of passion and fun-loving companionship, she was not going to blame Wyatt for walking away. He had asked for two weeks to explore this explosive attraction, and she had agreed.

This was the bright shining moment she had asked for and received. Some people never experienced such pleasure. They lived without knowing what happiness truly was. She'd done more living in a short span of time than she had in the past decade. How could she regret this?

Lana and Julia had their whole lives ahead of them, and were envisioning productive futures, while Elizabeth had a handful of broken promises and shattered dreams—compliments of her husband and his grandiose visions of power and prestige. No, she thought as she closed her eyes and drifted off to sleep, she wouldn't regret her time with Wyatt. He had made her unbelievably happy. She would remember that, no matter what happened, no matter how hard Lana and Julia tried to convince her that she had made a mistake. Even if this was a fool's paradise, she had basked in pleasure when she'd found her place in the sun . . .

The blaring phone caused Elizabeth to jerk upright, blinking to orient herself in the darkness. Bleary-eyed, she glanced at the clock. Who the devil was calling her at five o'clock in the morning? Even God didn't get up *that* early!

She groped for the receiver when another shrill jingle shattered the silence.

"This better be good or I'm going to strangle whoever is on the other 'end of the line—with the phone cord." Wyatt scowled, willing his heart to pry itself loose from his ribs and return to its normal resting place.

"Hello?" Elizabeth rasped drowsily.

"Liz? I called to remind you we're going to round up the cattle today," came the clipped voice.

"I remember."

"I'll be there at six-thirty to start the round-up. We'll do your cattle first."

There was a long pause.

"You aren't bringing that tenderfoot with you, I hope. We don't need that clown around. He won't know what the hell he's doing, and he'll just be in our way."

Elizabeth gnashed her teeth at Griff's snide comment. "Wyatt offered to help us."

"Great," Griff snorted. "Tell the sissy to bring a vacuum cleaner to sweep up the cow patties. Later, Liz."

The line went dead, and Elizabeth replaced the receiver in its cradle.

Wyatt braced himself on an elbow and raked his fingers through his tousled hair. "Is your neighbor always obnoxious at this hour of the morning?"

"I'm really sorry," Elizabeth apologized. "Griff doesn't take rejection well. He's making you his scapegoat."

Wyatt shrugged. "The man would have to matter to me before I cared what he thought. He doesn't and I don't."

"I'd like to get through today with as little conflict as possible. Roundups are always mayhem."

"I'll try to be on my best behavior," Wyatt promised as he rolled off the bed and headed to the shower. "I can't speak for Hollis, though. It seems he's spoiling for a fight."

It did, and that worried Elizabeth. It would probably be best if Wyatt took a wide berth around Griff, but if she asked him to remain at the house that might indicate she didn't think he could handle Griff. One bruised ego was enough.

Elizabeth padded toward the vanity to wash the sleep from her eyes. She squawked in surprise when she was abruptly tugged sideways and plunged beneath the shower.

Wyatt drew her body to his beneath the spraying mist. "I'm a firm believer in environmental conservation," he murmured against the sensitive spot on her neck. "Save water and share showers. That's my motto."

Tingling sensations began at the junction of Elizabeth's throat and shoulder, spreading like silken flames through her body. Slick hands glided over her, lathering her breasts with playful dedication. When Wyatt's fingertips skied down her hips to swirl over her inner thighs, Elizabeth's breath broke on a sigh.

He turned her in his arms so that she was facing him, so that he could savor the sight of her every luscious curve and swell. His hands and lips took eager turns at memorizing the feel of her fragrant skin.

He smiled in pure male satisfaction when he felt her shimmering around his questing fingertip. Sensual heat rippled around him as he teased her into breathless arousal and saw the need he had called from her receptive body mirrored in her dark eyes. She made him dizzy with answering desire, made him burn as she secretly caressed his gliding fingertips.

"Wyatt . . ." she gasped as shock waves of pleasure crested in her.

"Hmmm?" He questioned, nibbling at the corner of her mouth.

"I can't—" Her voice failed her when he moved his hand, igniting another pulsating flame that shimmered like sunbeams.

"Can't what?" he teased as he touched her intimately, feeling the warm rain of desire spilling onto his fingertips.

Her arms came around him, clutching him frantically to her as wild convulsions seized her. When he drew her legs around his hips and pressed closer, Elizabeth found the fulfilling cure for the fever that burned through her. She met him, matched him, took him with her to the sun . . . just as dawn burned away the darkness from the horizon.

"Lana?"

Lana propped the phone receiver against her shoulder and marked her place in the textbook with her forefinger. She'd been double-checking her lesson plans before dressing when her sister had called.

"What's wrong, Julia?"

"How do you know something is wrong?"

"I can tell by your tone of voice. Besides, you only call me when something is on your mind. More problems with your vet?"

"He isn't the worst problem at the moment. I was at Heart-strings yesterday."

"What were you doing there?"

"I don't know. That's just where I ended up when I felt the need to get away after John fired me and then rehired me."

"The homing-pigeon instinct," Lana diagnosed. "Heart-strings obviously means more to you than you were willing to admit to Mother."

"Don't start with me, Lana. I'm not your newest patient. Mother is," Julia insisted. "She and lover-boy McKenney were playing grab-ass on the portico. God, she doesn't act her age when she's around that man. She isn't herself these days. She's too lighthearted and playful for a woman who's about to lose Heartstrings. She should be brooding and sulking, but you wouldn't believe the way she and Wyatt were climbing all over each other. It was disgraceful!"

"He's still there?" Lana asked, surprised.

"He must be living there, even if he makes himself scarce on the weekends when we come home. His suitcase was in one of the spare bedrooms, but I'd bet my veterinary medicine degree that the spare bedroom isn't where he's sleeping."

Lana closed her textbook. This was serious. "Mother seems to be reaching out to recapture her lost youth. She's overcompensating for her anxiety. Since we aren't around, she doesn't perceive us an extension of herself anymore. She has lost touch with youthful vitality and is trying to recover it with this foolish infatuation."

"You can analyze her behavior from every which way, but what it boils down to is McKenney is taking advantage of Mother's vulnerability at this difficult stage of her life. We are both going to have to come at her from every direction—and with pinpoint accuracy—if we're going to stop this affair."

"The laser-beam theory," Lana agreed. "We will point out to her that she is desperately trying to stabilize her position by turning possible threats into justifications. She is using escapism, trying to live dangerously until the auction, because she perceives it as a danger and disaster."

"Do you know when the auction is supposed to be held?" Julia cut in.

"No, I haven't heard."

"Me either."

Lana was silent for a moment, the wheels of her analytical mind grinding. "Don't you think that's odd? It's been almost two weeks, but no date has been established. If McKenney is making contacts with big cattle corporations and well-to-do farmers and stockmen, you would think—"

"Oh, God!" Julia exclaimed, in a panic. "Do you think he might be angling to make a private bid for Heartstrings—not planning to hold an auction at all? If he woos Mother into selling out to him at a lower price, he could turn right around and take bids from his high-rolling associates."

"He's going to flimflam Mother and make himself a tidy profit at her expense," Lana predicted.

Julia muttered several epithets. "I knew his pretense of interest in Mother had to be a ruse. I just wasn't sure what he was up to. But it all makes sense now—the delays, the 'devoted' attention to her. He's romancing her for the ranch."

"We'll have to draw him out this weekend," Lana insisted. "Unless he can give us a confirmed date for the auction and produce the promotional flyers that should be circulating on his mailing lists, we can be certain our assumptions are correct."

"I don't think we should wait until the weekend. I'm going to Heartstrings as soon as I get off work tomorrow," Julia declared.

"I'll meet you there as soon as I can get away from school. We'll begin Operation McKenney. Hopefully, he'll be gone for good by this weekend."

"And I'll load the shotgun, just in case reasoning doesn't resolve this problem."

There was a slight pause before Lana said, "Better load two of them, sis."

Julia hung up the phone, assured that her psych textbook of a sister was, for once, prepared to do more than spin clinical theories.

Chapter Fourteen

The minute Griff Hollis wheeled beneath Heartstrings' gateway with his pickup and horse trailer, Elizabeth knew it was going to be a long, taxing day. Griff had two mounts with him—the one he usually rode and the wild-eyed, overbred Appaloosa he couldn't sell or give away. The Ap was going to become Wyatt's mount, Elizabeth guessed.

When Griff stepped down from his truck, his condescending smirk landed on Wyatt. Elizabeth winced, wondering how much guff Wyatt could actually take. Although he had promised to be on his best behavior, today was going to be an exercise in self-restraint.

"I guess you found time to help with the roundup, in between your household duties," Griff said for starters. "I saddled a horse for you, since I wasn't sure you knew how to do it yourself."

Two low blows in less than a minute, Elizabeth noted. She cast Wyatt a discreet glance, calculating how long it was going to be before he was ready to knock out a few of Griff's teeth. Elizabeth was ready *now*.

To his credit, Wyatt manufactured a semblance of a smile

and ambled over to unhook the tailgate of the horse trailer. "Neighborly of you to loan me one of your mounts."

"Yeah, isn't it?" Griff swaggered over to back the Appy out of the trailer. "The Ap has a lot of spirit, but he's good with cattle."

The minute the Appy clattered from the trailer he threw his head up to study his surroundings. Wyatt appraised the horse Griff had supplied for him. From all indications, Griff intended to bruise more than Wyatt's male ego.

"I'll go saddle a horse for you, Elizabeth," Wyatt volunteered, pivoting toward the barn.

"Need some help?" Griff mockingly called after him.

"Thanks, but I think I can manage," he tossed over his shoulder.

Elizabeth's dark eyes narrowed on Griff. "You realize, of course, that you're behaving like a jerk."

"Just because you've decided to put up with that greenhorn doesn't mean I have to." Griff scowled. "You should have told him to tend the home fires. He's probably better with dishes and laundry than horses and cattle. And when he's caught up around your place, you can send him over to mine to tidy up. My furniture needs dusting."

"You think a man is less of a man if he cleans up after himself?" Elizabeth smirked.

"*I* sure as hell don't bother with that sissy stuff," Griff said haughtily. "I have a cleaning *lady.*"

Elizabeth looked down her nose at him. "Pigs don't clean up after themselves, either, Griff."

"Come on, Liz, you know this guy isn't for you. We belong together. We're alike—same interests, same backgrounds. Let me cover your loan and save Heartstrings—"

"Hi, Griff," Vic greeted as he strolled toward the trailer. "Is Chuck still laid up?"

"Afraid so." Griff flicked a glance toward the barn. "But Mary Alice McKenney will be riding with us. That should be loads of help."

Vic muffled a laugh. "I'll get a horse."

About that time, Wyatt appeared from the barn, leading George and Chicago, carrying spare rope and the leather strips he had found hanging in the tack room.

Elizabeth eyed Wyatt curiously, wondering if he had decided to tie Griff's arms and legs in a Turk's knot and drag him merrily behind.

While Griff unloaded his sorrel gelding, Wyatt handed Chicago's reins to Vic and then glanced at Elizabeth. "What's the story on this Ap?"

"Hell on hooves," Elizabeth murmured confidentially. "He drops his head and bucks. About the time you're prepared for a leap, he digs in his hind legs and rears up. He's adequate around cattle and you can rope off him, but if he catches movement of another horse out of the corner of his eye, he'll buck or rear and you won't know which until he swallows his head or tries to perform the Swan Lake ballet by dancing around on his hind legs."

Wyatt nodded consideringly as he studied the Appaloosa. He walked over to apply the rope and leather straps to strategic positions on his unruly mount.

Griff was too busy gathering his lariat and pulling on his gloves to notice the contraption Wyatt was tying to the Ap until the ropes and straps were in place. A leather strip connected the poll of the headstall on the bridle to the saddle horn. A cotton rope circled the barrel of the Ap's belly and fastened in a slip hitch behind the cantle of the saddle.

"What in the hell is that?" Griff snorted.

"Improvised restrainers for misbehaving horses," Wyatt explained as he swung into the saddle with leisurely ease. "My father used to ride the rodeo circuit. He knew all the tricks of training difficult livestock. I'll be glad to give you a few more tips on your Appy after I see how it handles."

Griff scowled and reined toward the pasture gate. "You do that, McKenney, and then maybe we can swap recipes."

Elizabeth studied Wyatt's broad back as they rode toward the gate. She had the sneaking suspicion he hadn't simply worked on a farm in his younger days. More than likely he had lived on one. And why he was being so mysterious about that part of his background she couldn't help but wonder.

This was not the time to demand answers, however, she reminded herself. There were cattle to drive into stock pens before the stubble of last season's weeds could be burned from the pastures. Elizabeth wished she could afford to spray to control the weeds that deprived the prairie grasses of water and soil nutrients, but since the chemicals cost two dollars an acre, she would have to spend too much on this five-thousand-acre ranch.

As usual, some of Griff's cattle had come through the shared fences to graze with Elizabeth's herds. Seeing the Lazy H brands amid her livestock reminded Elizabeth of why she was hesitant to accept Griff's proposal. He overgrazed to such an extreme that his cattle were constantly bursting through to get to better grass and the high-protein cattle cubes Elizabeth used as a supplement.

The roundup of cows and calves in the first two pastures went smoothly, except for Griff's snide remarks and his constant attempt to commandeer the operation. Elizabeth wondered how much ridicule Wyatt could tolerate. After the first two hours, she suspected he had reached his limit.

The widespread herd of yearlings in the far pasture proved more difficult to secure than the cows and young calves. They were unfamiliar with this procedure, and they had a tendency to panic and veer off in all directions.

Griff took full advantage, bossing Wyatt around as if he were a complete idiot. The situation exploded when Wyatt was sent to work the corral gate where Vic was herding two nervous strays along the fence row. The timing was bad, and Elizabeth knew it. She was damned certain Griff knew it, too. He was purposely trying to humiliate Wyatt in front of Elizabeth and Vic.

Just as Elizabeth predicted, both strays tried to reverse direction. Vic wheeled to block their path and Damn It scrambled after them. The steers spun about to find Wyatt standing by the open corral gate into which they were to be herded.

The wild-eyed steers balked, rammed their heads through the fence wires and bulldozed their way into Griff's pasture. They never looked back as they thundered over the hill.

"Well, hell's bells, McKenney," Griff muttered. "Don't you have enough cow sense to back off? Everybody knows you can't drive cattle toward you. Too bad you didn't stay home and crochet an afghan. You would have been more help there."

Elizabeth saw the muscle in Wyatt's jaw twitch as he pivoted toward Griff who had ridden up behind him. While Griff sat his horse, smirking like the ruling cattle baron of Osage County, Wyatt uncoiled with lightning speed. His fist clenched on the front of his antagonist's shirt, sending Griff cartwheeling to the ground. Griff had only gotten to his knees when Wyatt grabbed him again, hoisting him to his feet.

Although both men were comparable in height, Griff outweighed Wyatt by a good thirty pounds, Elizabeth noted. She also noticed that Griff had been more anxious to shoot off his mouth than to back up his words with his fists. Wyatt, however, seemed agreeable to get his point across physically or verbally. Thankfully, he hadn't thrown a punch at Griff, though he looked as if he would like to.

"One more wisecrack, Hollis," Wyatt hissed as he stuck his face in Griff's. "If you keep pushing, you'll be making an appointment with your dentist to remove the teeth I knock down your throat."

Griff snarled back at him, trying to bluff his way through the intimidation and save face in front of Elizabeth and Vic. "As if you could, McKenney—"

Wyatt's elbow caught Griff in the chin, causing him to bite his tongue. Griff's temper snapped when pain shot through him, but a well-aimed knee to the crotch caused his legs to drop out from under him. He was still gasping for breath when Wyatt strode off to hop onto his mount.

Without waiting for Griff to catch up, Elizabeth and Wyatt reined toward the pasture to the northwest.

Wyatt let his breath out in a rush. "I'm sorry, Bet."

"He had it coming," she replied. "I just hope we can get through this roundup without a knock-down-drag-out fight."

"Worried about me?" he grumbled in question.

"No, you can obviously take care of yourself," she countered. "I'm only concerned that your knuckles might swell up when you rearrange Griff's face, so you won't be able to finish that afghan he thinks your crocheting."

The teasing remark cooled Wyatt's temper, and he chuckled aloud. "I'll gladly crochet an afghan if the two of us can cuddle up in it. I'd rather be known as a lover rather than a fighter."

"From all indications, you're an expert at both," she assured him before glancing back at her surly neighbor. "I don't think Griff is much good at either one."

The lunch Elizabeth provided during round- up turned out to be a grim affair. Griff sat in his chair, silently mocking Wyatt who didn't hesitate to help Elizabeth put food on the table. Equality, Elizabeth observed, was not something Griff recognized. It didn't dawn on him that she had been every bit as involved in the roundup as he was, yet she was expected to throw a quick meal together and he didn't even bother to offer to set the table. If there had been a remote chance Elizabeth might reconsider Griff's proposal, it evaporated as she watched him show his true colors.

After the foursome had wolfed down their meal, they mounted up to secure the last of the cattle in Heartstrings' pens before moving onto Lazy H pastures. Wyatt surveyed the grasses and assessed Griff's herds. The land was definitely overstocked. Lazy H Ranch had possibilities, but not with Griff at the helm. The cows were underfed, and the yearlings weren't as healthy as the ones at Heartstrings.

Wyatt frowned pensively as he stared at the house in the distance. His gaze swept the area, silently assessing the new farm machinery that lined the fence. He glanced at Griff and pondered the difference between Heartstrings and Lazy H.

"Something wrong, McKenney?" Griff demanded gruffly as he reined up beside Wyatt.

"I was just admiring the scenery."

"Well, don't think you'll ever have the chance to auction this place off," Griff grunted with his usual amount of disrespect.

"Thinking of selling out?"

"No!" Griff adamantly insisted.

Wyatt smiled mischievously. He simply couldn't resist returning the jibe after taking so much harassment from Griff. "Too bad. I have a few prospective buyers in mind who would take much better care of this place than you do. Elizabeth's progressive management looks to be more productive than yours. Maybe you should give Jerry Patterson a call and let him set up a proper nutrition program for your cows and steers."

"I'm doing fine without Jerry's advice," Griff growled sourly.

Green eyes glinted in the sunlight. "I'm sure that's what the last rancher said about consulting Jerry—right before his operation folded. Personally, I think you have your priorities backward."

"For damned sure and certain, nobody cares what *you* think." Griff jerked his horse around and bolted off to take command of the roundup.

Wyatt was still chuckling quietly when Elizabeth, wearing a concerned frown, glanced in his direction. He nodded at her, assuring her that fisticuffs weren't about to break out. No need, Wyatt thought, smiling to himself. From the look of things, Griff was already cutting his own throat. Why bother doing it for him?

Five hours later, Griff's cattle were penned up and the man had driven off, his horse trailer rattling behind his shiny black truck. Because of the wind and low humidity, he and Elizabeth had decided to postpone the pasture burning until the following morning.

Wyatt and Elizabeth were on their way back from unsaddling

the horses when two compact cars rolled into the driveway. Elizabeth groaned. A parent should be delighted to see her children return for a visit. She wasn't, not when she could predict the subject of the upcoming conversation—Wyatt McKenney.

Sure enough, Lana and Julia climbed out of their cars, looking judge-sober. After nodding an unreturned greeting to the hostile guests, Wyatt took his cue.

"I have a few phone calls to make to my contacts," he said before he ambled away, leaving Elizabeth with her daughters.

"How nice of you to come by for a visit," she said with pretended cheer.

"Now, Mother, you know Julia and I are here because we're concerned about you."

"I appreciate that, but I am managing just fine, thank you."

"Are you?" Julia questioned as she led the way to the covered portico. "I thought perhaps when Wyatt set the auction date, it might upset you."

"The date hasn't been set yet," Elizabeth replied as she plunked down on the bench to rest.

"No? It's been almost two weeks, hasn't it?" Lana reminded her mother. "Don't you think it's a little peculiar that your auctioneer hasn't scheduled the sale by now? And what about the proofs for the promotionals on the auction? Have you looked them over yet?"

Elizabeth squirmed uneasily. She supposed she should have been more curious about the details of the auction, but frankly she didn't want to think about the sale until the inevitable was upon her. Besides, this was Wyatt's vacation. He wasn't supposed to be tending to business.

"Are you suggesting Wyatt isn't as efficient as he should be?" Elizabeth inquired. "Do I need to remind you that he's been upgrading the looks of Heartstrings while he's on vacation?"

Lana inhaled deeply and stared grimly at her mother. "Julia and I have a theory . . ."

"So what else is new?" Elizabeth muttered.

"Mother, please listen without being defensive. We realize you've developed a certain fondness for Wyatt. We also realize you're facing a difficult crisis that might prevent you from logically assessing the situation. Julia and I are worried. We fear he might be preying on your affection for him and planning to use you for his own financial gain."

"Thank you so much for the vote of confidence," Elizabeth huffed. "You are saying that my personality and appearance are so lacking a man could not possibly appreciate me for what I am? That I am so blinded by my need to endure this crisis I'm not capable of analyzing this relationship?"

"Now, Mother," Lana patronized.

Elizabeth gnashed her teeth. Wyatt had been talked down to all day by Griff. He had finally lost his cool. Elizabeth wondered how much she could tolerate before she turned both of her daughters over her knees and gave them the spankings she'd obviously neglected to provide in their youth.

"All we want you to do is emotionally back away from this situation and take a good look at what you see," Julia insisted. "No date has been set for the auction, no promotions have been prepared for mailing lists. Obviously there is something appealing about this place or Wyatt wouldn't still be here. Has it occurred to you that he's offering to help just to endear himself to you before he offers to buy Heartstrings?"

Elizabeth gaped at her daughters as if *they* were the ones whose mental capacities were being questioned. "Just exactly what are you accusing him of this time?"

Lana took over before her sister's poor handling of the situation provoked a shouting match. "Given the facts as we know them—"

How diplomatic of Lana not to list these so-called facts, Elizabeth thought.

"—we cannot help but wonder if Wyatt might not be a con man setting up a scam. He could be pulling your emotional strings and manipulating you to arrive at a desired outcome. We don't want to see you victimized."

"All you have is Jerry Patterson's opinion of a man he knew

in college twenty-some years ago," Julia put in. "You haven't verified Wyatt's credentials or talked to his past clients. You've taken him at his word and in good faith. But what if he intends to persuade you to sell Heartstrings to him so he can sell it to other investors?"

"He may be trying to make a profit for himself," Lana added. "What if his generous offer to refurbish the ranch is part of the ploy to get you to sell out to him at a modest price? How can you be certain his intentions are honorable if there is no contract and no confirmation of the auction date?"

Elizabeth had to admit Julia and Lana were presenting reasonable concerns. It was true that Wyatt hadn't offered information about the sale, but Elizabeth had been reluctant to pose questions. She had vowed to live in limbo, ignoring the future. Not to trust Wyatt's ethics and intentions was to criticize her own ability to judge character.

God, what if she had been taken in by his charming smile, his refreshing sense of humor and her own awakened desire? Good grief, she could turn out to be just like Irene Truman!

No, Elizabeth hurriedly assured herself. She had the utmost faith that Wyatt had her best interest at heart. He had volunteered to assist in spiffying up the ranch for the auction to increase its value. He had given her gifts to express his affection.

Or delude you into trusting him? This strange new voice caused Elizabeth to wince.

Elizabeth rejected the negative thoughts Lana's and Julia's accusations had inspired. She was not going to let her daughters' suspicions distort her thinking. They were on the same psychological campaign they'd started the previous weekend. They simply didn't approve of Wyatt because they perceived him as a threat to their own relationships with their mother.

Elizabeth glanced sideways when the front door opened, announcing Wyatt's arrival. He had showered and changed into clothes that testified to his expensive tastes.

"I'm going into town for the evening," he informed Elizabeth before turning his attention to Lana and Julia. "I'm sure you young ladies would like to visit with your mother."

When he walked off, Julia muttered under her breath. "I'll say one thing for him, the man does put up a good front, doesn't he? He knows we're here to discuss this fling you're having, but he is so confident he has his hooks in you that—"

"Julia!" Elizabeth snapped.

"Yes, *Julia*," Lana added, flashing her sister a disparaging glance. "Why don't you go inside and find some scissors so you can trim your tongue."

"Fine, Miss Psychology, you try to reason with Mother. Maybe you can convince her there is legitimate cause for doubt here. And perhaps by the time our dear friend Wyatt offers to buy Heartstrings because he has become *so* fond of the ranch, Mother will demand that he pay a premium for the property instead of practically giving it away because she has the hots for him."

Julia glared at her mother as she reached for the doorknob. "I'm glad Dad isn't around to see this. How can you betray him—?"

"Betray him?" Elizabeth blustered, at the end of her tether. "You want to talk betrayal, do you? All right, now that you are both old enough—and supposedly mature enough—to deal with the truth, maybe you should know why your father didn't have time to spend with his family. There wasn't just another woman in his life, there were other women. One of them was his supposed secretary who—"

"How dare you tarnish his good name when he isn't here to defend himself!" Julia had erupted like Old Faithful.

"How dare you accuse Wyatt of misconduct when he isn't here to defend *himself*," Elizabeth countered. "If you want to discuss my being used for ulterior purposes, consider how I felt when I learned your father mortgaged Heartstrings without consulting me so he could expand the ranch operation during strained economic times. Ask me how I felt about this being the place he came back to after he'd entertained other women all evening."

"Dad would never do such a thing," Lana declared. "He was devoted to you."

Elizabeth gave her dark head a shake. "He was married to me, but his devotion lay elsewhere." Weary, she stood and sighed heavily. "And now if you will forgive me for leaving during your unannounced visit, I have to go to work. The money I make goes to paying off the debts your beloved father left behind—the ones he took on without discussing them with me. In case you're wondering, I'm not moonlighting at the Tall Grass Prairie Cafe to amuse myself. The next payment is due next week. If you doubt *that,* too, call Donna Henderson at the bank and ask her about the interest due on the improvement loan. Then ask her whose name is on the original contract—the one I inherited."

Julia watched her mother disappear into the house before turning a disgruntled frown on Lana. "Don't believe her. She's trying to confuse the issue and leave us questioning what's truth and what's fiction. Wyatt McKenney is the culprit here, but Mother doesn't want to admit it. She's defensive about the man who has bedeviled her."

While Julia stalked back to her car and left in a rush, Lana proceeded at a calmer pace, trying to sort out the emotional ramifications rationally. She evaluated the social and psychological levels in this complex situation, since it was her nature to gather data and determine how stimuli affected instinctive responses. She did realize, however, that she had relied upon a few unsubstantial conjectures in order to leapfrog to conclusions about Wyatt McKenney.

Although Lana was not positively certain her assumptions were accurate, she wasn't certain they weren't. As for Elizabeth's revelations about Bob Sutton, she found herself too emotionally tied to her father to want to see his memory tarnished.

Ah, emotion, Lana mused as she drove away. The befuddling factor that discredited hypotheses and conclusions. What if she and Julia were wrong about their father and about Wyatt McKenney?

And what if they weren't?

She vowed to sift through her textbooks, searching for similar behavioral patterns that might apply to her mother's case. This was a sensitive, complicated situation, involving midlife crisis, threatened self-image and counterphobias. The romantic involvement that might not be exactly what it seemed to Elizabeth was an additional complication. Julia's explosive nature had compounded the difficulties, and now Lana was about to blow a mental fuse in trying to sort everything out.

She slumped behind the wheel and switched on the radio. She simply was not in the mood to plow through the social dynamics. She preferred to listen to Garth Brooks croon about having friends in low places.

She considered how she would react to having Wyatt McKenney on *her* place—Heartstrings—intending to sell it for his own per- sonal gain. In truth, she thought she'd be very surprised to learn McKenney was on the up and up. His kind probably made a habit of singling out and seducing lonely widows before leaving them to gather up the pieces of their broken hearts while he trotted off to the bank to deposit his profits.

Chapter Fifteen

Elizabeth rolled over on her side, her hand instinctively moving to the empty space beside her. She glanced at the digital clock that glared in the darkness. After returning from work she had collapsed onto the bed and slept soundly for over an hour.

Headlights flashed against the windows and lanced off the walls, indicating Wyatt had returned from wherever he had spent the evening. She waited, expecting to hear footsteps approach, but there was silence. After several minutes she went looking for him.

Through one of the wide living-room windows Elizabeth saw his familiar silhouette. Perched on the bench on the portico, his long legs stretched out in front of him, he stared down the moonlit slope.

Elizabeth debated disturbing his reverie, wondering what thoughts were running through his mind. After Lana's and Julia's less than cordial attitude toward him, she wouldn't blame him if he packed up and returned to the City. Her daughters had made it clear that they didn't approve of him or appreciate his intrusion into their world—and into Elizabeth's life.

Mulling over Lana's and Julia's accusations, Elizabeth studied Wyatt's striking profile. True, he had been hesitant to discuss his past, his "other life." He had been very careful about keeping these two weeks a separate entity.

Of course, he *was* on vacation, she told herself when her daughters' wary suspicions began to hound her. He was not the shyster Lana and Julia made him out to be. He was caring and considerate, fun loving and wildly passionate—also successful, competent and trustworthy.

Elizabeth was *not* going "middle-age crazy" by following her heart and succumbing to this compelling attraction. She was mature enough—experienced enough—to know what she appreciated and wanted in a male companion. Perhaps she wasn't as worldly and well traveled as other women, but she was a reasonably good judge of people.

She had her two daughters pegged, didn't she? Know-it-all college grads who were not yet experienced enough to realize how much they *didn't* know about life. Their overprotectiveness had been activated because they perceived Wyatt as a threat to a structured re- lationship with their mother. They were being selfish by objecting to his presence, even though his nearness had a calming, satisfying effect on Elizabeth.

Wyatt was a man of character and honor, not a grifter scheming to bleed her emotionally and financially. And if those two troublemakers didn't stop trying to plant suspicions in her head, leaving her waiting for Wyatt to make a crucial mistake, she was going to knock their heads together! Elizabeth knew she was happier than she had been in years. Did Lana and Julia begrudge her that after all the sacrifices she had made for them and for Heartstrings?

She drew in a cleansing breath and opened the door to join Wyatt on the portico. Where the Heart-Stays, she mused. That was where she wanted to be. Wyatt was where her heart resided, and the rustic cabin in the wooded valley would remain her touch with tradition and heritage. She would keep it, that sym-

bol of stability. And she would have precious memories of her
time with Wyatt McKenney.

"Bet?" Wyatt glanced over his shoulder when he heard the
creak of the door. His breath froze in his chest as she floated
toward him like a vision—wearing absolutely nothing but an
impish smile. He wondered what would happen if Elizabeth
wandered outside his condo in the City—stark naked. She
would draw considerable attention, not to mention charges of
indecent exposure at OKCPD, he predicted. But out here, on
this isolated ranch where the night sky spanned forever and
tranquillity was the rule rather than the exception, Elizabeth
was free to do exactly as she pleased. It pleased Wyatt immensely that she was so uninhibited.

Pleasure and sudden arousal struck Wyatt as he watched
Elizabeth amble toward him, her lush body bathed in stardust
and moon shadows. He experienced a sense of relief that she
wasn't avoiding him. He knew Lana and Julia had come to
plead with their mother, to caution her against trusting him.
Wyatt had wanted to tell those two young females what was
what, but he knew it wasn't his place to interfere. Elizabeth
had made it known the previous weekend that she intended
to handle her family without dragging him into the conflict.

He knew he had to be more honest with Elizabeth. He
needed to disclose his true intentions, to explain himself so
there would be no misconceptions. But he had his own concerns to resolve, his own decisions to make. He had to know
whether she believed in him, despite her daughters' constant
warnings, despite the turmoil of losing Heartstrings and entering a new phase of her life.

Perhaps he shouldn't have been testing her the way he was,
but he had become suspicious and cautious over the years. Bad
experiences did that to a man, especially when he'd acquired
a great deal of wealth. Wyatt was searching for his own truths,
just as Elizabeth was searching for hers—with too damned
much help from Miss Amateur Psychiatrist and Miss Testy
Temperament.

Wyatt reached out his hand, drawing Elizabeth onto his lap.

"Mmm . . . I would've been back hours ago if I'd known I'd meet with such a *skin*tillating reception."

Elizabeth cuddled up against him as he nuzzled his chin against her shoulder. She didn't ask where he'd been or with whom. There was no alien scent clinging to him as there had been so many nights when Bob returned with his conjured excuses.

"If I'd known my reception would be well received I wouldn't have fallen asleep waiting for you," she murmured, pressing a light kiss to his clean-shaven cheek.

"That explains why you didn't have time to put on The Apron tonight," he said with a husky chuckle. "I like this outfit much better. It looks exceptionally well on you." His hand glided over her thigh, brushing her hip lightly before scaling her ribs to encircle the peaks of her breasts. "But I like you best of all when you're wearing nothing but me . . . and I'm wearing only you."

Elizabeth trembled at his tender touch, the caressing tone of his voice.

Paradise. Heaven on earth. That was where she was—and where she would remain just one more night. Tomorrow evening she would be driving off to the City to see what life was like in Wyatt's world. Then her sweet dream would end and she would have to deal with reality. But for tonight, they were alone in a galaxy of twinkling stars, caressed by whispering breezes and the light of a full moon. She had been granted another shining moment to add to her collection of unforgettable memories.

The thought prompted Elizabeth to tunnel her fingers beneath the buttons of Wyatt's Western shirt, feeling his muscled flesh relax beneath her inquiring fingertips. She would long remember how he felt, the appealing scent of his expensive cologne, the intoxicating taste of his kisses. Her senses had memorized him so well that she could close her eyes and feel his dynamic presence, hear the rich, resonant sound of his voice.

Heart-Stays, she thought as her hand swept over his chest

in an adoring caress. Her noble clan of ancestors had firm beliefs about being true to one's self and to what they deemed important. The heart, according to tradition, could find its own peace when given free rein. The soul of one's existence was the *knowing*, the *feeling* of absolute contentment. Elizabeth's heritage had kept her attuned to the very essence of life. She understood and accepted that innate feeling of belonging, of knowing what she needed and wanted. The remote cabin by Bird Creek was her soul, and Wyatt McKenney was her heart. Perhaps it was too late in life to fully enjoy her heart's desire, but at least she knew what it was. Some people never recognized what they really wanted and needed to enjoy inner peace. She trusted this deep-seated feeling, trusted this man, even though those around her were suspicious.

When Wyatt's hands and lips began to work their sensual magic on her body, Elizabeth let herself go, savoring his worshipping touch, longing to touch him in return. Flames seared her, smothering Lana's and Julia's words of caution.

There was only here and now. Only Wyatt. This was the only reality Elizabeth wanted or needed. The future was for young dreamers, those who were dissatisfied with the present. She was more than content. She lived and breathed for each marvelous moment that created its unique eternity.

"I love you . . ." she whispered as she arched into his caressing hand and felt the hard evidence of his desire straining against her.

Wyatt's muffled groan was his only response to her softly uttered confession, but she wasn't expecting a reply. Her affection was freely given, unconditional. She loved, asking for no obligatory assurances, no promises. She spoke of what she felt, of what she wanted Wyatt to recognize as basic truth— passion embroidered with selfless love.

His hands and lips whispered over her flesh with deliberate care, sensitizing every inch of her. His thumb teased her beaded nipples before he took each peak into his mouth and suckled gently. His caresses descended down her abdomen while he feasted on her, drawing one breathless response after another. His fingertips traced her softest flesh, savoring the warm nectar within.

She burned for him like a sweet, splintering fire and he longed to share her every sultry response, to feel her caressing him in every way imaginable. Her words had overwhelmed him, her generous yielding of passion stole his breath away. Wyatt wanted all of her, cherishing each splendorous moment until this obsessive fire burned itself out—temporarily.

"I need you," he rasped as he shifted her down beside him, still holding her intimately in his hand. "I want to taste you . . ."

Ripples of maddening pleasure swept through her as he nudged her legs apart and knelt before her. She arched upward as his lips grazed her aroused flesh and his hands whorled over her belly and thighs. His moist breath skimmed her as his thumb trailed lower, dragging another ragged moan from her parted lips. He delicately traced her with the heat of his tongue, sending pulsations spiraling through every fiber of her being, leaving her ablaze with tortuously sweet sensations that throbbed in frantic rhythm with her heartbeat.

Wyatt heard her soft gasp, felt her body shimmering around his lips, his fingertips. He wanted to give her every pleasure, to offer her the sun, as she was offering it back to him in a secret caress. Need vibrated through his body like a jackhammer as he touched her, tasted her. She was communicating with him in a sensual language that defied words and confounded thought. There was only indescribable pleasure that multiplied with each passing moment, each cherishing kiss and delicate caress.

He ached to give her more of the soul-shattering ecstasy that riveted him when he felt her body tremble in uncontrollable response. He wanted to feel her melting on his lips, his fingertips; shivering from a heat so intense and consuming that her life seemed to begin and end with his loving touch. He wanted to hold her suspended until he joined her in paradise, sharing passion's wild release, feeling tumultuous sensations diverge until they colored the night like glistening diamonds—each one a symbol of fiery pleasure given and shared.

"Wyatt? No . . ." Elizabeth caught her breath when immeasurable need burgeoned with each frantic pulse beat, doubling, tripling itself until it completely engulfed her, shaking the very foundations of her soul. "Not like this . . ." she whispered as ecstasy drenched her. "Not without you . . ."

Wyatt crouched before her and peered into her shadowed face, seeing passion etched on her beguiling features. "Yes, like this," he whispered as he unzipped his jeans. "And *with* me, too—all over again . . ."

He guided her quaking body to him, just as she had drawn him to her the previous night when she sent him out of his mind with the maddening want of her.

He came to her as gently as the wind whispering through the breezeways of Heartstrings, bracing a hand on the back of the bench, lifting her to him before slowly guiding her away. He teased her with his thumb with each penetrating stroke of his body, rocking her, loving her with the gentlest touch until her every breath was his name, until he felt her contracting around him, calling for him to share the phenomenal rapture of a passion defined only by their combined existences—one heart beating for the other in a melody as ageless as time immemorial.

Sensual flames engulfed Wyatt as fervent desire claimed his mind and body. He felt her melt and match each thrust until they were clinging fiercely to each other, tumbling through space like a meteor consumed by its own intense heat. Passion pulsed through him in reckless release, the jolt so electrifying that it seized him, transformed him, held him suspended in sublime infinity.

In the aftermath of ineffable passion, when Wyatt could breathe again and could remember why it was vital that he did, he opened his eyes to note exactly where they were. A shaky burst of laughter sprang from his lips as he stared down at Elizabeth who was still holding onto him as possessively as he was holding onto her.

She grinned and moved provocatively beneath him. "Very satisfying," she said, her voice raspy with fulfilled desire. "But hardly what I would call amusing. You and I must have different concepts of what lovemaking is supposed to be."

"I was just thinking that most people our age only do this sort of thing in a soft bed."

"Then I would have to say that they have become mundane and *we* aren't *most people,*" she assured him saucily. "Besides, the whole outdoors is more spacious and spectacular than a confining room."

Yes, Elizabeth would think that, he mused as he eased away and sank down to draw her back onto his lap. She was born of a clan attuned to the very essence of nature. They revered it, being integral parts of the land and the creatures that inhabited it. Wyatt imagined Elizabeth would define paradise as a blanket in the grass, beneath a canopy of stars and an Indian moon that burned orange against the black of night.

"You, my dear lady," he replied as he wrapped his arms around her and nuzzled his forehead to hers, "could never be called mundane. Free spirits like you are much too imaginative and unusual."

She was silent for a noticeable moment. "I wasn't always like this," she admitted. "I simply settled and existed instead of embracing life. I was never offered much encouragement in that department."

"Your husband was every kind of fool if he didn't appreciate what he had," Wyatt whispered.

Elizabeth smiled ruefully, and her arms curled around Wyatt's broad shoulders. "Bob's spontaneity never included me. I always wondered what I could have done to hold his interest, or if he was simply reaching out to hold someone who hadn't lost her youth—"

He silenced her with a quick kiss. "Like I said, Bet. The man was a fool. You will always be vital, alive and young at heart."

Elizabeth set aside the thoughts of her disappointing marriage and squirmed seductively on Wyatt's lap. "Thank you kindly, suh," she said with her best Southern accent. "But as I recall, you were the one who showed up at dinner in nothing but The Apron. I considered that extremely provocative and imaginative."

He grinned wryly as he set her onto her feet and stood up to lead her into the house. "You may appreciate aprons at dinner, but I prefer the way you show up for bedtime snacks. Come on, Bet, let's be utterly conventional and go to bed."

"I'm not the least bit sleepy after my catnap," she informed him, giving him a playful pat on the back pocket of his Levi's.

He looped his arms around her waist as they headed down the hall. "Did I say anything about going to sleep?"

"No, I guess you didn't."

It was a long while later—at least an eternity or two—before Wyatt or Bet gave the slightest thought to sleep on their last night together at Heartstrings . . .

"You're still here?" Griff muttered from atop his horse.

"Afraid so." Wyatt stepped down from the one-ton truck in which he had driven Elizabeth to Griff's pasture. With Vic Henderson's help they had loaded the gas-powered pump and water tank in the bed of the truck as a precautionary measure before meeting Griff to burn dead forage from the pastures.

Although this morning was the time Griff had designated for burning, Wyatt wasn't sure it was such a good idea, and he had told Elizabeth so. The wind was gusting and then dying down, making it difficult to second-guess the direction a fire might take when fed by fluctuating winds.

Wyatt had questioned Jerry Patterson the previous night about safety procedures for pasture burning in this region of the state. After explaining the variables Wyatt wouldn't have thought to consider, Jerry had handed him a weather-test kit. Equipped with enough knowledge about the fire triangle and con-trolled burnings in the Osage Hills, Wyatt decided this was not the day to set a torch to dry weeds. When he retrieved the psychrometer Jerry had given him for testing, Griff burst out laughing.

"What are you planning to do with those thermometers, McKenney? Preheat the fire to perfect oven temperature and cook lunch?"

Elizabeth flung Griff a reproachful glance. "Jerry gave Wyatt the device to ensure safety."

"Seasoned ranchers don't need new-fangled devices to start a damned fire, Liz." Griff snorted derisively. "You and I have been burning our pastures for the last five years. Good God, you've got to be kidding!"

Griff watched in ridiculing disbelief as Wyatt set the two thermometers in a sling and swung them around his head like the loop of a lariat. After Wyatt had achieved sufficient air movement to take a reading, he used a slide conversion chart to calculate the relative humidity.

Griff sighed audibly while Wyatt charted his findings in accordance with the fire triangle—temperature, wind speed and humidity. "Since when did Jerry resign as the district agricultural nutritionist to become the resident meteorologist?"

Wyatt defended his long-time friend. "Jerry is very knowledgeable about all facets of agriculture and ranching. It wouldn't hurt you to follow his advice occasionally." He glanced up at Griff, giving him a stare that Elizabeth couldn't quite decipher before he added, "You might not be where you are now if you had listened to Jerry."

Griff's tanned face puckered in a scowl. "I've had just about enough of you, McKenney. I don't care what you and your handy-dandy weather-wizard kit have to say. Today is a good day for fast burns to clear weeds and warm the ground for new spring growth."

Wyatt disagreed. "No, it isn't. According to the chart, it will be difficult to contain prescribed burning. There's not enough humidity in the air to keep the fire moving along the ground instead of climbing into cedars and oaks, causing a smoke inversion that can clog the valleys for days."

Griff scoffed at Wyatt's technical explanation. They made

him look less than informed and that bruised his male ego. Worse, the past few days Griff had been under stress for more reasons than he cared to name, especially in front of Wyatt McKenney who had insinuated he knew more about Griff's business than he should. Griff wasn't about to let McKenney deter him. The man was worse than a festering boil, in Griff's estimation.

"Fine, if you don't want to burn Liz's pastures, don't." Griff grabbed a box of wooden matches from his shirt pocket and glanced defiantly at Wyatt. "As for me, I'm going to get mine ready for spring grazing."

With that, he urged his mount forward, tossing matches in the dry weeds as fast as he could light them, leaving a trail of fire behind him.

"That son of a bitch," Wyatt muttered as he watched the flames catch in a gust of wind, preheating the grass before it was consumed in a wild burst of fire.

Elizabeth backed toward the truck when thick smoke and intense heat whirled in her direction. Alarm spread through her as she saw the fire racing along the fence row to engulf the cedars that skirted the creek. In a matter of minutes, billowing smoke and leaping orange flames filled the tree tops, sending sparks flying above the ground, as well as upon it. A sense of impending doom settled over her when the crackle of limbs and the hiss of flames became the terrifying sounds of a fire-breathing monster blazing into life to feed and devour.

If Griff had intended to set a backfire, he had failed miserably. There was no way to control the flames that swept past the fences that joined the Lazy H with Heartstrings. True, Elizabeth had hoped to complete the burnings and give the spring grass time to carpet the pastures and improve the appearance of the ranch before the auction. But this! This could evolve into a disaster!

The wind kicked up again, sending fire balls arcing through the cedars that lined the creek. Elizabeth glanced sideways, gauging the direction of the leaping flames. When she realized where the holocaust was headed she gasped in horror.

"Oh God, no!"

Wyatt wheeled around to see the stricken look on her face. He wasn't familiar enough with the area to understand what had put her into such an upset state, but there was no question that she was distraught. She made a mad dash for the one-ton truck and its water tank. Wyatt barely had time to climb into the cab before Elizabeth floorboarded the accelerator and zoomed off, literally plowing through a closed gate in her haste to outrun a fire that was already blazing out of control.

"Not Heart-Stays," she whispered brokenly as she flew across the pasture at breakneck speed. "Please God, take everything else away from me if you must, but not that!"

Wyatt, who had braced his arms against the dashboard, his feet on the floorboard, jerked his head up to see tears streaming down Elizabeth's cheeks. His gaze darted to the inflamed creek and then swung to the hill in front of them. He had the sickening feeling that the far side of this particular hill was where the quaint cabin—forever burned in his memory after the night he had spent there with Elizabeth—was located. He had not, however, thought the place held such sentimental value for Elizabeth.

The look on her tear-stained face was living testimony to how much she cared about that cottage where her ancestors had lived. She was already driving like a maniac, trying to overtake the fire-breathing dragon that was swallowing grass and trees in blistering gulps. The unsecured water tank in the bed of the truck was slamming against one sideboard and then the other as she swerved around the rugged terrain, trying to miss jutting limestone boulders. Another jolt at high speed would launch the tank out of the truck for sure!

"Bet, slow down!" Wyatt barked, trying to break her hysterical trance.

"Not Heart-Stays," Elizabeth chanted between sobs. "Please, not Heart-Stays."

Wyatt did the only thing he could do; he held on for dear

life as the truck bounded over the limestone peak of the hill and skidded across loose rock. The truck fishtailed and soared down the slope that was fast becoming familiar to Wyatt. He could see the dirt path leading from the graveled road to the creek, the adjoining pasture he had trekked across with Elizabeth when she'd first taken him to the cabin.

"Damnation," she burst out when the flames raced over the rise and swooped toward the valley on a draft of wind.

If she could reach the cabin in time to douse it with water she might be able to salvage her ancestral home. The small cemetery on the hillside above the cedars was already dancing with flames, and Elizabeth's heart burned in her chest like a scorched tombstone. She could almost hear haunting voices calling to her from the hissing flames. She had failed to protect the relics and traditions of the Heart-Stays clan. The one sacred memorial of a proud people who had been shunted aside in the name of progress was being blackened with smoke and singed with flames.

Dear God in heaven, if she couldn't save Heart-Stays she would lose her anchor in a sea of uncertainty. Knowing she could keep the rustic cottage in the peaceful valley beside the creek was what had kept Elizabeth going these past two weeks. If she had Heart-Stays, she knew she could endure whatever fate dealt her.

Lana wanted to talk about having one's security and stability threatened, did she? Well, losing Heart-Stays was the last straw. Damn Griff for turning her peaceful sanctuary into a raging inferno.

Sobbing, Elizabeth slammed on the brake and launched herself out of the truck. She bounded up to the gas-powered pump in the blink of an eye, trying to prime it with frenzied haste, while casting apprehensive glances at the approaching fire.

The pump motor refused to spark to life, and Elizabeth cursed it colorfully.

"Here, Bet, let me do it."

She peered through her tears to see Wyatt beside her, his face grim. Sobbing, she allowed him to ease her out of his way

so he might adjust the choke. With two quick jerks on the
rope, the gas pump sputtered and coughed its way to life.

"You drive," Wyatt instructed. "I'll soak the walls and roof.
Keep circling the cabin, but if the heat becomes too intense,
we'll have to back off." He grabbed her hand as she lurched
around. "Don't take any dangerous chances. Do . . . you . . .
understand," he said slowly and succinctly.

"No," Elizabeth blubbered, beside herself with anguish. "I
don't understand why I should have to lose Heart-Stays, too!"

Chapter Sixteen

Wyatt braced one hand on the sideboard of the truck and grabbed the hose for the water tank. Streams of water dribbled down the wooden shingles and trickled off the eaves of the rustic cottage. Hurriedly, Wyatt turned the nozzle toward the porch as Elizabeth circled the front of the cabin and then veered west.

Smoke drifted toward the cottage like the cloud of doom. Wyatt practically ripped the buttons of his shirt in his haste to peel off the wet garment and tie it over the lower portion of his face like a mask. The damp cloth enabled him to draw a few cleansing breaths when the black cloud descended and hell's inferno followed after.

Elizabeth had already made four speedy circles around the cabin by the time he hammered his fist on the back window of the cab, gesturing for her to head for safe ground. For a moment he swore she was going to defy him, to make the supreme sacrifice to save Heart-Stays. He met her teary gaze in the window and saw the very spirit of her existence doused like a candle flame when she finally admitted defeat.

Wyatt slumped against the water tank as the truck bounced

across the rough terrain. He made a pact with himself, there and then, to see that Griff Hollis paid full retribution. That bastard had known damned good and well what might happen when he set his pasture ablaze so close to Heartstrings property. And very soon, Wyatt would know exactly why Griff had done it. He had placed a few calls the previous afternoon after his last clash with Hollis. Wyatt had the niggling feeling Griff was a man with ulterior motives. He wanted to know what they were, and after this last disastrous fiasco, he wanted revenge— pure and simple. Elizabeth did not deserve this!

The instant the truck skidded to a stop, Wyatt slung a leg over the sideboard and hopped down. He wanted to offer Elizabeth the compassion she so desperately needed while they waited to determine whether their attempt to fireproof the cabin with water had been successful.

She was sobbing when Wyatt opened the door to pull her into his arms. "It's all right, Bet," he murmured as he cradled her trembling body close.

"No, it isn't," Elizabeth whimpered. "It will never be all right again. You just don't understand . . ."

Wyatt grimaced and said nothing, lost to painful memories of his own past, forcing himself to think only of Elizabeth's needs during this traumatic moment that had broken her spirit. He had considered her to be exceptionally strong-willed, a fighter when it came to meeting difficult challenges. But this blow had knocked her legs out from under her.

It was as if someone were threatening to unplug her life support system, depriving her of survival. This cabin, Wyatt realized, was her source of strength and spirit. Elizabeth Smith Sutton had dissolved into tears when she risked losing the very roots of her existence. Though she had insisted that this cabin and the acreage surrounding it be excluded from the auction, Wyatt hadn't realized then just how important keeping Heart-Stays truly was to her.

He could feel Elizabeth quivering in his arms, feel her pulse pounding against his chest while she waited for the worst and prayed for absolution. If this cabin were spared, she would endure. Wyatt was sure she had convinced herself of that. And if she lost this secluded cottage in the once-peaceful valley that now raged with flames, her heart would be torn out by the taproots.

Elizabeth drew a deep breath and turned in Wyatt's arms, welcoming his support—physically and emotionally. She watched in grim resignation as the crowning fire leaped from the peak of one cedar to the next, watched the underbrush explode in flames. A gust of wind sent another wave of heat rippling around the cottage, uplifting debris that danced in fiery destruction.

Elizabeth held her breath when smoke rolled over the cottage and swirled skyward. The time of reckoning had come . . . and she couldn't stand to watch!

"Oh God, please!" she wailed as she lurched back around to bury her head against Wyatt's sturdy shoulder.

Her clenched fingers dug into his taut muscles, her rigid body was plastered to his. Her nails scored his bare shoulders while she whispered chants to the powers that be.

The wind died down in the aftermath of a fierce gust, and the flames followed their course along the underbrush that lined the creek, burning all the way to the water's edge. Fire seared grass and limbs, crackling and popping as it consumed what had once been the habitat of quail, wild turkey and deer.

But the rustic cottage in the very soul of Heart-Stays country stood like a monument amid the charred remains and smoldering coals. Trees, once evergreen and now black, reminded Wyatt of gnarled, crippled hands reaching toward a smoke-filled sky.

Elizabeth mustered her nerve and glanced sideways. Her ragged breath caught at the dispiriting sight of naked branches scorched by devastation. Her spiritual haven was in ruin, save for the antiquated cottage standing in a haze of smoke. The very heart and soul of her ancestry had survived, awaiting the rebirth of spring. It would be years before sheltering trees would shade the land along the creek, but there would still be peace, the knowledge that all had not been lost.

"Bet?" Wyatt watched, concerned, as Elizabeth shrugged out of his arms and strode away, as if called by silent voices that only she could hear.

In the distance a siren whirred, and dust billowed along the gravel road to the south. Wyatt presumed someone had called the fire station in Pawhuska. He doubted it was Griff. More than likely Vic had seen the towering cloud of smoke and sought reinforcements. Wyatt wondered how many acres this wildfire would consume before it met with obstruction. For certain, Heartstrings would be plagued with a black eye until bulldozers could rake away the charred remains.

By the time Wyatt caught up with Elizabeth she had ambled through the gate of the cemetery located on the rise overlooking what had once been a peaceful valley and tree-lined creek. She now crouched beside a sooty mound of stones, staring pensively at the small plaque beside it.

Sensing a presence behind her, she glanced back, allowing Wyatt to see the fresh tears that swam in her eyes. "My great-grandfather lost his tree," she murmured.

Wyatt's brows furrowed in a bemused frown. "I'm sorry, Bet. I don't understand the significance."

She wiped away tears with the back of her hand and came to her feet, gazing down the blackened hill to the creek. "One of the sacred customs of the Osage was Sending Away the Spirit," she explained in a wobbly voice. "The fourth day after the death of a warrior, a strong, sturdy tree was selected and a portion of the bark was cut away. The bare trunk was stained red to commemorate the man's passing spirit. The tree was bidden to travel with the God of Day on its endless journey. The evergreen was a life symbol, for the Osage sincerely believe that death is the beginning of a glorious, never-ending life."

Wyatt could think of nothing appropriate to say, and so he said nothing at all. He simply waited until Elizabeth strode toward the truck. She was coping with her loss pensively while he was asking himself how many different ways he could murder Griff Hollis without getting caught.

Damn that arrogant son of a bitch, Wyatt fumed. The man

refused to listen to reason. Although it was understandable that Griff wanted to ridicule the intruder who had become his rival for Elizabeth's affection, Wyatt couldn't fathom why the man would go to such foolish extremes. What had Griff proved today? That he was the most bullheaded bastard in Osage Hills—or what was left of them after he'd practically burned the place down!

Well, Griff Hollis was going to discover that he had roused a sleeping lion. Hollis hadn't endeared himself to Elizabeth with this stupid stunt; he had alienated her. And Wyatt was prepared to hold a grudge on her behalf, even if she felt charitable.

He sighed heavily, knowing she probably did. Heart-Stays had survived the holocaust. Elizabeth was prepared to be content with that.

But Wyatt wasn't . . .

"Are you all right? What the devil happened?" Vic questioned when the truck pulled into the driveway. "I called the fire department when I saw smoke rolling down the hills."

As Wyatt had predicted, Heartstrings had suffered a noticeable black eye from Elizabeth's pyromaniacal neighbor's tossing of lighted matches left and right. Though Griff had set a backfire, it had shot off in the wrong direction . . . or had it? Couldn't prove it by Wyatt.

Vic was still yammering while Elizabeth and Wyatt climbed down from the truck. "Did you see the swath that blaze cut before the fire trucks could cut off its source? If they hadn't foamed the timber, the flames would be all the way to Big Heart by now!"

Elizabeth reached down to absently pat the dog that trotted up to greet her, and then she ambled toward the house to shower and change. The smell of smoke evoked an unpleasant memory she was anxious to escape, even though she knew the sight of charred trees and pastures would remain with her for weeks to come.

"Is she okay?" Vic questioned after Elizabeth was out of earshot.

"No, she almost lost the cabin she's so attached to," Wyatt said grimly. "We were planning to leave tonight for the City so I can conduct an auction. But I think it's best if we take off as soon as I can convince her to go. Will you hold down the fort until Julia and Lana get here?"

"Sure, I'll tend to whatever needs to be done," Vic assured him. His gaze drifted northwest. "This fire didn't barbecue any corralled beef, did it?"

Wyatt gave his sooty head a shake. "The cattle weren't in its path. Griff—The Torch—Hollis managed to miss them."

Vic frowned. "Griff did this?"

"All by himself," Wyatt grunted sourly. "Nice guy, your neighbor. With friends like him, there's no need to worry about attacks by hostiles."

When Elizabeth emerged from the shower, having had another good cry while she bathed, Wyatt was perched on the edge of the bed. "Bet, I want you to come with me, right now. I have some errands I really must see to before tonight."

Elizabeth wrapped the towel around her and gaped at him as if he were insane—or she was, she wasn't sure which. "Leave now?" she said hollowly. "Leave after—"

"*Especially* after," he emphasized. "There's not a damn thing you can do here except look at the eyesore and stew over it."

"You think out of sight, out of mind applies here?" She inhaled deeply and shook her wet head. "I think you'd better make this trip alone. You and I were only trying to postpone the inevitable anyway. You have your world and I have mine—what's left of it. Once all the arrangements for the auction have been made, you won't be coming back this way. And in time you—"

"Damn it!" Wyatt went into a temper.

Outside the window the dog barked, and Wyatt muttered a few choice oaths. Willfully, he marshaled his composure. The fire must have ignited his fuse, he decided. *Thank you Griffin Hollis—you bastard—wherever the hell you are.*

"I want these last few days with you, Bet," Wyatt continued in a calm voice that belied his inner turmoil. "And you need to get away more than you realize. We promised ourselves this time together. Vic offered to oversee the chores, and your daughters will be here to help him. And I thought you intended to call that vet Julia's been sparring with, to let them fight it out this weekend."

Elizabeth remembered telling Wyatt of her mischievous plan to request John W. Casey III's presence at Heartstrings while Lana, Brad and Julia were in attendance. The scheme didn't sound so amusing to her now, not after the place had practically burned down before the foursome could tear it down.

Yet, much as Elizabeth thought she needed to remain at Heartstrings, she wondered why. She didn't know—she truly believed Julia needed this time to settle her ongoing feud with her boss. If Elizabeth's instincts were correct, Julia and John had been skirting the real source of their conflict. And Elizabeth had anticipated this last weekend with Wyatt, seeing him in his own element. But after her world had come dangerously close to going up in flames . . .

"Bet, there's no way I'll be able to concentrate on my job this weekend if you're here. *No way,*" Wyatt adamantly assured her as he approached. His hands curled around her elbows, holding her at arm's length, demanding her full attention. "The chores will be done during your absence. Give us this time together."

Finally, Elizabeth nodded agreeably and tried to elevate her droopy spirits. "Okay, I'll go. I just hope you remember I'm not all that crazy about taking your Caddy. The seats in that darned thing practically hug you when you sink down in them. I don't like being caressed by a car."

Wyatt breathed a sigh of relief and grinned at her remark. Resilience. That was what Elizabeth Smith Sutton had going for her, among her other redeeming qualities. Her irrepressible spirit and sense of humor always came bouncing back, even if they occasionally needed time to recoup after she was thrown for a loop.

"That fact has been duly noted already," Wyatt confirmed. "You'll be relieved to know that I do have a pickup at home. You won't be sentenced to the curse of a luxury car for more than a few hours. I'll even sell the damned thing first chance I get."

"Shave the mustache *and* sell the Caddy?" she asked in feigned astonishment.

When Wyatt noticed that familiar sparkle in those luminous eyes that were so dark they shined like obsidian, life breathed back into him again. When Elizabeth hurt he bled, when she was hurting, he had the homicidal urge to bleed whoever had caused her hurt. Griff Hollis was dead meat. The next fire Hollis saw was going to be the blaze around the stake he was tied to.

Wyatt knew he was being spiteful. But damn it, the man deserved to pay through his upturned nose. Wyatt had never claimed to be perfect, however, when it came to Elizabeth he was fiercely protective.

"You can let go of me now," she prompted. "I said yes. No need to squeeze my arms off."

Wyatt unclasped his hands and stepped back a pace. "Why don't you call Casey III while I shower," he suggested. "I'm anxious to know if he accepts your weekend invitation."

So was Elizabeth. Of course, by now it might be too late. Julia might have quit again—immediately after being fired. The thought put a faint smile on Elizabeth's lips as she made a beeline for the telephone.

To Elizabeth's amusement, John W. Casey III accepted the invitation without question or hesitation. She'd expected as much. She didn't bother informing the vet that she wouldn't be around to referee any shouting matches. That would be Lana's department. The dear girl did so love to apply her psychological knowledge to resolving problems. But then, Lana might find herself up to her analytical neck in her own conflicts with Julia. It should be a most interesting weekend, Elizabeth predicted. The bee's nest would really be abuzz when Lana and Julia read the note Elizabeth left on the dining-room table, explaining her whereabouts.

Elizabeth inhaled a purifying breath and grabbed her suitcase to pack for the trip. She was not going to dwell on the near disaster. The cottage was safe—scorched but still standing. She was thankful for that. No matter what else happened, Heart-Stays would be waiting for her when she needed the tranquillity and sense of belonging it had always provided. And there, the memory of her time with Wyatt would also reside. The world could burn down around her—almost had— but within those walls was safety, security and serenity.

The view outside the rustic cabin had been marred by Griff's carelessness. He had been out to show Wyatt that he didn't need newfangled contraptions to tell him what to do and when to do it. And his defiance had backfired—literally. Elizabeth wondered when Griff would skulk over to apologize for his destructive tantrum.

She had been involved in enough pasture burnings to know that sometimes even the best-laid precautions went up in smoke. Containing fires was often difficult. On more than one ranch in Osage Hills flames had whirled off in the wrong direction. It was a risk everyone took, come spring.

Without burning, pastures were never as productive for grazing livestock. The cost of spraying chemicals on weeds was prohibitive, as were the restrictions and regulations the Environmental Protection Agency had placed on the use of these chemicals. It had reached the point where ranchers had to pass a test in order to acquire a permit to purchase pesticides and weed preventatives. Before long, Elizabeth suspected Uncle Sam's regulations would require weeds to be handpicked, buried six feet deep in environmentally safe containers which could only be purchased—at great expense—with yet another certificate that was signed, notarized and delivered in triplicate.

Elizabeth shook her head and chortled at her wandering thoughts. Very soon, she wouldn't have to concern herself with the battles ranchers and stockmen faced. She would be tucked in her cracker-box home, knitting sweaters for Damn It so he wouldn't catch cold when she took him for daily walks down car-lined streets before imprisoning him in a fenced yard.

Gawd, Elizabeth, why don't you depress yourself a little more while you're at it? Hmmm?

"I really do wish you would clam up," Elizabeth muttered at the ridiculing voice.

"What did I *say?*" Wyatt questioned behind her.

Elizabeth jerked upright and whipped around, feeling like a blathering fool. "I wasn't talking to you."

He glanced around the bedroom and laughed softly. "And my doctor thought *I* needed a vacation?"

Elizabeth snapped her suitcase shut and strode toward the door. "Let's get this long ride over with, shall we?"

"I'm so thrilled that you are anticipating my company," Wyatt teased.

"You, I can take," she assured him. "The *Caddy* I can leave."

Wyatt closed the door behind him and made a silent vow to keep Elizabeth so well entertained that she didn't have time to fret about the fiasco caused by her firebug neighbor. They would remember this weekend for a long time to come, he promised himself.

It was certainly going to have to last Wyatt for two weeks because he had to fly to Alabama Sunday afternoon before hopping a plane to Texas in the middle of the week. And thanks to his previous no-nonsense schedule he'd be flying off into the Wild Blue Yonder to touch down in Colorado for the National Cattlemen's Convention. He'd stopped the world so he could get off for two weeks. Now the carousel had cranked up again.

As they drove away from Heartstrings, Wyatt watched Elizabeth's gaze drift to the charred strip of land that lay before the blackened hill, spoiling what had once been a breathtaking view. He contemplated what she'd said about expecting him to follow his out-of-sight-out-of-mind policy with her. She was right, of course, he thought to himself. When she was out of his sight for two weeks, he'd probably go out of his mind.

Then they would both be talking to themselves in padded rooms—in some quaint little sanitarium for the middle-aged crazies of the world. They would be in their own separate rooms, of course. Lana and Julia would insist on that.

Chapter Seventeen

"Is Mother out of her ever-loving mind!" Julia spewed after reading the note on the dining table.

Lana scuttled over to retrieve the piece of paper. Having read the message on it, she laid it on the table, trying to approach the situation with her usual detachment. That wasn't easy.

"This is obviously another outcry for help, for our attention," Lana diagnosed. "We've been so busy that Mother feels unloved, unwanted and neglected. She hopes to find the affection that's been missing from her life by turning to Wyatt McKenney—no matter how artificial and temporary his interest in her might be."

"Thank you, Dr. Joyce Brothers," Julia sniffed sardonically. "Now that you've reasoned out the how-comes and what-fors, what are we going to do to resolve the problem?"

Lana tapped a well-manicured forefinger on the note. "Mother left Wyatt's phone number in case of emergency. The first order of business is to call and leave a message for her to get in touch with us. *I* will talk to her when she returns the call."

"I can deal with Mother," Julia muttered defensively. "I am, after all, the oldest."

"But not necessarily the wisest in this matter. You are too confrontational and reactionary. I keep telling you, we have to handle Mother with kid gloves right now. Giving up Heartstrings is a terrible emotional blow to her. I would very much like to see her come through this with her sanity intact."

"Too late," Julia declared. "Running off with that devious gigolo testifies to her instability. He's setting her up for the fall, I'm certain of it. This weekend, he'll wine and dine her and then he'll give her his spiel about wanting to buy the ranch. His contacts are probably circling around like vultures, waiting to swoop down and pluck up Heartstrings. Then Wyatt will swagger off with his wallet bulging."

"And matters will be all the worse for Mother," Lana prophesied. "She'll be beside herself with guilt because she fell for the scam and tried to degrade Dad to justify this fling. She'll be humiliated and left to find a new niche—with a meager nest egg—because she didn't sell out to the highest bidder."

"Good God, you should see the burned area from an airplane!" Brad groaned as he strode into the house unannounced.

Lana had left her car at the airport for Brad, and he'd raced to the ranch the minute he landed his plane.

"Talk about an ugly scar. This won't help the resale value of Heartstrings one bit. And worse, you have to drive through that burned area around the creek just to get here. It's a wonder the house and barn didn't go up in flames. If the wind had switched direction you might not have had a place to come home to."

Julia glanced at Lana. "No place to come home to," she repeated musingly.

Reality struck hard and swift. There had always been Heartstrings to come to when the going got rough in the outside world. Julia had made a habit of saddling up Chicago and trotting off across the pastures to collect her thoughts and rejuvenate her spirits. Coming home had been the cleansing balm that healed all wounds.

This was where she came running after her clashes with John W. Casey III. Just where was she going to go when she needed to escape after Wyatt sold off Heartstrings as if it were just another piece of property? To a cramped apartment like the one she rented in Bartlesville? To Lana's compact place in Skiatook? What a depressing thought!

Julia had to have breathing space. In that, she was a great deal like her mother. And so was Lana, beneath all that intellectual and psychosocial blather.

"Lord, I'm beginning to understand why Mother turned into a fruitcake," Julia murmured as her gaze swept the comfortable, homey surroundings she had taken for granted—until now. "I can't even imagine what it's going to be like not to be able to come back here."

Lana's dark eyes followed her sister's gaze around the room. Like Julia, she felt desperate, despite her attempt to remain objective. Some things demand subjectivity, Lana realized. Some feelings refused to be labeled and classified. The uneasiness in the core of her being shattered her sense of stability, caused emotions to bubble and churn, seeking release. She knew—without ever comprehending *how*—what her mother was undergoing. It was as if something very rare and special were about to be whisked away, and she was driven to fight back.

This ranch wasn't just Elizabeth's chosen line of work, Lana realized. It was her life, or it had been until she'd tried to substitute Wyatt McKenney's spurious interest in her for her love of Heartstrings. *That* was the crux of the problem, the cause of these reckless attempts to find new meaning and purpose. Once Elizabeth's emotional substitute vanished, she would be a rudderless ship adrift.

Lana glanced out the window, seeing the black strip of land that had been desolated by the fire. She couldn't help but wonder if Wyatt might have been responsible for starting the blaze that marred the view. That con man might have deliberately set the fire, hoping Elizabeth would agree to reduce the price of the ranch when he made his bid.

Bleakly, Lana stared at her sister. "We *have* to save Heartstrings, Julia. We both have stable incomes now. We have to secure loans so Wyatt can't get his hands on our ranch and Mother won't have to leave the only life she knows."

"I can't exactly call my job stable," Julia grumbled. "It's a day-to-day challenge, determining whether I'll be fired before I resign."

"Well, you're going to have to resolve your conflicts with your boss, and that's all there is to it," Lana insisted. "We're going to apply for loans to lessen Mother's burden. When she comes home, we'll assure her that we want to finance this endeavor. She'll have her life and her stability back, and we'll have the heritage she's battled to preserve for us."

"And I'll help in any way I can," Brad promised. "I've always loved this place myself. And when the two of us are married—"

"Married?" Lana echoed, still entangled in emotions she was having difficulty controlling. His abrupt comment had only made matters worse. She wasn't prepared to deal with that now! "We haven't discussed a permanent commitment and all its ramifications. I thought we'd decided to allow ourselves ample time to know and understand each other. This is not the time to discuss our future, not with this serious crisis to resolve."

"*You* decided we needed time," Brad muttered, offended that his informal proposal was being shunted aside. "I was ready to get married when I took the job with the aviation company in Tulsa, but all you could talk about was how you were going to save all your students from themselves."

Lana gaped at the man she thought she knew so well. "All this time I thought you were in total agreement with me. I thought we communicated our feelings and had no secrets. Why didn't you tell me what you were thinking so we could discuss it?"

"Probably because you would've analyzed him to death the way you do everybody else," Julia put in. "I've been wondering how long he was going to let you lead him around by the nose before he stood up to you. He's spoiled you rotten, catered to your whims. If you cared as much about him as you do about your amateur 'psychiatrics,' maybe this romance would finally get somewhere, just like Mother said. Brad has been in a holding pattern for a year, waiting to get runway clearance with you."

"Julia!" Lana huffed, her dignity offended. "What a cruel and disgusting thing to say. And who, I would like to know, gave you the right to speak on Brad's behalf? How can you possibly know what he is feeling? Have you been secretly envying our stable relationship?"

"Now wait a minute—" Brad was allowed four words, but he didn't get to finish a sentence before the two sisters were at each other's throats.

"Envy you?" Julia hooted sarcastically. "Only a snail could appreciate the speed at which you and Brad travel, getting absolutely nowhere. Envy you because you are so well organized and methodical? No way, Lana. Sometimes I wonder if the two of you set an alarm clock to determine when you should kiss each other good night. There's no spark, no spontaneity. Why would I envy something as dull as that?"

"Now hold on, Julia—" Another four words and Brad was interrupted again.

"Haven't you ever heard of logical and reasonable?" Lana demanded of her sister. "If you were intellectually inclined rather than emotionally wired, you might be able to settle into a nurturing relationship instead of flitting from one man to another without finding whatever it is you think you're looking for."

"And you need to give way to impulse occasionally," Julia smirked at her self-contained sister. "God, you probably even schedule your disagreements with Brad. If I were Brad, I'd be flying around, looking for someone to appreciate me instead of pick me apart to determine what makes me tick. Both of you need to get a life."

"I cannot believe you are saying these things at a time like this," Lana all but yelled—a first since her preschool years. "Mother is in dire straits and you are criticizing my relationship with Brad. As if you had a life, Julia. You can't even interact with your boss without instigating a fight. You're the equivalent of tossing a match into gasoline. If someone even looks at you the wrong way you go into one of your manic-depressive mood swings and the whole place goes up in flames."

"Lana, I think we need to talk—" Seven words! Brad was on a roll!

"Oh, shut up, can't you see I'm trying to deal with my neurotic sister."

Brad's eyebrows jackknifed and then flattened over his narrowed eyes. "Are you implying that *I* am less important on your priority list than your hair-trigger-tempered sister? Well, thanks one helluva lot, Lana. Maybe Julia knows me better than you do. I've been catering to you instead of saying exactly what's on my mind. Maybe I'd like to throw away the alarm clock and schedules and do whatever comes naturally for a change. And maybe," he added with a sneer, "your mother is the only one around here with any sense. Elizabeth is amusing herself instead of brooding and stewing over what tomorrow brings. At least she has today and all its enjoyments."

"Clam up, Brad," Julia snapped. "This is none of your business. You can't even handle Lana, so don't presume to understand Mother."

"And maybe you've got Elizabeth and Wyatt figured all wrong," Brad retaliated. "He seems like a nice guy to me."

"You would say that, being a man." Julia sniffed. "You men have a nasty habit of defending each other's flaws because they are basic characteristics of your gender."

Lana added her psychological two cents' worth. "Brad is not like other men."

"Oh, thanks." Brad scowled. "Just what does that make me? A eunuch? Well, I've got news for you, sweetheart, these physical urges you think I control with such ease have me taking cold showers."

"See there, Lana, I told you men were all alike," Julia piped up. "Brad's been deceiving you the same way Wyatt is deceiving Mother. You never really know what's on a man's mind until you light a fire under him to smoke out hidden truths. Brad's repression is a smoldering volcano. *He's* the physical and emotional minefield around here."

"The hell I am!" Brad objected. "You're the wacko, not me. No wonder you don't date anyone over a couple of months at a time. Since I've been seeing Lana you've gone through boyfriends like an elephant through sacks of peanuts."

"I'm looking for the right man instead of settling," Julia said in her own defense.

"Yeah, well, I pity the poor guy who *settles* for you."

"Bradley Phelps, I will not have you crucifying my sister. It is quite obvious that you are using her as a scapegoat to relieve the pent-up anger you actually feel toward me." Lana lifted her chin and stared him in the eye. "Come on, walking land mine, air your griefs on their true source," she dared him.

"Why? So you can psychoanalyze my comments and the subconscious emotions from which they sprang? No thanks. Julia's right. I belong in an airplane. At least I can get off the ground!"

"What is going on in here?" The voice came from the portico.

"Hell and damnation, what's *he* doing here?" Julia groaned in dismay.

John W. Casey III invited himself inside after the yelling died down. He wore an amused smirk that was directed at the feisty blonde whose blue eyes were spitting fire at him. "From the sound of things, you've managed to cause disruption at home as well as at the clinic. What did you do this time, Julia? Give injections of loco weed? I must admit I'm relieved to discover you wreak as much havoc on other peoples' lives as you do on mine. Is this the oldest child battling for control again?"

"I suppose you think you have my sister all figured out," Lana snapped at John.

"If I had her all figured out, I wouldn't have to gird myself up for battle every day before going to work with Miss Attila."

Julia glowered at the unwanted intruder. "Lana, Brad, I don't think you've had the misfortune of meeting my obnoxious boss, Ivan the Terrible."

Lana looked the tall, lanky vet up and down. "Don't tell me. Let me guess. You are also the oldest sibling of your family, hence your power struggle with Julia."

"Gawd, Lana," Brad moaned. "Don't start analyzing the man already. You don't even know him, except by reputation, and that from Julia's distorted point of view." He whirled around when Lana's head snapped up and she glared furiously at him. "I've had enough. I'm leaving!"

"Escapism," Lana called after him. "You're retreating because you feel incapable of dealing with difficult situations. In laymen's terms, one might say you were a coward."

Brad rounded on Lana, his face puckered in a thunderous scowl. "Go to hell. And take your neurotic sister with you." When Lana blanched and gaped at him as if he were a maniac, he expelled a snort. "How's that for spontaneity? And here's another impulsive shocker for you, sweetheart. You and I are finished, *kaput*. Find yourself another cadaver. I'm tired of being patient and understanding and at the bottom of your list of priorities. If I can't be *on top*, then I'll find someone who likes me in that position."

The door slammed shut; Damn It barked his head off, and Lana wailed. "Brad, come back here this instant!"

Julia watched her sister race out the door, her customary composure gone. She was yelling Brad's name as he roared off in her car. Julia's car threw gravel as Lana spun it around to give chase.

John stared out the spacious windows, watching the two vehicles speed off in a cloud of dust and then he studied the charred stretch of land that slashed the grand view in half.

"What did you do? Burn the place down during one of your temper tantrums?" he questioned.

"I thought I only had to endure your sarcasm five days a

week. I hope I'm getting paid overtime for this additional torment. Just why are you here?" Julia demanded to know.

"Your mother invited me for the weekend."

"Mother?" Julia parroted in astonishment. "Why would she do that?"

John grinned. "Maybe she likes me."

"Well, that explains it. She has developed exceptionally bad taste in men lately."

"I don't know about that. I like Wyatt McKenney."

"You would," Julia grumbled as she wheeled toward the back door. "If you're staying, then I'm leaving."

"Escapism," John taunted her, his gaze focusing, like radar, on shapely, denim-clad hips. "Besides, you don't have a car, *coward.* Lana took it."

Julia swung around and lifted her chin. "I have a horse. And from the back end, my horse bears a striking resemblance to you."

His gaze narrowed thoughtfully. "If you'd said that at the clinic I'd have fired you on the spot."

"Well, show some gumption, Casey III, and fire me on *this* spot. I'm tired of sparring with you and everybody else. All of a sudden my world is turning upside down. Nothing's going right!" she shouted at him before she stalked off.

"Julia, come back here, damn it!"

The speckled dog barked and scampered off behind Julia. John was on Damn It's heels, but his eyes were on the sassy blonde who always managed to get a rise out of him—in more ways than one. He asked himself if that was one of the reasons he picked fights with his temperamental assistant who looked as if she belonged at a model agency rather than an animal clinic.

The truth was, he liked the looks of Julia, liked to argue with her to sharpen his wits. He wondered if he would ever work up the nerve to tell her so. But then, a man never wanted to give too much ground to a woman like Julia. The inch he gave could turn out to be several miles of rough road . . .

* * *

Elizabeth stood in the middle of the spacious condominium in west Oklahoma City, studying the modern furnishings that reminded her of a sterilized emergency room. Everything had its place and remained in it—the glass-topped coffee table and end tables, the stiff-backed sofa and matching chairs. The only objects in the living room that had a warm appearance were part of Wyatt's impressive collection of Western Art. The paintings and prints by famous artists looked sadly out of place in this cold, austere surrounding that was more of a headquarters than a home. By his own admission, Wyatt wasn't here very often. Elizabeth could see why, too. Although the furnishings were expensive, they weren't inviting. This was evidently home and office, a place where business was conducted before bedding down for the night.

While Wyatt placed several calls in his office, Elizabeth stepped into the bedroom. Her gaze fell to the stiff brown bedspread and pillow shams. The room could have been situated in any number of motels. It was impersonal, showed no signs of life. In fact, if one could judge a man by his home, Elizabeth would have had to say she didn't know the Wyatt McKenney who lived here. The owner of this condo was nothing like the man she'd met at Heartstrings.

She had the inescapable feeling that Wyatt had simply existed here. There was no memorabilia to signify places where he had been or things he had done . . .

"It isn't Heartstrings, is it?" Wyatt questioned from behind her.

She turned toward him and smiled compassionately. "No, it isn't, not to me, at least. What is it to you, Wyatt?"

He heaved an audible sigh. "This is the place where I hang my hat on my way through town," he confessed as he glanced at his watch. "I need to pick up some flyers from the printers, meet with a prospective client and stop by the hospital to check on my fellow auctioneer before we dress for dinner. I'll be back in an hour." He dropped a hasty kiss to her lips before pivoting toward the door. "There are refreshments in the fridge if you need a snack."

Elizabeth watched him leave, pitying him. How could anyone sit down and relax in a place like this?

She wandered over to open the thick drapes, only to find herself staring at another set of brick condominiums, the two buildings separated by a lawn the size of a door mat.

God! She could never live like this, not after having five thousand acres to stretch out in. Her early, forced retirement was going to be a living hell! She couldn't knit enough sweaters to keep herself occupied. What in the world did she think she was going to do with herself day in and day out? Climb the walls without a ladder? For certain, she would have to apply for a full-time job. But she'd go bonkers if she was cooped up in a place like *this* with a view like *that!*

Pausing at the door of the office, Elizabeth studied the neatly organized desk and file cabinets. Only one picture hung on the wall. It was an aerial photograph of a farmhouse, barn and sheds. Wheat fields surrounded these structures, and cattle peacefully grazed in plush spring pastures. Elizabeth presumed the farm was the one on which Wyatt had lived during his childhood—the one he had casually mentioned in passing.

It niggled her that he was so closemouthed about his past. Why, she wondered, was he so hesitant to share his private thoughts with her when he was so open and giving in passion, so attentive and considerate when they were together? It made her think he was leading a double life . . .

She chastised herself. "Good grief. There you go again, letting Lana's and Julia's ill-founded suspicions undermine your thoughts."

Wyatt had done nothing to deserve her criticism, and she wasn't going to spoil their last few days together by interrogating him the way Lana and Julia thought she should. After he'd checked his calendar to confirm the auction date, the proofs for the promotions would be mailed to her. There was no great rush. She hadn't intended to sell until the spring grasses were lush and thick and the loan came due. There was

time left for Elizabeth to fully accept the fact that she was
leaving Heartstrings and that her love for Wyatt would become
no more than a sweet memory, broken only by occasional visits
before time and distance cooled the fires that now burned so
bright.

You should never have told him you loved him, she reflected
as she wandered around the massive office desk. It had probably made him uncomfortable because he was afraid she would
expect a permanent commitment. Still, it would have been
comforting if Wyatt had said he cared a little . . .

Careful, Elizabeth, that nuisance of an inner voice cautioned
her. *You know perfectly well what happens when you give and then
expect something in return. If you expect nothing then you can never
be heartbroken or disappointed. Be true to yourself and to Wyatt. You
told him how you feel. Don't play the woman scorned. Let your love
for him be enough.*

"God, you're a noble so and so," Elizabeth grumbled at her
other self.

*Better to give than to receive, especially if the giving is from the
heart.*

"What is this? A cliché festival?"

Inhaling determinedly, Elizabeth retrieved her suitcase to
change into the elegant black evening gown Wyatt had given
her. She was going to enjoy herself. While her daughters were
fighting it out at Heartstrings, worrying themselves silly about
their mother, she was going to be running around and having
the time of her life. She and her daughters had exchanged
roles for the weekend. They would stay home and fret, just as
Elizabeth had done during their teenage years.

This was her weekend to end all weekends, and she was going
to revel in every last moment of it!

"Lord, this place is magnificent." John Casey III stared
across the rolling pasture that stretched out for miles. "How
can you even consider giving it up? If I had Heartstrings I'd
hold onto it with both fists."

Julia swiveled her head around to peer at John's striking profile. "Do you really think so?"

John shook loose from his trance. "Do I really think so *what?*"

"Do you think this is spectacular, or are you just trying to be nice for once in your life?"

John nudged George up beside Julia's mount and looked straight into those blue eyes that danced with irrepressible spirit. "You should know me well enough by now to realize I'm not accommodating."

"You can say that again," Julia razzed. He had left himself wide open for a jibe.

For once John let her have the last word. When they were at the clinic, armed with surgical instruments, they made a practice of cutting each other to pieces for sport. But John didn't want to do that here. This was . . . different.

"There is something compelling about Osage Hills country," he admitted, his attention shifting to the limestone peaks that tumbled to the sprawling valleys below. "It's so peaceful it lures you into thinking you've found paradise, your private corner of the world."

Julia smiled and decided not to play the antagonist. For some reason she didn't feel as defensive and competitive around her all-too attractive boss now. She was more at ease on her own turf than she was in *his* clinic, utilizing *his* supplies, following *his* orders. Here, they were equals, a man and woman enjoying a remote area that appeared to be untouched by human hands—except for that blemished strip of pasture scoured by fire. Julia purposely avoided that section of the ranch when she went riding.

"Lana and I thought we could give up Heartstrings. We thought we had no sentimental attachment that couldn't be replaced with a few photographs and our childhood memories. But letting go isn't quite as easy as we'd figured," Julia confided.

"Mother is having a terrible time making the adjustment. And Lana and I can't do it either, even after we tried to convince Mother it was time for her to begin a new phase of her life. This ranch is part of what we are, and it's like tearing off an arm to lose it. This upheaval put Lana and me at each other's throats and caused her spat with Brad." Julia sighed heavily. "It feels like the world is coming apart."

John considered that comment, and he silently agreed. Heartstrings was wild and unrestrained and so was Julia. She was a free spirit. And a bit of a loose cannon, if ever there was one, he thought with a wry smile. He ought to know, since he had witnessed her explosion an hour earlier.

"There's too much heritage and history tied up in this ranch to let some streamlined cattle corporation move in and tabulate the property in terms of profit and loss columns," Julia said as she stared into the distance. "The Heart-Stays clan founded their original village here. This was the very pulse beat of a people who had once been free to roam over thousands of miles at whim.

"When other members of the tribe sold their allotted lands and tried to venture away from their heritage, as the whites urged them to do, my great-great-grandfather fought to preserve this stronghold. He bought up all the land he could afford and held this place together so that Heartstrings would become the enduring symbol of the Heart-Stays clan.

"The younger tribesmen would return for annual celebrations, longing to reclaim the old customs and traditions," Julia continued. "They came to regret giving up their piece of history. Lana and I don't want to make that same mistake. We owe it to our heritage to prevent this property from falling into uncaring hands."

John studied Julia while she spoke, noting the feeling in her voice. Her mesmerizing tone was doing crazy things to his pulse, not to mention other effects it was having on him.

It suddenly occurred to John that he hadn't wanted to understand Julia because he took mischievous delight in sparring with her. It amused him to set off her hair-trigger temper and watch the sparks fly. That was also very safe. Better to make war, not love with Julia. She sharpened his wits with her quick rejoinders, and she kept the clinic jumping. Before John had hired her—fresh out of vet school—the clinic was just the place John went to do the job he had been educated and trained to do.

He had the inescapable feeling that the impulse to go chasing after Julia—after he'd fired her and she'd stormed off—was the same one that had compelled him to accept Elizabeth's invitation to the ranch. He had reached the point where he wanted to do more than work beside Julia in the clinic, nettling her until those gorgeous eyes blazed and she gave back to him as good as she got.

It was becoming increasingly evident to John that instigating petty arguments was his shield against the crux of the problem. He felt drawn to that fire he sensed burning inside Julia. His provoking taunts were nothing but a smoke screen for feelings he was reluctant to expose after suffering first-degree burns in a love affair that had turned out to be painfully one-sided.

Despite his wariness of becoming seriously involved, John felt himself gravitating toward Julia while their horses stood shoulder to shoulder on the limestone peak. When Julia turned to stare at him, his gaze instinctively dropped to the lush curve of her mouth. The current of awareness that surged through him was worse than plugging himself into a two-twenty-volt receptacle. And when their eyes met at close range, John felt the earth wobble on its axis. He was about to cross over a dangerous line that could leave him vulnerable. He wondered if Julia was feeling the same crosscurrents of emotion while she stared back at him.

"If you don't want me to kiss you, you better tell me now," he said hoarsely. "Otherwise, I'm going to find the answer to the question that has been hounding me for months."

"I don't want you to kiss me," Julia replied, her voice crackling noticeably.

He leaned closer, his lips a fraction of an inch from hers. He stared into eyes as clear and blue as the spring-fed pond that glistened in the valley below. "Why not, Julia?"

She drew in a shaky breath and licked her lips. John inwardly groaned at the gesture that succeeded in making him even more aware of that honeyed mouth.

"I don't want you to kiss me," she burst out, "because I'm afraid I'm going to like it—damn it!"

As was his custom, Damn It barked when his name was called. When he romped forward, George and Chicago bolted sideways. John and Julia teetered off balance. Their heads thunked together and they had to scramble to keep their seats when the horses stepped around the dog that barged between them.

John jerked upright in his saddle. He told himself that he had been saved in the nick of time, that he would probably have come to regret the kiss. He also told himself that he was turning out to be a first-rate liar if he actually believed that baloney.

He glanced tentatively at Julia and groaned at the sight of her. The breeze had whipped her shiny blond hair around her face, as if it had been tousled by a lover's hand. The knit blouse she wore hugged the full swells of her breasts, revealing their beaded peaks beneath the clinging fabric. He stirred her as much as she stirred him and it showed—in both of them.

John's willpower caved in. He couldn't stop himself from reaching for her; he was tired of trying to pretend he saw her as nothing more than his assistant at the clinic. "Come here, Julia. I'm afraid I'm going to like kissing you, too . . ."

When his arm curled around her waist and he swung her into his saddle, facing him, Julia realized why she was so sensitive to everything this man said and did. This infuriatingly impossible man, who teased her every chance he got, had the uncanny knack of setting sparks to more than just her temper.

She was very aware of the lean columns of his thighs beneath her legs, of the breadth of the chest against her suddenly sensitive breasts. And sure enough, when his full lips slanted over hers and his arms came around her, hot sparks ignited an undeniable fire.

"Damn, I was afraid it was going to be like this," John rasped when he finally had to come up for air, hating the fact that he couldn't hold his breath for at least thirty minutes at a time.

Julia's arms settled over his shoulders. She tipped her head back and smiled impishly at him. "You'd better kiss me again, just to be on the safe side," she suggested. "We don't want to leap to any hasty conclusions."

John's grin affected every feature on his handsome face. "I've got news for you, little lady, there is nothing about the way we kiss each other that's anywhere near the *safe* side."

Julia's senses reeled when he bent her over his arm and stole the breath clean out of her. This was even worse than she'd expected. When John W. Casey III got down to the serious business of kissing, Julia was utterly defenseless. And for all the times she wanted to shoot the man for aggravating her, she suddenly wanted to kiss him to death! Who would have believed that the man she swore she hated was the one she was clinging to—as if she never meant to let go!

Chapter Eighteen

Elizabeth was introduced to so many people at the cocktail party held in one of Oklahoma City's posh hotels, she couldn't begin to keep the names and faces straight. She had received dozens of compliments on the sequined gown, but none of them meant as much to her as Wyatt's smoldering gaze roving over her like a warm caress.

Wyatt had been an attentive companion—for the most part. There were times when an associate dragged him away for a private conference, but he always returned to wrap a possessive arm around her or lean close to ask if she was still enjoying herself. And surprisingly, she was. Most of Wyatt's acquaintances in the horsey set were amicable and fun loving. There were, however, a few exceptions.

Elizabeth was approached by the worst of the lot after Wyatt had been hauled away by an oversize man with a bald spot on the crown of his head. She sensed trouble the instant the willowy, immaculately dressed brunette appeared beside her, an empty champagne glass in one hand and a full goblet in the other.

"So you're Elizabeth Smith Sutton," the woman said, a slight slur to her words.

Elizabeth smiled cordially. "Yes, I am. Nice party, isn't it?" she added for lack of much else to say.

The brunette's glassy eyes were wandering all over her, sizing her up. For what? Elizabeth couldn't imagine. She felt like a horse on the auction block, being appraised for strengths and weaknesses.

"I've attended classier parties." The brunette brought the glass to her lips and sipped freely. "But this is standard protocol, of course. Wining, dining and complimenting prospective buyers is part of the strategy to ensure they are full of self-importance before bidding at the auction."

"You are in the horse-breeding business, I take it." Elizabeth glanced discreetly around the reception room, wishing Wyatt would magically appear. The brunette was not Elizabeth's idea of a good time. Much too stuffy for Elizabeth's down-home tastes. Give her Irene Truman any ole day.

The brunette helped herself to another sip of champagne, diamond and ruby rings sparkling on her long, manicured fingers. "Yes, I'm in the business. This affluent widow dabbles in race horses and cutting horses to amuse herself. And of course, I own stock in the Remington Race Track and am on the board for the Quarter Horse Association."

Elizabeth didn't know whether she was supposed to applaud or curtsy before the brunette, who was her own biggest fan. She decided to shrug her off instead. "Because that amuses you, too?" she questioned teasingly.

The brunette obviously didn't have a sense of humor, despite her vast financial holdings. "You aren't one of *us,* are you?" she said, her nose in the air.

"No, I don't own race horses," Elizabeth responded, ignoring the haughty tone and condescending glance.

"I thought not. And I suppose Wyatt bought the dress for you. It looks like something that would suit his tastes."

Geez, who *was* this witch and *where* had she stashed her broom?

The statuesque brunette inhaled more champagne until she was holding two empty glasses. "You won't be able to keep him. I hope you realize that, Elizabeth Smith Sutton. I intend to have him, and I will be waiting to get him back when he tires of you. I don't doubt he will."

Elizabeth was thinking seriously about offering the vamp a glass of champagne—right in the face. But she restrained herself.

"Well, shit," Wyatt muttered when he glanced aside to see that Deidre Delaney had cornered Elizabeth. Of all the guests at the party this one Wyatt had promised himself Elizabeth would avoid. So much for good intentions.

"Excuse me, Alex. I'll be back in touch with you tomorrow." Wyatt zigzagged across the crowded room to rescue Elizabeth.

"There you are, darling," Deidre enthused.

Elizabeth was positively certain the brunette had at least two faces—one for prospective female rivals and one for Wyatt. Suddenly the vamp was all smiles and provocative charm.

"Hello, Deidre," Wyatt said in a neutral voice. "Thank you for keeping Bet company. More champagne?" He directed the question to Elizabeth.

"Please." Deidre thrust her glass at Wyatt and then turned him around, patting him on the tush as if it were a habit. "I'll keep Bet busy until you get back with my drink."

Wyatt muttered under his breath and strode off, though he had intended to draw Bet away to refill *her* glass.

"Sooo . . . tell me, how long has this fling of yours been going on?" Deidre slurred in question.

Elizabeth thought it over and decided she had two options. She could smack Deidre a good one or she could retreat. Retreat seemed the better part of valor, in this instance.

"Excuse me, Deidre, I think I'll freshen my drink."

When Elizabeth spun about, her gaze locked with Wyatt's. Halfway across the room, he rolled his eyes and shook his head, as if to apologize for leaving her in Deidre's clutches. She actually felt sorry for him. He looked more uncomfortable about the situation than she was.

"Sorry, Bet," he apologized on his way by her. "I'll be back in a second."

Elizabeth watched Wyatt hand Deidre her drink. When he tried to make a hasty departure, she grabbed his arm and brushed her well-displayed bosom against his elbow. Although Elizabeth cautioned herself against leapfrogging to conclusions, she suspected Deidre and Wyatt had been close. She hoped that Deidre had been during one of Wyatt's more indiscriminate phases. It was no compliment to be in the same category with that vampish lush!

A moment later, Wyatt returned, straightening the tie Deidre had been toying with. "If you're ready to leave, we can go any time."

Elizabeth smiled wryly. "What's the matter *dah*ling?" she asked with a wild flutter of eyelashes. "Afraid Deidre and I are going to have another chat?"

Wyatt chuckled at her playful antics and expelled the breath he swore he'd been holding for five minutes. "Yes," he openly admitted. "Deidre is an expert at leaving wrong impressions."

"Born troublemaker?"

"And then some," Wyatt muttered as he propelled Elizabeth toward the exit.

"Old girlfriend?"

Wyatt stared straight ahead. "Old wife."

His tone was so completely devoid of emotion that Elizabeth wasn't sure how to take the comment. She didn't know whether Wyatt was deliberately suppressing anger and hurt or if there really was no feeling left in him for Deidre.

"And you'd rather not talk about it. Right?" she predicted.

"Right," he said as he ushered her toward the car.

Elizabeth let the matter drop and sank down into the plush leather seat that molded itself around her like a glove. She was disappointed that Wyatt never mentioned his past when *she* confided the problems of her marriage. She believed in being open and honest. Wyatt obviously preferred to keep the doors to the past closed and locked. It made her wonder if she was going to be behind one of those doors that was never reopened.

Pensively, Elizabeth sat on her side of the car while Wyatt negotiated the traffic to reach the condo. Oh good, she thought. They were headed back to the sterile rooms Wyatt called home and she was supposed to forget all about her awkward encounter with Deidre, the ex-wife with an attitude and a desire to recover what she had lost.

How long ago had Deidre lost Wyatt—and why? Elizabeth wondered. As usual, Wyatt was keeping his own counsel, refusing to elaborate.

"It was over a long time ago," he said four miles later.

Well, that's a start, thought Elizabeth. She waited, wondering if her silence would compel him to continue without her having to come right out and pry.

Silence was a part of conversation, Elizabeth noted. When one party said nothing, the other usually felt obliged to fill in the empty spaces.

"Well?" Wyatt said after a tense moment.

Elizabeth smiled to herself. Now, what was it Lana called this classification of games in transactional analysis? Catapulting through *structural diagrams* to achieve the *social paradigm*—or something to that effect.

"Well, what is it you expect me to say?" she threw out a question in response to his question.

Wyatt grumbled under his breath. "You aren't making this any easier."

"I'm trying *not* to make it difficult for you."

"But you really would like to know what happened between Deidre and me," he speculated.

"Only if you want to tell me." Boy, she was getting pretty darn good at this, wasn't she? Lana would be so pleased.

"Are you trying to patronize me?"

"No, I'm being a receptive listener. Lana maintains that listening to what people *say* and *don't say* is a necessary requirement for good psychiatry."

Wyatt gave a crack of laughter and inhaled a cleansing breath, feeling the tension drain for the first time in a half-hour.

She glanced at him, noting that the tense lines that had bracketed his sensuous mouth and eyes had vanished. "Feeling better now?"

He veered down a side street and came to a complete stop. Without preamble, he reached over to pull Elizabeth toward him, despite her restricting seat belt. He kissed her hard and then slumped back in his bucket seat. *"Now* I feel better."

On that declaration, he reversed direction and pulled back onto the main thoroughfare to head to his condo.

Elizabeth sat there, reasonably certain that all Lana's psychoanalytic flapdoodle was a waste of time. If her daughter accomplished one damned thing by crossing levels of structural diagrams, she didn't know what it was. But then, she had received a chuckle and a kiss from Wyatt. He was apparently feeling better, knowing that she wasn't going to fly into a jealous rage because she had encountered his ex-wife. Still, Elizabeth couldn't help but be curious. That was only natural.

The minute Wyatt closed the door to his apartment, his thumb hooked beneath the spaghetti strap of Elizabeth's gown, gliding it provocatively down her shoulder. He gave the same attention to the other thin strap, lowering the black, sequined gown until it was gaping over her breasts.

When his palm slid over the dusky crowns, Elizabeth set her curiosity aside and yielded to the pleasant sensations pulsing through her. She wasn't going to have this weekend spoiled by insecurity or jealousy. This was her present, and she had vowed to revel in it.

"I love the way you make me feel when I'm with you," Wyatt whispered against the curve of her throat.

She noted that he hadn't said he loved her, only that she made him feel good.

Stop analyzing, she scolded silently. This is about making precious memories, not future plans. You had commitment once upon a time and realized it was a charade of empty promises and disappointments. Just enjoy Wyatt while you can. He's here with you, and that is all you need to know, all that ultimately matters.

Elizabeth reached up to push the black jacket from his shoulders. She then removed his tie. When his shirt joined the other garments on the back of the nearest chair, she raked her fingers across the broad expanse of his chest, evoking a quiet purr of masculine pleasure.

Wyatt's hand gently cupped her breast, kneading her sensitive flesh. "After this, being without you is going to feel like hell, because this is as close to heaven as I'll ever need to come."

Heaven, Elizabeth silently agreed as he took her lips beneath his. He touched her with such incredible tenderness that she was melting in his hands, beneath his persuasive kiss. Her body reflexively arched toward his caresses, sensation after sensation burgeoning until her breath came in ragged spurts. With deliberate care, Wyatt eased her from the gown and divested her of her undergarments, greeting every inch of the supple body that was revealed to him.

The night light illuminated the way to the bedroom that Elizabeth had found as impersonal as a motel room, but there was nothing cold about it now. It was the most intimate of places, and it held a quiet promise of the ecstasy to come. Elizabeth welcomed each wondrous moment, each familiar touch of his hands, his lips, his aroused body.

Wyatt crouched beside her on the bed. His hands flowed over each curve and swell like a tide sweeping over the shore, erasing all that had come before, leaving her hungrily craving what would come after. With each light stroke of his hand he sought out a sensitive point, reveling in her uninhibited responses, feeling her sensual pleasure intensify until it throbbed through him just as surely as if she had touched him. He wanted to feel her unfurling around him with each sensation that blossomed deep inside her.

He had never been able to take pleasure from Elizabeth without giving of himself in return. He had never experienced a woman the way he experienced her. There had never been anything remotely impersonal about their lovemaking, and there never could be, not when she was such a delicious treat to his senses that he virtually absorbed her until her sultry scent was a vital part of him.

Each muffled moan he drew from her challenged him to provoke another and yet another. He wanted to give her the heat of sunshine, to feel it diffusing through her. He wanted her to touch the stars, feel them shimmering through her body. He wanted his caresses to sear her like lasers until she burned so hotly for him that the pleasure spilled over him and made him burn just as hotly for her.

"Come here . . . *please,*" Elizabeth whispered urgently. Staggering pulsations were riveting her with each penetrating stroke of his fingertip. Ribbonlike streams of pleasure spiraled through her, intensifying, multiplying until they completely consumed her.

"Not yet, Bet, maybe not even tonight. Maybe not even until morning," he said with a seductive smile. "I can come only once, but you can fly away and return again and again . . . for both of us . . ."

His lips brushed over hers as his thumb circled her aroused flesh, his tongue filling the dewy recesses of her mouth, his fingertips penetrating her throbbing core with maddeningly tender precision. When he withdrew his hand from between her legs and traced her belly with the moist evidence of her desire for him, Elizabeth quivered beneath his feathery touch. He repeated the erotic gesture as his lips drifted down to skim the hard rise of her nipples.

Flames coiled in the core of her as he retested its silky heat with his fingertips. He then traced her inner thighs with deliberate provocation until for her all sensation centered on his stroking hand, until she breathlessly waited to see how many more ways he could torment her with incredible pleasure.

He suckled and tugged at her nipples until her nails clenched on his forearms. When he placed his hand atop hers and drew it over the pebbled peaks, then guided it to the flat plane of her stomach, he heard her breath catch, felt her body tremble.

"Wyatt?"

"Yes, Bet?" he questioned against the satiny curve of her hip.

"What are you . . . doing?"

He smiled against her skin as he took her hand with his on a journey of discovery. "Letting you feel why I enjoy touching you so much."

"I don't think—"

"Good." His tongue flicked between her fingertips as he settled her hand against her inner thigh. "Don't think at all, not when this is about feelings . . ."

Elizabeth's breath evaporated when his lips whispered over her hand and then his mouth moved over her, penetrating with an intensity that left her shivering. Dissolving beneath his intimate touch, she forgot to breathe when his lips skimmed her fingertips, sharing the warm rain of her own response. He made her so wildly aware of each bold caress, each sensual movement of his hands and lips that Elizabeth not only discovered how much he pleasured her, but how her fervid reactions affected him. He was taking pleasure in her body. She could feel his hand trembling above hers; was aware of the erratic rush of his warm breath as he seduced her into undefinable rapture.

"Oh, God . . . Wyatt . . ." Elizabeth moaned deliriously.

"Enough?" he questioned against her shimmering flesh.

"More than . . ."

His reply was a husky growl and the erotic flick of his tongue. Elizabeth came undone, whirling in sensations so vivid and intense that she cried out his name with each frayed breath. His hand stilled, his lips settled over her, waiting for her to drift down from the towering peak of splendor. And then he began again, so slowly, so tenderly each pronounced ache surged with aftershocks that held her suspended in wild splendor.

"Sweet mercy! You have . . . to . . . stop!" Elizabeth said on a shattering breath.

"I can't. I'm obsessed with making love to you," he admitted as he guided her legs farther apart with his knees. "I—"

When Elizabeth twisted away to fold her hand around his rigid flesh, Wyatt's breath lodged in his chest. Her thumb brushed the velvety tip of his arousal, circling him until she had summoned a silver drop of desire. And then she tasted him, teased him with flicking tongue and skimming lips.

She kissed the soft yet steel-hard flesh she caressed, cherishing his intake of breath and the quaking of his body. And when each raspy breath became her name, she drew away, giving him time to battle for the control she sensed he had come dangerously close to losing.

She knew him in the most intimate sense, she realized. She had discovered how to make him burn in her hands and on her lips. She had learned what pleasured him mildly, what drove him to the very brink. She had mastered his passion as skillfully as he had mastered hers. She could prolong each sensation, as if she were striking the delicate strings of a harp, making his masculine body hum. It gave her immense gratification to know that she could read him as she had been able to read no one else. And she fully comprehended what he meant about *pleasure given* being as satisfying as *pleasure taken*.

When she measured the throbbing length of his masculinity with her moist tongue, Wyatt swore he needed something to anchor himself to. His body arched toward her whispering kisses and evocative caresses, and his mind tumbled off balance. Thought was nothing more than the translation of sensation. All he knew was what he felt her doing to him. The seething needs she instilled in him took him to the very edge of desperation and left him dangling. And just when he was certain he could endure no more of this exquisite torture, she held him gently in her hand and waited for him to regain control of his raging passion.

When she teased him once again with her tongue, Wyatt made a ragged sound and squeezed his eyes shut against the hot chills that bombarded him. "Damn, Bet, I wanted this to last all night. I'm not sure I'll survive another minute."

"Challenge yourself," she lovingly teased.

"I already did . . ." His breath hissed out in pleasure more vivid than pain. He was being seared from inside out. White-hot sensations scored a burning blow, pulsing through nerve and muscle until he was literally shaking with intense need.

"Bet, no!" Wyatt gasped as passion billowed out of control like a wildfire sweeping along its devastating course to consume and devour.

And when his control shattered, she was there beneath him, guiding him to the answering heat of her own ardent need for him. His body covered hers as elemental abandon seized him. The world spun away in a dizzying blur, and Wyatt had nothing to hold onto except Elizabeth . . .

And she was all he needed, wanted . . .

He clutched her to him, reminding himself to be gentle, knowing he wasn't—couldn't be—when ungovernable sensations overpowered his mind and assaulted his body. He thrust forward, burying himself deeply, yet not deeply enough to satisfy the wild hunger that spurred him into a merciless rider.

When he found shuddering release, he was drifting in a dimension of space so far removed from reality that he was completely disoriented. A street light that was shining outside his bedroom window appeared to be the moon glowing against the fluffy clouds of heaven. The arms that lovingly held him and the soft words that broke the breathless silence were surely those of an angel.

He was dead, of course. There was no other explanation for the euphoric sensations that rippled through him. This was what the afterlife was like, Wyatt assured himself. This consummate sense of inner peace, this sublime and incomparable satisfaction. *Paradise found* . . .

"I love you . . ."

Elizabeth's soft words came to him like a soft echo. He really should move, he knew. He should follow that hauntingly sweet voice until he could find reality. But she had made love to him so thoroughly there was no going back to that impersonal room with just a dresser, closet and bed, not when he was perfectly content in paradise . . .

Elizabeth smiled to herself when she felt Wyatt slump against her, heard his rhythmic breath against her shoulder. She held him as he unconsciously held her while he slept. She savored their closeness in the aftermath of passion. For her, this was where loving really began. When desire had run its fiery course, she needed to hold, and to be held, tenderly. The weight of his body pressing into her was welcome. This was where she wanted him to be—not on his own side of the bed after his physical need had been appeased.

He didn't even have to say he loved her, for she had convinced herself that he did. She had lived with a man who had fallen out of love with her. She knew what that was like. This was not like that. Whatever the reason, Wyatt couldn't bring himself to say the words, but he *did* care for her. Maybe he didn't love her deeply. He did care, though. And even if Deidre was correct in saying that Elizabeth couldn't keep Wyatt for very long, she had his affection now. When he went back to his busy life and hectic schedule, she would take comfort in knowing that, for a time, they'd had it all.

She let go of the last cautious string to her heart and put her complete faith and trust in Wyatt. Despite Lana's and Julia's doubts, she was now certain he would never intentionally hurt or deceive her. He might be a man who refused to look back, but he was honorable and trustworthy just the same.

On that comforting thought, Elizabeth followed Wyatt into sleep, letting her dreams take up where reality left off . . .

Chapter Nineteen

Julia wore a path on the carpet, then checked her watch for the tenth time in ten minutes. It was after eleven o'clock, and she didn't know where her sister was. After pacing the floor for another quarter of an hour, she saw headlights approaching.

"Well, it's about time," she muttered to the room at large.

The door creaked open and Lana wobbled inside to plunk herself down on the sofa. Her dark eyes were glazed and when she expelled an exhausted breath, Julia was thankful there was no open flame nearby.

"You've been drinking?" Julia questioned in shocked disbelief. Lana never drank. She never did anything to threaten her high morals or distort her analytical thought processes.

"Brilliant deduction, Sherlock," Lana mumbled as she propped her feet on the coffee table. "They don't serve much soda pop at the Silver Stallion."

"The Silver Stallion?" Julia parroted. "Good God, Lana, that dive caters to the worst types in town! What are you trying to do? Get yourself mugged and mauled?"

Glassy eyes lifted, attempting to focus on Julia. "I was being impulsive."

"In a bar?" Julia howled. "That's not spontaneity; it's stupidity!"

Lana's left shoulder lifted in a shrug. "Nothing happened. Some big bruiser announced to the patrons that I was Liz's kid and if anybody bothered me he'd beat the shit out of them."

Julia bit back a grin. Her prim sister rarely uttered a foul word, either.

Lana's head swiveled to scan the room. "Where's the vet?"

"Taking a shower."

"I think I'll join him. That would be impulsive."

When Lana tried to stand up, Julia shoved her back on the couch. "You aren't showering with anyone. You're going to bed."

Lana's dark lashes swept up, and she set her chin at a determined angle. "I'm not going to bed until Brad comes back."

Julia heaved a sigh and knelt down in front of her sister. "Lana, he's obviously not coming back tonight."

Tears pooled in Lana's eyes, and her lips quivered. "He's not coming back at all—ever—is he?" she wailed.

About that time John ambled into the living room to see Lana fling herself at Julia, blubbering and sobbing. He watched Julia gather her sister in her arms and consolingly pat her on the back. For all Julia's sass and spirit she could be very compassionate with those she loved. She could also be very passionate . . . John halted that tantalizing thought before it left him smoldering.

"All this time I thought Brad and I had the perfect relationship," Lana slurred out. "I thought we understood each other. But he's just like the rest of them, isn't he? You were right, Julia. All men are bastards."

John smothered a grin when Julia grimaced and glanced at him over Lana's ruffled head. His brow quirked as he waited to see if Julia would confirm that.

"They're not all as bad as I thought," she replied, holding John's amused gaze. "Some of them have a few saving graces."

"Not Brad," Lana said between shuddering gulps. "He deceived me. He didn't express his inner feelings. He thinks I'm a boring prude! And after all the time I spent nurturing and analyzing our relationship, he walked out on me!"

"Do you want him to come back, Lana?"

"Yes, so I can tell him to go to hell," she spluttered.

"Maybe Brad is home by now. You could tell him how you feel over the phone," John suggested.

Lana twisted around to stare up at the sandy-haired vet. "Isn't there some place you should be about now? We don't need you here pestering my sister. You do a superb job of that at work. I can certainly understand why Julia dislikes you—"

"Lana," Julia said warningly.

It was a waste of breath. Lana's bottled frustration came bubbling out.

"My sister happens to be one of the best-trained, most knowledgeable vets in the state—the world maybe. She has the background and certificates to prove it. If you had any sense—"

"Lana—"

"—you would appreciate her," Lana continued without taking a breath. "Yes, she has spunk and grit and I wish I were more like her. You men just aren't impressed by a woman's determination and assertiveness. It just makes you defensive."

John made note of the fact that, even though Julia and Lana had been snapping at each other earlier, they were very protective of one another. Obviously they fought *with* each other on occasion, but they didn't hesitate to fight *for* each other.

When John didn't take the hint and leave as Lana thought he should, she staggered to her feet and glared at him through blurry eyes. "Where's the shotgun, Julia? I'll blow the bastard away, and you won't have to tolerate him anymore."

"No one is going to shoot anybody," Julia said reasonably. "John is staying the night."

"Not with you!" Lana railed. "Wyatt may have bowled

Mother over with his charming deceit, but I'm not about to let this—this jackass pester you!"

"He's not a jackass," Julia corrected.

"That's what you said the other day."

Julia flushed with embarrassment as she met John's twinkling silver eyes. "That was the other day. I've reevaluated my opinion since then."

"Why?" Lana glowered at John, who was doing his damnedest to keep a straight face. "Because he turned on his limited charm to get what he wants from you? Physical satisfaction and psychological control? Well, don't trust him, Julia. He's trying to manipulate you."

"I think you should go to bed before we both have to be treated for hoof-in-mouth disease," Julia muttered uncomfortably.

Lana thrust her shoulders back and jerked up her chin, very nearly throwing herself off balance. If it were not for Julia's supporting arm, she would have flipped over the arm of the couch. "I don't want to go to bed, now or ever. I want another drink to forget what I don't wish to remember."

"And that is . . . ?" John prompted in stifled amusement.

"That all men are jerks, just like Julia said."

"I'd really rather you didn't quote me," Julia mumbled. "Come on, sis. You'll feel better in the morning."

"No, she won't," John guaranteed, being absolutely no help at all. "She'll swear her head is about to explode."

Julia scowled into his ornery grin. "Thank you, Mr. Optimistic."

John strode forward to lend a hand when Lana balked at Julia's attempt to herd her toward the bedroom.

Lana flung up a limp-wristed hand to deter him. "Stay away from me, you—"

Julia clamped a hand over the lower portion of her sister's face, smothering several unflattering descriptions. "I will deal effectively with John," she assured Lana. "I'll practice all your psychoanalytic theories on him, don't worry."

Lana pulled Julia's hand away from her mouth while she

was being shepherded toward her room. "Those theories don't work worth a damn. Just look where it got me with Brad. All he wanted was to sleep with me, and that's what John wants with you."

"Lana! I do wish you would give your tongue the rest it deserves."

"Why? You never do. You say what you think, whether anyone wants to hear it or not." She set her feet and nodded determinedly when a thought bobbed into her beer-logged brain. "Maybe I'll call Brad and tell him what I think of him. Hand me the phone."

Julia tried to object. "You aren't going to—"

"Yes, she is," John cut in, ushering Lana toward her room. "I think maybe Brad needs to hear what Lana has to say right about now."

Julia snapped her head and glared at John's mischievous smile. "No, she'll tell him off."

"Trust me on this one, Julia. Sometimes a man needs to be told off. It wakes him up to what he's about to lose if he doesn't get his act together."

His meaningful glance melted Julia's resistance. "So now you're the resident psychiatrist, are you?" she asked teasingly.

John leaned out to flip back the bedspread. "No, I'm a man and I happen to know how a man thinks and why he behaves the way he does when it comes to women."

When Lana tried to grab the hem of her T-shirt to jerk it up and over her head, Julia clamped down on the garment to hold it in place. "Maybe you'd better wait in the hall," she suggested to John.

He chuckled and ambled off. He was having a helluva good time watching Julia deal with her inebriated sister. He was also highly amused that the intellectual one of the pair was doing some high flying herself. He couldn't wait to see how Lana handled the hangover that would greet her when she crash-landed.

When John closed the door behind him, Julia released the

hem of the shirt and dialed Brad's number. After four rings, Brad answered the phone.

"Brad? Julia."

"Don't you start on me," he muttered. "I don't want to be analyzed to death again today."

"I doubt you will be," Julia assured him before she thrust the phone at Lana, who had tugged on her nightie and flounced onto the bed. To her sister she said, "Okay, let him have it with both barrels if it makes you feel better."

Lana inhaled deeply and let loose her firepower.

"I'm not sure what Lana's tirade is going to accomplish," Julia murmured confidentially to John while they eavesdropped from the hallway. "And, by the way, the woman you hear yelling into the phone is *not* my sister."

John chuckled at the comment. "Maybe not, but Brad might be finding out for himself that Lana isn't always deliberate and methodical. From the look and sound of things, there's a lot of you in Lana—buried beneath that stockpile of knowledge she prides herself on having acquired." He studied Julia's lively features for a thoughtful moment. "Did you ever wonder if your sister tried to become your exact opposite because she felt she couldn't compete with you?"

"God," Julia groaned. "Don't tell me you have analytical tendencies, too!"

John ignored that. "Lana said she wished she could be more like you—more spirited, more spontaneous. She may be afraid to try because she considers you the expert. Tonight may be her attempt to test the waters and shed a few layers of self-restraint."

"So I'm to blame for my sister's behavior?" Julia prodded. "Thank you *so* much."

John curled his hand beneath her chin and grinned down into her lovely face. "No, but Lana is right about one thing." His voice dropped huskily. "I'd rather be sleeping with you."

Julia blushed profusely, and for the first time in her life, she was at a loss for words.

"Am I too honest for you, Julia?"

She nodded, desperately trying to recover her powers of speech.

John had never been good at communicating with women, especially not after his broken engagement; he'd been hurt badly. But Julia was different. She wasn't the least bit deceptive or pretentious. She was what she was—take it or leave it. John had been fighting the strong attraction long enough to see it for what it was. And what it *was* had become hopelessly compelling. He was hooked on this feisty blonde whose interests and background coincided so perfectly with his. Julia tested him, challenged, amused him.

Smiling tenderly, he bent to brush his lips over hers in a whispering kiss. "Well, if you aren't going to sleep with me, I guess I'd better bed down for the night. Six o'clock chores are going to come early after this fiasco with your sister."

When John withdrew, Julia blinked. "That's it? Just like that?"

He laughed at her owl-eyed expression. "Did you think I planned to rush you? I'm simply stating my feelings so you'll know where I stand. Brad tried to suppress his needs because he thought Lana would come around eventually, so she assumed he was more interested in an intellectual relationship. I, on the other hand," he said with a broad grin, "would get physical with you here and now. But I want you to know it isn't just for the weekend. Good night, Julia, sweet dreams . . ."

When John sauntered off, Julia stared after him. She thought of the past, of the men who had lasted two months at the most, and finally understood why. She had been looking for Mr. Right in the wrong places. He was here, under her nose, and he had been since she'd accepted the job at the animal clinic months earlier.

The realization was like having a spotlight glaring in her eyes. She was in love with John W. Casey III, son of a well-to-do rancher who lived near Ponca City. *His* family's ranch wasn't in financial difficulty, and Julia had envied him the security that gave him. At the same time, she had felt an attraction that she had been fighting quite admirably, if she did say so herself. It had always been there, though, simmering beneath her shield of defense, since the first time she met John.

Hearing John admit that he desired her left Julia feeling hungry and reckless. She wanted to explore the realm of her relationship with John, to enjoy him instead of constantly battling him.

A pensive frown knitted her brow as she shut off the lights and headed for bed. Had her mother experienced that same compelling need when Wyatt had walked into her life? Were Elizabeth's feelings for Wyatt caused by more than the loss of Heartstrings and fear of starting life anew?

Surely not, Julia convinced herself. Her mother was too old to be battling the flood of sensations that swept through her when John kissed her. Besides, love couldn't be the underlying emotion in Elizabeth's case . . . could it?

The curious thought trailed off when Julia passed Lana's bedroom door. Lana was still shouting the walls down, attaching a few choice curses to Brad's name. Julia wondered if Brad had hung up on her, or if he had simply gone deaf.

Julia nearly choked on her orange juice when she glanced up from the kitchen table to see Lana shuffling toward her. Lana's dark, shoulder-length hair looked as if it had been styled by a cyclone. Her puffy eyes were streaked with red and her T-shirt was inside out. Julia had seen better-looking road kill.

John took one look at Lana and camouflaged his laughter with a cough. "Morning, Sunshine. Don't we look bright and cheerful."

Sporting a headache that threatened to tear her skull apart, Lana transfixed him with a sour gaze. "Why are you still here? Hasn't Julia gotten rid of you *yet?*"

Julia blanched. Lana was still not herself. Her customary diplomacy was buried beneath a hellish hangover. "John will be staying for the weekend. He's going to help check cattle and do chores. Mother said a few cases of foot rot and shipping fever needed attention."

Lana plunked herself down at the table and propped her throbbing head up with one hand. "Sounds like the perfect pastime for a vet." She flung John a snide glance as she reached for her glass of orange juice. "Hope you don't get kicked where it hurts while applying medication."

"Lana, lay off, will you? John hasn't done anything to you. You're scapegoating."

"Don't try to talk psychiatry to me," Lana muttered grouchily. "I've decided to quit thinking before I speak."

Julia sipped her juice and was silent for a moment. "How did your conversation with Brad go last night?"

Lana lifted her tousled head—it felt like a mushy pumpkin. "I would appreciate it if you wouldn't mention What's-His-Name in my presence for the next century. It's officially over. I told You-Know-Who that he could stick it up his you-know-what."

John grinned into his orange juice. This was a very different Lana from the one he had met briefly the previous afternoon. Her shell had cracked wide open. "Well, I suppose we'd better get at the chores. The meteorologist is predicting rain by afternoon."

"Nothing like a little gloom to dampen spirits," Lana said bleakly. "It might as well rain. It will suit my mood." Her bloodshot gaze lifted to take in her sister, and she swallowed audibly. "I hope you can manage without my help this morning. I think I'd better go back to bed so I can die in peace."

"Maybe you need a drink to get you going," John teased.

The glower she gave him could have melted the glass in his hand. John was reasonably certain this would be the first and last time Lana used liquor to try to drown her troubles. Troubles, John had learned years ago, had gills and fins and they could swim.

* * *

Elizabeth had attended her fair share of farm sales and auctions over the years, but she had never been to an affair quite as sophisticated as the quarter horse show held at Heritage Hall. The facility was first class and those in attendance were either wealthy or they lived well beyond their means. If the latter possibility were so, Elizabeth knew perfectly well what would happen when the local banks called in debts.

Watching Wyatt commandeer the auction so confidently impressed Elizabeth beyond words. He had fastidiously studied the pedigrees and bloodlines of the horses to be sold, and his resonant baritone, amplified by a microphone, brought the chattery clientele to attention immediately. Wyatt wasn't just good at what he did; he was terrific. It was little wonder he was highly paid to perform his duties. When bidding hit a lull, he would impart information about the breeding stock and cutting horses, offering background and occasionally relating an amusing anecdote about the owners of the animals.

Elizabeth sat there, her mouth gaping, while Wyatt rattled off incoming bids and called in reluctant bidders with the flick of a hand or a nod of his dark head. He had such a commanding presence that the entire function came to life while he was on the podium behind the sale ring. His attendants were trained to respond to a nod or a glance from him, so Wyatt kept the sale moving like a well-oiled machine. Elizabeth was glad she had the chance to see him in action.

In the lonely days to come she would recall how he looked, standing in front of a large crowd. While he was jet-hopping from one far-flung auction to another, she would be doing her daily chores, wishing Wyatt were beside her . . .

Her sweeping gaze fell on Deidre Delaney, the ex-Mrs. McKenney, who was bidding on a leggy chestnut colt with spot and snip markings on its dark face and white stockings that extended just below the knees of its front legs. Although Wyatt gave no sign that he was doing anything except accepting another bid, Elizabeth was aware of the provocative smiles Deidre cast in his direction.

Elizabeth tried to overlook the niggling jealousy that

hounded her. She had no reason to compete with that snobbish lush. Deidre Delaney fit what Lana called the Beautiful Bitch Syndrome. Still, Elizabeth told herself that what Deidre and Wyatt had was over long ago, that they would have patched up their differences if he had wanted to.

Deidre had evidently married again, hence the name Delaney. And Wyatt had admitted that he had become obsessed with his work, was practically married to it, in fact. Considering his schedule for the next two weeks, Elizabeth had to agree. He pushed himself hard, or at least he had done so until his physician had prescribed a vacation.

When Deidre's bid wasn't raised, Wyatt pronounced the stud sold. Deidre smiled craftily at Elizabeth. If that was a symbolic gesture, Elizabeth refused to participate in the game she chose to play. Deidre could sit and gloat for all Elizabeth cared. The wealthy witch had just bought herself a colt, and everyone at the auction knew how much she had paid for it. Big damn deal.

A few hours later, the auction was concluded, and people milled around the auditorium while buyers paid for and collected their purchases. Deidre was sashaying toward Wyatt with a drumroll walk that would have done Irene Truman proud. Elizabeth looked the other way. She wasn't going to be a victim of Deidre's vampish games. If Deidre was making a desperate play for Wyatt's attention in an attempt to rekindle the flame, then it was her privilege to give it her best shot.

Too bad Deidre didn't know Elizabeth had no hold on Wyatt, that they avoided speaking of the future and of commitment. She could have saved herself a lot of trouble and expense. Elizabeth had the sneaking suspicion that Deidre had bid on the stud, which had brought the highest price of the day, just to impress her acquaintances and Wyatt.

Deidre's comments on the previous evening suggested that buying and selling registered stock was only an amusing pastime for her. Elizabeth couldn't help but wonder if she saw Wyatt as a prize she had somehow allowed to slip away and that she wished to reacquire.

Despite her noble intention of *not* monitoring Deidre's activities, Elizabeth's gaze was drawn to the podium. She gnashed her teeth when she saw Deidre push up on tiptoe to plant a kiss right smack on Wyatt's lips.

Remain calm, that's what Lana would say. Recognize the stimuli that triggers impulsive responses. Resist . . .

Elizabeth took a purifying breath and reassured herself that she did not really want to claw out Deidre's eyes or yank out her hair. She was not angry or jealous. Deidre was not her social better, and she had no reason to feel inferior.

Having given herself that silent pep talk, Elizabeth sought out a familiar face from the previous evening and struck up a conversation. She refused to glance toward the cashier's desk, where transactions were being carried out under Wyatt's supervision—and with Deidre's presence. Damn it, the woman was worse than hydrogen atoms attaching themselves to oxygen!

Breathe, Elizabeth.

She tried, she really did!

Chapter Twenty

"Elizabeth?"

Elizabeth pivoted to see one of the men who had been working in the show ring standing beside her. She judged him to be in his midthirties. He was dressed in a stylish Western suit and boots, as Wyatt was.

"I'm David Saunders, one of Wyatt's assistants," he said. "Wyatt asked me to tell you he's going to be tied up for several hours. One of the buyers is being a little difficult and insists on double-checking registrations and pedigrees."

As if Elizabeth couldn't guess who dreamed up that excuse to waylay Wyatt.

"A regional Quarter Horse Association meeting has been called," David went on to say. "Since Wyatt is on the board, he'll have to stay." He handed Elizabeth the keys to the Caddy. "Wyatt thought you might like to wait for him at his apartment."

Elizabeth glanced toward Wyatt, who was hunched over the cashier's table, rifling through files while Deidre was perched at his shoulder like a pet parakeet.

"Yes, I think that would be best," she agreed. "Problem is,

I'm not familiar enough with the City to find my way to the apartment."

"No problem." David handed her the map Wyatt had drawn. "You won't have any trouble. The condo is easy to reach. Stay on I-40 west until you intersect the bypass. It will take you north to the condo."

Elizabeth studied the diagram that indicated the landmarks she remembered. "I think I can manage with this. Thank you."

"Wyatt said to tell you he was really sorry about the delay. I'll bring him home when he can get away."

While David weaved through the crowd to rejoin Wyatt at the podium, Elizabeth stared at the keys in her hand, sighed and strode off.

To Elizabeth's surprise it was raining when she walked outside the gargantuan facility. Another spring thunderstorm appeared to be ripping through the state. By the time she reached the Caddy her hair was plastered to her head and her simple cotton dress was glued to her skin. Soaked, she stuck to the leather seat.

Thunder boomed overhead as Elizabeth steered the car onto the highway, following the directions on the map. After twenty minutes she pulled into the parking lot and skedaddled toward the condo. The austere apartment did nothing to elevate her soggy spirits. She kept picturing Deidre clinging to Wyatt like Spanish moss.

"Forget about it," she told herself as she headed for the bedroom to retrieve dry clothes. This was their last day. Wyatt had a flight to catch the following afternoon—which meant a hasty trip to Heartstrings to drop her off before rushing back to the City. She shouldn't be fretting over Deidre Delaney. The woman had already proved she could pull strings and lure Wyatt away.

Feeling unbearably lonely, Elizabeth decided to call home, even though she risked being lectured by mothering daughters. The phone rang five times before a groggy voice answered. Elizabeth frowned at the raspy tone.

"Lana? Is that you?"

"Mother? Where are you?"

"In the City."

"With *him*?"

Elizabeth blinked at the hiss in Lana's voice. This didn't sound like the Lana she knew. "Are you all right?"

"No, I broke up with that despicable jerk I've been dating."

"What happened?"

"I discovered he wasn't the man I thought he was. I hope you don't learn the same thing about McKenney, but I won't be surprised if you do. Men can be more underhanded than I ever believed possible!"

Elizabeth held the receiver away from her ear when Lana's voice reached a wild pitch. For a moment, she almost forgot it was Lana talking and not Julia.

"I tell you, Mother, you can't trust any of them. If you do, you'll be sorry."

Them, Elizabeth presumed, were the males of the species.

"You think you have the ideal situation, the perfect match and wham! The qualities I thought What's-His-Name appreciated and admired about me are the very ones that annoy him most. There is no such thing as total honesty in the male-female relationship. If you think there is, you're kidding yourself, just as I was. And mark my words, Mother, Wyatt McKenney is just like You-Know-Who. All that polite attentiveness was just a sham. Wyatt wants something from you. I'm certain he's using you to turn a profit on Heartstrings. You think he hangs the moon? Just wait until he drops it on your head!"

"Lana, if you don't mind—"

"Has he scheduled the auction yet?" Lana persisted.

"I'm not sure."

"Mother, for God's sake, show some initiative and find out!" Lana all but yelled. "Check his calendar to see if he penned you in. If he's luring you into selling to him so he can make the profit, you'll be confined to a limited income while he's snickering his way to the bank."

"I don't think Wyatt is working a scam," Elizabeth declared.

"No? Well, I didn't think What's-His-Name would announce we were through and storm off, either. Now he's gone and I've wasted an entire year on that jackass. As for you, there's no need for you to worry about selling Heartstrings," Lana told her mother. "Julia and I have decided to take out loans to pay the debts. We don't want to let Heartstrings go. Your behavior lately suggests you're fighting the trauma of this any way you can."

"You are going to take out loans?" Elizabeth repeated, bewildered. "I didn't think you cared about Heartstrings."

"Well, we do!" Lana adamantly proclaimed. "I may not have a boyfriend, but I'll be damned if I lose the home I always come back to!"

Elizabeth had anticipated a shakedown at Heartstrings when she left it in her daughters' hands. She had not, however, expected Lana and Julia to rally to her rescue. They were good kids, for the most part, and it was generous of them to offer to hold Heartstrings together, but Elizabeth didn't want to tie their hands financially when they were just starting out.

"I appreciate your offer," she told Lana. "But it's time to let go. We can keep the cabin and a few acres. That will be enough."

"No, it won't!" Lana loudly objected, leaving Elizabeth's ears ringing. "I'm on Spring Break, and come Monday, I'm going to the bank to draw up a contract. Julia is planning to do the same. That is that. You don't need Wyatt as a substitute for what you think you're about to lose because you aren't losing Heartstrings. Now, when are you coming home where you belong?"

"Tomorrow."

"Don't wait, Mother," Lana implored. "The man is bad news, I'm certain of it. The ride he's taking you on will only hurt you. And for heaven's sake, don't agree to any arrangement he suggests! That shark plans to gobble you up for a between-meal snack."

Elizabeth was growing concerned about Lana. The daughter who studied basket cases was becoming one. The one who never raised her voice or became ruffled by any situation was spewing like Mt. Vesuvius.

"Let me talk to your sister," Elizabeth demanded.

"Don't bother. She's flipped out."

"What do you mean she flipped out?"

"I mean she has suddenly decided the vet is her dream come true. He's switched tactics with Julia. The sneaky rascal is all smiles and come-hither glances. It's sickening. Julia can't see what he's doing, but I know he's trying to charm her into submission so she'll follow him around the clinic like an obedient puppy. That six years age difference is to his advantage. Like I said, men always want something, and they'll say and do practically anything to get what they want. John W. Casey III sees Julia as a challenge to conquer, a free spirit to be broken. Wyatt McKenney sees you as a way to pad his savings account. And You-Know-Who is just an ass—"

Lana's voice broke. For the first time since Elizabeth could remember, her younger daughter was bawling her head off.

"Pull yourself together. Just because you and Brad had a quarrel—"

"A quarrel?" Lana said between sobs. "A quarrel! We had a battle that made the war zone in the Persian Gulf look like a tea party! He called me a pseudo-intellectual prude who had no emotions of my own—said I stuck my nose in psychology books just to find a personality that might fit the image I'd designed for myself. Can you believe he said that?"

"I'm sure he was upset," Elizabeth replied. "And obviously you were, too."

"Upset doesn't begin to describe having my illusions shattered," Lana blubbered. "Mother, come home. I need you. Heartstrings needs you. And we've got to talk some sense into Julia before she makes the worst mistake of her life. Brad told her she couldn't find a man who would put up with her feisty temperament, so now she's out to prove that she can. John Casey would be the worst possible match for her!"

Elizabeth was torn between her desire to spend one last night with Wyatt and her need to be there for her daughter. Julia, she felt certain, was compatible with John. She'd noticed all the signs the minute she'd seen the two of them together—fighting an inevitable attraction.

Lana, on the other hand, was undergoing a metamorphosis that was long overdue. She had always taken herself too seriously. Becoming the immovable force to counterbalance Julia, she had suppressed that natural sibling rivalry by becoming Julia's opposite. Now, suddenly, Lana's true nature had broken through her reserve. The poor kid needed reassurance.

"Are you coming home, Mother?" Lana questioned between sniffles.

Elizabeth took a deep breath. She wanted to say no, but she had to say yes. "All right, Lana. I'll be home as soon as I can. But it might be late this evening before we can get there."

"We?" The disappointment was apparent in Lana's scratchy voice.

"We," Elizabeth confirmed. "You are wrong about Wyatt."

"Then ask him about the auction," Lana challenged. "Promise me, Mother."

The line went dead and Elizabeth stared pensively at the receiver. She had always wondered how long Brad would allow Lana to play by her rules, all in the name of logic and respect. Those two had become a comfortable habit neither had wanted to break. Whatever happened next, they both needed to retreat a step and assess their true feelings for each other. Elizabeth would have liked to stick her nose into their business and offer advice, but she was not one of the involved parties. Damn, sometimes motherhood was the pits. This was one of those times . . .

The phone jingled, jostling Elizabeth from her musings. When the answering machine clicked on to take the call, Elizabeth pivoted to check the weather report on the TV. She hoped she and Wyatt wouldn't have to drive through a downpour to reach the ranch.

"Wyatt, this is Emmet," the caller said. "I got the lowdown on that ranch you wanted me to check out in Osage County."

Elizabeth wheeled around, her heart hammering. She was

afraid to hear what was about to be said . . . and afraid not to.

"Your instincts were right, as usual," Emmet went on to say. "The loan against that property is about to be called in. The banker wants to get out from under it as soon as possible. You could buy the place if you can cut a quick deal. I put out feelers like you asked to see who might be interested in picking up that ranch. Crowley Cattle Company is looking for a place to set up an operation since the environmentalists pushed them out of New Mexico. I also got word that a Florida corporation needs to invest for capital gain. You could roll that property over and make yourself a helluva profit, minus my commission, of course. Call me when you have the chance. I want to keep these two fish on the line and let them bid against each other. They're both hungry for a buy, and Osage County suits their needs. If you can get your hands on the ranch, dirt cheap, you can smile all the way to the bank."

Elizabeth half collapsed against the wall, as if she'd suffered a body blow. She stared in disbelief at the answering machine, her heart shriveling up as she took one agonizing breath after another. Had she so completely misjudged Wyatt? Obviously!

She'd been lured by the charm of a wizard who created believable illusions with smoke and mirrors. She had sailed off on a magic carpet ride, refusing to look down to see how far she could fall. She was a naive, gullible and unsophisticated fool—a prime target for deception.

She had refused to listen to Lana, Julia and Griff Hollis who had been more objective. They had been outside the sensual web Wyatt had spun around her. He had convinced her to give them two weeks to get to know each other, had refused to discuss his past or his plans for the auction. Why? Wasn't it glaringly apparent now? He intended to sweet-talk her into selling to him so he could enjoy a big profit rather than just the auction commission.

Cursing, Elizabeth stormed toward the calendar that rested on the edge of Wyatt's desk. She checked the listings of appointments. The scheduled dates of auctions did not include a possible listing for Heartstrings. He had been holding her off, waiting until she fell beneath his spell, waiting until she—utter fool that she was—fell in love with him and agreed to his request! He'd done all the right things that might indicate he cared—given her seemingly devoted attention, a bouquet of flowers, an expensive gown.

No wonder he hadn't returned her confession of love. He'd been playing with her emotions. He'd made no comment, no profession of affection, so she couldn't accuse him of lying to her, now could she? He had simply been hiding deeper truths. He probably intended to ask to buy the ranch this very night. That was what this weekend was about. Wyatt had whisked her away from her family who constantly issued warnings before he presented his private bid for Heartstrings.

Elizabeth swiped at the tears that scalded her cheeks and all but ran to the bedroom to gather up her belongings. She didn't bother leaving a note. As soon as Wyatt heard the message on the machine he'd know she had discovered the truth about him. She'd offered him honesty, and he had repaid her with deceit. She'd fallen in love with him, and he had used her! God, Elizabeth had thought she was long past the hurt a man could evoke. She had been through this once already. She'd thought Wyatt was different; well, he was exactly the same.

Elizabeth snatched up the phone to call a taxi. She didn't care if she had to spend the night at the bus depot. She was going to be long gone when Wyatt returned. And furthermore, he could have his ex-wife back. They deserved each other! They were a perfect combination—genuine bitch and full-fledged bastard!

Maybe she should march home and marry Griff Hollis. It would be a mercenary act, but it would prevent Heartstrings from becoming a financial burden to Lana and Julia.

Look on the bright side, Elizabeth told herself on her way out the door. You won't have to worry about Griff breaking your heart, because you don't have one left.

* * *

"Thanks for the lift, David." Wyatt climbed out of the car and poked his head back inside. "I'll meet you at the airport tomorrow afternoon."

When David sped off, Wyatt dug into his pocket for his keys and then jogged toward the condo. He was going to compensate Elizabeth for this delay. What should've taken an hour at the most had spanned four hours, thanks to Deidre's manipulations. She could really be a pain in the ass.

Wyatt raked his hands through his damp hair and glanced around the quiet apartment. He had expected to see Elizabeth propped on the sofa, occupying herself by watching television, but she was nowhere to be seen.

"Bet?"

No answer. Wyatt smiled mischievously. She was obviously in the shower. He peeled off his tie and jacket on his way down the hall. His anticipatory smile evaporated when he noticed Elizabeth's suitcase were gone. Damn it, surely she hadn't gotten upset about Deidre. He had tried to assure her that he had no intention of going back to what had been a costly and heartbreaking mistake.

Another thought occurred to Wyatt, and he lurched toward the office. Knowing Lana and Julia, they might have attempted to persuade Elizabeth to make an early return. Maybe their urging had sent their mother rushing off. But why hadn't Bet left him a note? The fact that she hadn't done that didn't bode well. What could possibly have made her flee without so much as a good-bye?

Wyatt switched on the answering machine. He listened to the call from a prospective client in Kentucky who rattled off information and requested a return call. The second message came from the president of the National Cattlemen's Association. The third call was the one that had Wyatt swearing.

Feeling as if he had taken a fist to the solar plexus, he dropped into a chair. The worst possible thing had gone wrong. He could almost see Elizabeth listening to the incriminating phone call that sent her racing off, completely disillusioned.

"Thanks a helluva lot, Emmet." Wyatt scowled. The message had gotten worse with each sentence.

Tension knotted inside him. After two weeks of unparalleled pleasure, the stress was back in triplicate. One poorly timed phone call had destroyed his peace of mind. His last night of heaven had turned to hell.

He'd intended to tell Elizabeth the whole truth tonight—all of it. He'd wanted to make his private bid for Heartstrings the right way, at just the right moment. He'd been procrastinating, giving her all the time she needed, taking the time he needed. But now he'd waited too long and Emmet had unknowingly destroyed the trust he had established with her.

"Shit," Wyatt muttered as he grabbed his mobile phone and headed for the door. He wished the Caddy could sprout wings and fly. No, on second thought, he'd take the truck. Elizabeth hated the Caddy . . . but not quite as much as she now hated him.

Lana and Julia were standing in front of the window when Wyatt drove up in a late model, crimson, extended-cab pickup. Rain hammered on the tiled roof of the house as he dashed toward the portico to meet the *un*welcoming committee. Lana and Julia greeted him at the door with identical glares.

"Where's Mother?" they chorused.

Wyatt gaped at the pretty dragons who blocked his path. "Isn't she here?"

"No, when I talked to her, she said the two of you might come down late tonight," Lana reported, her dark eyes flashing with hostility.

Wyatt did a double take. He could have sworn Julia was the feisty one. So what the hell had happened to Miss Self-Discipline? Whatever it was, she was projecting her anger on Wyatt. He was getting nowhere fast with Lana or Julia.

"I think Elizabeth overheard a misleading phone call on my answering machine and decided to make her own way home," Wyatt reported. "I was hoping to explain to her that—"

"Oh, I'm sure you were," Lana sniffed sarcastically.

Julia butted in. "Look, Wyatt, we both know what you're up to. You're trying to make a killing on this ranch. Mother is your means to a profitable end."

Wyatt gnashed his teeth until he nearly ground off the enamel. "You're mistaken."

Waste of breath. He could stand here until Judgment Day and never convince Lana and Julia that his intentions were honorable. Elizabeth's daughters had resented his intrusion since he'd arrived. They had never trusted him and never intended to. He was up against two stone walls. Hell!

"I think it would be best if you left," Lana insisted, looking down her nose at him. "We won't be needing your services. Julia and I have decided to get loans to help Mother keep Heartstrings. The ranch is no longer for sale. Find yourself another gambit. It isn't going to be Mother."

Wyatt's gaze bounced back and forth between two pairs of narrowed eyes—sizzling blue and flashing brown. "You'll never get loans without collateral."

"Maybe not," Julia said. "But no matter what happens to Heartstrings, you won't get it at a rock-bottom price to sell to the bidder of your choice. Mother must realize by now that you're up to no good."

That did it. Wyatt had been as courteous as he knew how—for as long as he could stand. Exasperation was eating him alive. He was losing something priceless, and he wasn't going to back off just because Miss Lah-de-dah and Miss Lah-de-dee were restricting him from the premises.

"I happen to care very deeply for Elizabeth—"

"Yeah, right," Lana scoffed.

"No matter what you think or believe," Wyatt plowed on, "I was trying to save Heartstrings, not sell it out from under you. Your mother is too much a part of this ranch to leave. I can see it in her eyes and hear it in her voice when she speaks of the heritage she doesn't want to lose. If you think my interest in Bet is mercenary, you have misjudged me. And you've failed to give your mother credit for being the warm, kindhearted and intelligent woman she is. She made me happy when I was with her, and I think I made her happy. But you two are trying to destroy what was between us, just because I don't fit into your future plans for your mother."

Wyatt inhaled a deep breath and stared at one determined face and then the other. "I guess you would have to know what true happiness is before you could understand what I'm trying to tell you. Until you do, you'll never believe that all I want is Bet, however she'll have me."

Wyatt lurched around and walked off in the rain, knowing he had made a long drive for nothing. Elizabeth, wherever she was, believed the absolute worst about him. Lana and Julia would be there to reinforce her low opinion, and Wyatt would be flying from here to hell and back, unable to defend himself!

"Damn," he muttered as he swung himself into the truck. How was he going to reach Elizabeth after she'd had two weeks to harden her heart against him?

And how was he going to get through the tormenting nights without her?

As Wyatt drove away, he asked himself where Bet could have gone to avoid him. If she'd anticipated that he might follow her, she could have rented a motel room in the City. It could take all night to track her down . . .

Heart-Stays, he thought suddenly. Maybe she had gone to the cabin. That was one place he knew she sought out to revive her spirits.

Wyatt felt his hopes rising as he sped through the rain, looking for the muddy path that led to Heart-Stays. To his bitter disappointment, Elizabeth wasn't in the cabin that now stood among the blackened skeletons of trees.

He did the only thing he could do. He left a note, hoping she would find it before he caught his flight. If she did, she might be willing to listen to an explanation when he tried to call.

Wyatt retrieved the sleeping bag that he and Elizabeth had shared on their first night together. He placed logs and kindling in the hearth, and laid the sleeping bag before it, leaving the room just as it had been, just as he would always remember it. Everything was just the same—the rain, the inviting pallet. All that was missing was the heat of the fire—and the generous passionate woman who had sent him up in flames.

"My gawd, girl, what on earth happened to you?" Irene Truman croaked when she found her bedraggled friend standing on her doorstep.

Elizabeth ambled through the door when motioned inside. She was so cold she couldn't stop shaking. But it wasn't just walking in the rain from the bus station that had chilled her to the bone. Her crash course in reality had put an icy glaze around her heart and sent shivers through her soul.

After leaving Wyatt's apartment, Elizabeth had caught the evening bus from Oklahoma City to Tulsa. The two-hour layover had given her plenty of time to sort out her thoughts and emotions. During the trip from Tulsa to Pawhuska Elizabeth asked herself how she could have been so gullible. She'd been around for forty-five years. She should've known better!

Irene steered Elizabeth to the sofa and shoved her down onto it. "You just sit tight, sugar. I'll get us some coffee."

In two shakes, she was back with two steaming cups. She sank down across from Elizabeth, peering intently at her. "Now tell me what the devil happened. You look like you lost your best friend. Heck, I thought *I* was your best friend!"

Elizabeth had once thought Wyatt her best friend. She had been able to talk to him so easily, even if he hadn't opened up to her. Now she knew why. God, nothing was worse than being deceived by those you trusted explicitly.

Elizabeth inhaled shakily. The tears she'd held in check came flooding out. "Oh, Irene, I've been such a fool! I thought Wyatt and I had something special. Come to find out, he only wanted to get Heartstrings cheap and sell it for a big profit."

"Well, that bastard!" Irene huffed, watching helplessly as Elizabeth broke down and cried her eyes out.

"The girls warned me that he wasn't what he seemed to be.

But I decided to trust my instincts. I should have remembered I didn't have good luck with Bob, either."

Irene groaned miserably. "This is all my fault. I was the one who encouraged you to take the chance. I wanted you to get out and enjoy yourself a little. You've worked entirely too hard the past ten years, without rewarding yourself with any pleasure."

"I've worked for nothing," Elizabeth's voice cracked with defeat. "I have managed to humiliate myself and lose the ranch. Worse," she wailed, "I have to admit that my children have more sense than I do!"

Elizabeth muffled several sniffs and struggled for composure. "I was wondering if you could drive me home. I may as well get Lana's and Julia's I-told-you-sos over with tonight. They'll top off a horrendous day."

"Sure, hon." Irene surged to her feet. "I'll get us a jacket. And if you don't feel up to working tomorrow night, I'll take your shift. It was supposed to be my day off, but heck, I don't have a thing planned."

"No, I'd rather keep busy," Elizabeth insisted as Irene disappeared down the hall.

"Are you sure?" her friend called back.

Elizabeth blinked back another flood of tears. She wasn't sure about anything anymore. She had once again discovered that what she'd believed and trusted in with all her heart wasn't necessarily so. She had seen only what she'd wanted to see in Wyatt McKenney, blinded by her own attempt to find new meaning in her life. But she had learned what she'd always known to be true. The only thing she could count on in this world was Heartstrings. It never failed her. She, however, had failed her heritage, and she had let the man she had dared to love tear her heart into jagged pieces.

Chapter Twenty-one

The phone rang as it had every hour on the hour since Wyatt drove off. When Julia reached for the receiver, Lana flung up a hand to forestall her.

"Let it ring. I'm tired of hanging up on that shyster."

"It could be Mother," Julia reminded her.

Lana flounced back on the couch beside John. "Oh, all right, but if it's McKenney, cuss him out for me."

"You've already done that three times," Julia said as she picked up the phone.

"Is she home yet?" Wyatt posed the same question for the fourth time. He breathed a relieved sigh at getting Julia rather than Lana. That girl had become hell on wheels!

"No, she isn't. I thought this call might be from her. Lana wanted to let it ring."

"Julia, I appreciate your loyalty to your mother, but I want to talk to her the minute she comes in."

"Hang up on him, Julia."

"Give the guy a break," John put in. "Whatever happened to that business about being innocent until proven guilty?"

"You *would* take his side." Lana sneered. "Just stick to vet medicine and keep your nose out of our family business."

Wyatt overheard the voice in the background. Who couldn't? The calm, soft-spoken Lana was shouting. "Julia, do something with your sister," Wyatt grumbled. "She has developed symptoms of the psychological disorders she studied."

"You're telling me," Julia muttered.

Since Julia hadn't hung up on him, Wyatt took a chance. "Elizabeth makes me happy," he repeated emphatically. "I don't want to lose her, and I don't want to see you lose Heartstrings, either. Before you *forget* to tell Elizabeth I've been calling, ask yourself what I have to lose, rather than gain, by selling the ranch out from under you."

Julia turned her back on Lana who was glaring at the phone—more specifically, at the man on the other end of the line.

"I want the chance to explain, Julia," Wyatt implored. "That's all I'm asking."

"Will you *please* hang up the damned phone before he sabotages your thinking!" Lana snapped, making a wild gesture with her arm.

The glass of Coke John had lifted to his lips went flying before Lana's flailing arm. Ice and liquid splattered down his shirt.

"Will you calm down!" John growled, at the end of his patience. "Ever since Brad pointed out a few of your flaws—"

"He assassinated my character, that's what he did!" Lana yelled in correction.

"And you crucified him, so that makes you even. If you weren't so crazy about the guy you wouldn't be biting everybody's head off."

"Crazy about him?" Lana blared. "I hate him!"

"I've got to go," Julia said into the phone. "World War III is about to break out."

Wyatt hung up the cellular phone and veered off of the interstate to reach his condo. He would have given anything to be at Heartstrings, even if Lana-the-lunatic had turned it into a war zone. Anything was better than facing the unbearable loneliness of knowing he was losing the love and respect of the woman who'd brought happiness back into his life.

Well, by damn, if he couldn't have Bet, he would at least ensure that she didn't have to lose something precious to her.

On that thought, Wyatt picked up the mobile phone and dialed Emmet Costain. Emmet—friend, accountant and financial advisor for McKenney Enterprises—had gotten Wyatt into this disaster and he could damned well make sure that Elizabeth was justly compensated.

"Damn, that's cold!" John hissed when an ice cube dribbled inside his shirt and settled on his chest, freezing flesh. He peeled off the soaked shirt, only to find Julia snatching it from his hands.

"I'll rinse it out before stains set in," she volunteered before striding toward the kitchen.

"The least you could do is pick up the ice cubes," John grumbled at Lana as he grabbed ice that had slid between the cushions of the sofa.

"Why? Because I'm a woman and you think women are supposed to clean up the messes men make?" Lana sniped. "Julia is right. You are a male chauvinist pig."

John had had all he intended to take from the brooding female venting her frustration on him. What could have been a romantic evening of listening to the patter of rain and cuddling up with Julia to watch a late-night flick had been spoiled by this psychologist from hell.

"I've had it with you," John muttered.

"Good, then leave. I don't want to see my sister hurt."

John stuck his face into hers and growled. "That's not what you want at all. Since you and Brad broke up, you want everyone else to be as miserable as you are."

Gasping in outrage, Lana gave John a shove back into his own space. When he tumbled off balance, he grabbed her arm to anchor himself. She let out a furious squawk as she was jerked off the couch, then landed atop John. Wedged between the divan and coffee table, Lana and John squirmed to free themselves from each other.

The front door opened and Elizabeth strode inside, halting abruptly when she noticed the wriggling bodies on the floor. "What is going on?"

Two heads popped up, and Elizabeth gaped at the bare-chested vet who was lying under . . . Lana?

"Mother!" Julia appeared at the kitchen door. Her gaze leaped to John and Lana who found themselves in incriminating positions—Lana straddling John's hips. The wounded look on Julia's face had John scowling and attempting to untangle himself to stand up.

"Julia—"

"Don't speak to me!" she sputtered, glaring. "Lana tried to warn me that the only reason you came here this weekend was to—" She slammed her mouth shut and whirled around. The back door rattled when she stormed outside.

"Thanks a lot," John muttered at Lana before he stalked off to track down Julia.

Lana flounced on the divan, arms crossed on her chest, glaring at nothing in particular. "Men! Why couldn't they have been confined to another planet? Pluto sounds like a good place for them."

Home, thought Elizabeth. Three-ring circus though it was, she was glad to be here, even temporarily.

Lana shot her mother a quick glance. "By the way, things aren't always what they seem. What you thought you saw John and me doing wasn't what we were doing at all."

Elizabeth nodded remorsefully. "No, things aren't always as they seem, are they? A man wandering out of a woman's bedroom bare-chested can be as misleading as a man lying bare-chested beneath a certain woman's sister. And what you think someone feels for you can be an illusion."

On that philosophical thought, Elizabeth propelled herself toward her bedroom to cry herself to sleep. It had been one helluva long day.

* * *

Bleary-eyed, Elizabeth crawled out of bed to face her morning chores. The ringing phone had awakened her three times before midnight. Each time she'd picked up the receiver and then replaced it without a word. She figured Wyatt was calling to talk his way out of the hole he had dug for himself, but she was through listening to the lies. Her "dream weekend" had ended in a nightmare. She just wanted it to be over, to forget how she had humiliated herself.

While Elizabeth and Lana were loading cattle cubes in the one-ton truck, Griff Hollis slopped through the water holes left by the previous night's rain. He motioned for Elizabeth to join him at his truck.

Elizabeth climbed down from the overhead storage bin, irritated by Griff's attitude. *She* was supposed to come to *him*. Women catering to men, that's the way he thought things ought to be.

Griff rolled down the window and tried to look properly apologetic, even though Elizabeth didn't buy it. "I tried to call you last night to tell you I was sorry about the burn, but your phone must be out. It was making a clicking noise."

Griff cleared his throat and stared straight ahead. "Liz, I'd like to make things work between us. I keep telling you that auctioneer isn't for you and that we need each other. I'd like to put the past behind us."

"Griff, I've—"

He flung up a leathery hand. "Just let me finish. I said some things I didn't mean because I was frustrated by McKenney's interference. But the bottom line is that I'd like to have you and Heartstrings."

Elizabeth glanced toward the house when the back door squeaked open. Julia and John came strolling out, hand in hand. Despite the dreary mood she was in, a smile tugged at Elizabeth's lips. It appeared that John and Julia had resolved their differences. Julia looked happier than she had been in months. Elizabeth was glad someone around here was enjoying life.

When she swiveled her head around to give her attention to Griff, her gaze landed on the object lying on the floorboard of the passenger side of the cab. A suspicious frown knitted her brow. Flashbacks of the night she had been forced off the road while driving Wyatt's Caddy popped into her mind.

"What are you doing with that fog light, Griff?" she questioned accusingly.

Griff refused to meet her probing stare. "I was doing some coyote hunting. I've seen packs of them prowling my north pastures."

Elizabeth wasn't buying any more lies, not from anyone. "You were the one who forced me off the road and blinded me with a fog light so I couldn't tell who it was, weren't you?"

Griff's eyes widened in surprise; then he muttered under his breath. "Hell, Liz, I didn't know that was you. I thought it was that pesky auctioneer. After we tangled I just wanted to get even."

"You were trying to get even by wrecking his car?" Elizabeth fumed. "I blamed teenage pranksters. Come to find out it was you! I suppose that *accidental* burning that ruined the looks of Heartstrings and very nearly burned down my cabin was your way of getting even with me for refusing to accept your proposal. God, no wonder Patty divorced you!"

"And no wonder Bob ran around on you." Griff sneered contemptuously. "I probably would've ended up doing the same thing if I'd married you. And furthermore, I hope you have to sell out for little or nothing. If I'm going to lose, you should, too!"

Elizabeth frowned in confusion as Griff slammed his truck into reverse and tore off. She didn't understand what he meant about them both losing.

When Elizabeth turned around, Julia and Lana were staring at her. There was no doubt that they had overheard what was said about their father. Neither Julia nor Lana uttered a word.

They simply turned back to their tasks, leaving Elizabeth to hers.

Well, Elizabeth thought as she drove off to feed the cattle, she was well rid of Griff and Wyatt. As Lana had said, Pluto sounded like the perfect planet for the male gender. Pluto or hell. Elizabeth was generous enough to let them take their pick.

Julia and John had filled Elizabeth in on the details of the spat that had ended Lana's year-long courtship with Brad Phelps. By six o'clock Sunday evening, Elizabeth was ready to ship her younger daughter off to the very same planet she had consigned all men to.

While Elizabeth was quietly nursing her broken heart, Lana was storming around, spoiling for fights. Elizabeth had never seen her daughter in such a pestilent mood. Lord, when the rug was pulled out from under Lana, she forgot all her training in psychology. Elizabeth was beginning to wonder how long she had kept this schizophrenic personality of hers under wraps. The poor kid didn't know who she was these days. Manic-depressive mood swings didn't begin to describe her abrupt and decisive changes of temperament. And worse, Lana was planning to spend her spring break at Heartstrings. That should be fun, Elizabeth thought dispiritedly. She and Lana could cheer each other up—or something.

The festering boil that was Lana's frustration came to a head after supper. A very humble and miserable looking Brad Phelps showed up at the door. He was ready to talk reconciliation, Elizabeth decided. He wouldn't have shown up in hostile territory if he wasn't. She stood aside, watching Brad and Lana stare at each other. They were both hesitant to take the first step toward a truce.

"Well . . . I better get back to Bartlesville," John declared, breaking the awkward silence.

"Thank you for helping with the chores this weekend," Elizabeth said appreciatively.

"It was my pleasure." John turned toward Julia and smiled.

"I can't think of any place I would rather have been than here." He glanced wryly at Lana, who hadn't taken her eyes off Brad. "Of course, things could have been even better if a certain someone—who shall remain nameless—hadn't spent all her time eating her heart out and taking her anger out on everyone."

Julia wrapped her arms around John's waist and was rewarded with an affectionate hug. When Lana's gaze darted in her direction, she grinned at her sister. "Well, don't just stand there, Lana. If the rest of us had to be miserable right along with you while Brad was gone, the least you can do is let us know whether you're glad he's back."

The teasing remark spurred Lana into action. She had only taken two steps in Brad's direction when he surged toward her, lifting her off the portico to kiss the breath out of her, right in front of anyone who cared to watch. Everybody did. Even the wind that swept through the breezeway seemed to breathe a sigh of relief.

While Lana and Brad were clinging to each other and whispering apologies, John smiled down into Julia's upturned face. "Take as much time as you need tomorrow to get your business at the bank in order," he insisted. "I'll hold down the clinic until you get back."

When Julia walked John to his truck to say a private goodbye, Elizabeth took her cue and made herself scarce. She was glad Lana and Brad had made peace. Lana certainly functioned better when she could count on Brad's affection and support.

Elizabeth wondered if Lana had begun to realize what a stabilizing factor Brad had become in her life. Maybe the weekend feud had been good for both of them. They had backed off long enough to measure the true strength of their feelings and to reevaluate each other. Perhaps they had learned a valuable lesson.

With Damn It on her heels, Elizabeth strode toward the barn to saddle George. She had certainly learned *her* lesson well. Romance was for youth, not for a middle-aged woman who had tried to grab hold of something that was no more than an illusion. She was going to have to be content with seeing her daughters happy. Perhaps that would compensate for the loneliness and the deep sense of betrayal that filled her soul. She doubted it, but that was probably as good as it was going to get. It would take months to turn off the precious moments that had been shattered by Wyatt's deceitfulness. And it would take years to forget what a fool she'd made of herself!

In pensive silence, Lana and Julia walked out of the bank in Pawhuska Monday afternoon. They had both sat down suddenly when Donna Henderson had informed them that Wyatt had wired money to pay off both loans that had been hanging over Heartstrings for the past decade. As of Monday morning, the ranch was operating in the black.

"What is his angle?" Julia questioned her sister.

Lana glanced toward the very old, five-story triangular building that graced Main Street and frowned pensively. "Do you remember last night when you and Mother found John and me on the floor together?"

Julia blinked at the abrupt change of topic. "Of course, I do. What does that have to do with this?"

"I recall Mother making the comment that things aren't always what they seem." Lana turned her full attention on her sister. "We might possibly have misjudged Wyatt McKenney and his intentions toward Mother."

"You are referring to the Bare-Chested Incident," Julia speculated.

Lana nodded her dark head and strode toward the car. "When we saw Wyatt coming out of Mother's room, we presumed the worst. And when Mother was enjoying herself for the first time in years, we were writing her reckless behavior off as an attempt to escape the reality of losing Heartstrings."

Julia frowned consideringly as she eased beneath the steering wheel to start the car. She kept hearing Wyatt's words ringing in her ears as she drove toward the ranch.

She made me happy when I was with her and I think I made her happy, too. I guess you would have to know what true happiness is before you can understand what I'm trying to tell you.

Only now that she and John had come to terms did she comprehend what Wyatt had meant. The way she felt when she was with John defied description. She knew Lana was feeling the same way now that Brad was back in her life. Her sister was her old self again, except she wasn't taking herself or her psychoanalysis as seriously as she once had. Lana had loosened up considerably after the eye-opening experience of nearly losing Brad. They had both become more open with their affection, making certain that those around them knew how they felt about each other.

Now the only one around here who was going through the paces of life without enjoying herself was Elizabeth. She was merely existing. It was even worse than it had been before Wyatt walked into her life. There was no spirited twinkle in her eyes, no lively smile. A black fog had settled over her soul.

"Lana, I think our overprotective instincts have done more harm than good in this instance. In fact, I'm afraid we're guilty of meddling and accusing an innocent party of crimes he may not have committed."

Lana was silent for a moment. "I suppose you heard what Griff said to Mother yesterday . . . about Dad."

Julia sighed audibly. "I heard. Again, it appears that things aren't always what they seem. Mother has suffered more than we ever realized." She stared at the gravel road and the rolling Osage Hills for a long moment. "Wyatt must love Mother a lot to do what he just did," she mused aloud. "It cost him a bundle to pay off the debts, but he has no guarantee that we might be willing to let him explain or to accept him. In fact, he has no guarantee that we'll even tell Mother who actually paid off those loans, at least not soon enough to do him any good."

Lana admired the scenery around the home they had very nearly lost before she'd recognized its value to her. "Do you remember how we used to complain about Mother trying to run our lives and tell us what to do?"

"Yes, I rebelled vocally—you tried to analyze why a parent felt the obsessive need to retain control," Julia said with a chuckle.

"And now that our roles have been reversed," Lana contended, "I can see that caring and concern provoke a certain protectiveness that can't be helped. When someone means a great deal to you, it's only natural to want the very best for that person. And when it comes to Mom, I'm not sure anyone will ever be quite good enough."

"So what you are saying is, like it or not, we should keep our noses out of Mother's personal business, just as we expect her to back off and let us live our own lives."

"Absolutely," Lana confirmed, grinning mischievously at her older sister. "Just as soon as we finish poking our noses into Mother's business *one last time . . .*

Chapter Twenty-two

Elizabeth set herself a grueling pace during the following two weeks, while Lana spent the remainder of her spring break with Brad, planning their small wedding to be held at Heartstrings on the first of June. Julia was back at the animal clinic in Bartlesville, happy as a clam. Elizabeth had offered to work longer shifts at the cafe to occupy her time, but nothing eased the loneliness, the torment she was enduring every hour of every day—and night. Sweet mercy, the nights were the worst. All that kept Elizabeth going was the knowledge that she wasn't going to lose Heartstrings.

Lana and Julia had told her that they had managed to secure loans to pay off the debt. Elizabeth fully intended to keep her job at the cafe to help her daughters pay the loan back. Together, they would find a way to keep Heartstrings for future generations.

Elizabeth and Vic had finished burning pastures. They had been especially careful after the incident with Griff. These days, Elizabeth saw nothing of Griff Hollis. When his starving cattle broke through the fences, looking for nourishment, she and Vic corralled them and hauled them back where they belonged. There would be no more neighborly gestures on Elizabeth's part after what Griff had spitefully said and done. Whatever he was doing with his time these days Elizabeth didn't know—or care.

As for Wyatt McKenney, she knew he had abandoned his attempt to make money off of her. The phone had stopped ringing long ago. That had been a relief, because she didn't think she could stand to hear that deep baritone voice without coming apart at the seams. She was still too raw inside, too mortified about being so thoroughly deceived.

After pulling weeds from the garden behind the house, Elizabeth climbed to her feet and worked the kinks out of her back. Now that she knew she was staying at Heartstrings she could plant vegetables for canning and freezing. Processing food would keep her busy on those long summer nights, she assured herself.

Glancing toward the freshly painted barn and outbuildings, she heaved a tired sigh. Heartstrings looked good. She wished she felt and looked as cheery as the ranch. At least she had gotten something from Wyatt, she mused. A hollow consolation. *His* labor for the price of *her* broken heart.

Impulsively, she strode toward the barn to saddle George. She had a few hours to spare before Lana and Julia, and the men in their lives, came home for the weekend. Elizabeth knew their visit was a mission of mercy. Her family planned to console her, to distract her. And when they arrived, she would manufacture a smile and pretend she had recovered from disillusionment and heartache.

Bless their hearts, Lana and Julia had refrained from saying they had told Elizabeth so. They had been very supportive and had committed themselves to the loans to save the ranch they had begun to value as much as she did.

Before Elizabeth realized it, she was reining George down the hill toward the cottage. Despite the blackened trees that surrounded the creek, the familiar sense of peace settled over Elizabeth. She should have come here sooner to rejuvenate her

spirit, but the cottage held one very vivid memory she hadn't
been sure she could face.

*Remember the good times you had with Wyatt, even if they were
only illusions.* That ever-present voice! *Don't dwell on the bad
times. You knew it wouldn't last forever going in, Elizabeth. But you
were incredibly happy for a time. Remember only that.*

"Don't you have anyone else to talk to, damn it!"

The dog yipped at the sound of its name, and Elizabeth
managed a feeble smile. She had her faithful friends—George
and Damn It—and a family who cared about her. Life wasn't
so bad. And her alter ego was right—again. Although she
hadn't expected her liaison with Wyatt to end in betrayal, she'd
known it would end eventually. She should concentrate on the
pleasurable moments she and Wyatt had shared. Even if he
had not been sincere, she had felt whole and alive for that
short space in time—for the first time in her life.

Having delivered herself the consoling advice, Elizabeth
tethered George by the porch and stared toward the crystal
clear pond. In time the beauty of the area would be restored.
She and Vic could cut down the charred stumps and let the
grass around the creek fill in the bare spots like lush green
carpet. The trees that had survived could be trimmed. Her
serene paradise would endure, just as it always had, despite
the disappointments and scars.

Elizabeth pivoted toward the door and strolled into the
cabin. The sight of the sleeping bag spread before the hearth
caused her heart to skip several beats. The memories she and
Wyatt had made here came rushing back, pricking her soul.
She hadn't known what true loneliness was before she'd lived
for Wyatt's playful smiles, the deep resounding sound of his
laughter, the warmth of his touch. Now she could measure the
depth of the emptiness inside her, feel the extent of the ache
that knew no boundary.

"Damn him!" Elizabeth wilted to her knees on the pallet,
and when she did, she spied the note Wyatt had left behind
two weeks earlier.

Whatever else you believe, Bet, know that I love you.

Tears pooled in her eyes until the written words blurred. Tortuous emotion swirled through her, shattering the last of her composure. For two weeks Elizabeth had tried to project an air of calm, of control; but the note tore the fragile shell that housed her emotions.

"If you really loved me, you had one helluva way of showing it," she cried out to the watery vision that swam before her eyes.

"I told you how I felt about you every time I looked into your eyes, every time I touched you. Weren't you listening, Bet? I was communicating from the heart . . ."

When the deep voice rolled toward her, Eliza- beth twisted around to see Wyatt's muscular frame dominating the cabin. The world shrank to the space he occupied, and the only air she breathed was the remembered scent of him. Valiantly, she fought her vulnerability, steeling herself against the allure she had discovered to be a clever delusion.

"What are you doing here? I thought you'd be off making money at someone else's expense by now," she said crisply.

Wyatt peered down at a tear-streaked face surrounded by windblown brown hair. "I canceled my trip to Colorado," he explained as he drank in the sight of her.

Elizabeth wiped away the stream of tears, muffled a sniff and rallied around her bruised pride. "If you came to try your hand at sweet-talking me into selling Heartstrings to you, it's too late. Lana and Julia assumed the loan so we can keep the ranch. Take your bid somewhere else, Wyatt."

Wyatt gave his head a contradicting shake. "Lana and Julia didn't assume the loan. They didn't have the collateral to bor- row that kind of money. You really should've questioned them about it." He smiled wryly. "Obviously, you had something else on your mind."

Elizabeth's head snapped up, and she glared at his confident grin. "You think I've been pining away for you instead of pay- ing attention to business?"

"It looks that way to me," he took great pleasure in observing.

"Of all the egotistical, conceited—"

"I love you," he declared softly, sincerely.

"And cows jump over the moon," she flung back, refusing to fall prey to whatever will-o'-the-wisp had brought him back to torture her all over again.

"Would you like to hear the explanation of the phone message you overheard from Emmet?" he asked, still smiling in that infuriating way that made her so angry.

"No, I would not. You've had two weeks to conjure up plausible excuses, and I've had time to count all the ways you betrayed me."

"You are going to be difficult, I see."

"I am going to be *sensible*, you see," she assured him, elevating her chin stubbornly.

Wyatt propped himself against the doorjamb and crossed his arms over his chest. He had always been spellbound by the fiery sparkle in those onyx eyes. Elizabeth may have become disillusioned and belligerent—definitely belligerent—but she was spirited. He adored that about her. Occasionally she had her legs knocked out from under her, but you simply couldn't keep her down, Wyatt was proud to admit.

Elizabeth was definitely a survivor, and this cottage was her source of revitalization. She was the lucky one. Wyatt had been so miserable he hadn't been able to stand himself until he had received the call from Lana and Julia. *They* had invited *him* for the weekend, if he could make the arrangements. Imagine that! They had also thanked him for paying off the loans and had apologized for thinking the worst about him.

Of course, gaining Lana's and Julia's trust was mere child's play compared to winning Elizabeth's back. The battle royal had just begun. She was going to question and reject everything he said.

"What would you say if I told you I was the one who paid off both loans?" he asked her.

Her chin tilted a notch higher. "I would call you a liar. And if I discover you actually *did* pay off the loans, which I doubt, I'd assume you have another scheme up your sleeve."

"I do," Wyatt frankly admitted. He strode forward to tower over Elizabeth, who was sitting Indian-style on the pallet. He could almost feel those proud Heart-Stays' ancestral spirits gathering around her, providing moral support.

"Fine, let's hear it, McKenney. Just what money-making scheme brought you back to Heartstrings this time? And this better be good," she challenged. "I'm not as gullible and trusting as I once was."

When Wyatt crouched before her, his playful smile evaporated. He became dead serious. His future happiness was at stake. He faced a kangaroo court of one prepared to believe the worst. He only hoped the line of defense he had mentally rehearsed would be convincing. Otherwise, it was going to be one miserable drive back to the City in that Caddy Elizabeth hated so much.

"There was no money-making scheme to take over Heartstrings," he told her honestly. "I didn't set an auction date or print flyers because I wanted to make my own private bid."

"That's just what I thought." She sniffed resentfully. "After romancing the ranch, you expected me to sell out to you for a modest price because—imbecile that I was—I fell in love with you. Luckily I discovered your underlying motive in time." She glared at him and continued, "And by the way, please extend my appreciation to your friend Emmet. He saved me from being a bigger fool than I'd already been."

Wyatt stared straight in her eyes, despite the hostility he saw in them. "My bid was not for money, Bet. It was a bid for love. I knew I wanted this ranch the first time I sat down on the portico and heard the wind whispering to me through the breezeway, saw the rolling hills stretch out before me like some quiet, secluded kingdom in lost-but-not-forgotten dreams. But as much as Heartstrings appealed to me, I also knew it would be nothing without you. I wanted to give us the time we needed to know each other. I had to be absolutely certain that what you felt for me had nothing to do with saving this ranch. I didn't want to be just an escape from your financial burden. I had to be sure it was *me* you wanted above all else."

Elizabeth frowned ponderously, remembering what Irene had said about low-maintenance marriage prospects who could provide financial security. "You thought I saw you as a means to an end," she murmured. "And of course I reinforced that concern by considering Griff's proposal."

Wyatt nodded somberly. "It has happened to me before Bet. I had to know for certain that I was important to you, without the money, with or without Heartstrings. I didn't want to be your meal ticket or your salvation. I wanted to be wanted just for myself."

"But I don't understand. Why didn't you—?"

"I didn't expect you to understand," Wyatt interrupted. He reached out to trace the sensuous curve of her lips, and he smiled sadly. "But *I* fully understood what *you* were going through, what you were feeling, because I have been there myself. I remember the sense of guilt, failure and frustration— the feelings that were haunting you when you thought you were losing Heartstrings."

Wyatt sank down beside her, looped an arm around his bent knees and heaved a deep sigh. "I had to give up the homestead my great-grandfather staked in the Land Run of 1889. I felt the same way you did about holding onto tradition, but I lost my heritage. I didn't want to see you lose yours."

Elizabeth stared at him, noting the faraway look in his green eyes. She had the feeling that, at long last, she was about to discover the truth about his past.

"My family was reasonably well off. That was the main reason Deidre married me," he told her in a voice devoid of emotion. "I was young, and I thought I was in love. Her family had been in the horse-breeding business for years. She was used to money, and she expected me to provide it for her. Her affection never went any deeper than my wallet, though it took me a few years to admit that humiliating fact to myself."

Elizabeth remembered the willowy brunette who had seemed cold and heartless. Then she thought of her own disappointing marriage to a man who had been more interested in her inheritance than her affection. She was beginning to understand why Wyatt was so sensitive about wanting to be appreciated for the man he was, not the wealth he'd acquired.

"When Deidre and I began having marital problems I involved myself more deeply in auctioneering, spending more time away from home. I knew I had made a mistake by marrying her, that I had been blind to her faults and her selfishness.

"I didn't even realize her drinking problem was so serious until it was too late. One weekend, while I was out of town, she had a traffic accident after she'd been drinking heavily. The motorist she sideswiped was critically injured. Although the laws pertaining to drinking and driving weren't as strict as they are now, it cost me my family's ranch to pay the hospital bills and to prevent Deidre from serving time in jail."

"Oh God, Wyatt, I'm so sorry," Elizabeth commiserated.

She thought her life had been filled with trials and disappointments, but Wyatt had suffered far more than she had. Bob had very nearly cost Elizabeth the ranch, but Deidre *had* made Wyatt lose his heritage.

"I was down—broke," Wyatt continued grimly. "Deidre was already gone when the money ran out, but she rebounded quickly. She and Keith Delaney were married two days after the divorce was finalized. Keith was twenty years older than she was, and he catered to her every whim. I doubt she ever loved him back, but his money made her as happy as a woman like Deidre is ever going to be."

"And that's when you became an obsessive money-making machine," Elizabeth guessed.

Wyatt nodded affirmatively. "At first I drove myself to get Deidre out of my mind, to forget what she had cost me. I had failed to hold on to what my family had scratched and clawed to build into a successful farm and ranch operation, and making money became a compulsion that compensated for my loneliness. It became a way of keeping track of how far I had come from scraping rock bottom.

"I was in a position to be at the right place at the right time to make a great deal of money. I hired an efficient financial advisor who helped me invest wisely. I kept waiting for my ranch to come up for sale, but it was developed into an industrial site and I realized I'd never get it back. So I simply threw myself into a profession that became the only driving force I could understand."

"And now that you've come so far, Deidre sees you as suitable marriage material again?" Elizabeth met his gaze, probing deeply. "Do you still love her, Wyatt, in spite of everything?"

He smiled ruefully. "She killed all feeling I had for her when I gave all I had to spare her and then she left me. To be honest, I feel nothing but pity for Deidre. I know for a fact that I could take time off and spend months doing everything within my power to please her, but she has become so self-centered and self-indulgent she can never truly be happy. I think she only wants me back to prove to herself that she can acquire whatever she thinks she desires. It's only a game with her. She has no love to give, no concern except how others can benefit her. She's not as open and generous as you are. She never will be."

"Just how did you get mixed up with her in the first place?" Elizabeth couldn't help but ask.

Wyatt chuckled humorlessly. "She was one of the most sought-after beauty queens on campus, and I didn't have the sense to look deeper than her alluring appearance. I promised myself never to make that mistake again." He looked up, his green eyes glittering with sincerity. "And then I found you, the one woman who detested my luxurious silver Caddy and my expensive suits. And when I was absolutely sure you cared about me and not what I owned, a misinterpreted message from my financial advisor sent my hopes and dreams tumbling down around me."

"Just what *was* that phone call about?" Elizabeth wanted to know.

Wyatt smiled sheepishly. "Pure vengeance."

Elizabeth blinked, bemused.

"After Griff Hollis' marriage proposal and his 'accidental' burning spree, I had Emmet check up on him. Your neighbor isn't quite as financially stable as he wanted you to believe. The bank is foreclosing because he hasn't been paying the interest or principle on his loans. I think his motive in asking you to marry him was to salvage what he could from his ranch and settle down on Heartstrings."

"Why, that sneaky bastard!" Elizabeth was outraged.

"My guess is he wanted to spoil the looks of Heartstrings before the auction. Griff anticipated that you would take his offer, for fear you wouldn't receive the worthy bids this ranch deserves. He was counting on your fierce need to keep Heartstrings to sway you toward him."

"Wait until I get my hands on a shotgun," Elizabeth muttered resentfully.

Wyatt laughed at her burst of temper. "I considered that myself, but I decided to cut a little deeper than simply filling his hide with buckshot. The Osage County ranch that Emmet was discussing is the Lazy H. The bank foreclosed, and the ranch is now owned by McKenney Enterprises. I've decided not to sell it off, but to combine it with Heartstrings . . . on one condition . . ."

Elizabeth gaped at him. "You bought five thousand acres at three hundred dollars an acre, *and* you paid off my loans? Damn, Wyatt, just how rich *are* you?" She immediately flung up her hands when she realized what she'd said. "Don't answer that question. I don't want to know. Besides, it's none of my business."

He told her anyway, adding, "In the first place, I got the bank to sell to me for one hundred dollars an acre, so they could get out from under the long-standing improvement loan Griff has been using to keep up appearances. And in the second place, I want *my* business and *your* business to be *our* business. But there is one stipulation I ask for paying the loans so you can keep Heartstrings."

Elizabeth eyed him warily. "What's the catch, McKenney?"

Wyatt reached for her then, tumbling with her onto the pallet where they had first made love one dark and stormy night.

"Not *what's* the catch. *Who* is the catch," he corrected before dropping a long-awaited kiss on her lips. *"You* are the catch, Bet. I want Heartstrings to be my home because this is where *my* Heart-Stays. I want to retire from jet-hopping and enjoy the money I've made for a change, to travel when we want to get away for a few days, then come back to this land that feels so right to me. But this ranch is no good to me without you. Will you marry me, Bet?" he asked, his heart in his eyes.

Elizabeth wormed loose, sat up and turned her back on him.

"Bet?" he questioned apprehensively. "What's wrong?"

"I can't marry you," she told him, refusing to meet his incredulous gaze.

"But I thought you loved me."

"I do. That hasn't changed and it never will," she assured him.

"Then why not, damn it!" he blared in frustration.

The dog barked and came romping inside with its tail wagging.

"I wish you'd give that dog a regular name," Wyatt scowled. "I can't even cuss around here without having it brought to my attention. Now why the hell won't you marry me?"

Very slowly, Elizabeth swiveled her head around to reveal the impish smile that played on her lips and the playful sparkle in her eyes. "I can't marry you because you own a Caddy."

The love shining down on him told Wyatt all he'd ever needed to know. He chuckled delightedly as he pulled Elizabeth down on top of him. "First the mustache and now the Caddy? Lord, you are one demanding lady. What other sacrifices do you expect me to make to have you?"

Elizabeth bent to brush her mouth over his smiling lips and then she said very softly, very sincerely, "I want you to love me as much as I love you, for the rest of my life . . ."

Damn It barked his head off and bounded outside when the sound of an approaching vehicle broke the tranquillity of Heart-Stays.

Wyatt reluctantly sat up, drawing Elizabeth with him. Damn, the most peaceful paradise on earth was suddenly crowded with unwanted intruders. Maybe he should purchase property on the moon.

In less than a minute Elizabeth's two daughters and their boyfriends were filing into the cabin, grinning smugly—every last one of them.

Elizabeth glanced accusingly at her offspring. "Why didn't you tell me who paid off the loans?" she demanded without preamble.

"Wyatt asked us not to," Lana replied as she wrapped an arm around Brad's waist. "The psychological impact of his unexpected arrival was supposed to be—"

"Lana," Brad teased affectionately. "Aren't you forgetting something?"

Obviously Lana and Brad had made a pact that he would caution her when she launched into her analytical spiels.

"Sorry," Lana apologized before turning her attention to Elizabeth. "So what's the verdict, Mom? Do we get to keep Wyatt for our very own, or is he history?"

Elizabeth peered adoringly at Wyatt and smiled. "We're keeping him, if he agrees to lose the Caddy."

Wyatt stared into Elizabeth's fathomless eyes, feeling every last bit of tension evaporate, and his heart swelled with the love he had almost lost. "Consider the Caddy gone."

"So what's for supper, Mother?" Julia inquired while she stood contentedly wrapped in John's arms. "John and I are starved. We had to vaccinate, cut and brand two semi loads of steers today."

"Spaghetti," Wyatt announced for Elizabeth. "I'll cook if I can find The Apron."

When Elizabeth burst out laughing at the reminder of his revealing apron, Lana and Julia eyed her curiously.

"Inside joke," Wyatt explained as he cuddled Elizabeth possessively to him. "And thanks for dropping in to check on us. We do appreciate your concern. Close the door on your way out."

Julia and Lana took their cue and reversed direction, but not before exchanging glances with Elizabeth to make certain their mother understood that they had given Wyatt their stamp of approval. Elizabeth breathed a relieved sigh. Now the family dinner table wouldn't be a battleground.

"Now then, where were we?" Elizabeth questioned when the door creaked shut.

Wyatt's green eyes glittered with hungry desire. "We were accepting bids on very valuable property—your heart and mine."

When his roaming hand glided over her hip and brushed the peak of her breast, Elizabeth felt that familiar spark leap to life. It was here at Heart-Stays that she had discovered a new beginning, here that life had taken on new meaning for her. The promise in Wyatt's smile again filled her with happiness and a newfound sense of wonder.

"I love you," she murmured as she instinctively arched toward his worshipping caress, his cherishing kiss.

"How much, Bet? More than Heartstrings?" he asked, his words vibrating against the sensitive point beneath her ear.

Elizabeth turned his face to hers, holding his unblinking gaze. "If Heartstrings was the price I had to pay to have your love, I would give it away to someone who appreciated it as much as I do," she told him. "But you, Wyatt McKenney, are the man who owns my soul."

The look in her eyes assured Wyatt that she meant what she said; she belonged to him.

"Just try to leave me, pilgrim," Elizabeth dared him, doing her John Wayne impersonation. "You'll find the seat of your breeches peppered with buckshot. You should know by now that what I love with every beat of my heart I fight to keep." Her teasing smile vanished as she matched him caress for arousing caress. "And you're the one I love the best of all . . ."

Wyatt gathered Elizabeth in his arms and his heart, knowing he would gladly pay any price to keep this vibrant, spirited woman in his life. She was his source of strength, of happiness.

Here, on the rolling prairie and timbered creeks of Osage

Hills, they would begin the best halves of their lives, sharing their love, satisfying their need for wide-open country where one can be in touch with nature and all of creation.

Heart-Stays, the very pulse beat of Heartstrings, like the hallowed spires of Camelot, was a mystical place, its almost tangible spirit bringing peace, understanding and contentment.

It was here that Wyatt could reclaim his lost past and anticipate a bright future, here that his soul had found its perfect match. *His* heartstrings would be forever tied to this warm, generous woman who had effectively proved that her love for him was genuine and everlasting.

Love, Wyatt had learned, wasn't just a bid; it was an all-encompassing promise that whispered over the rolling hills and radiated through the endless vault of blue sky like eternal sunshine . . .

That was the last rational thought he entertained before Elizabeth showered him with a deluge of wild, sweet sensations, taking him with her to that unique dimension they created when they were in each other's arms.

A Note to Readers

This story is very special to me because of my Osage Indian heritage and my birthplace, Pawhuska. The Osage Hills are rich in the history and customs of my ancestors, a people who lived in reverent unity with creation. Their deep appreciation for the land is a concept other cultures have always had difficulty understanding. I hope, in some small way, that in *A BID FOR LOVE* Elizabeth has conveyed a sense of that tradition which deserves to be honored and passed down through generations.

And finally, I hope Elizabeth and Wyatt will serve to remind all of us that love, laughter and romance never lose their invigorating sparkle, no matter at what age we experience them.

Warmest wishes,

Carol Finch
aka Gina Robins and
Connie Feddersen